THE WOLF OF SARAJEVO

ALSO BY MATTHEW PALMER

Secrets of State

The American Mission

THE WOLF OF SARAJEVO

MATTHEW PALMER

G. P. PUTNAM'S SONS / NEW YORK

G. P. PUTNAM'S SONS
Publishers Since 1838
An imprint of Penguin Random House LLC
375 Hudson Street
New York, New York 10014

Library of Congress Cataloging-in-Publication Data

Palmer, Matthew, date.
The wolf of Sarajevo / Matthew Palmer.
p. cm.
ISBN 9780399175015
1. Political fiction. I. Title.
PS3616.A3435W65 2016 2015025533
813'.6—dc23

International edition ISBN: 9780399576904

Printed in the United States of America
10 9 8 7 6 5 4 3 2 1

BOOK DESIGN BY MEIGHAN CAVANAUGH

This one's for you, Mom

The belief in a supernatural source of evil is not necessary; men alone are quite capable of every wickedness.

—JOSEPH CONRAD, *Under Western Eyes*

He who fights with monsters should look to it that he himself does not become a monster. And when you gaze long into an abyss the abyss also gazes into you.

—FRIEDRICH NIETZSCHE, *Beyond Good and Evil*

We have met the enemy and he is us.

—POGO

SREBRENICA, BOSNIA
JULY 12, 1995

PROLOGUE

It was mid-July, but the concrete floor of the old tractor factory was as cold as death. Meho Alimerović sat propped up uncomfortably along an outside wall, the heat from his body leeching slowly into the raw bricks. His head rested against a pitted metal sign that advertised in faded red letters the SREBRENICA TRACTOR COLLECTIVE.

His nose itched. There was no way to scratch it, not with his hands tied tightly behind his back with wire.

When the siege lines broke, Meho had sought shelter at the UN compound where the Dutch battalion of peacekeepers had their headquarters. The whole Srebrenica enclave was supposed to be a safe area protected by the United Nations. Hundreds of others had the same idea. The Dutch had shut the gates and posted guards to keep them out. There was no room at the inn.

Meho looked to his left and right. There were maybe four hundred of them packed in tightly like matchsticks in a box. They were men and boys, the youngest ones looked to be no more than twelve or thirteen. The women and girls had been separated and taken somewhere else. Meho shuddered to think about what was almost certainly happening to them right now, at least to the pretty ones.

His sister, thank god, was in Sarajevo with their parents. Amra worked with him. She was a journalist too and good with people and languages. But she did not have Meho's foreign connections or his ability to move through the siege lines that encircled Sarajevo like a hangman's noose. Amra had wanted to come with him to Srebrenica to get out of the open-air prison that was Sarajevo even if only for a couple of days. It was lucky that he had said no. If they had taken his sister, it would have made him insane. He would have fought his well-fed captors with their shiny black guns slick with oil and sweat and he would be dead already.

As it was, death would wait. But Meho knew that her patience would not be tested today. Death would feast soon enough.

Why else would they separate the men from the women and children, with "men" defined very loosely to include boys just barely old enough to hold a gun? He could see it on the faces of their captors. They were little more than boys themselves, but their faces were set hard with the grim look of men who had an unpleasant but necessary job to do. And they harbored murder in their hearts.

The men holding them were not regular army, neither the Yugoslav National Army nor the Bosnian Serb Army. They were paramilitaries. Meho recognized the stylized lizard patches on their shoulders as the unit badge for the Green Dragons. Not as bad as

Arkan's Tigers, perhaps, but a close second. Bosnia was awash in paramilitaries, many of them appropriately enough named for poisonous insects or other creepy-crawlies. There were the Yellow Wasps and the Scorpions, the White Eagles and the Red Ants, New Byzantium and the Serbian Guard. Most were "weekend Chetniks," regular guys with regular jobs who took a few days off every week or two to hunt men for sport and pillage defenseless towns for profit.

The various combinations of colors and animals were almost comical and certainly juvenile, like children playing with exceedingly dangerous toys. Under siege in Sarajevo, drinking smuggled coffee and liquor by candlelight, Meho and his friends would joke about imaginary groups like the Purple Cocks and the Gold Fish.

It didn't seem so funny now.

In spite of this, a single hot cinder of hope flickered in his chest. Eric would come. Eric would save him. Him if not the others.

Eric was his employer and, Meho hoped fervently, more than that. Eric was his friend. And his friend had friends. In the American embassy. In the UN system. In the Bosnian government. Even in the Bosnian Serb "capital" in Pale. Eric would come. Eric would save him.

The man pressed up firmly against Meho's right shoulder had bad breath and his clothing stank of onions and stale cigarette smoke. He looked to be in his sixties and was thin to the point of emaciation. It was hard to imagine that he posed much of a threat to the future of Greater Serbia, but there he sat, waiting along with the others to learn his fate.

To Meho's left was a teenager, fifteen or sixteen years old at the most. He was crying softly but trying not to let anyone see. Meho pretended not to notice.

A few men whispered to one another, their voices muted and indistinct. Most sat silently.

Meho shifted again, but no matter which way he turned, the wire seemed to dig even more firmly into the soft flesh of his wrist.

The older man to his right looked at Meho appraisingly.

"They won't kill us all," he said confidently. "There are camps, like the ones the Germans and Croats used to have back in the last war. They'll send us to one of those. My father was in one of the camps for a while. It was bad, he said, but he lived. We will too."

"I'm sure you're right," Meho agreed in a voice lacking all conviction.

The older man seemed to reassess, maybe spurred by Meho's own doubts, maybe by his own fears.

"But just in case," he said. "If you should make it and I should not, I have a brother in Sarajevo. His name is Emir Safetović and he runs . . . ran . . . a bakery in Ilidža. Tell him that Sulejman is buried somewhere in these mountains and that he should find my bones and bury them next to my wife."

Meho nodded, confident that this was a message he would never have the chance to deliver.

"Is there a message you might have for someone?" the old man prompted him. If it was a fair trade, it would not be such bad luck. It was a small enough kindness that Meho could offer him.

"Tell my sister Amra Alimerović from Vratnik that I love her." He paused, thinking seriously about what he would want to leave behind. "And I have a friend, an American named Eric. Tell him something for me."

"Yes."

"Tell Eric . . . tell him that it's not his fault."

"And he will understand?"

"Yes, he will."

The old man leaned toward Meho as though he wanted to shake hands to seal their pact, pulling up short when he remembered that his hands were bound.

The metal doors on the opposite wall swung open with a loud crash. A tall, broad-shouldered man swaggered through them onto the factory floor. His black jumpsuit was starched and creased. The pants legs were tucked into black leather boots that gleamed with a fresh coat of polish. The butt of an automatic pistol protruded from a low-slung tactical holster strapped to his thigh. His face was obscured by an emerald green balaclava, and as ironic as it seemed to Meho that he would recognize a man by his mask, there was no doubt as to his identity. At that moment, whatever hopes Meho might have harbored for salvation were extinguished. The old man was wrong. They would all die that night.

This was Captain Zero. Commander of the Green Dragons. The Butcher of Bijeljina.

Captain Zero was a sociopath of the highest order, with a reputation for cunning as well as ferocity. The Dragon was also something of a firebug. Arson was his calling card and the balaclava was his trademark. As far as Meho knew, no one had seen the captain's face. No one had taken his picture. A few in the foreign press had speculated that he was scarred or deformed in some way, like the Phantom of the Opera, but no one knew anything for sure.

The captain walked up and down the line of captives, assessing them as though picking out the choicest cuts at the butcher shop. They were not men, only meat.

Zero stood in front of Meho in what was approximately the middle of the room. And then he did something that scared Meho more than the time a sniper's bullet had whipped inches past his ear and shattered the window of his car.

He took off his mask.

It was a death sentence.

Meho tried to look away, but he could not. He was trapped by the Dragon's gaze as neatly as the little tailorbird had been hypnotized by the cobra in that Kipling story about the mongoose. The captain was no more than two meters from Meho, and his eyes were so dark that they seemed to be made up of only pupils with no visible irises. To Meho, they looked like two polished onyx marbles.

The eyes were mirrored by a shock of thick black hair. Beyond that, Captain Zero was perfectly ordinary-looking. The kind of man you might see waiting in line to buy bread at the bakery or a coffee and pastry at the corner café. Just a man.

Captain Zero offered Meho a reptilian smile and an unspoken communication.

I am going to kill you tonight, he seemed to say.

I know, Meho thought back. His pulse hammered behind his eyes.

Captain Zero turned to his lieutenant, the man who had seemed to Meho to be in charge before the paramilitary leader had arrived.

"Get them up and outside," Zero said.

Uniformed thugs rousted the captives and lined them up, marching them outside into the cool dark night.

The low growl of a diesel engine got louder as they moved through the woods. Emerging in a field, Meho saw a yellow backhoe digging a long trench in the earth by the light of the moon. The trench looked just wide enough for a man to lie down in. A grave.

There were other trenches, Meho saw. And other groups of men and boys. Thousands of them gathered in the dark to be slaughtered like spring lambs.

The rest of Meho Alimerović's life was a blur. He was lined up with the others alongside the trench as the Green Dragons began to execute their captives.

Captain Zero did his part with the pistol from his thigh holster. As the paramilitary leader worked his way murderously down the line, Meho measured his life in gunshots. He would be dead in eight gunshots. *Seven. Six.*

He thought about running, but that would be both futile and somehow undignified.

It's not your fault, Eric. I should have known better. I shouldn't have come.

Five.

Four.

There was a man on the other side of the trench holding what looked to be a video camera. Who would want to record something like this? It was a snuff film on an industrial scale.

Three.

Two.

The man to his right stiffened as the captain put his gun to the base of the man's skull and blew a hole through his head. He tumbled forward into the trench, needing only someone to place his feet in the shallow grave with all the others before he could be bulldozed under.

One.

Meho could feel the hot steel of the gun barrel burning the hair and skin on the back of his skull as the captain bade him farewell.

"Good night, Turk," he whispered.

Zero.

TWENTY YEARS LATER

NOVEMBER 14
3:28 P.M.

There was not enough time. Thirty-two minutes. At four o'clock or near enough as to make no difference, he would kill her. There would be no peace. The country would slide inexorably and tragically into war, and Eric would lose another friend who deserved to live. Bosnia's fate and the life of a friend were balanced on a knife-edge with no room for error.

"Drive faster."

The car careened around a tight corner in the warren of narrow streets on Sarajevo's outskirts. The back bumper scraped loudly against the side of a van parked halfway up on the sidewalk. Up ahead, Eric could see the building where he believed the shooter was hiding. But that's all he had. A belief. A theory. One grounded in experience both long and recent, but a supposition nonetheless. *What if he was wrong? What if the shooter was somewhere else? What if his skills had eroded to the point where he chose to do his serious killing with a car bomb rather than a scoped rifle?* If Eric was wrong, he would miss this one window.

The room for self-doubt was almost infinite. But Eric could not afford to doubt. It would make him weak. Indecisive. It would kill his friend. He would not allow that, Eric swore. He would not let them kill her.

But it was so late.

There was so little time.

And the costs of failure would be unacceptably high.

He must not fail. He would not fail.

Not again.

Never again.

FORTY DAYS EARLIER

SARAJEVO
OCTOBER 5

1

The ghost was right where he had left him. Same place as always. The corner of Ulica Zmaja od Bosne and a nameless side street, standing there stiff and startled as the blood ran down his chest, belly, and legs to pool on the cement sidewalk. It was the ghost of the first man Eric Petrosian had watched die. It could just as easily have been him. There was no particular reason that the anonymous sniper had picked the man six feet to his left rather than Eric. It was happenstance. Karma. Luck.

Inasmuch as Eric could remember, there had been nothing especially different about the man who would become a ghost. He had been about Eric's age, about his height and build, dressed in jeans and a dark winter coat. But he was dead and Eric was not, and that was ultimately the difference that mattered.

In a way, of course, the man had been fortunate. He had simply died. The paramilitaries who specialized in this kind of long-distance murder typically tried to wound their targets first so that they could kill the rescuers before finishing off their initial victim. All wars were cruel. This one had been vicious.

The ghost faded as he always did, and the pool of blood sank into the cracked pavement like a cooling rain into parched earth. They were only memories, a distant echo of the siege that held the city close in its iron grip for almost four years.

Every time he passed this spot, Eric saw the ghost, if only fleetingly. In this, he was hardly alone. Nearly every Sarajevan was haunted by ghosts. At least those old enough to remember. The end of the siege was some twenty years in the past. The city had never really moved on, however. The Bosnian War was very much a piece of unfinished business.

It was a beautiful crisp day. Early October was the time of year when Sarajevo was at its best. In six weeks or so, the streets would be awash in runoff from seemingly unending rains, and a few weeks after that the city would be shrouded in clouds of smog from the soft brown coal that the poorer residents still burned for heat. Today, however, the sky was a perfect cerulean blue bowl balanced upside down on the ring of dark mountains that girded the Bosnian capital. It would have been easy to pretend, if Eric allowed himself the luxury of self-delusion, that all was well. But somewhere up in that clear blue sky, the invisible specter of war hovered over a city that had known far too much of it.

Eric glanced at his watch. He was running late. *Better pick up the pace,* he thought. The ambassador was not famous for his patience. If he had had more time, Eric would have chosen a circuitous route for the short walk from the embassy to the ambassador's residence, one that bypassed his ghost. But he was in a hurry.

The ambassador's residence was something of an oddity. It was aggressively modern in a society that valued the traditional, antiseptic in a city that never quite felt clean. The guard at the gate recognized Eric and waved him through without asking to look at his badge.

"*Dobar dan,* Rasim," Eric said by way of greeting.

"*Dobro došli, gospodine,* Eric." *Welcome.*

Ambassador Prescott Wylie was sitting on the veranda at the back of the house nursing a glass of tomato juice that Eric knew was a mere stalk of celery away from being classified as a Bloody Mary. It was ten o'clock in the morning. Wylie liked to think of himself as a modern Churchill, but he had really been successful only in his emulation of the British Bulldog's prodigious drinking habits.

The American ambassador to Bosnia was physically imposing, and he had gotten far using his bulk to intimidate colleagues as well as foreigners. He had played linebacker at Dartmouth, and even after three decades of diplomatic dinners, he was still more big than fat. Eric was not impressed by either Wylie's bulk or his brain. The ambassador's father had been both a Dartmouth alum and an American diplomat of some renown. Eric suspected that it was his legacy status, rather than any actual talent, that accounted for Wylie's career success.

The ambassador was not alone. The Nordic blonde sitting across from him with a relatively restrained double espresso in front of her was familiar to Eric from the papers and by reputation. Annika Sondergaard was a Danish politician, a former foreign minister and current High Representative of the Union for Foreign Affairs and

Security Policy. The Union in this case was the European Union, the block of twenty-eight mostly wealthy states that Bosnia theoretically aspired to join. Hers was a highfalutin title if ever there was one, and Sondergaard had staked much of her political credibility on an all-out effort to keep Bosnia from sliding back into chaos.

The U.S.-backed Dayton peace agreement had ended the fighting in Bosnia in 1995 but left behind a divided system of government that had proved to be entirely unworkable. Bosnia was composed of two "entities," the borders of which roughly tracked the front lines from twenty years ago. On the map, the Serb-controlled Republika Srpska with its capital in Banja Luka seemed to squeeze the Muslim-Croat Federation from the north and east like a vise. Sarajevo's central government was weak and fractious. Real power was held at the entity level. The negotiators at Dayton had understood full well the inherent fragility of the system they devised, but it was the best they could do at the time. The priority had been to stop the fighting. A viable unitary state, it was assumed, would emerge over time. But it hadn't worked out that way.

The new High Rep had her own ideas about what the country should look like, and she had outlined the principles in her New Compact for Bosnia, a proposal that was already being referred to in European capitals as the Sondergaard Plan. Eric did not doubt her sincerity, but Sondergaard was one in a long line of senior public officials whose ambitions of Balkan peacemaking were animated in no small part by dreams of a Nobel Peace Prize. Most quickly found their plans undone by the intransigence of a three-sided conflict that had been given twenty years to set.

The High Rep looked older in person than she did in the papers. *Worn down by the weight of office perhaps,* Eric thought. Or maybe she just photographed especially well. Still, she was a striking woman with an angular face and sharp cheekbones that gave her something of an air of haughty indifference. Even sitting down, she looked tall. There was a reason the local press had dubbed her the Valkyrie, and the political cartoonists invariably drew her with a horned helmet and metal breastplate.

"You're late," the ambassador observed with a hint of irritation.

And you, sir, are drunk.

"My apologies, Ambassador. I couldn't get the deputy speaker of parliament off the phone."

"He does go on," the ambassador acknowledged, seemingly mollified now that he had established his dominant position in front of the attractive woman. "I don't think you've had the chance to meet High Representative Sondergaard."

"Not yet, no. Pleasure to meet you, ma'am."

The High Representative looked him up and down as though he were a blind date. It was not an unpleasant sensation.

"Good to meet you, Eric," she said, once she had finished her brief assessment. "The people in the EU mission here tell me that you're the man to know in this town."

Eric shrugged.

"They exaggerate."

Eric sat at the table, and the waiter brought him his usual, a cup of strong and bitter Turkish coffee poured straight out of a slender copper *džezva*. The finely ground Turkish-style coffee that served as the region's universal lubricant was one of the legacies of five hundred years under Ottoman rule and—as far as Eric was concerned—perhaps the single greatest gift that any culture had ever given another.

"Hvala," he whispered sotto voce to the server by way of thanks.

"Petrosian. That's Armenian, isn't it?" the High Representative asked.

"On my father's side," Eric replied, knowing full well why she had asked. With his brown skin and vaguely almond-shaped eyes, he did not look especially Armenian. It would be kinder, he decided, to assuage her curiosity without making her ask a question she might fear was intrusive. "My mother was Cambodian."

"Was?"

"Yes, she passed away when I was young."

"I'm sorry."

Eric nodded in acknowledgment of her sympathy but said nothing. He did not like to speak about his mother. When his father had smuggled her out of Pol Pot's Cambodia, she had left a part of herself behind. A part of her that died along with nearly every member of her extended family. Eric had been the one to find her body, a ten-year-old boy confused and uncertain as to why his mother would be sitting in the car in the garage with the engine running. To this day, exhaust fumes had a kind of Proustian power to send him back in time to that awful moment.

"You were here before," Sondergaard said to him in a manner that was almost, but not quite, a question. "During the war, I mean."

"I was."

"As a diplomat?"

"A journalist. Stringing for the wire services. Reuters and UPI mostly."

"What convinced you to cross over?"

"I thought I could do more good in this job. Make more of a difference."

"And have you?"

"Jury's still out."

"Cambodia, Armenia, Bosnia. They all have something in common, don't they?"

"Yes, they do."

Prescott Wylie looked confused. Eric turned to him.

"Genocide."

Annika Sondergaard, he decided, would have made one hell of a psychiatrist.

"So tell me what I need to know about the guest of honor."

Sondergaard was clearly talking to Eric, but the ambassador jumped in to answer the question.

"Bakir Hasović is one of the linchpins on the Federation side," he said. "If your plan is going to get traction, you are going to need to make sure that he's supportive. His position is deputy prime minister in the Federation government, but that undersells his importance. As the head of the Bosniak Unity Party, he's the key to the coalition. If the BUP pulls out, the government falls. That lets Hasović punch well above his weight."

So far, all pretty much in line with the briefing that Eric had given the ambassador earlier that morning to prep him for this meeting. Diplomacy was an odd business that operated according to its own arcane rules. It could, in particular, be rigidly hierarchical and rank conscious. As a consequence, it was often the case that the person speaking in a meeting knew much less than the younger, more junior people taking notes or sitting along the back wall. It was just the way things worked. Eric's job was to advise the ambassador in private and defer to him in front of others. He had never been especially good at the second part, to Wylie's occasional irritation.

Prescott Wylie was competent enough in his own way, but he was a newcomer to the Balkans who had spent most of his career well to the west of where the Iron Curtain had once been drawn across the continent. Most of his previous assignments would have fit neatly into the group of countries that Washington wags referred to derisively as the Chocolate Makers. Wylie did not speak the local language, and he had not had enough time to develop any kind of real feel for the culture. Living inside his bubble of drivers and bodyguards, armored cars, and translators, it was unlikely that he ever would. This was a manageable shortcoming as long as he was willing to listen. In their nine months together, however, it had become clear to Eric that Prescott Wylie was quite taken with the sound of his own voice.

"So what approach would you recommend I take with Hasović to get him to see things my way?" Sondergaard asked the ambassador. "Our way," she corrected herself.

"I'd suggest playing to his sense of patriotism. Go with the big picture: bringing Bosnia into the twenty-first century and the European family of nations."

It was a stock answer that could have applied to just about any conversation with just about anyone on just about anything. It was also, Eric knew, absolutely wrong. This was not at all what he and Wylie had discussed earlier that morning. Hasović was a crook. You didn't appeal to a crook's conscience; you appealed to his wallet. Wylie would never forgive Eric, however, for challenging him in front of Sondergaard. He held his tongue. The ambassador was just getting warmed up.

"Hasović is a Bosnian nationalist," Wylie continued. "He needs to understand your plan as the last best chance to keep the country together. He has no love for the Serbs, but I am convinced that he loves his country and ultimately shares our vision of a unitary Bosnia with room enough for all."

Eric almost choked on his coffee. The only thing Hasović loved was money.

"That's very interesting," Sondergaard said, even as her tone made clear that it was not.

The ambassador's butler appeared in the doorway. He was a Bosnian Croat of indeterminate sexuality who affected the manners of an Edwardian-era majordomo that he seemed to have acquired by watching pirated DVDs of *Downton Abbey*.

"Deputy Prime Minister Hasović is here, Mr. Ambassador," he announced in his passable English, with an accent that somehow merged Slavic with faux British.

"Show him in."

They all rose in greeting as Hasović was ushered into the room. He was short and dark and built like a wrestler. His black hair was styled in an early-Elvis pompadour held in place by so much mousse that it looked almost shellacked. He wore a dark suit with a white shirt and no tie. The top two buttons of the shirt were undone, doubtless to offer his interlocutors a better look at the thick gold chain around his neck that was the Bosnian gangster world's equivalent of a Zegna tie.

Hasović's hands were big and beefy, and his grip was just a little too strong, an effort to dominate rather than a greeting.

"Please." The ambassador gestured to the table once the initial round of introductions were done. "High Representative Sondergaard doesn't have much time, I'm afraid, so we need to get right to business. But first, coffee? Something stronger?"

No business in the Balkans was ever transacted without a cup of coffee to smooth the discussion and maybe a shot glass of *rakija* or homemade brandy to set the tone.

Hasović took a Turkish coffee with no sugar and a glass of plum brandy. Bosniaks were nominally Muslim, but Eric knew few who didn't drink.

"I suppose you know why I'm in Sarajevo," Sondergaard began. Hasović's English, while not perfect, was adequate. Eric was along for the meeting in part to help with translation should that be necessary.

"More or less," Hasović replied. "You are here to sell me a plan."

"Not sell, really, but perhaps persuade. My view and the views of my colleagues in Washington and Brussels is that Bosnia is again slipping toward war. For a brief moment, it seemed that Zoran Dimitrović's election in the RS marked a turn for the better, and for a year or so, Bosnia seemed to be moving in the right direction. But the last six months have been little short of disastrous, and violence seems increasingly likely."

Hasović nodded as though only half listening. He knew all of this.

"The ambassador tells me that you are a patriot. I hope that you appreciate the urgency of the situation, the need to overcome not only the legacy of the war but the legacy of the peace as well. Bosnia needs a new deal and a new political framework. And I need your help to get there."

Hasović's eyebrows had lifted in what struck Eric as amusement at Sondergaard's description of him as a patriot.

"Madam Ambassador," Hasović said. "You are still new to this part of the world. With all respect, we have seen many emissaries come with many plans. Almost all of them fail, and the envoys depart leaving those of us who live here to suffer the . . ." He turned and looked at Eric. *"Posledice."*

"Consequences."

"Hvala."

"We must all take risks in the service of peace," Sondergaard said.

"After you, Ambassador."

Sondergaard and Hasović sparred for another twenty minutes, with Ambassador Wylie occasionally interjecting his own views as though reminding the principals that he was still there. Eric took notes, but it was clear that the BUP leader was not buying the line about a twenty-first-century Bosnia. Hasović may not love the status quo, but he had learned to benefit from it. Change was risk, and Sondergaard and Wylie had not done enough to spell out the potential benefits.

Then Hasović said something that seemed to Eric like an opening.

"The burden always seems to fall most heavily on those who have been a failed initiative's most committed supporters," Hasović continued. "Political leaders suffer. Business suffers. The position of the Bosniak Unity Party is really quite delicate. We are faced with some potentially serious setbacks. I have to consider the good of my party as well."

Eric understood what Hasović was saying, and he also knew that neither Wylie nor Sondergaard was in a position to grasp its significance.

"You do know, Mr. Deputy Prime Minister, that the international community would want to protect key public enterprises in the transition to a new unitary political system . . . to ensure continuity of certain services."

Eric was breaking protocol by speaking up, but if there was a chance to capitalize on the opportunity Hasović had given them and potentially get him behind the Sondergaard Plan, it was worth pissing off Wylie. Hell, pissing off Wylie might even be a good enough reason to do it.

Hasović's eyes narrowed as he considered what Eric had said. This was language he could relate to.

"What kind of businesses are you talking about?" he asked carefully.

Eric glanced briefly at Wylie and Sondergaard. The ambassador looked like he had just bitten into a rotten piece of fruit, but the High Representative gave him the briefest and subtlest of nods. *Go ahead.*

"Basic services, really. Electricity. Water." Eric paused and looked Hasović squarely in the eyes. "Trash collection."

Blue Line Sanitation, the quasi-private company that had the lucrative contract for trash pickup in the greater Sarajevo municipal area, was under the nominal control of Hasović's son-in-law. In reality, it was an open secret that Hasović called the shots and had first claim on the spoils. Blue Line Sanitation was the single most important source of funding for the Bosniak Unity Party, which was run more like a for-profit company than a political party. For Hasović's profit, actually. In the last few weeks, there had been talk that Blue Line might lose the contract to a rival company with close ties to the powerful interior minister. Hasović could not allow that.

"So what would happen to existing contracts for city services?"

he asked smoothly, as though the question were of mere academic interest.

"Well, some of the details still need to be worked out, but I think it would be reasonable to consider a freeze on public tenders that would keep the current arrangements in place for a fixed period."

Eric looked at Sondergaard as he said this. He was freelancing and wanted to make sure that he had her buy-in. Again, the High Rep nodded. *Keep going.*

"What kind of period?" Hasović asked.

"Three years or so." Eric had just pulled that number out of thin air.

"I would think five years would be more . . . patriotic."

"You may be right, but that would no doubt require some up-front assurances that the plan could win the support of the key partners in the current coalition government."

"The BUP is prepared to throw its weight behind a plan that recognized the need for continuity as well as change," Hasović suggested.

"Publicly?"

"Of course."

The rest was details.

When Hasović left, the three internationals sat back at the table for a postmortem.

"You seemed quite sure of yourself there, Eric," Wylie said with an edge of anger in his voice. "Don't you think you might have promised too much in that exchange?"

"Almost certainly. But I didn't want to miss that chance, and I didn't think that either of you knew about his commercial stake in the trash business."

"Like Tony Soprano?" Sondergaard asked lightly.

"Only without the class," Eric agreed.

The ambassador polished off his "tomato juice" and gestured to the server for a refill.

"You need to remember whose mission this is," he said sourly.

"Yes, sir. Apologies for overstepping."

Wylie turned toward Sondergaard, now all charm and tact.

"Madam High Representative, I hope we haven't committed you to something you will have trouble delivering on."

"Not at all," she said. "I think we're in a better place than I had dared hope we would be at this point."

"My government certainly recognizes the importance of your initiative. Is there anything else I can do for you? Any way I can help?"

"Well, there is one thing you could give me," she replied.

"Name it."

"Him." She pointed at Eric. "Just for a month or two."

"He's all yours," the ambassador agreed without so much as a glance in Eric's direction.

"I'll try not to break him."

"Don't worry. I tried. I didn't succeed."

MILAŠEVCI, BOSNIA
OCTOBER 9

2

The drive from Sarajevo to Banja Luka was only about four hours, but it was a trip through hundreds of years of turbulent history. This was one of the world's great civilizational fault lines, the blurry boundary between East and West, Christian and Muslim, Ottoman and Hapsburg. The Romans fought the Illyrians in the mountains that lined the road north. Soldiers loyal to Samuel of Bulgaria had patrolled these valleys in the late tenth century before losing a war to the Byzantine Empire. Most recently, Croat, Serb, and Bosniak forces in the wars of the 1990s had battled for control of the towns and villages that empire after empire had sacked and rebuilt in the same locations with the same geographic and strategic logic. The Balkans, Churchill had once observed, produced more history than they could consume.

Eric and Annika sat in the back of the high-end Land Rover that was part of the EU mission's vehicle fleet. *The EU,* Eric thought, *for all of its shortcomings as America's premier partner in global diplomacy, made excellent cars.* Even traveling the rough mountain roads, the ride was smooth and quiet and the High Rep was using the opportunity to get briefed in advance of what was likely to be a critical meeting.

"What do you know about Zoran Dimitrović?" she asked Eric.

"Not enough," he admitted. "He's been on the political scene for some time, but up until recently, only in a decidedly minor-league role as the head of a marginal right-wing political party called the National Party. Then, about eighteen months ago, the RS government fell and there were new elections. The National Party took off. Dimitrović all of a sudden had money and that bought him new friends in the media, the police, and the business community."

"Where did the money come from?"

"That's the thing. Nobody seems to know. But Dimitrović and the National Party went from polling near the 5 percent threshold for making it into parliament to almost 40 percent. And it happened in the political equivalent of overnight. I've never seen anything like it, and I'd be lying if I said I understood how it happened."

"I suspect that your ambassador would be able to offer an explanation," she suggested slyly.

"Sure. Just not one based on evidence. I could tell you that Dimitrović is really an alien overlord from another galaxy sent here to enslave us all, starting with Banja Luka. It's an explanation, but not an especially likely one."

Annika laughed.

"I like you, Eric," she said.

"Thank you, Madam High Representative."

"Oh, please don't call me that. I hate it when people have to stop and take a breath before that god-awful title. Annika is fine."

"It does make it easier," Eric agreed. "In truth, I appreciate the opportunity to work with you on this. What you're doing . . . what we're doing . . . is tremendously important."

"You see the same thing coming as I do, don't you?"

"War."

"Yes. What happened when Dimitrović came to power?"

"Now the story gets really quite odd. Dimitrović was a nationalist, remember, a hard-liner. But he comes to power in the RS and almost immediately adopts a pro-Western agenda. He wants Bosnia in the EU and NATO. He scales back ties with Serbia. He works to strengthen the central government, even when that means agreeing to transfer some powers from the entity level to Sarajevo. That's something we've been pushing for unsuccessfully for years. And this is all from a guy who's rumored to have the Serbian cross tattooed on his behind."

"So it's a Nixon-to-China story? The hard-liner looks to open up to the world, and because his nationalist credentials are unimpeachable, he's inoculated against charges of being a sellout."

"That's the way it looked to us," Eric agreed. "For a while."

"Then what happened?"

"For about ten months or so, Dimitrović was a dream partner for us. We were getting everything we needed out of the relationship. Then, about seven or eight months ago, something changed. Something important. And I'm sorry to be vague on this point. It's just that we don't entirely understand what happened. But the Dimitrović administration suddenly began to backtrack on all of its commitments. The RS pulled out of the joint institutions and stopped paying taxes into the central coffers. Police liaisons were withdrawn; the Serbs who had been working in various international organizations active in Bosnia quit in response to threats against their families; and trade ties were cut. And most worrisome, the paramilitaries reappeared like the dead coming back to life in some zombie movie."

"The same groups that were active during the war?" Sondergaard asked.

"Many of them, yes. Not the Tigers, thank god. But the Yellow Wasps, the Scorpions, the Green Dragons. They're all back and they're playing a major role in the RS. It's scary."

"What about the new group?"

"The White Hand?"

"Yes."

"Again, we know a lot less than I want to. It's a new group, but an old name. The White Hand was the name adopted by a cabal of military officers back in the early part of the twentieth century. They were led by an army colonel who was looking for leverage in opposing a parallel secret military organization called the Black Hand that also sometimes went by the name Unification or Death."

Annika looked skeptical.

"This is real history, I promise you. I know it all sounds terribly melodramatic. But the guys who did this were all absolutely invested."

"In what?"

"Well, the Black Hand wanted to unify the Serbs, Croats, and Slovenes in a single state modeled after German and Italian unification, all under a Serbian king. There's good reason to believe that

Gavrilo Princip, the guy who shot Archduke Franz Ferdinand in Sarajevo and triggered the First World War, worked for the Black Hand. So it's not like the group was just a footnote."

"And the White Hand?"

"The White Hand won a power struggle with the Black Hand and gradually accumulated more and more power, mostly by exercising control over the king, Alexander Karadjordjević."

"What happened to them?"

"Tito. When the communists came to power, the members of the White Hand were imprisoned or executed. A few fled abroad."

"And now they're back?"

"It's more likely that it's a new group of people who have appropriated the name. The leader is someone who calls himself Marko Barcelona."

"Hardly sounds like a local name. Is he a Spaniard?"

"It's probably a nom de crime. Some of the gangsters in the ex-Yugosphere style themselves after the place they made their bones. Joca Amsterdam. Misa the Kraut. That sort of thing. Almost no one in that line of work uses their real name. Barcelona is one of the big points of entry for cocaine from South America. So the best guess is that he was somehow involved in the drug trade."

"Best guess?"

"We know hardly anything about him. He uses the nickname Mali, which means *little one* in Serbo-Croatian. That could be meant literally or it could be a joke. Maybe he's a dwarf. But maybe he's two meters tall and a hundred and fifty kilos."

"It could mean he has a tiny penis," Annika suggested mischievously.

"Could be. Or maybe the name Tripod was also in the running. We don't know. Mali is secretive beyond the point of paranoia. I've never seen a picture of him. I don't know where he lives. Some people think he's entirely fictional and the real leader of the White Hand is someone else altogether who is hiding behind a made-up character."

"What do you think?"

"I think he's for real, but I wouldn't rule anything out. This place can be down-the-rabbit-hole weird. Whoever he is, the power that Mali and the White Hand have accumulated in a remarkably short time is real enough. The Hand does Dimitrović's bidding, and the few politicians who have crossed the president have reason to regret it."

The Land Rover stopped. Eric leaned forward to get a look out the front window.

"The road is closed," the driver said to him in Serbo-Croatian.

A row of oil barrels painted white stretched across the two-lane "highway" that connected Sarajevo and Banja Luka. There were no workmen anywhere in sight, no machinery and no indications of any major construction on the road up ahead. A sign with an orange metal arrow pointed the way to a detour on a dirt track that seemed to run up into the mountains and then parallel to the highway.

"Something about this doesn't feel right," Eric said to Sondergaard.

"I agree. What do you think we should do?"

"Smart thing would be to turn back."

"Probably. But this meeting with Dimitrović is important. Without him, we don't have a peace deal."

"What do you think, Munib?" Eric asked the driver.

He shrugged. "Road needs the work. Maybe they have just yet no to start it."

Munib's English was of the rough-and-ready variety, but he spoke it quickly as though speed would somehow compensate for the errors. After years in the region, Eric had no trouble with this particular variant of fractured communication.

"We can try the detour. Take it slow and see what we find," Eric suggested.

Annika nodded. "I do want to get to Banja Luka," she said. "There's so little time to work with."

Eric understood her urgency. "Let's try it, Munib."

The dirt track was rough but not especially difficult for the Land Rover. About two kilometers down the road, however, Munib had to stop again. Two sizeable logs had been laid across the road. A gray-green tarp strung up in the trees kept the sun and the rain off the three men sitting at a wooden table alongside the roadblock. Their guns were leaning casually against a tree.

Instinctively, Eric turned to look through the rear window. There were two more men behind them. They carried their AK-47 rifles in their arms, not pointing the weapons at the Land Rover but not pointing them away either.

"What do we do?" Annika asked. "Run?"

"No, that would be a terrible idea. They'd be quite likely to shoot."

"So what should we do?"

"Talk."

He opened the door and got out. Sondergaard was right behind him.

The three guards stood. Two of the men retrieved their rifles, and the three guards walked toward Eric and Annika. It was likely, Eric knew, that the one man without a Kalashnikov was in charge. He looked to be a little older than the other two, in his twenties rather than his teens, and he had a full beard. The younger men looked more like they just had not shaved for a few days. They were wearing army uniforms, but they did not all match. Their boots, in particular, were an assortment of different styles. This was the trademark of the paramilitaries, a mixed assortment of clothing and weapons and equipment, whatever they had been able to scrounge or steal. There was a unit patch sewn on the left shoulder of their uniforms. It was shaped like a shield with a cartoon wasp, its stinger dripping blood. The Yellow Wasps.

In the Bosnian War, the Wasps had been responsible for the ethnic cleansing and looting of Zvornik. They were indiscriminate, killing Serbs as easily as they killed Muslims or Croats. The Wasps' original leadership was still incarcerated in The Hague, found guilty by the International Criminal Tribunal for the Former Yugoslavia of crimes against humanity. That someone would seek to revive the Yellow Wasps seemed itself a crime.

Eric could hear the two men with rifles arguing fiercely with each other in Serbian. Their disagreement was about him.

"He's a Turk, just look at him," said the soldier with a pronounced belly and the forearms of a butcher.

"Fuck you. No way. He's a Gypsy, a fucking Gypsy. He's practically black." The second Wasp was lanky and thin and pale. He looked less like a real soldier and more like a university student acting in a play about a virulently nationalist paramilitary.

Eric and Annika stopped, and let the triad of soldiers come to them.

The leader spat into the dirt. A few flecks of spittle clung to his beard.

"What's your business in the independent state of Republika Srpska?" he asked.

"Independent state?" Eric replied. "Last I looked, the RS was part of Bosnia and Herzegovina."

"Not for long," the Yellow Wasp officer answered. "This is the border checkpoint. You need a visa if you want to cross."

"This is Annika Sondergaard, the European Union's High Representative, and my name is Eric Petrosian. I'm the political counselor at the American embassy in Sarajevo. We have a meeting with President Dimitrović in Banja Luka, and I don't think he would appreciate your shaking down his guests."

"I'm not interested in what Dimitrović thinks," the Wasp replied. That in itself was a very interesting data point.

"Who do you work for then?"

"None of your damn business."

Eric translated the brief exchange for Annika's benefit.

"I say we turn back," she said.

"Agreed."

"We'll be returning to Sarajevo," Eric said to the Wasps. "But you will be seeing us again."

The two armed men raised their weapons, and when Eric looked over his shoulder, he could see that the men behind him were now pointing their guns at the Land Rover. Their driver, who remembered the war all too well, kept his hands visible on the steering wheel.

"Not with that nice car," the Wasp captain said. "You can walk back to the road from here."

In his eyes, Eric could see the same frightening mixture of avarice and nationalist fervor that had led Bosnia down the road to hell two decades earlier. He could feel his anger rising. He sure as hell was not going to give in to this kind of blackmail and intimidation.

Eric took a step toward the Wasp captain.

"You had better tell your men to put those guns down," he advised, with what he hoped was a confident smile. "It could get them killed."

"By you? A Gypsy?"

"Oh, no. I don't do that kind of thing. But, you see, I work for the government of the United States of America. There are people I work with who do that sort of work regularly."

"I don't see them here," the Wasp said sneeringly.

Eric pointed up into the clear blue sky.

"Do you see that little black dot?" he asked.

Despite himself, the Wasp leader looked where Eric was pointing.

"No."

"Look carefully. It's very small. But it's there."

"What about it?"

"It's an unmanned aerial vehicle. You might call it a drone, but don't do that around the people who fly it. They're very sensitive. In any event, it's monitoring us. The woman I'm traveling with is rather important. If you shoot at us, the Reaper pilot controlling that aircraft will hunt you down and kill you in these mountains. I'd hate for something like that to be necessary."

"I don't believe you," the captain said, although it was clear that he was less than 100 percent certain. "The bombs would kill you too."

"These are the very latest Reapers," Eric replied. "They're equipped with more . . . personal . . . capabilities. It wouldn't take more than a few seconds, and from what I've been told, there should be very little pain. The rounds it fires are remarkably accurate but also quite large. Again, I'd really be sorry to see something like that prove necessary."

Without waiting for orders, the two armed men in front of them lowered their weapons. The captain gestured palms down to the two behind them, and Eric knew that they had lowered their guns as well.

"I have a little gift for you," Eric said.

He pulled something out of his pocket and extended his hand. The Wasp captain reached out, and Eric shook hands with him, pressing something into his palm as he did so.

The paramilitary leader looked at it. It was a coin with an American flag on one side and the Great Seal of the United States on the other.

"What is this?" he asked.

"It's a challenge coin," Eric explained. "If you can produce the coin the next time we see each other, I have to buy you a drink. If you don't have it on you, you buy me one. We're friends now."

The Wasp smiled, showing a mouth full of yellow-brown teeth. He pocketed the coin.

"Now, why don't you ask your boys to move those logs so we can get on our way to Banja Luka."

The Wasp nodded and patted the pocket where he had placed the challenge coin.

He barked instructions to his subordinates, who were soon pulling on the ropes that opened a gap in the log barrier.

When they were back in the jeep and through the checkpoint, Eric explained to Annika what he had done.

"There's a drone following us?" she asked.

"Of course not. But they don't know that. All these guys have seen too many movies. It seems to them like just the sort of thing we would be able to do. I used that."

"But then why give him the coin at the end? It seems like a mixed signal to me. You risk confusing the dog."

"We'll be back this way. We may need him to want to help us without the constant threat of an invisible drone. What I did helped him save face. It looks like he won because I gave him something even if it's only a trinket from the embassy gift shop that cost me a couple of bucks."

"They teach you to do things like that drone story in your school for diplomats?"

"Oh god, no," Eric said laughing. "That's not a diplomat thing. I learned that kind of bullshit as a journalist."

Zoran Dimitrović's office was on the top floor of an early-twentieth-century Italianate bank building that had been converted into a presidential villa. It was neither vast nor imposing. The scale was appropriate, however, for Banja Luka, a city of some one hundred and fifty thousand on the banks of the Vrbas River. It would never rival Vienna or Budapest, but Eric appreciated the city's wide-open green spaces and provincial charm. During the war, Republika Srpska's government had operated out of an old ski center in the mountain town of Pale. Banja Luka was at least a real city.

In the 1990s, Banja Luka had been a magnet for Serbs displaced from the parts of Bosnia under Muslim or Croat control. Many had stayed on after the war. The fighting had touched the city only indirectly. The notorious Manjača concentration camp built by the army on a mountain just south of town had held thousands of prisoners. The camp leaders, who had presided over a brutal regime of torture and murder, had been convicted of war crimes by the international tribunal in The Hague.

The president's chief of staff met them at the villa's wrought-iron doors and escorted them up the marble stairs to the office. Oil paintings featuring dark colors and somber themes hung heavy on the walls. It had been more than eight months since Eric had been in the building. He and Ambassador Wylie had met frequently with Dimitrović when he had first taken office. Cutting ties with the American embassy had been one of the first signals that something fundamental had changed in Banja Luka. The presidential palace seemed less dynamic than it had on Eric's last visit. Most of the offices they walked past were empty and looked like they had been for some time.

The president was waiting for them just inside the door to his office. He was only in his midfifties, but his hair was already turning from gray to white. He kept it cut short. His blue suit looked tailored and his tie looked expensive. Italian, Eric suspected. Dimitrović was tall, even for a Serb, almost six foot four, but he was stoop-shouldered and walked with a slight limp, an old war wound, it was rumored, even though no one seemed to know exactly where he had served in the fighting.

Dimitrović greeted Annika coolly. There would be nothing friendly about this meeting.

"Nice to see you again, Mr. Petrosian," Dimitrović said, as he shook Eric's hand. It was clear from his sour expression, however, that this was a lie. It was not the last one that Eric expected to hear over the next hour.

"Nice to be remembered, Mr. President," Eric offered in return. This, at least, had the virtue of being true.

The furniture in Dimitrović's office was a mishmash of styles. Eric sat in an overstuffed armchair that was too soft and too low to be comfortable. Sondergaard was seated on a love seat directly across from the president.

Dimitrović's plus-one was young and fit. He did not offer his name and Dimitrović did not introduce him. He looked more like a bodyguard than an advisor. There was a small pin on the lapel of his jacket that seemed like the kind of thing Diplomatic Security or the Secret Service used to differentiate levels of access. He took a seat along the wall behind Eric and Sondergaard so that he was looking across the room at Dimitrović rather than facing the guests. It was unusual behavior. Eric could not recall ever seeing anything like it.

"Madam High Representative, welcome to Republika Srpska," Dimitrović began, as two middle-aged women in matching uniforms distributed coffee and cookies. "I believe this is your first time in my country."

Dimitrović understood English well enough, but he spoke it with difficulty. Eric translated his Serbian for Sondergaard.

"Actually, this is my third visit to Bosnia," she replied.

"I don't include the Federation. I mean the RS."

"As your country?"

"Maybe not yet as a member of the United Nations. But my first loyalty is to Republika Srpska and its people."

"Well, the future of your people will be determined by the decisions that you make in the next few weeks. You know why I'm here." Sondergaard leaned forward on the love seat to underscore the urgency of her message. "Bosnia is at the edge of a precipice. You know what lies at the bottom. We all do. We've seen it before, close up. I want to help you step back from the abyss. But I need your help."

"I don't believe we are at the edge of anything," Dimitrović replied, and then paused to allow Eric to translate. "We are already falling. We have been falling for nearly twenty years now. Bosnia is a trap, pure and simple. It is a pit with smooth sides from which we have not been able to climb out. Look with clear eyes at the real lessons of the breakup of Yugoslavia. Ethnic cleansing was an ugly reality, but it worked. The places in the former Yugoslav space that are the most stable and successful are those places that were most effective in eliminating their restive and quarrelsome minority populations. Slovenia is the easiest example; it didn't have many minorities to start with. But look at Croatia. The Croats expelled nearly all of the Serbs and they have little cause to regret it. The same is true for the expulsion of Serbs from their ancestral home in Kosovo. It is those places that cling to the fantasy of multiethnic harmony that are the hardest to govern and the most backward politically. The peoples of the Balkans do not want to live together. They want to live at peace as neighbors with good fences between them. The sooner you in the West understand that basic reality, the easier it will be to talk about real solutions."

"Such as?"

"A new Congress of Berlin. The big powers agreed to a rational redrawing of borders once before. But the last time around, Europe and America insisted that the Tito-era administrative boundaries of Yugoslavia's republics were sacrosanct and could not be changed. This is ridiculous. If Yugoslavia could be so casually disintegrated, what is so special about Bosnia? Kosovo was not even a republic. It was a Serbian province that you chose to strip away and give to the Albanians. Why should we not have the same rights if we don't wish to live together with the Croats and the so-called Bosniaks? If we wish to live on our own, who are you to tell us that we cannot?"

"So yours is the discredited dream of a Greater Serbia?" Sondergaard asked incredulously. "Have we not already seen the terrible consequences of that ambition?"

"I am no more interested in being ruled from Belgrade than from Sarajevo. We Bosnian Serbs have fought for our freedom and we have won the right to self-determination. And we are determined to chart our own way forward, unburdened by the ineffective Dayton institutions."

"You do appreciate that the Congress of Berlin set the stage for World War I. None of these decisions are made in isolation. I offer you an alternative vision. Community. Union. Cooperation. These stand in opposition to the idea of separation and isolation. Yours is a dark view of human nature, Mr. President."

"Yes," Dimitrović agreed readily. "Yes, it is."

"There was a time not so long ago when your views were different. When you supported Bosnia's membership in the European Union and even NATO. When you worked in favor of a unitary

Bosnian state that did not distribute rights and responsibilities to its citizenry on the basis of their ethnicity and family name."

"Times change. I assure you that my views are sincere."

Dimitrović was looking over Sondergaard's shoulder, Eric noticed, as though seeking approval from the young "advisor" sitting along the back wall.

"So you no longer see Bosnia as a future EU member state?" the High Rep asked.

"I no longer see Bosnia as a state."

"Even at the risk of war?"

"Yes. Even then."

"What happened to you, Mr. President? You came to power promising support for a unified Bosnia. You started to make good on that commitment, then you moved away from it without any sort of warning."

"Perhaps the scales fell from my eyes," Dimitrović suggested, with a dismissive wave of his hand. "The only past that concerns me is the past injustice that has been done to my people."

"There will be a peace conference in Sarajevo in three weeks' time. Will you participate?"

"In my capacity as a hypocrite? I don't see how that would be possible. History is our guide. A history of man's inhumanity to man. We learned under the Ottoman pashas the importance of solidarity and will not surrender it to your artificial concept of unity."

"Will you at least send someone to represent you at the conference?"

Dimitrović again looked to the back wall before responding.

"If you force me to be blunt, I will be. Republika Srpska is not interested in the Sondergaard Plan. We have our own plan."

"Which is?"

"You'll see."

On the way out, Eric made certain to walk over to the "advisor" and shake his hand.

In the car on the way back, Eric asked the visibly dispirited High Representative if she had noticed the man's pin.

"No," she admitted. "But he didn't really seem the type for jewelry."

"It wasn't jewelry," Eric agreed. "It was more like a unit badge."

"For which unit?"

"It was a white hand."

"That's interesting."

"Ain't it. I think we may be looking at this all wrong."

"In what way?"

"We'd been assuming that Dimitrović was using the White Hand as an instrument of his personal power, a way to consolidate influence in his office. What if it's the other way around?"

"Meaning?"

"What if the White Hand is in control of Dimitrović?"

"Well, that would certainly complicate things, wouldn't it?"

On the drive back, Annika looked out the window at the verdant mountains only just beginning to change their summer colors for the muted tones of fall. In a few months, the Bosnian landscape would appear harsh and unforgiving, but for the moment, it was hard to credit that life in a place this beautiful could be anything but peaceful and comfortable. Settlements were spaced out along the road almost at regular intervals like mile markers.

Half an hour outside Banja Luka, they had to stop as a column of ten tanks crossed the highway, a mix of Yugoslav-era M-84s and Soviet surplus T-55s. In a field to one side, regular army troops were digging in, building firing positions for towed artillery that was pointed south toward Sarajevo. It was just an exercise, Eric knew, but there was a sense of urgency to the scene as though the soldiers involved expected to be doing this again for real at some point soon.

"Take a look at the flags," Eric said. The lead tank was flying a tricolor flag with horizontal stripes of red, blue, and white. Similar flags were flying from the antennae of the self-propelled guns digging in for whatever exercise was under way.

"What is that? Serbian?"

"That's the flag of Republika Srpska."

"I thought Bosnia had a unified army now. Wasn't that the one major accomplishment of post-Dayton integration?"

"It was," Eric agreed. "But that deal has broken down and the army has splintered. Most of the heavy weapons belong to the RS now."

"Is Dimitrović right, Eric?" Annika asked sadly, after they had navigated their way past the army encampment. They were driving through a small town of crumbling timber-and-wattle homes. It had been a mixed village before the war, with most of the villagers identifying themselves as Yugoslavs to the census takers. Now, the village was almost entirely Serb and it had something of the air of a ghost town. The High Representative's mood seemed to match that of the town, tired and forlorn.

"Right about what?"

"This," she said, gesturing out the window. "That the people here can't live together, that they won't live together, that they're better off apart."

"The old ancient hatreds argument?"

"Yes. What if it's true? What does that mean for Bosnia's future and what we're trying to do?"

"I don't think it is true," Eric said, trying to project conviction, knowing how easy it was for peacemakers in the Balkans to slip into a kind of fatalistic despair about a region that seemed to work so hard at resisting accommodation and compromise. "Or rather, I don't think it's necessarily true. The reality is that the ethnic groups in this part of the world have lived together in relative peace for longer than they've been killing one another. Mixed marriages were common here before the war."

"And what about Srebrenica? Or Jasenovac?" During the Second World War, the Nazi puppet regime in Croatia had murdered hundreds of thousands of Serbs, Jews, and Gypsies. The most notorious death camp, Jasenovac, was a cultural touchstone for the Serb side every bit as powerful as Srebrenica was for the Bosniaks or as Vukovar, the object of a vicious three-month siege at the outbreak of the Yugoslav wars, was for the Croats. Bosnia did not have a single history. It had three self-contained narratives.

"This isn't Disneyland," Eric said. "History here offers up plenty of violence, shocking violence. And it's often organized along ethnic lines. But history is not destiny. When Tito died, the Communist Party held Yugoslavia together with Scotch Tape and glue for ten years. But in the end, it couldn't survive the end of the Cold War and the disintegration of the Soviet Union. Nationalist feelings had been suppressed under the communists, not eliminated. Ethnic nationalism was there right under the surface. It offered people a sense of identity, of belonging. The violence didn't have to be a part of that picture. A few leaders—Milošević on the Serb side, Tuđman in Zagreb, and even Izetbegović in Sarajevo—used nationalism to promote themselves. To take power. The more they took, the more they wanted, and like Mao said, 'It's easy to ride the tiger. What's hard is getting off.'"

"But the hatred, the intolerance, it all seemed so real, so visceral. Was it all just made up?"

"Oh, it's real enough. The anger is real. The bitterness is real. The sense of historical grievance on the part of all the parties is real. Just about everyone in this part of the world carries around a mental ledger of historical injustices, and the books are never balanced."

"But aren't the Serbs the ones responsible for what happened here?"

"Depends on where you want to start the narrative. It's largely true if you want to start the clock in 1991. But the Serbs don't start it there. They look back to 1941. Some go back to the Battle of Kosovo in 1389 as the starting point. And we in the West don't always understand it. Did you ever read Rebecca West's book *Black Lamb and Grey Falcon*?"

"Well, I bought it, but I'd be lying if I said I read it."

"It is awfully long," Eric agreed. "Eleven hundred pages to describe a six-week trip through Yugoslavia in the thirties. She's not a great writer either, but she was a very perceptive observer. She wrote that Westerners who spend time in the Balkans have the unfortunate habit of adopting one of the nationalities as their pet, the one that can do no wrong. As she put it, 'Eternally the massacree and never the massacrer.'"

"So Jasenovac explains Srebrenica?"

"No. Nothing can explain Srebrenica. And nothing can justify it. It was a singular act of evil."

"Can we just ignore the history? Tell them it doesn't matter?"

"We can't. It's a part of what makes this place what it is. It makes the people who they are. I saw something similar up close with my grandparents. They were from a village near Trabzon on the Black Sea where they grew the sweetest grapes on planet Earth, or so my grandfather assured me. His family were farmers. My grandmother's father was a shopkeeper. They were only teenagers when the Ottoman troops started burning the Armenian villages. The soldiers drowned tens of thousands in the sea and left the bodies floating on the surface like pack ice. My grandparents were the only two people from their village to survive. They eventually drifted to America on a postwar tide of refugees, got married, built a good life. But they never really left the village. Even after almost seven decades in sunny Southern California, they considered themselves villagers from Trabzon. Old Grandpa Petrosian had a photograph of his family's farm, a sepia-toned picture of grape arbors and haystacks that he kept on his desk. Both the land and the genocide had worked their way deep into his soul, into his blood and bone. It was who he was."

"And they never went back to the village? Just to see it again."

"Go to Turkey? No way in hell. They wouldn't even eat turkey."

Annika's smile was tired but genuine.

"I hope you don't mean to tell me that it's all hopeless."

"Not at all. We can't ignore the history, but that doesn't mean we should let it be the driver of policy, to dismiss them all as prisoners of their own prejudice. We overcome it. And that means we have to understand it. To share in the historical memory."

"Memory does seem to be something of a local specialty in the Balkans. It's like what Talleyrand said about the Bourbons: 'They have learned nothing and forgotten nothing.'"

"Yes," Eric agreed sadly. "They remember. They remember everything. Even things that never happened."

JASENOVAC
MARCH 20, 1942

3

The gruel was thin and tasteless, a few lumps of starch mixed with water from the river that had not been boiled long enough to sterilize it. Natasa pushed away the battered tin cup that was almost her sole earthly possession with an expression of disgust. Her cousin, Ivan, pushed it back.

"You have to eat, Natasa."

They were sitting on the back steps of the barracks. The wood was slick with mud and slime, but there was no place else. They were lucky. Most of the prisoners ate standing up. A few crouched in the muddy yard bent over their cups and bowls like dogs.

"Eat," Ivan said, gently this time.

"I won't. It's disgusting."

"It's life, Natasa. If you don't eat, you die."

"I'll die anyway."

"Maybe," Ivan acknowledged. "Maybe even probably, but if you don't eat, you'll end up a *muselmann* first."

The *muselmanner* were the living dead. Skeletons. They were empty husks who had lost the will to perform the most basic human functions. They would not eat or sleep or clean themselves. Some shuffled mindlessly through the camp moaning softly. Some cowered in the darkest corners of the common buildings, their rough cotton pants soiled with urine and feces. They were no longer human. The Croatian guards called them *muselmanner*. It was the German word for Muslims. The Croatian fascists, the Ustaše, must have picked it up from their Nazi overlords.

"Why do they use that word?" Natasa asked, as she grudgingly took a sip of the dirty water that passed as soup.

"I think it's because of the ones who lie curled up on the floor like Muslims in prayer. Don't worry about it, Natasa, don't worry about anything except living one more day."

Ivan smiled and Natasa felt warmer even though the March weather was damp and cold. The winter had been harsh. Thousands of prisoners had died of malnutrition and exhaustion. Thousands more had been judged too weak to work and sent to the brick factory. What happened there no one knew for certain, but no one ever came back from the factory. The clouds of ash that spewed from the factory's tall chimney were thick and black and reeked of death.

Natasa finished her soup and firmly rebuffed Ivan's efforts to give her the last few swallows of his serving. Ivan was only a few years older than Natasa—twenty to her fifteen. But he acted as though he were the grown-up and Natasa the child. She did not mind so much. She wanted so desperately to be a child.

He had always been protective of her even back in the village near Mount Kozara, where the fields were fertile, the streams clean and clear, and the larders full of smoked meat and cheese, apricots and honey. That was before the madness.

Ivan's father and Natasa's mother had been brother and sister. They were dead, along with their spouses. Natasa's father had died back in the village resisting deportation by the Croatian fascists. Her mother had died in the fall from typhus. Ivan's father had died before the war, and his mother had been taken to the brick factory soon after their arrival in the camp. She had always been somewhat frail.

There were a few others in the camp who Natasa knew, even a couple of distant relatives. But Ivan was the only one she was close to. This was not a place you made friends.

There was nothing alive in the camp. No trees. No grass. No flowers. Nothing beautiful. Everything was colored in muted shades of gray and brown. Outside the barbed-wire fence, the landscape was covered in ash from the furnaces.

In truth, Natasa was not entirely sure why they were here. Ivan said it was just because they were Serbs, and the blue ribbon pinned to her thin jacket marked her as a Serb as clearly as the Jews were identified by their yellow stars and the communist Partisans by a red badge. Only the Gypsies were not marked by a color, and they largely kept to themselves in a part of the camp that was if anything even more squalid and fetid than the block of wooden shacks where Natasa and Ivan worked and slept. It was unfair, Natasa complained. They had not done anything wrong—nothing except to be born Serbs. But that seemed to be crime enough.

A pack of guards in their warm black greatcoats marched into the yard as though they were on parade. Weapons hung over their shoulders or across their backs like oiled serpents.

"Oh, to be young . . . and fascist," Ivan said, with the wry smile that not even a year in a concentration camp had been able to take from him.

"They do seem happy," Natasa agreed.

The guards spread out, kicking a few of the prisoners to their feet.

"Up, you bastards," Natasa heard one of the guards shout as he slammed a leather boot into the ribs of an older man who was slow to rise.

The prisoner, a Partisan to judge by the red badge on his threadbare jacket, lay in the mud on his side unable to or unwilling to stand. It was hard to believe that this old man was a fearsome guerrilla fighter. Maybe he was being punished for a son who had joined the communists. The guard swung one leg back as though preparing to kick him again then seemed to change his mind. There was no point to it. The prisoner was too weak to be of any value. Instead, he pulled a fingerless leather glove from the pocket of his greatcoat and strapped it tightly to his right hand with practiced ease. A short curved blade was built into the glove. It stuck out like the sharp spur on the gamecocks that the village men used to wager on. The guards called it the *Srbosjek*—the Serb cutter. It was good for only one thing, cutting throats. But that it did very, very well.

Within seconds, the elderly prisoner was lying dead in a puddle of mud and blood. The guards left him there. A team of prisoners on corpse duty would be by soon enough to add him to the pile of bodies waiting to be dumped into mass graves or burned in the great ovens at the brick factory.

Natasa felt nothing at watching the old man's death. It was one of hundreds of murders she had witnessed. One of thousands of dead bodies. Death would come for them all. A part of her, the part that was still a girl from a large family in a small village, despaired at her own lack of feeling. This act of senseless violence should have filled her with horror. That it did not, that she had grown numb to the brutality of the camp, made her wonder if in some important way she was not already dead.

"Come on," Ivan said, helping her to her feet. "Let's get to the factory before little Adolf takes an interest in us."

He rose unsteadily to his feet. Malnutrition brought on spells of dizziness and vertigo. Ivan extended a bony arm to Natasa to help her to her feet. The skin on the back of his hand was like parchment paper. The veins under the skin stood out in sharp relief. Her cousin had once been handsome, with strong features and curly brown hair. The features had hardened into something vulpine, and his head was shaved to deter lice. Ivan was no longer handsome, but he was her whole world. Natasa did not know what she would do if she lost him. It would be the end of her.

They shuffled through the camp toward the factory where they stamped sheet metal into bowls and plates for the Croatian army. It took almost five minutes to cover the three hundred meters. None of the prisoners had the energy to do more than push themselves forward at a speed just above a pace that would earn a kick or a club from one of the guards. No one seemed to care. The goal of Jasenovac was not efficient production. The goal was extermination. The world had gone mad.

"Factory" was perhaps too grandiose a term for the building where they worked. It was just a single-story wooden structure, no different from the overcrowded barracks. The carpentry was shoddy, but the roof at least did not leak. The machines inside were valuable. The factory was a relatively good work assignment. The prisoners who worked the fields or those sent to dig coal in the mines did not last long. The factory work was at least indoors.

This was a shift change. The factory never closed. The machines ran twenty-four hours a day, and the prisoners worked in twelve-hour shifts. The guards would have worked them harder, but the death rate among the workers was too high. The prisoners were expected to die when the Croats told them to, not on their own schedule.

Natasa went about her job like an automaton, moving slowly to conserve energy. If they were lucky, there would be beans for dinner. If not, it would be half a litre of turnip soup. The diet offered barely enough calories to stay alive.

Natasa's job was to dip the bowls into a vat of enamel and stack them to dry. She did it again and again, thinking of nothing. Ivan was working the stamping machine alongside a tall blond girl from Zagreb named Jelena. Natasa and Ivan were from a village and they were used to hard physical labor. Jelena was the daughter of a physician, and she had trained as a pianist. She was stick thin and her blond hair was falling out in clumps, but there was a vestige of her former beauty that had survived life in the camp. Tuberculosis had given her skin a glow that could almost have been mistaken for health.

Ivan was sweet on Jelena. Natasa saw him pull something from his pocket, a small hunk of black bread, it looked like, and press it into Jelena's hand. She tried to give it back, but not too hard. The second time he pressed it on her, she kept it.

One of the guards had seen them, however. And not just any guard.

He was an enormous villager from Herzegovina with a face as round as the moon and a sadistic streak that was well known to the prisoners, who called him the Hand of Satan. He was one of the guards who always wore his *Srbosjek* and he used it without provocation.

"What's in your pocket?" he demanded of Jelena

She looked at her feet.

"Nothing," she said dully. It was a mistake. You should always make eye contact with the guards when you lie to them, Natasa knew.

Jelena turned out the pocket of her coat. It was empty.

The guard reached for her wrist and turned her hand over. The crust of bread was clutched in her palm.

"Food in the factory is forbidden," he said menacingly. The Hand of Satan reached for a wooden truncheon at his belt.

"Stop!" Ivan screamed, as he stepped in between Jelena and the guard. "The bread is mine. I brought it into the factory. The punishment is mine."

"Very well," the guard agreed.

He slipped the truncheon back into the holster on his belt. Natasa stood rooted to the floor.

With a single smooth motion, the guard swung his Serb cutter across Ivan's throat. Her cousin's neck was so thin that she could hear the scraping sound as the razor-sharp knife cut into the bone.

Blood arcing from Ivan's neck fell on Jelena like a red rain, soaking into her clothes and the piece of bread she still held in her hand.

Natasa slumped to the cement floor, her vision gray and blurry.

The guard hit Jelena casually with the back of his hand, knocking her head against the stamping machine. The doctor's daughter fell alongside Ivan. Dead maybe. Maybe not. It didn't matter.

The guard turned to look at Natasa as though seeing her for the first time.

"Clean this up," he commanded.

SARAJEVO
OCTOBER 12

4

For a brief moment when she walked through the door, Eric was twenty-one years old again and in love. She had not changed. Not really. Her hair was still chestnut and still shoulder length. She was fit and strong, with broad shoulders and a trim waist. There were a few lines around her eyes and at the corner of her mouth. She had to be well into her forties by now, Eric knew, but she sure did not look it.

A complex cocktail of emotions produced an almost physical pain in his chest right above his heart. It was a mixture of regret, desire, and nostalgia. He had loved this woman fiercely and passionately as only a young man can. That was a long time ago.

There was more than one kind of ghost.

“Hello, Sarah.”

“Hello, Eric.”

"It's been a long time."

"Yes."

They were in Eric's office in the CAA, the controlled access area that housed the ambassador's suite, the political and economic sections, and the defense attaché's office, those parts of the embassy that handled classified information. That Sarah was there on her own meant that she was still with the government and that she still had her clearances. He should not have been all that surprised to see her. It was bound to happen at some point.

Eric got up from his desk and embraced Sarah Gold for the first time in twenty years. The skin on her cheek was cool where his lips brushed it. She took his hand and squeezed it firmly.

"I'm so glad to find you here, Eric."

"It's nice to see you," Eric replied, and he was surprised to realize it was true. Time had blunted the sharp edge of hurt as it always did. Eventually.

Unconsciously, almost instinctively, he looked at her left hand. There was no ring. That did not really mean anything, however. Many of the women in her organization did not wear their rings. The perception of availability could at times be exploited.

"I need to talk to you," Sarah said, and there was a note of urgency in her voice.

"Sure. Sit down."

"Not here. Can we go someplace?"

Eric glanced at the clock on the wall. It was almost seven.

"Dinner?"

"I'd like that." She smiled and his heart skipped a beat or two before settling into a slightly faster rhythm. *Don't be an idiot,* he chided himself. *She left you, remember?*

Unbidden, an image of her chestnut hair fanned out across a white pillowcase sprang from his memory. His old apartment, the one across the road from the Holiday Inn where he and the other journalists used to drink away the dark nights of the siege. But that was before Sarah. Once they met, it had been just the two of them huddled together in the dark as the shells fell on the city, drinking red wine rather than the Scotch that Sarajevo's close-knit community of war correspondents guzzled like expensive water.

He took a step back from her and tried to pull himself away from the past. The past was a trap. He had known that since he was ten years old. It was full of lies and promises unkept. And death.

"How about the old place?" he asked.

"Is it still there?"

"It is."

"Still good?"

"Just as good."

"That would be fabulous."

Eric locked up his office, logging off the various computer systems and pulling the blinds shut against prying eyes. The Bosnians didn't have much of an intelligence service, but the Russians and Chinese were both active in Sarajevo. There were still a few people working in the suite so he did not need to set the alarms.

"I'm done for the night," he told his staff, as he and Sarah headed for the door.

One of his officers looked up briefly from his monitor and nodded in acknowledgment. "Have fun, boss. Be good."

Outside, it was already dark and growing cool. Eric offered Sarah his arm and she took it. They fit together neatly, just like they always had.

It was a fifteen-minute walk at a leisurely pace from the embassy to Kod Jasne, a small, unassuming restaurant on the outer edge of Baščaršija, the old part of Sarajevo on the north bank of the Miljacka River. It was the most vibrant part of the city, with good restaurants and numerous bars and cafés that featured hookah water pipes and the fruit-flavored tobacco called *shisha*. Fifty years of communism and four years of war had tried and failed to erase Sarajevo's Ottoman-era charm. And Baščaršija was ground zero for the city's vibe of bohemian cool.

Kod Jasne was one of the few restaurants that continued to operate more or less without a break through the siege. Jasna, the matronly proprietress, had had a relative in the UN who was able to smuggle in enough meat and flour and coffee and sugar to keep her in business. Eric and Sarah had been regulars, along with a small group of international journalists, diplomats, and spies. Other spies, Eric corrected himself, looking over at Sarah's profile. He had not known what she did for a living when they first started seeing each other. He suspected, of course, that she was not really a press officer. She wasn't the type. But they had been lovers for more than six weeks before she had told him that she was with the CIA.

On the walk to Kod Jasne, they caught each other up on the intervening twenty years. Eric told her about joining the Foreign Service, working on the soul-crushing visa line in the Mexican border town of Ciudad Juárez, almost quitting, sticking it out, and making it through the diplomatic equivalent of dues paying with his sanity mostly intact before embarking on a career that included tours in Ankara and Phnom Penh as well as two stints in Sarajevo, a year in Kabul, and two years at the U.S. Mission to the United Nations in New York.

"So you finally made it to Cambodia," Sarah said. She knew about his family and his mother's suicide. "Did you find what you were looking for there?"

"No," Eric admitted. "I'm not sure it exists."

After six months of searching, Eric had found a cousin in Cambodia, seemingly the only relative on his mother's side who had not been lost to the killing fields. They had shared a meal and a few drinks and Eric had listened to stories of his mother when she was young and innocent. There was nothing in those stories that he could connect to the beautiful but deeply sad and damaged person who could not process what had happened to her and her family. Eric remembered finding her body in the garage and feeling not horror or anger but relief. He had been happy for his mother and relieved that as her son he had not been an anchor tying her to a life that she could no longer live. It was a complex emotion for a ten-year-old, one he was still wrestling with.

For her part, Sarah told him that after Bosnia she had moved over to the Middle East department with postings in Jordan and Israel as well as Egypt and Iraq. About two years ago, she had moved back to Washington to take charge of the Balkan Action Team at Langley. She did not mention anything about a husband or kids. *She would have, wouldn't she?* Eric asked himself. If she had them. But maybe she suspected that he still had feelings for her and wanted to use them to manipulate him. It was the kind of thing the CIA taught the new recruits at their famous Farm in Virginia. It was not really fair to think that way, however. Sarah would tell him soon enough why she had sought him out after so many years.

Sarah was easy to talk to. She had always been easy to talk to. Talking had never been their problem. Srebrenica had been their problem, or at least Eric's inability to shake off the moral outrage and the depression that followed. Eight thousand murder victims, and all Eric could do was think about his own pain, his own loss. It was, he now understood, the narcissism of youth.

They passed a building on which an anonymous graffiti artist with more passion than imagination had spray-painted SMRT SRBIMA in angry red block letters. *Death to Serbs.*

Sarah stopped to look at it and shook her head.

"Just like old times."

"Yeah. Things are getting tense. You can see this kind of stuff all over town."

Two women walked by them in the opposite direction dressed in loose dark-colored tunics with their heads covered in the *hijab*. Observant Muslims.

"That's new," Sarah commented. "I remember there were more miniskirts and high heels than *hijab*s back in the day."

"Yes," Eric agreed. "Bosnia is changing. It's more conservative and the communities are still drifting farther away from one another. It's a matter of identity. Being Bosnian doesn't mean as much as being Bosniak for most people, and that means Islam is fundamental to your sense of self. So you get more Bosniaks fasting during Ramadan or adopting traditional dress codes. The Serbs, for their part, have embraced their Saints' Day celebrations and mark the new year on January 13. The Croats are actually going to mass on Sunday and taking communion. The major ethnic groups are all circling the wagons."

"Who are they afraid of?"

"Each other."

"What a mess."

"You said it. Bosnia is deeply unloved. Everyone sees something in it that they hate. The Serbs reject the state—Bosnia and Herzegovina. Their country is Republika Srpska. The Bosniaks hate Dayton and the two-entity structure that split this country in half and makes it essentially ungovernable. And the Croats hate the Federation that makes them a minority in their own patch of Bosnia. They want a third entity that the other two groups will never agree to."

"Is there a way out?"

"There's Sondergaard."

Sarah scoffed. "Another do-gooding Nordic? Hasn't Bosnia seen enough of them?"

"No. This one seems different to me."

"How so?"

"She's tough. She's not going to shy away from the hardball politics of this place."

"Tough enough?"

"We'll see."

"And you're working for her now from what I understand."

"Word gets around."

"That's what words do."

The look she gave him was ambiguous, hard for Eric to interpret. But whatever she was hinting at, it seemed important.

Eric stopped abruptly, catching Sarah by surprise.

"Is this it?" she asked.

"It is." The building in front of them had wooden walls covered in green paint that was sun faded and peeling. He pointed to a hand-lettered sign over the door that advertised Kod Jasne.

"Everything looks so different," Sarah commented.

"The city has changed a lot since the old days. It's changed in the three years I've been here. Even old buildings like this one are surrounded by so much new construction that it can be hard to get your bearings."

"I'll say. I hardly recognize the place."

She pointed to something on the ground.

"But I recognize that," she said. "Are there many of them left?"

It was a Sarajevo rose. City residents had poured red enamel into the scars left in the sidewalks and streets by shells or mortar rounds that had taken at least one life. The pattern was distinctive and unforgettable, and the roses were a symbol of both Bosnian defiance and crippling sorrow.

"Fewer and fewer all the time. When they dig up the streets or sidewalks for various construction projects, they don't bother to replace the roses. There are only a handful left."

"I remember that one," Sarah said.

Eric nodded.

"Me too."

It had been a rainy day in April when a mortar round had landed right on that spot, sending a shell fragment into the brain of a young woman who had been waiting in line for a table at the restaurant. Eric and Sarah had been inside, and were among the first to go to her assistance. There had been nothing they could do, however, except hold her hand as the life drained from her body. They had stopped going to Kod Jasne for a while after that. Ghosts.

Jasna was still there, and she greeted Eric and Sarah like they were old friends.

"So good to see the two of you together again," she said, as she led them to the table in the back corner that had once been "theirs."

Jasna's decorating style sprawled right on the border of kitsch, occasionally veering over the line as it did with the collection of porcelain cats scattered throughout the room. The chairs were low, more like stools, and the tables were made of large copper trays balanced on wooden stands. The floors were covered with several layers of Turkish kilim. The kitchen was open and connected directly to the dining room. This was now fashionable in trendy restaurants in the West, but Kod Jasne had always been like that. It had once been Jasna's house.

There were no menus. Jasna fed her guests whatever she had made that day. Today it was *ćevapčići*, sausage-shaped kebabs that were one of the reliable staples in the Balkans. Jasna made hers from a mix of beef and lamb. They arrived hot off the grill with a round flatbread called *somun* and a mix of sides and salads, all chosen by Jasna. Nothing goes better with *ćevapčići* than beer, and the local stuff, Sarajevsko Pivo, was pretty good. Eric and Sarah each had a pint.

Balkan food was not sophisticated. It was largely based on village cooking traditions. There was not a lot of variety to it, but the ingredients were all fresh and locally sourced, and the recipes had stood the test of centuries. Sarah slathered a piece of bread with *kajmak*, a spread made from sheep's milk that was halfway between butter and cheese, and a roasted-pepper-and-eggplant dip called *ajvar*.

"God, I missed this stuff," she said. "You can't get this kind of thing anywhere else in the world."

Dessert was baklava made with walnuts rather than pistachios and drenched with honey. Demitasses of bitter Turkish coffee kept the sweetness of the baklava from being cloying. In Bosnian culture, coffee meant that it was time to move from social talk to business. Washington culture was not really all that different in that respect.

"Tell me, Sarah," Eric said, as he sipped his coffee. "What are you doing in Sarajevo? And what does it have to do with me?"

"My team is worried about Bosnia."

"We all are."

"Our predictive models all point toward some sort of conflict—maybe even a renewal of open war—in the next six to twelve months."

"How much did you pay for that model? 'Cause I think I could have got you the same prediction for a hell of a lot less."

Sarah smiled. She had many different smiles. And Eric thought of the last time he had seen that particular one, a little off center, producing just one dimple on her right cheek. The last time he had kissed her.

"You're in the wrong line of work," she said. "You should have gone into consulting."

"Tell me about it."

"Anyway. Our analysts have been watching things deteriorate over the last eight months or so. The critical variable seems to be the rise of Marko Barcelona and the White Hand. Dimitrović's government and the paramilitaries in the RS are operating more or less under his direction, even if that's not anything you or I might recognize as control."

Eric nodded. He knew all this.

"At first, we'd been operating under the assumption that Mali was an extension of Dimitrović, that Dimitrović himself created the

White Hand for his own purposes. The Hand was a tool for undermining the Bosnian state and giving himself an alibi for breaking his commitments."

"But lately you've started to think that maybe the reverse is true," Eric suggested. "That Mali is controlling Dimitrović. That maybe Dimitrović built the White Hand but lost control of his creation. A kind of Dr. Frankensteinović."

Sarah's smile was different this time. The soft one that meant she was impressed.

"That's about it," she said. "It would explain Dimitrović's one-eighty on changing the Bosnian constitution and trying to make this place into a viable unified country. Mali has a different agenda."

"What is it?"

"Himself."

They finished the coffees. Jasna brought them each a small glass of brandy, her family's personal home brew, she whispered conspiratorially, so the other diners would not overhear. For old times' sake, she explained. Jasna's *rakija* was made from quince and smoother than the typical plum-based moonshine.

"So what does Mali have on Dimitrović?" Eric asked.

"We're not sure yet," she admitted. "Something big. Something important. We had one source in Dimitrović's camp who reported that there was a disc or a tape. Dimitrović was evidently bitching about it one night and our source was there. But he didn't know what was on it."

"Can you use him to try to get more on this? Something more specific."

"We can't ask him anything anymore."

"Sleeping with the fishes?"

"The worms."

"That works too. So where do I fit into this?"

"I want you to help me find out what Marko Barcelona has over Zoran Dimitrović. What's his leverage and how can we counter it."

"I'm just a regular diplomat, Sarah. This is really more your organization's sort of thing, isn't it? Don't you have some Jason Bourne type you can wheel out for something like this? Someone with substantially more muscle mass." Eric was fortunate to get his height from his father's side and stood a hair under six feet tall. But his build was from his mother, lanky and whip thin. He was in good shape and strong, but although he was a regular at the embassy gym and ran every weekend with Sarajevo's Hash House Harriers, Eric was never going to be anything but skinny. The rectangular hipster glasses he wore did nothing to make him look tougher.

"I'm not looking for someone with massive biceps," Sarah replied. "I need someone with a bulging Rolodex. No one in the U.S. government has anything like your range of contacts in Republika Srpska. You know everyone who matters in Banja Luka and Zvornik and all of the one-cow towns in between. I need your help. Bosnia needs your help."

"Okay. I understand that. But why the cloak-and-dagger? Why not do this through channels? Set up a task force. Have me seconded to it. Why are we having this conversation at Jasna's rather than the ambassador's office?"

"Eric, you've grown cynical over the years."

"Just a little more cautious maybe."

"Don't get me wrong. A little cynicism is a good thing. It'll help keep you sane . . . and alive. But only in small doses. Too much can be poisonous."

"Like love or oxygen?"

"God, you are a child of the eighties. That's very sweet."

"And you are a clever girl."

"Ain't I though."

"But back to my question."

Sarah's smile vanished like a mirage. She bit her lower lip and looked quickly around the restaurant, looking for anyone who seemed out of place. The gesture seemed somehow mannered, a moment staged for Eric's benefit rather than a piece of genuine tradecraft.

"We have a leak," she confided. "Someone on the inside. Maybe CIA. But maybe State or one of the other agencies. There's not enough data to be sure. We don't know if it's someone working directly for Dimitrović or if Belgrade or Moscow is passing him stuff, but we have to believe that anything we do through channels will get to Banja Luka. That's what we think happened to our source in Dimitrović's office. We only get one shot at this, so we need to be extremely careful. We're doing this with a small team."

"How do you know the mole's not part of that team?"

"We can't know. But we're playing the odds. The smaller the number of people who know what we're doing, the less the chance of exposure."

"Do you have authority for this?" Eric asked.

"It falls under our group's standing authorities. We've got a letter from the Langley lawyers that says so."

"Can I bring Wylie in on this? Let him know what I'm doing."

"I'd rather you didn't."

"Why not?"

"I don't trust him to keep his mouth shut. He's a braggart and a drunk and kind of a gasbag."

"You've got his number," Eric agreed, with a rueful shake of his head.

"Wylie's already cut you loose," Sarah added. "You work for Sondergaard now. You don't need to account for your time to him. Or to Sondergaard. Not really. She'll be in and out of Bosnia. You'll still be available to her when she needs you. But you'll also be available to me. I need you, Eric."

Sarah leaned toward him, and over the powerful smells of grilled meat and mint and cardamom, Eric picked up a hint of her perfume. L'Eau d'Issey. The same one she had used when they were together. Was she still wearing the same perfume or did she put it on just for him, hoping that he would remember? Of all the senses, scent offered the most direct connection to memory.

Eric sighed. He could rationalize his choice in professional terms any way he chose. On the surface, it was about the future of Bosnia. But if he was going to be honest with himself, this was as much about the past as it was about the future. Sarah and Srebrenica and a garage in suburban Orange County. Ghosts.

"What do you need me to do?"

"Take me to Banja Luka. Help me meet some people who might be in a position to know what's going on and what Mali is using to control Dimitrović if—in fact—that's what's happening."

"And then?"

"What do you mean?"

"There's always more."

She smiled that "I'm impressed" smile again.

"Really?"

"Really."

"Maybe so," she agreed. "We'll see. But we have to hurry. There's no time to waste."

"Because of Sondergaard's conference?"

"No. Because whatever it is that Mali has . . ."

"Yes?"

"We're not the only ones looking for it."

GENEVA
OCTOBER 13

5

As a matter of principle, he hated code names. Too much artifice; not enough value. He used them, of course. It was an integral part of his chosen profession. It was tradecraft. But he did it reluctantly. For this op, he had been saddled with an especially clunky sounding code name—Klingsor. It sounded like something best treated with a shot of penicillin. Fuck it. If he was going to be Klingsor, then he would be fucking Klingsor.

Klingsor and his team had their mark. They were targeting a Geneva-based lawyer named Emile Gisler. Kundry—Klingsor tried to use the code names for the op even in his private thoughts to minimize the risk of a slip over the radio or the phone—had told him that their mark almost certainly had the package. Kundry wanted it something fierce. It was Klingsor's job to get it.

Klingsor and Kundry had worked together before. Kundry was a solid professional, one of the best he knew. But there was something about this current op that did not feel quite right. It seemed ad hoc, made up on the fly, and cobbled together from bits and pieces of capabilities. But Klingsor the Sorcerer had performed miracles for Kundry on more than one occasion. Odds were he could do it again.

Geneva was a god-awful place to do this kind of thing. The Swiss liked things neat and tidy. The national sport of Switzerland was ratting out your neighbors to the police, and static surveillance quickly drew a host of disapproving glances followed by a visit from a friendly member of the Kantonspolizei acting on an anonymous inquiry from a "concerned citizen." It was better to keep moving even if the logistics were a little more convoluted as a consequence.

"Klingsor," said a voice in his ear. The receiver was no bigger than a hearing aid and connected via Bluetooth rather than the Secret Service–style spiral cord that practically screamed "I'm a spy." "This is Echo Three. I have eyes on target, southbound on rue des Rois. Gray suit. Red tie. Black briefcase in his right hand."

Echo Three could just as easily have been describing himself. Geneva was a city of bankers and bureaucrats, and they dressed the part, anonymous men who could have stepped right off the canvas of a Magritte painting if bowler hats ever came back into fashion.

"This is Echo Four. I have acquired the target."

"Echo Three. Dropping contact."

Klingsor did not want to do it this way. Too many things could go wrong with a snatch and grab, and the consequences of a fuckup could be quite severe. But Gisler's office had been a dry hole. Klingsor's team had tossed the place pretty thoroughly. It had taken no more than ten minutes to crack the safe. There had not been anything inside. Just gold, gaudy jewelry, cash, and a thick stack of bearer bonds. Nothing really valuable. No information. The package was no doubt secured in one of the several hundred safe-deposit boxes that Gisler maintained for a client list that included drug dealers, Central Asian autocrats, the more respectable sort of terrorist—think Red Brigade rather than al-Qaeda—and "controversial businessmen" from east of the Urals. Gisler was not too picky as long as the check could be expected to clear. Kundry had ordered the snatch and grab, which is why Klingsor found himself sitting in the passenger seat of a panel van cruising through the streets of Europe's most antiseptic city.

At least it was dark.

Gisler was on his way back to his apartment from the bar where he spent most nights drinking. He liked to drink. And eat. Their mark was something of a bon vivant with a penchant for fine dining and the build to prove it. Gisler was as close to perfectly spherical as Klingsor had ever seen a man achieve. Klingsor listened in on the radio as Echoes Two through Four traded coverage of the lawyer back and forth, always keeping him in sight but never giving him a chance to spot the coverage by overstaying their welcome. They were a good team. Klingsor was proud of them. This next part was the tricky bit.

Klingsor pulled a black balaclava out of his pocket and slipped it on over his head. Echo One did the same.

The van crept carefully down rue du Diorama, turning left onto rue de la Synagogue just as Gisler reached the intersection. This was a quiet part of Geneva, which even on a good day could not be mistaken for Berlin or Milan. At twenty minutes to midnight, there was no traffic. The one security camera covering that intersection had come down with a nasty virus. It would show a continuous loop of nothing in particular for the next three hours before the virus took its own electronic life.

Echo One slid the van door open. Echoes Three and Four had come up alongside behind Gisler wearing masks like Klingsor's, and in one carefully choreographed motion, they muscled the rotund Swiss lawyer into the back of the van before he had time to so much as protest. Had he tried, he would have had a hard time making himself heard with the palm of Echo Four's hand pressed firmly over his mouth. Echo One closed the door and the driver pulled away from the curb. The whole thing had taken no more than six seconds. It was textbook.

"What a fat tub of lard," Echo Three complained. He said it in German. They had agreed as part of OPSEC that all conversation would be in German. It was not Klingsor's best foreign language, but his Hochdeutsche was more than adequate, and it was the one language other than English that all members of the team had in common.

The lawyer had recovered from the initial shock. He did not seem especially surprised at what had happened. With the kind of clients Gisler routinely dealt with, Klingsor supposed that kidnapping was no doubt an ever-present risk.

"Who do you work for?" Gisler demanded, once Echo Four had removed his hand. He tried to stand up, but Echo Four pushed him back onto the floor of the panel van using just enough excess force to make the point.

"Tell me who you work for," Gisler insisted again.

"You don't want to know," Klingsor answered. He put as much menace as he could into the phrase. He wanted Gisler afraid. As he spoke, he leaned forward and let his jacket open up far enough that the well-padded lawyer could see the butt of Klingsor's Glock sticking out of its holster at his waist.

"Do you want moncy?" Gisler asked. "I have money. Enough money." The fear was already starting to eat away at his bluster. That was good.

Klingsor said nothing and his team was disciplined. They followed his lead. He wanted Gisler to imagine the worst. His thoughts would settle inevitably on his own particular and personal fears. He would do a better job of frightening himself than Klingsor ever could. Quiet was most effective in raising anxiety, and anxiety made men like Gisler talkative.

It was a twenty-minute drive to the parking garage. The building was only half finished. The company that owned it had recently sold it to another developer with an address on Cyprus that was little more than a post-office box and a tax credit. That company was controlled by Klingsor's employer. The deal would ultimately fall through. But for now, work on the garage had been suspended while all involved did due diligence. They would have it all to themselves.

Echo Three unlocked the gate, and the van took a circular ramp down three stories into subterranean Geneva.

"It'll be quiet down here," Klingsor explained to Gisler. "And private. We have some things to discuss."

"What do you want from me?" Gisler asked. The lawyer did not try to put on any kind of display of false bravado. His double chin quivered with evident fear. He was sweating heavily, Klingsor noted. His shirt was already soaked through at the collar.

"Just one simple little thing," Klingsor said.

"What is it?"

"Be patient."

The van stopped. Klingsor opened the door and Echo Four hauled the lawyer to his feet by the collar of his bespoke suit jacket. The sound of ripping cloth testified to both Echo Four's freakish strength and Gisler's substantial bulk.

A plain steel door was set in the wall of the garage next to where the van had parked. Klingsor opened it with a key from a chain around his neck and Echoes Three and Four hustled Gisler inside. The room behind the door was little more than a raw concrete cube. In the center of the room was a dentist's chair. A metal table held a range of tools, some sharp and shiny, others dull and blunt. A car battery sat at the far end of the table with a pair of jumper cables lying next to it.

It was all for show.

Klingsor had no intention of torturing Gisler. It was not that his organization was above that sort of thing. But that was not his department. There were specialists for that, and Klingsor respected what they did. They were professionals. Klingsor, however, was an expert on human psychology. The manipulation of fear. He was quite good at it, almost an artist, really. And that is what this was, a kind of performance art. He could leverage the full range of emotions. Greed was a reliable old standby, and lust had its place, particularly with the young and naïve. But fear was his favorite. It made the strong weak and the weak bare their souls. If Klingsor did his job correctly, Gisler would be back at his apartment in a few hours unharmed. At least physically, at least for now. What might happen to him when his client discovered that his lawyer had misplaced the package left in his keeping was not Klingsor's concern.

Echo Three stripped Gisler of his jacket and tie, and forced him down into the dentist's chair. The chair was Klingsor's idea, a trademark of sorts. For most people, there was an almost Pavlovian response to the chair. The association with pain was strong and deeply rooted. The chair set the right tone.

I am going to hurt you.

The skin on the lawyer's face and neck was pale and clammy. There were dark circles of fear sweat under his armpits. Klingsor bent over him. With the mask on, only his eyes were visible, eyes that Klingsor knew how to use to create the impression of a window to a dark and twisted soul. He liked to believe that wasn't true. He was a devoted family man, with two daughters he adored and doted on. He was a good churchgoer and generous to his many friends. This was a job. But he was introspective enough to recognize the corrosive effects that this particular art form could have on the psyche. Every man had his limits.

I'll take a break after this job, he had promised himself, go someplace warm and lie around for a while, maybe put in for a transfer to a different department, something with less travel. He had tried that once or twice before and had been denied. He was, they had assured him, too valuable in his current position. Well, fuck them.

Klingsor stared at Gisler from behind his mask, willing his eyes to be as cold as polished stone.

"You have something I want."

"Tell me," Gisler croaked.

Water dripping from the ceiling had formed a puddle in the

middle of the room. There was a broken pipe somewhere. The effect was suitably dramatic.

"You are keeping a package for a man. You may not even know what's in it. But it is very important to me. I want it. Tonight."

"I keep almost everything in safe-deposit boxes," Gisler pleaded. "The banks are closed. They will not open until nine."

Good, Klingsor thought. They were already discussing the terms of the handover. This should not be especially difficult.

"Tell me where."

"All over the city. What is it you're looking for?"

"A package left in your care by a man named Marko Barcelona."

Gisler looked confused.

"I don't have the faintest idea who that is."

"Don't fuck with me," Klingsor said menacingly. "This is not a game."

"No," Gisler agreed. "I'm telling you the truth. What's his real name? Maybe I know him by something else."

This was a problem. Klingsor did not know. Marko Barcelona was an obvious alias, but nobody seemed to know who he really was. And Klingsor's organization was usually pretty good at that sort of thing.

"He's the head of the White Hand," Klingsor answered. "A Bosnian criminal organization. Sometimes he goes by Mali. Other than that, he uses no other name that we know of. It's likely that the package contains a tape or a disc or a memory stick. Maybe it's just the URL to a site on the dark web where it's sitting on an anonymous server, but I will have it from you."

Klingsor sensed that this was the time to imply a more direct physical threat. Gisler was right on the edge. His complexion was waxen and pale. His shirt now soaked all the way through with sweat. His breathing was heavy and ragged, and he stank of fear.

On the table was a power drill. Klingsor picked it up and pretended to examine it carefully. It was an older Makita, covered in stains that were supposed to look like dried blood but were really nail polish. The drill bit was long and had a quarter-inch router head at the tip.

"You don't need that," Gisler gasped. "I'll tell you everything you want to know. Please."

The lawyer stiffened and tried to clutch at his chest, coming up short because of the restraints.

"He's having a heart attack," Echo Three said. There was no hint of panic in his voice. They were all experienced professionals.

"Be careful. Could be a trick," warned Echo Four.

Echo Three gave him a dismissive look.

"Him?"

"Okay. No."

"Get the defibrillator from the van," Klingsor instructed.

Echo One retrieved a bright red hard-plastic case from the back of the van. He popped it open and pulled out a pair of paddles. Then put them down.

"The fuckin' battery's dead."

"Didn't you check that?" Klingsor demanded.

"No," Echo One admitted.

"Can we plug it in somewhere?"

Echo One held up the plug. It had a British-style three-prong connector. It would not fit the European plugs in a Swiss parking garage.

"What the hell?" Klingsor asked.

"We got the kit from the London office," Echo Four said.

In Klingsor's experience, really serious fuckups were rarely the result of a single major mistake. Rather, it was a series of small things that went wrong in just the right way, each one compounding the consequences of the error or oversight that preceded it. In the world of after-action reviews, there was even a word for it. The "snowball." Klingsor could feel that he and the team were already trapped in a snowball that was rolling downhill and picking up both speed and mass. Force equals mass times acceleration, and they were in for one hell of a hard hit at the bottom of this hill.

"Can you hook the defibrillator up to the car battery?"

"It's just a goddamn prop. It's got no juice."

"Let's try CPR."

"Aw, fuck. You might as well sacrifice a chicken."

Klingsor ignored him, although he knew that Echo Four was almost certainly right. CPR was not a high-percentage strategy. But it was the best of the available options. The only alternative as near as he could see was to sit on his ass and hope that Gisler did not die.

Like everyone else on the team, Klingsor had the right training. He forced air into Gisler's lungs while Echo Three compressed his chest at the prescribed intervals. They kept it up for some time after it was clear that the lawyer was dead.

Ordinarily, his first call would have been to a specialized team that his organization kept on standby to clean up messes like this one. But this op was different. There was no safety net. Klingsor would have to rely on the assets at hand and wing it. He hated winging it.

His first call—his only call, really—would be to Kundry, who was going to be royally pissed.

LANGLEY, VIRGINIA
OCTOBER 15

6

Officially, it was the South-Central Europe Long-Range Planning Group. Nobody called it that, at least nobody who worked below the seventh floor at CIA headquarters in Langley. To everyone else, even if only to those who bothered to talk about it at all, it was the Island of Misfit Toys.

On the org chart of the European Directorate, the office floated off to one side, tied into the hierarchy by only a few tenuous dotted lines. On paper, the group was responsible for red-celling U.S. policy in the Western Balkans, trying out various scenarios, and developing the pros and cons of particular responses so that there would always be something on the shelf to respond to just about any conceivable contingency. It looked good on paper. In Washington, a lot of things look good on paper.

But that did not fool Victoria Wagoner. As director of the

Long-Range Planning Group, she was queen of the Island of Misfit Toys. Except that she had her own name for it. Exile. She felt like some obscure European potentate from another century who was too high profile to kill but too awkward to have hanging around the palace. It was easier to stick an extraneous royal in a tower somewhere, with or without an iron mask. Or maybe on some island. Elba would do nicely, thank you.

For Vicky, known universally as VW since starting in the intel business as an analyst on East Germany at the tail end of the Cold War, the Long-Range Planning Group was her own personal Elba. And after almost two years in the group, she still was not certain just what she had done to deserve exile. She had given twenty years of her career to the Western Balkans Division. She had been one of the first to anticipate the bloody breakup of Yugoslavia, and she had had the guts to put her prediction on paper. For a while at least, that had made her something of a minor deity in the narrow professional circles she traveled in.

She knew why Clark had been sent to the Island. He was an asshole with a serious anger-management problem who had picked an unwinnable fight with senior management one too many times. Linda Marigliano had had an affair with her boss that ended badly. She had filed a sexual harassment suit and lost. Her prize had been a transfer. This is where the losers of the European Directorate's turf wars and policy battles washed ashore like so much bureaucratic flotsam. In the private sector, they probably would have been fired, which would have been merciful. It was hard to fire civil servants, even those in sensitive national security positions. That's what the Island was for. Other directorates had their own version. It was as if a gulag archipelago stretched across the organizational charts and personnel systems of the CIA and almost every other U.S. government agency. There should be some kind of club, VW had long thought, a system of lapel pins and a secret handshake. They could hold meetings with their own peculiar rituals like Freemasons or Boy Scouts. Lord knows they had the time.

Why VW was on the Island was not clear to her. To the best of her knowledge, she had not crossed any of the higher-ups in any significant way. She had not flunked the part of the lifestyle polygraph where they asked about drug use, gambling, or sex with farm animals. She had not published any spectacularly wrong products that had contributed to a decision to invade one or more small countries. Her batting average on predictions was, in fact, well above the median.

For two years, VW and her team had turned out a steady stream of useless reports on a range of hypothetical events, none of which had come to pass. Albania had not fallen under the control of a drug trafficking narco-boss with ties to the FARC in Colombia. Serbia had not gone to war with Kosovo in a quixotic attempt to take physical possession of the Serb-majority municipalities north of the Ibar River.

But now there was Bosnia in danger of melting down into a new round of ethnic violence. The indicators were increasingly stark and worrisome. They should be hitting all kinds of alarm bells. The Bosnian army had effectively split, with most of the guns again going to the Serbs. The paramilitaries were back on the scene, and low-intensity acts of ethnic violence had become commonplace. In a town near the Croatian border, someone had thrown a hand grenade into a Serbian elementary school, killing two children and seriously injuring a teacher. Bosniak nationalists had bulldozed a Croatian war memorial. One of the few remaining mosques in Republika Srpska, a historically significant Ottoman-era building in Zvornik with a graceful minaret, had been recently firebombed. The Scorpions were claiming responsibility.

The LPG had identified a breakdown in governance in Bosnia as a real risk as far back as five years ago, but not in exactly this way. No one had seen this coming.

VW had devoted her life to the CIA. She had no children and no husband, and had long ago entered the age group where her odds of getting married closely paralleled those of being killed by a terrorist. Hell, since she worked at CIA headquarters, her prospects for winding up on the business end of a terrorist operation may well have been slightly better than those for being on the receiving end of the Question.

VW was a little overweight—okay, maybe a little bit more than a little—and a little bit frumpy in how she dressed. Her colleagues had never cared. All that mattered in the Directorate of Intelligence was the quality of your mind—and VW had analytic acumen in spades.

She deserved better from the Agency. At the very least, she deserved an explanation for her ostracism. It would never, she knew, be forthcoming. The system did not work like that.

She had tried to make the best of it.

When Dimitrović had come to power and announced his support for a new post-Dayton Bosnia, everyone had been hopeful that Europe's most dysfunctional state had at long last turned the corner. The mainstream analysts fell back on the standard clichés in lauding Dimitrović's conversion on the road to Damascus or his "Nixon-to-China" moment for Bosnia. From the very beginning, however, VW had had her doubts. Dimitrović was a classic alpha wolf, lean and crafty and hungry. His turn to the West struck her as manufactured. At best, it was tactical; at worst, it was deceptive. Under her direction, the Island of Misfit Toys had put forward a number of analytic red-cell reports that challenged Dimitrović's bona fides as a reformer. As she knew they would, the reports had sunk into the bureaucratic swamp without a sound or trace.

But after six months of the new leader's extraordinary and unprecedented progress in building a unified state, even VW had started to come around.

Dimitrović's fall from grace, his regression to chauvinistic nationalism, had been as sudden as his earlier embrace of "brotherhood and unity" with the Federation's Bosniaks and Croats. It had caught everyone by surprise. It was exactly the kind of thing that the Long-Range Planning Group was supposed to forecast. And they had missed it.

At least they were still working the problem, VW consoled herself. It seemed like the mainstream analytic office covering the Western Balkans had simply stopped trying. They produced almost nothing in the way of serious analysis. They seemed to be working hard, or at least late, but there was no product to show for it.

VW stirred the cold dregs of coffee in a mug embossed with the CIA's eagle and shield. Maybe she should take a walk down to the cafeteria for a fresh cup. It might help clear her head. But there was a significant risk at this time of day of running into a friend, a colleague, or an acquaintance from her earlier life, back when she had been somebody. She could not stand the expressions of sympathy for her state of exile. They were too close to pity. She would rather drink her coffee cold and bitter.

On the desk next to the coffee was a file with an orange Top Secret cover sheet. Inside was a report that her political-military unit had been working on. There were some indications in the intelligence that an old military airfield near Bijeljina was being used to fly in guns and ammunition from Russia. Putin, she knew, looked at the RS as a wedge that he could drive between the Balkans and the West, as well as a way to validate his ethnic landgrab in Ukraine and punish the Europeans and the Americans for their sanctions policy. It was even possible that the mysterious Marko Barcelona was secretly working for the Kremlin. That was a theory worth exploring as a red-cell exercise. The report on her desk contained some interesting speculation, but it was short on hard evidence. It would be nice to have some surveillance imagery and maybe signals intelligence from the airfield.

VW picked up the phone on her desk and dialed from memory.

"Hello."

No one at the CIA ever answered the phone with a given name, or even the name of the office. Either you knew who you were calling or you did not. And if you did not, then fuck off.

"Bob, it's Vicky."

"VW. Hey. How's life on the Island?"

"I don't think you're supposed to say that out loud."

"Oh, yeah. Sorry. Didn't mean to be rude."

Bob Landis was an engineer, a nuts-and-bolts techie who had long ago crossed the Rubicon into management but had never quite lost the social ineptitude characteristic of his profession.

"What can I do for you?" Landis asked.

"I need a favor."

"What is it?" Landis's tone shifted from conciliatory to cautious.

"I need a couple of hours of drone time in Bosnia."

"They aren't drones, VW, they're . . ."

"Unmanned aerial vehicles. I know. My turn to apologize. I certainly don't want to hurt their feelings. But I do need some UAV time and I'm hoping you can help me out."

"Who do you want to kill?"

It was a joke. Sort of.

As a consequence of what had once been known in government circles as the Global War on Terror—often abbreviated with the ugly uneuphonious acronym GWOT and later gifted with the much more frightening moniker the Long War—the CIA had acquired a large and sophisticated air force all its own. The Agency operated a fleet of Reapers and Predators and other more exotic UAVs that it used for collecting information and, more recently, for something referred to euphemistically as kinetic operations. Assassination.

Landis had once built drones. He had been a part of the team that had the idea to mount a Hellfire missile on a Predator. And he had watched by live satellite feed as his creation was used in battle for the first time, killing a group of innocent scrap-metal collectors in Afghanistan because one of them was tall and in some way resembled Osama bin Laden. Since then, this kind of operation had become routine, standardized with kill lists and checklists and "safeguards" intended more to ward off any potential congressional investigation than to ensure that collateral damage was kept to a minimum.

Much of the work was done by contractors. The CIA did not actually like getting its hands dirty. Landis's job was to manage the schedule for the drones.

"You know who I want to kill, Bob. Whoever the son of a bitch is who sent me here. But I'll do that job myself. For now, I need something a little more prosaic. Just some overflights, imagery, and SIGINT on an airfield near Bijeljina that we think the Russians may be using."

"Sorry, VW. I got nothing for you."

"Waddaya mean? If I need to wait a few days, that's okay. This is potentially significant, but it's not hair-on-fire urgent."

"No, I mean I don't have anything for anyone at any time. All of the UAV time has been earmarked for another program indefinitely. The relevant satellite time too. It's out of my hands."

"What program?"

"I don't know."

"How is that possible?"

"It's a director-level code. I don't know the name of the actual program. And I sure as hell don't know what it does."

VW knew better than to ask him for the code. There was no way he was going to give that out.

"Where are the assets?"

"You mean physically?"

Landis had stopped thinking of the UAVs as actual aircraft operating in the real world. To him, they were just hours of flying time and maintenance schedules on a spread sheet.

"Yes. Physically."

"Same place."

VW knew where that was, a clandestine airfield in eastern Slavonia that the CIA rented from the Croatian government at an exorbitant cost.

"So whatever it is they're doing is still in the Balkans?"

"Probably. But it's not the kind of question I ask."

"So what can I do to get what I need? Are there any other assets available?"

"You could put in a request to transfer an airframe from Ukraine or Syria ops on a temporary basis," Landis suggested.

"And the odds of success on that?"

"Statistically indistinguishable from zero," he admitted.

The Balkans had once been the highest-priority issue on the international agenda, but those days were long gone. Moving assets from a hot place like Ukraine was simply not a realistic option. VW would have a better chance of building her own UAV in the garage of her Alexandria town house and flying it over the Atlantic like Charles Lindbergh with a remote control.

"What's going on?"

"Damned if I know."

"Good-bye, Bob."

She hung up.

VW sat at her desk stirring the cold coffee without drinking it. She needed to think.

Something was going on in her region. Something that she was being kept out of. It was infuriating, an insult on top of an insult, salt rubbed into the wound of her exile. But there was something else as well, a spark of intellectual curiosity. It was a puzzle. VW liked puzzles and she was very, very good at them.

There was, she realized, a back door. There was always a back door. In this case, it was the contractors. One of the ironclad laws of government was that contractors would demand their time and a half for every minute of mandatory overtime. The CIA's UAV fleet was operated exclusively by a corps of contractors. Eventually, permanent staffing patterns in the intelligence community would catch up to twenty-first-century reality . . . but likely not until the twenty-second century. It was the nature of government.

Among the more ignominious duties that she had been assigned that were consistent with the terms of her exile to the Island was being the backup comptroller for budget and finance in the Office of Russian and European Analysis. In truth, the demands on her time were not especially onerous. She was merely the backup, after all. But it did mean that she had administrative access to the time-and-attendance software from her desktop. She fished a pocket of Nescafé from her desk drawer and mixed it with water that was almost but not quite hot enough from the machine in the break room. With a sigh, she sat down at the computer to review the overtime charges for the last three months.

It took longer than she had bargained for, but once VW got her teeth into a challenge, she rarely let go, and by nine p.m. that evening, she had found what she was looking for. Contractors from BlueSky Solutions, a Beltway bandit with ties to General Atomics—the company behind both the Predator and Reaper UAVs—were consistently billing overtime to a program identified only by an eleven-digit number. This was the director-level code that Landis had referred to. This worked well enough for the time-and-attendance software, but VW knew that the T&A figures would need to be reconciled with the accounting program that managed the massive flow of money in and out of the subregional budget for operations. The budget software would not accept the code; it would require the program name to be input into the correct field.

VW toggled over to the accounting program and searched the database for the entries that corresponded to the suspicious time-and-attendance overtime charges. It was not hard to find. All of the overtime for BlueSky Solutions had been charged to a single program. Parsifal. VW had been working on Balkan issues for most of her career, and she had never seen this program name in any of the operational files.

"What the fuck is Parsifal?" she asked out loud to an empty office.

SARAJEVO
OCTOBER 16

7

"I have a lead." Sarah's eagerness was visible in the athletic hunch of her shoulders and the bright gleam in her eyes. Her body seemed almost to quiver, like a hunting dog that had spotted a bird in the brush and was holding point.

"What sort of lead?" Eric shook his head and laughed. "Even asking that question makes me feel like a character from *Law & Order*."

"Not here."

They were standing in the embassy's expansive atrium, a corner of which had been given over to a coffee bar. Eric had just gotten his usual morning fix, a double espresso straight up, when Sarah had arrived looking like she had already had several shots.

It had been four days since Eric had agreed to help her. Since then, Sarah had passed through the embassy on several occasions, but she never stayed for long. Eric expected that she was there just to use the commo facilities and read the traffic.

"My office?" he suggested.

"Not there either."

"My office isn't secure enough?"

It looked to Eric as though there was something Sarah wanted to say in response but that she had changed her mind.

"Maybe I just feel like some fresh air," she said instead. "It's a beautiful day out. Let's go for a ride."

"I have a meeting at two."

"Cancel it."

"Where are we going?"

"I'll tell you in the car."

Sarah was like that. She had always been like that: secretive and demanding, maddening and passionate, selfish and generous. Eric had loved her for her dualities even as they had made him crazy. Part of him wanted to refuse on principle, but he knew that he could not.

Twenty minutes later, they were in Sarah's car, a rented Peugeot 308, headed north on the major road leading to the RS.

It was unseasonably warm, with clear blue skies and just enough of a breeze to keep the diesel fumes from settling over the city like a shroud.

"Okay, what's the big lead?" Eric asked. "Was it Colonel Mustard in the billiard room with the candlestick? I never trust a guy with a mustache big enough to do double duty as a comb-over."

"Nothing so dramatic, I'm afraid. But I've been working my old network in Srpska along with some of our more recent acquisitions. It can be a slow process. A mentor of mine once told me that operational intel work is like being a spider on a web trying to read the vibrations of the various threads. If you can feel them, the vibrations will tell you that you've got prey trapped, how big it is, and where it is on the web. But you have to keep a light touch. If you grab the threads too hard, you can't read the vibrations.

"In any event, one of my old assets got word to me that he had something on Mali that he was willing to share. There'll be a price, of course. This guy was pretty mercenary back in the day. But he worked cheap, and I think I can cover his fee out of what I can dig out of the station's couch cushions."

"So where are we going?"

"Zvornik."

Zvornik was a depressed postindustrial town on the banks of the Drina River. Although right across the river from its sister city in Serbia, Mali Zvornik, or "little Zvornik," Zvornik had been 60 percent Bosniak before the war. The paramilitaries had zeroed in on Zvornik early in the conflict. Arkan's Tigers and the Scorpions had been the most aggressive, running concentration camps, blowing up mosques, and stealing everything that was not nailed down. Decades after the fighting, Zvornik was still a hotbed of ethnic nationalism.

"Do you have security of some kind for this little exercise?"

"Well, I'm traveling with a big strong man," Sarah said flirtatiously.

"Where is he? In the trunk? Maybe you should let him out. Give him some air."

"You're still funny, Eric. I always liked that about you."

Eric was somewhat chagrined at the way Sarah's simple compliment delivered a strong shot of dopamine to the pleasure center of his brain. It was clear to him that his feelings for her had not entirely faded. *No good can come of this,* he warned himself.

"Who's the contact?"

"His name is Viktor Jovanovski."

"Macedonian?" Eric asked. In the former Yugosphere, the "ski" ending to a family name was usually either Macedonian or Bulgarian.

"On his father's side. His mother was a Bosnian Serb and Viktor grew up in Zvornik. Dad was a small-time criminal, but his son made the big leagues, or at least triple-A ball. He was with the Scorpions during the war and made a small fortune smuggling cigarettes and gasoline. As a sideline, he also worked for me. Agency reporting indicates that he's still a serious player in the black economy and that gives him a reason not to be happy about Marko Barcelona."

"New guy muscling in on his territory?"

"Pretty much. These are apex predators. Their position depends as much on reputation as on capability. A mob boss like Viktor can't be seen as being scared of a guy like Mali. Otherwise the pack will tear him to pieces."

"It almost sounds like you feel bad for the guy."

"I don't have an ounce of sympathy to spare for Viktor. But I need to understand him if I plan to use him."

"And what does he want from you? He made contact, no? And nothing's for nothing in this part of the world."

"He's probably hoping that I can get a Reaper to drop a Hellfire on Mali's house."

"Is he right?"

Sarah laughed.

"Not my department."

"What makes you think you can trust this guy?"

"Self-interest rightly understood."

"Okay, but I'm skeptical that your old friend Viktor has read much Tocqueville."

"He may not recognize the line, but he'll understand the concept. Believe me, if there's anything Viktor knows, it's what's best for himself."

It was not a long distance to Zvornik as the crow flew. But they were not crows. Although the road was in decent shape on the relative scale used in judging Bosnia's roads, it was circuitous, winding up and around the steep peaks of the Majevica mountain range. Spindly trees somehow clung to life on the nearly sheer black-rock cliff faces on either side of the narrow road. This was wild Bosnia, the old Balkans of bears and wolves and mountain clans that had refused to bend the knee to the Ottoman invaders. The high mountain passes had been tamed by brute-force Yugoslav engineering but never entirely subdued. Sarah drove the mountain road expertly, just on the edge of control, downshifting into the turns and steering the agile Peugeot around the occasional rockfall.

Five kilometers before the border with Republika Srpska, Sarah pulled off the road, and Eric changed out the Peugeot's Bosnian license plates for a set of Serbian plates from the trunk that began with the two-letter code used for cars registered in Mali Zvornik. The guards at the makeshift border crossing wore Scorpion patches on their uniforms. Zvornik was their home turf. Two bored-looking paramilitaries waved them through the checkpoint with only a quick glance at their license plates. It was not their job to harass the locals.

Twenty minutes from the checkpoint, the road split. Sarah slowed to make the turn to Zvornik.

"Stop here," Eric said impulsively.

They were in a small village called Konjevići. There was no road sign, no store, no obvious reason to stop at this particular crossroads.

"Turn right," Eric said.

"Zvornik's to the left."

"I know. I want to make a stop first."

"Are you sure?"

"Yes."

"Have you been back there since?"

"No."

"Are you ready?"

"I don't know."

"Okay. Let's go."

The secondary road was rutted and washed out in places. The Peugeot was built for the autobahns and smooth tarmacs of Western Europe, and nearly bottomed out crossing a couple of deep gullies. Thirty minutes of hard driving brought them to a small black-and-white sign with an arrow that pointed to the left. SREBRENICA-POTOČARI GENOCIDE MEMORIAL.

Sarah stopped and looked at Eric questioningly.

He nodded.

"Turn here."

The parking lot was empty. Srebrenica was a Serbian town now, and with the uptick in tensions between the Federation and the RS, the flow of tourists and visitors from Sarajevo had slowed to a trickle. The memorial itself was striking. Rows of small, Egyptian-style obelisks that looked like miniature Washington Monuments covered acres of ground. Each one a grave. To one side was a graceful arc of gray granite, a memorial wall with names and birth years. The victims of Srebrenica. There were more than eight thousand names on the wall. It was stark and powerful.

Eric and Sarah stood at the edge of the cemetery. The sheer number of graves was daunting, a mute testament to man's capacity for evil.

"Can I help you?"

Eric almost jumped out of his skin. The voice was right behind him, and he had been so lost in thought that he had not heard anyone approach.

Turning, he saw a wizened old man bent over almost double and using an old shovel as a cane. *There are few things,* Eric thought, *more macabre and redolent of mortality than a shovel in a graveyard.*

"Are you looking for someone in particular?" the man asked. He spoke in Serbo-Croatian with a Bosniak accent.

"Yes," Eric answered. "I'm looking for a friend."

"What's his name?"

"Meho Alimerović."

The old man arched one of his eyebrows, and he stiffened as though trying to stand straight.

"Alimerović, you say." He stared intently at Eric through eyes that had grown milky and dim with age.

"Yes, Meho Alimerović. He would have been twenty-five years old."

"Follow me."

"You know where he's buried?"

"I know where all of them are. It's really not that difficult. They don't move around all that much."

The old man was surprisingly sure-footed. The blade of the shovel crunched into the gravel path with each step. The steles, Eric noted, were engraved with a name and two dates. The first dates spanned decades, but on every grave the second date was the same: July 1995.

"Your friend is one of the lucky ones," the attendant said. His accent was so rural that it was a little hard for Eric to follow.

"Lucky?"

"He's all here. Some of the other graves have only bits and pieces. When the Serbs saw they were starting to lose the war, they dug up the graves and scattered the bodies. They used heavy machinery and they weren't especially careful. Most of those buried here would never have been identified without DNA testing."

The man stopped in front of one of the thousands of identical steles.

"Here's the one you're looking for, Eric," he said.

Eric's attention snapped from the stele to the graveyard attendant.

"You know who I am?"

"I've been waiting for you."

"For how long?"

"Twenty years."

"You were here that night, weren't you? You were here with Meho."

"I was. Along with thousands of others."

"And you survived."

"A few of us did. Those too old to be any kind of threat. And I was a considerably younger man back then. I suppose they didn't want to go to the trouble of burying us all."

"And he told you about me?"

"Yes."

"That he was here because of me."

"No. Quite the opposite, in fact. He asked me to give you a message. He told me to tell you that it was not your fault. In truth, it was a strange message. I asked him if you would understand it, and he assured me you would."

Eric did and he felt a hot flush of shame at the memory. From beyond death and across twenty years, Meho reached out to him to offer succor. But Eric could not accept. It was his fault. It was his responsibility, his pride and vanity and ambition. The graveyard swam in his vision behind a wall of tears that he fought back, knowing even as he did so that this was just another act of pointless pride.

"How did you know it was me?" Eric asked.

"Who else could it be? Meho hasn't gotten many visitors. Two women, his sister and his mother. That's all. No friends before you. Where are his friends?"

"Dead."

"All of them."

"All that mattered."

"I'm sorry," the old man said. "There were so many. So very many."

"Too many," Eric agreed.

"I looked for you after the war. In Sarajevo. But I couldn't find you. All I knew was Eric the American."

"I was gone by then," Eric said. "I left not long after . . . this."

The caretaker nodded his understanding.

"I'll leave you to grieve in private. May the blessings of Allah be upon you. Thank you for coming here, even after all these years."

He walked away slowly, leaving Eric and Sarah alone at the grave.

Eric bowed his head. He wished that he believed in God. It would have been easier if he did. He laid his palm on the top of the stele. The marble was cold to the touch.

Forgive me.

"There's nothing to forgive."

Had he said that out loud?

Eric looked over at Sarah.

"I know what you're thinking," she explained. "We went over this a thousand times before . . . we stopped seeing each other. I know why you wanted to come here. It's not your fault. It's Captain Zero and the Green Dragons and the Yellow fucking Wasps. It's not your fault. It's not Meho's fault. It's not my fault or the fault of the poor DUTCHBAT veteran who wakes up in the middle of the night in a cold sweat because he was here and he was armed and maybe he could have done something even though his orders were to stand by and watch. It's not your fault. Meho himself just told you that."

"You don't understand . . ." Eric began.

"Don't I?"

"No. Listen. By early July 1995 the situation in Srebrenica was deteriorating pretty quickly. The whole city was supposed to be a UN safe area protected by a Dutch batallion, but it was clear to the Bosnian Serbs that the Dutch weren't willing or able to fight to defend the city. So Ratko Mladić and the Bosnian Serb army were going to go ahead and take it. We could all see it coming. The regular staff reporters were too nervous to go to Srebrenica and see for themselves what was happening. A few of us stringers wanted to go.

I was ready to go, but I asked Meho to go first and scout around for a few days. I told him I would join him later. I had someplace to go first."

"Vienna?" Sarah asked resignedly.

"Yes."

"To be with me?"

"Yes. Just for the weekend like we'd planned. Then I was going to Srebrenica to meet up with Meho. He wasn't supposed to be there. He wouldn't have been there if it wasn't for me."

"Or me."

"You didn't know. I did. It was dangerous and I asked him to do it."

"He was a grown-up. Meho made his own choices. Don't take that away from him."

"He was a fixer. He worked for me. He would have done anything I asked. If I had asked him to go to hell and get me an interview with Satan himself, he would have done it. I should have known. I should have been more careful. It's my fault."

"It's the past, Eric. You need to let it go."

"The past is never dead. It's not even past."

"Faulkner was an alcoholic prick."

Eric smiled in spite of himself. Only Sarah.

"Yes, he was. But he had his moments." Eric paused, struggling for the right words. "According to the State of California, my mother's cause of death was suicide. But it was really murder. Pol Pot and the Khmer Rouge killed her as surely as they killed her father and mother and brothers and everyone else who mattered to her. They stripped her of her past, and it was more than she could bear. Before her, my father's family fled Armenia steps ahead of the genocide. I heard all their stories about their village near Trabzon. Their own paradise lost. And then Meho. Three generations of genocide. The defining features of my life."

"I understand, Eric. I do. My mother's parents had numbers tattooed on their forearms. The years had blurred them, but they were still legible. They were both at Bergen-Belsen although neither would ever talk about it. They met there, actually. Never again. That's why we do this. That's why we are here. Don't lose sight of the good we can do."

Eric reached out again to touch Meho's grave with the tips of his fingers, as though performing a benediction.

"Why today, Eric? You've been living in Bosnia for years and you haven't come here before. Why now?"

Eric turned from the grave to look Sarah in the eyes. They were standing inches apart, and he could feel her hot breath on his skin, as intimate as a kiss.

"Because being with you is a bridge to the past. It's like it was all the day before yesterday. I had to come here eventually, and I'm glad I could do it with you."

Sarah took his hand.

"This war wasn't about him or you or me. It was much bigger than all of us. We were all of us caught up in its wake and tossed about like bits of sea grass in the ocean. You and I washed ashore, is all. Meho didn't make it. He was my friend too, Eric. I loved him same as you. But I buried him and I mourned him and I moved on. Time for you to do the same."

Sarah was right. He knew she was right. Eric nodded as though he agreed with her. But it was a kind of lie. He would never be able to let go of the past.

Sarah shook her head. She seemed to recognize the lie.

"Come on," she said resignedly. "Let's go."

Another ninety minutes of driving brought them to the outskirts of Zvornik. The transition from sylvan wilderness to the urban and industrial was shockingly abrupt. On the far side of a sharp curve, the city appeared like a concrete spaceship that had landed in a farmer's field. It was an ugly town, comprised mostly of two- or three-story buildings, many half finished as though the owners had overreached and run out money for windows and doors and roof tiles. Many of the homes had a kind of gap-toothed quality, missing something even if it was hard to pin down exactly what.

On the edge of town, there was a complex of large factory buildings, all of them shuttered and silent. For political reasons, Marshal Tito, the unquestioned ruler of Yugoslavia from the end of the Second World War until his death in 1980, had spread industrial production across the country's six republics. One factory in Croatia might make the soles of work boots while another factory in Macedonia made the uppers and a third factory in Slovenia stitched them together. When Yugoslavia broke up, many of these inefficient socially managed factories lost their reason for being. Eric knew of at least one former steel plant that had been given over to growing mushrooms.

Their route took them past the Bijela Džamija, the White Mosque. A week ago, it had been a graceful link to the region's Ottoman past. But the firebombing had put paid to that. The dome had collapsed and the marble-clad minaret was streaked with black. The air smelled of smoke and diesel. Bright yellow police tape was strung mockingly around the mosque, as though the police would really investigate the crime with an eye toward possible arrests. The cops were just going through the motions, and the crime scene tape was just so much bunting. It was oddly festive.

"Do they know who did this?" Sarah asked.

"Almost certainly the Scorpions. This was ground zero for the chitinous bastards."

Sarah stopped the car.

"I want to look at this," she said. "And remember what this is all about."

"Do we have time?"

"Viktor's not going anywhere. He's got nowhere to go."

Sarah pulled the Peugeot up onto the curb. They stood side-by-side on the sidewalk in front of the mosque, close but not touching.

"It's already started, hasn't it?" Sarah said.

"Yes."

"Can we stop it?"

"I don't know. But I'm sure as hell going to try."

She took his hand and squeezed it hard as if they were shaking on a deal.

"Bježi! Pusti me!" It was a girl's voice shouting "Go away. Leave me alone."

A knot of boys in black leather jackets embossed with red scorpions rounded the corner. They surrounded two young girls wearing headscarves and long dresses in dark colors. The girls were hunched over, afraid. The boys were taunting the older girl, who could not have been more than sixteen.

"Come on, you little Muslim bitch. What's the going rate for a Turkish whore? Five dinars? I think you'll have to do me for free." One of bigger boys grabbed the girl's right breast. She screamed and tried to push him away. The second girl, who was no more than ten or eleven, looked confused. Eric could see that she had Down syndrome.

"Are you armed?" Eric asked Sarah.

"You're goddamn right I am."

"Try not to kill anyone."

"No promises."

Eric strode quickly toward the girls and their tormentors. Sarah was right behind him.

"That's enough, boys," he shouted.

The Scorpions turned to face him, no longer laughing but deadly serious in the face of a challenge.

"Go home, old man," one boy said dismissively.

"Not without the girls," Eric said calmly.

"You can have the little one. This one's coming with me." The boy who said this was the biggest and, Eric suspected, the ringleader. He put his arm possessively around the older girl, who struggled in vain to get away.

"Let her go right now, or my friend here will put a bullet between your legs. That should cool you down a bit."

A gun had appeared in Sarah's hand as if by magic. It was now leveled straight at the Scorpion's groin.

He let go of the girl and reached behind his back.

"I wouldn't do that," Eric said. "It might hurt. A lot."

The boy seemed suddenly unsure of himself.

"Go ahead," Eric suggested. "Give her a reason."

The Scorpions slunk off, leaving the girls free and at least temporarily safe.

The young girl with Down syndrome hugged Eric, pressing her face into his jacket. He patted her back awkwardly.

"Are you two okay?" he asked the older girl.

"Yes, thank you. Come on, Edita, we need to get home." The girl's eyes were red and brimming with the tears she had been fighting to hold back.

"We'll take you," Sarah said. "I don't think those poisonous bugs have gone far."

The girls accepted the ride gratefully.

"Why are you still here?" Eric asked, as they drove the few short blocks to the address the girls had given them. "Zvornik is hardly a safe place for Bosniaks."

"Our mother is sick," the older girl, whose name was Aida, explained. "We have nowhere else. No family. We'll survive here."

"No, you won't," Sarah said, and there was bitterness in her voice. "You have to leave."

"To go where?"

"Sarajevo."

"We have no place to live there."

"I can help you with that," Eric said. "A friend of mine is the head of a group that helps resettle people from the RS in Sarajevo. I'll put you in touch."

They brought the girls home, and Eric took their contact information. It would be easy enough to bring the family to Sarajevo and get them set up with a temporary place to live and maybe even a job.

Twenty minutes later, they were back on the road driving to their rendezvous with Jovanovski.

"You do understand what we just agreed to," Sarah said sadly. "What we decided to do."

"I do," Eric said. "We just agreed to take part in the ethnic cleansing of Zvornik. Ain't life a bitch."

ZVORNIK
OCTOBER 16

8

Sarah turned off the main road onto a side street and stopped in front of a charmless building with a sign in Cyrillic letters identifying it as Vitez, which means *knight*. A Balkan *kafana* was a kind of hybrid bar/coffee shop. Men would get their morning coffee at their favorite *kafana*, maybe a beer in the afternoon, and something stronger in the evening with a little music thrown in for good measure. The *kafana* was a full-service establishment and the linchpin of Balkan social life.

Vitez was decidedly down-market.

"Nice place."

"Not much to look at," Sarah agreed. "But it's one of the places where Viktor and I used to meet when he was an active asset. It's quiet and out of the way. The owner is discreet and the beer's cold."

The inside of Vitez matched the grim exterior. The thick clouds of smoke from the generations of men chain-smoking cheap, foul-smelling cigarettes had left a gray film over nearly every visible surface. The windows were clouded with grime, filtering the sunlight to a weak, sickly yellow. The furniture was mismatched, and the tabletops were pitted and scarred.

The bar might once have been handsome. It was made of dark wood with a marble top, but the wood was discolored and the marble was stained and cracked. Most of the bottles lined up along the wall behind the bartender had no label. Some of the bottles had once held Coca-Cola or orange juice. Home brew.

"That's Viktor," Sarah said sotto voce, pointing to a table in the back of the room with just the sparest movement of her head.

The man sitting at the table Sarah had indicated was large even by the outsize standards of the Balkans, a region that turned out NBA-caliber basketball players and heavyweight judo champions at a prodigious rate. Eric estimated that Viktor was somewhere north of two hundred and fifty pounds, most of it muscle. He wore a white silk shirt, and a trace of tattoo across his neck and chest hinted at a large swath of ink under his clothes. From what Eric could see, it looked like a professional job, not a crude prison tattoo. His hair was cut short, almost military in appearance. He was alone but talking animatedly on a cell phone.

Eric could not see a weapon of any kind, but he knew that a man like Viktor would never be far from a gun—or a bodyguard. One or more of the other men in the *kafana* were no doubt on his payroll. But the dozen or so patrons all looked like they would have been right at home in the cantina from *Star Wars*, and there was no way to be sure which ones belonged to Viktor.

They walked over to the table and sat down across from Sarah's one-time asset.

"Hello, Viktor," she said in English.

"Stinky, I'm going to call you back," Viktor said into the phone before hanging up. "It is nice to see you, Sarah. Long time." Viktor's English was accented but more than adequate. The former Yugoslavia's criminal class was multilingual. It was good business.

"Yes, and it would be impolite to remind a girl of just how many years it's been."

"It will be the secret between us." The Serbo-Croatian language had no articles, and even Slavs who spoke English well had trouble with "a" and "the," often picking between the two seemingly at random.

"I'm glad you reached out to me, Viktor. I need your help with a little problem."

"I will listen. But first, tell me who is Gypsy friend with four eyes." The Serb nodded with his head in Eric's direction. Eric was used to the various reactions that his skin tone elicited in the casual racists who populated the region. Some insisted he was black. Some thought him an especially swarthy Greek. Gypsy was a common conclusion. Almost no one guessed half Asian.

"This is Eric. He's from the embassy and he's working with me."

"Good to meet you," Eric said in Sarajevo-accented Serbo-Croatian. "But I should probably tell you that I'm not a Gypsy. I'm a grave digger."

Viktor laughed and slapped the table with a meaty hand that was so hairy it might have belonged to a gorilla. Gypsy was the nickname for the fans of the Red Star Belgrade soccer club. Their arch rivals, Partizan, were known as the grave diggers after their black uniforms.

"I like this one," Viktor said to Sarah. "He can stay."

"Glad you approve." The note of irony in Sarah's reply would not have been lost even on someone whose English was considerably weaker than Viktor's.

"I hear you are asking questions about Mali Barcelona," Viktor said. "That can be . . . unhealthy."

"So are cheese fries and chili dogs, but you won't see me cutting those out of my diet anytime soon."

Viktor probably missed some of the nuances of this. There was no regional equivalent of a chili dog. But he likely got the gist.

The crime lord motioned to the waiter. He pointed at the cup of coffee in front of him and held up three fingers. The rules of hospitality were inviolable.

"Sarah, you have been working too hard," Viktor said. "There is more to the life than chasing poor law-abiding criminals through the mountains. Look at how that has gotten you. Forty-three years old. Divorced after a three-year marriage. No kids. No boyfriend. The small apartment in the not-so-good part of city. You are still pretty girl. You could do better. Leave Mali alone."

Eric was taken aback about how much Viktor seemed to know about Sarah's life. He knew more than Eric did, for sure. The news about Sarah's divorce and current relationship status was interesting. The bit about the size of her apartment was just showing off. He wanted Sarah to understand just how much he knew about her. Where did he get that kind of information?

Sarah seemed unfazed and unsurprised.

"You're working with him, aren't you?" she said. "You're Mali's boy now."

Viktor shrugged.

"I like to think we are colleagues," he said. "It is the relationship of a mutual benefit."

The waiter arrived at Eric's elbow and placed three cups of coffee on the table along with three glasses of water. It was the same coffee as was served in Sarajevo, but here in Republika Srpska it was known as *domaća*—domestic—rather than Turkish. On the back of the waiter's hand, Eric saw a tattoo of a barbed scorpion's tail that disappeared under his sleeve. Eric glanced quickly around the room and realized that it had emptied out. The other patrons were gone. The waiter's shirt was untucked. Maybe he was just sloppy, or maybe he was concealing a weapon of some kind at his waist. The situation was starting to look both unstable and, as Viktor had observed only a few minutes earlier, unhealthy.

"I believe that renewing our earlier relationship would be even more beneficial to you than whatever arrangement you have now with Mali," Sarah said smoothly. *She was a professional,* Eric thought, with no small amount of admiration. He cast another quick look around the room. Even the bartender had vanished. It was just the four of them.

"What are you offering?" Viktor asked Sarah.

"Whatever you want . . . in exchange for what I need."

"Which is?"

"A tape that little Marko has been using to blackmail Zoran Dimitrović. It might be a disc or a memory stick or a software file.

But whatever form it's in, I want it. Every last damn copy. If you can get it for me, or help me get it, I'll make you a rich man."

Viktor's laugh was harsh and barking.

"I am the rich man. Mali offers me far more than money."

"What?"

"Power."

Sarah looked at Eric, and although her face was calm and impassive, he could see the muscles in her jaw were tight. She was nervous. She had reason to be. This was not going the way she had hoped.

"What do you mean, Viktor? What kind of power? Political power? You want to be the next minister for transportation in the RS government? Doesn't seem like your style."

"Mali has plans. He is a man of the vision. I like this vision. This future. There is room in it for the man of my talents."

Eric felt a shadow cross over the conversation, the shadow of war and death.

"Are we done here?" Sarah asked.

"Not quite, I'm afraid. Mali, he asked me to give you the message. So that you do not forget to stay out of his business."

Viktor stood, leaning forward on the table to glower at Sarah and Eric. It was a practiced look, one Eric was certain he had used countless times in countless displays of dominance meant to intimidate rivals or marks. Understanding it as a show did not make it any less effective.

Eric looked quickly over his shoulder and saw that the "waiter" was about five feet behind them with his right hand resting casually behind his back, almost certainly on the butt of a pistol or the handle of a knife.

"You are supposed to rough us up?" Sarah asked innocently. "Drop us in front of the embassy from the back of a speeding car? Doesn't seem like such a good idea. My government will hunt you down and squash you like a roach."

"Mali tells me that you will not report this. That you aren't even acting for the American government. That you are . . ."

Sarah moved with speed and power, and she lunged across the table with a telescoping metal baton in her right hand. Eric had not noticed it. She must have slipped it out of her purse while Viktor was delivering his soliloquy. The tip of the rod caught Viktor in the throat just below the Adam's apple, and he went hard to the floor.

Acting on instinct and reflex rather than experience or training, Eric shoved the chair he had been sitting on backward toward the waiter. The heavy wooden chair slammed into his kneecap and tangled his legs, throwing off his timing as the Scorpion foot soldier tried to draw a snub-nosed pistol from his waistband. By the time the ersatz waiter had his weapon out of its holster, Sarah had had time to close the gap. The blunt tip of the rod smashed onto his wrist, and Eric could hear the dry crack of breaking bone. The gun fell from his hand and clattered on the concrete floor.

Sarah shoved the tip of the baton like a lance into the man's solar plexus, and he doubled over, exposing the back of his skull to a sharp blow that sent him sprawling forward on his face. He did not move.

Viktor, however, was trying to regain his feet, clawing at his throat as though gasping for air. Sarah walked up to him and delivered a calm, almost clinical shot to his temple with the baton. The big man joined his associate in blissful unconsciousness.

Sarah looked over at Eric. She was not even breathing hard.

"Nice assist with the chair."

"Not sure you really needed it."

"Maybe. Maybe not. We'll never know. But you did good. First time?"

"Yep."

"You can get to like it."

"I don't think so. Let's get the hell out of here."

"Agreed. We can talk in the car."

"Damn right we will." Eric was angry and he wanted Sarah to know it. She had not been straight with him. "You owe me some answers."

"You'll get them," Sarah promised.

Eric wanted to believe her, but he could not.

MOSTAR
OCTOBER 23

9

To look at it now, it was hard to believe that Mostar had been the site of some of the most intense and vicious fighting of the Bosnian War. This city had been the focal point of the fighting between Croat and Muslim forces before Washington had forced a peace and a shotgun wedding between the two sides in a Federation that neither had ever fully embraced. The centerpiece of Mostar was Stari Most, an elegant bridge made of white limestone that arched gracefully over the Neretva River. The bridge had stood for more than four centuries, and a rotating cast of conquerors and foreign overseers had marveled at its otherworldly beauty: Ottomans and Austrians, the Wehrmacht and the Red Army, Yugoslavs of all flavors and the nationalist splinters left after the country's disintegration. All had trod the bridge's cobbled street as rulers.

Then, in 1993, a Croat artillery unit had targeted the bridge, hitting it with some sixty shells before it finally collapsed into the Neretva, leaving behind two towers on opposite banks with stubby stone arms reaching out across the river straining to touch. The Croatian Defense Council claimed that the bridge was of strategic importance. In truth, it had held little military value. The shelling of Stari Most was an assault on culture, an act of killing memory. The Croat paramilitaries had wanted to erase any trace of shared heritage, of Islamic achievement.

In this, as in so many other things, they had failed. The bridge had been rebuilt after the war at considerable expense, using as much of the original stone as possible. Still, while the physical gap across the river had been repaired, the rift between the two sides had never really been closed.

Eric told Annika something of the history of the bridge as they walked from the old mosque on the left bank to the bazaar area on the opposite side of the Neretva. The sky was the color of slate. It had been raining lightly off and on all day, and the cobblestone streets were slick. They took their time.

At the midpoint of the bridge, the High Representative of the Union for Foreign Affairs and Security Policy stopped to take a selfie.

"For my Facebook page," she explained somewhat sheepishly. "At the end of the day, I'm still a politician."

Eric nodded absentmindedly. He was distracted, thinking about Sarah.

They had had it out on the ride back to Sarajevo. Sarah clearly knew more than she had let on about what leverage Marko Barcelona had on Dimitrović. She had been holding back on him. Even more worrisome, she had not really pushed back against Viktor's accusation that she was essentially freelancing, operating without official sanction from their government. How Mali could know that seemed an important and interesting question. But neither as important nor as interesting as whether or not it was true.

"Is it?" Eric had demanded. "Is it true?"

"It's complicated," Sarah had replied.

"Bullshit. It's yes or no. Do you have the authority for what we're doing out here, or did you put our necks on the block on spec, just looking to see what you can turn up?"

"Eric, the CIA is a bureaucracy, and like all bureaucracies, it sometimes wants things that it cannot ask for. You need to see that we are doing the right thing."

"Where's the line, Sarah? What separates an informal effort from a rogue operation?"

"Success," she countered. "And secrecy."

The drive back to Sarajevo had seemed to take a very long time.

With a conscious effort of will, Eric shunted all of that off to the side. That problem was for later. He was in Mostar to introduce Annika to someone he thought could help them.

"Can this really work?" Annika asked, as they neared the café where Eric's friend had agreed to meet them. "What you've proposed is more than unorthodox, it's . . ." The High Representative was at a loss for words.

"Nuts?" Eric suggested.

"Yes. That just about sums it up."

"Got any better ideas?"

"No," Annika admitted. She looked tired. The burden and responsibility of peacemaking was weighing heavily on her. They were not succeeding, and the consequences of failure were too awful to contemplate.

"So why not at least put this on the table?" Eric asked.

"Why the hell not," she agreed.

It started to rain again just as they reached their destination, a café with a view of the old bridge and the somewhat unimaginative name View of the Old Bridge. Much of life in the Balkans revolved around the café. This is where business was done, friendships sealed, and courtships conducted. The View of the Old Bridge had been in business for more than a century, and it had not changed all that much over the years.

A few patrons looked at them with unabashed curiosity when they stepped inside. Annika was well known to those who read the papers and Eric's look—which was mainstream for New York or London—was decidedly exotic by local standards. He had long ago learned to tune it out.

The café was open to the street, with a mix of tables inside and in a fenced-off garden area out front. Eric led Annika to a table in the garden under an awning that shielded it from the rain. The man sitting at the table was young and looked even younger than his thirty-four years. Black hair framed a face that was arresting if not conventionally handsome. His ice-blue eyes were his dominant feature and together with his easy smile were the key to his considerable appeal to women. He wore jeans and a black T-shirt. A copy of the Sarajevo daily *Oslobođenje* sat on the table next to his coffee.

He rose when he saw Eric and folded him into an embrace.

"Good to see you, my friend."

"And you. Annika, this is Nikola Petrović, leader of the political opposition in Republika Srpska."

"Such as it is," Nikola said modestly.

He took Annika's hand and held it for just a moment too long, an invitation. Nikola was incorrigible, but Annika, Eric was quite confident, could handle him.

They sat at the table and ordered coffee. The rain was heavier now, running off the awning and wrapping them in a curtain of water and sound. Eric realized that Nikola had chosen the table deliberately. He did not want their conversation to be overheard. It was why they were meeting in Mostar, far from the reach of the RS state security. It was so easy to slip back into the old paranoid behaviors.

"Nikola is the head of the Social Democratic Party," Eric said to Annika, as though she were hearing this for the first time. In reality, he had already briefed her thoroughly in advance of the conversation, but it would be helpful for Nikola to hear the thinking behind the proposition Eric was about to put to him. "The SDP was part of the governing coalition with Dimitrović's National Party when it was backing a unitary Bosnia and eventual EU and even NATO membership. When the National Party turned back to the dark side—or however you want to describe it—the Social Democrats left the government and set themselves up as the loyal opposition."

"How many seats do you control?" Annika asked Nikola.

"We have seventeen deputies," Nikola said.

"And how many seats are there in the RS assembly?"

"Eighty-three."

"But the SDP has allies," Eric hastened to assure her.

"Powerful allies," Nikola added with a grin.

"Dazzle me."

"Well, the United Party of Roma—that's the Gypsies—have two

seats. The Party of Pensioners—that's the graybeards and the blue hairs—have four. And Youth of the Left—that's the longhairs—have three. That's pretty much it, bringing my grand coalition up to a total of twenty-seven opposition parliamentarians."

"About a third of the assembly," Annika suggested.

"Missed that mark by zero-point-seven assemblymen. Believe me, I've done the math. And there are a couple of guys in the ruling party who would easily count as zero-point-seven human beings at the most if we were allowed to keep score that way."

Annika laughed, and it seemed to take years off her age. It was nice to see her start to relax.

Nikola too seemed to sense that Annika was warming to him, and while his motives may well have been less than pure, he was clearly doing everything he could to radiate charm.

"Nikola, how much do you know about what Annika is doing in Bosnia?"

"Just what I read in the papers."

"The Sondergaard Plan may be Bosnia's last, best chance to avert another war. Another terrible war. The peace conference is going ahead with or without Zoran Dimitrović in two weeks. That doesn't give us a lot of time to prepare."

"Then why are you wasting a precious afternoon on me?"

"We need your help."

"To fix Bosnia?"

"Yes."

Nikola looked at Annika, his blue eyes focused on the High Rep as though she were the only person in the world. *It was a neat trick,* Eric thought. One he would do well to learn.

"How much has our friend Eric taught you about Bosnia?" Nikola asked.

"More than I knew two weeks ago."

"Has he introduced you to the wonders of Mujo and Haso?"

"What is it?"

"Not what, who. Muhamed and Hasan are the quintessential Bosnian everymen. Simple village folk who somehow are always coming out on top near the end.

"In any event, Haso goes fishing one day at the height of the war and catches the magic goldfish. 'Let me go,' the fish says, 'and I will grant you a wish. Anything your heart desires.'

"So Haso shows the fish the Contact Group map that had been proposed by the big powers as a way to split the country up among Serbs, Muslims, and Croats, and bring peace to Bosnia. Things weren't going so good with that. And Haso says to the fish, 'I want you to draw the lines on the map in such a way that everyone's happy and there's peace in our time.' The fish takes a good long look at the map and says: 'I can't do that. I don't think anyone can do that. Do you have anything that might be more within the scope of my power?'

"'Well,' Haso says. 'There's my wife, Fata. I'd like Fata to be beautiful.'

"'Bring her by,' the fish says. So Haso goes home, and he collects Fata and brings her to the lake and presents her to the fish. And the fish takes a good long look at Fata and says: 'Let me see that map again.'"

Annika laughed. Eric smiled. He had heard the joke before. He had heard all of Nikola's ten thousand jokes before. But Nikola told them well.

"So what do you want me to do?" Nikola asked. He seemed genuinely puzzled that an EU diplomat might be in need of his assistance. His confusion was not without foundation. What Eric was about to offer defied conventional political logic.

"We want you to represent Republika Srpska at the peace conference in Sarajevo," Eric explained. He tried not to make it sound like "We want you to grow wings and fly," but it came awfully close.

Nikola snorted.

"My joke was funnier."

"I'm not joking."

"Come on, Eric. I'm the leader of the opposition. It's a parliamentary system. The opposition is like a third tit. I can't even fix a parking ticket. How am I supposed to speak for the RS at a bloody international conference?"

"Easy," Eric said calmly. "You represent the RS public. Not the government. Not Dimitrović. Think about it. The people who voted for him voted for his platform. They wanted Europe. They wanted a functioning state. They wanted peace and reconciliation. There were plenty of far-right loonies on the ballot. They didn't win. Dimitrović won and you won. Now you still represent those positions—the positions that won the democratic election—and Dimitrović does not. He's not the guy the people voted for. You are. You can speak for them. They asked you to speak for them."

"That's a little . . ." Nikola was not certain how to finish the sentence. For the first time ever in their long friendship, Eric saw that he was at a loss for words.

"Bold?" Eric suggested. "Visionary? Brilliant?"

"No, that wasn't where I was going. Lunatic is closer to what I was thinking."

"It was Dimitrović who broke faith with the electorate," Eric insisted. "It was all a giant game of bait and switch. Step forward and let the people know that they still have a champion."

Nikola looked over at Annika helplessly.

"Don't look at me," she said. "Eric's right. You can do this. We need you to do this. You may well be the only thing standing between the Bosnian people and another bloody civil war."

Nikola looked unhappy.

"Don't put that on me," he pleaded.

"No one can put it on you, Nikola. You have to take it. You have to accept it. No one can force you to."

"But how would it be legitimate? How could it? I only have a third of the assembly."

"Legitimacy is in the eye of the beholder," Eric said. "If enough people believe that what you are doing is fair and just, the legitimacy will follow naturally from that."

"This sounds almost like a coup," Nikola insisted.

"Nope. You're not overthrowing the government. You're representing the majority of RS voters who chose peace and reconciliation when they were given the opportunity. Come to the conference. Speak for them. Give them a voice."

"You know that they might just kill me and dump my body in the Drina."

"I can get you protection."

"Easy for you to say."

The rain had let up and the clouds broke. The sun peeked out uncertainly, and the wet limestone of Stari Most glistened like the scales on the brook trout that the local fishermen pulled from the green waters of the Neretva. Nikola noticed it as well.

"All you need is a pigeon with an olive branch and you'd be Noah." Serbo-Croatian did not distinguish between pigeon and dove.

"Do I get my own miracle?" Eric asked.

"You mean me?"

"Yeah."

Nikola turned to look at the bridge, and it seemed to Eric as though he were staring back into the past.

"Do you know the story of that bridge?" he asked Annika.

"Some of it. Maybe not all."

"Suleiman the Magnificent commissioned it to replace a rickety old wooden thing that wasn't up to the job. Three times the architects built a stone bridge and three times it collapsed. The pasha, who did not want to look bad in the eyes of the sultan, was not especially forgiving of the failures. He had them impaled. Mimar Hayruddin, knowing that the penalty for failure was a horrible death, built a bridge of timeless beauty that stood for four hundred years. Maybe success must be built on the back of failure."

Eric did not interrupt. It was a truism of diplomatic practice that when the guy on the other side of the table was negotiating with himself, you did not try to stop him. Nikola was bringing himself around to the right conclusion.

"So are you ready to join me?" Annika asked. "Are you ready to help build this bridge?"

Nikola turned his gaze away from the bridge and looked intensely first at Annika and then Eric.

"Let's do it," he said.

Eric had not realized that he had been holding his breath, waiting for Nikola's decision. There was still a great deal of work to do, but there was now at least a path forward.

While the odds were long, they had a chance. Bosnia had a chance.

MOSTAR
JULY 1566

10

On the day before the bridge was opened, Mimar Hayruddin prepared for his own funeral. It seemed a reasonable precaution. This was the third attempt to span the mighty Neretva with stone. Suleiman the Magnificent himself had ordered it to be done, and what the sultan ordered had best be done. Even the impossible. Especially the impossible.

The architect of the first attempt had been a casual acquaintance of Hayruddin's. His bridge had collapsed before the keystone of the arch could be laid. The architect still guarded the approach to the bridge on the left bank of the river, or at least what was left of him did. His skeleton and the small bits of flesh and cloth that clung to the bones sat propped up by the sharpened stake that ran from the pelvis bone along the spine and out the mouth. The local bey's executioner had learned the trick from a descendant of Vlad the Impaler of skewering a man from ass to mouth in such a way that no major organs were damaged. Those so punished could live for days, begging for death with their eyes.

The second architect had been a genuine friend, a fellow apprentice of Mimar Sinan's, the lion of Ottoman architecture. His friend had promised, rather foolishly, to deliver the bridge on an ambitious and optimistic schedule. He had run into problems when the riverbed had shifted under one of his pillars, causing cracks in the structure that had made the bridge unstable. He had been fortunate to catch the bey at a bad moment. In a fit of pique, the governor had simply killed him on the spot.

The third architect had been a rival of Hayruddin's, a man whose sole talent consisted of self-promotion. Arrogance did not span rivers, however, and his moldering corpse occupied a stake not far from his predecessors'. His death had been a blessing to the field of architecture.

Now the task of constructing the bridge over the Neretva had fallen to Mimar Hayruddin. He had not wanted the responsibility, but it was difficult to say no to the sultan. For six years he had labored on the project, and what had begun as duty had grown into a labor of love. The bridge was beautiful. His bridge. It arched over the green Neretva like the neck of a swan. Hayruddin had used local stone for the bridge, a kind of limestone with the luster of marble. The builders had joined the stones with metal pins, and Hayruddin had mixed a mortar of his own design that included horsehair and egg whites. The towers at either end of the bridge were slender and elegant rather than squat or utilitarian. They added to the bridge's grace and beauty.

Yes, the bridge was beautiful. But was it strong? Tomorrow the bey would watch as a team of oxen hauled a large sledge loaded with bricks across the bridge. The slender swan's neck of the bridge seemed so delicate, so fragile, that many of the builders believed the span would simply snap under the weight. Builders. They did not know math. But they did know stone. Hayruddin would give them that.

If the bridge failed, Hayruddin would die, most likely with a spear skewering him from tail to tip.

"I am ready to die," he murmured to himself.

"What did you say, Master?"

"Don't call me that," Hayruddin said automatically.

"Yes, Master."

Tahir was only eleven, but he was clever. Two years ago, Hayruddin had caught him stealing food. The bey would have taken his hand. Hayruddin put the boy to work. And he had fed him. *If you feed a stray,* Hayruddin thought ruefully, *he will never leave.* The boy had become his valet, somehow making himself indispensable. Hayruddin had been teaching Tahir draftsmanship and math. Not a merchant's math. The kind of math an architect would need. Tahir was a quick study. He had an eye and the potential to be a great architect one day.

"Tahir."

"Yes, Master."

"If I die tomorrow . . ."

"You will not die, Master. The bridge is strong."

"If I die tomorrow, there is a bag of coins hidden in the back room. Silver and a little bit of gold."

"Yes, Master. I know where it is."

Hayruddin's eyes narrowed.

"Behind the loose brick in the corner near the desk," Tahir added helpfully.

"And you were not tempted to steal it?"

"No, Master. I love you."

Hayruddin actually had to blink away a few tears at that. The prospect of dying in the morning had made him soft.

"If the bey kills me tomorrow, take the coins. There is more than enough to get you to Istanbul. Find a man called Sinan. He is an architect, the finest in the empire. Give him this."

He handed the boy a piece of paper folded into thirds and sealed with red wax.

"It's a letter," Hayruddin explained. "Sinan will take you in and finish your education."

"Yes, Master," Tahir said obediently.

Hayruddin turned to the rest of his preparations. Tahir drew a bath and Hayruddin scrubbed himself with a harsh soap made of sheep fat and ashes until his skin was raw and red. The bey was unlikely to offer him the appropriate funeral rites. If his corpse could not be washed as custom proscribed, then he would at least go to his death clean.

Hayruddin laid out a fresh tunic. White. The color of death.

His papers were in order. He wrote a farewell letter to his wife in Istanbul. They had no children.

Tahir helped him lay out his clothes for the morning.

"You should eat, Master," the boy said. "I can fix you something."

"No, thank you, Tahir. I am not hungry."

"Do not worry. You will not die tomorrow. The bridge is strong. It will stand forever."

"Oh, Tahir, my son," Hayruddin said. It was the first time he had called him that. "Nothing stands forever."

GENEVA
OCTOBER 25

11

At one time, in his youth, Klingsor had briefly flirted with the idea of going to law school and following in his father's footsteps as a corporate attorney. Even as a young man, however, he had enough self-knowledge to know that the law was not for him. It was too staid. The work would be tedious, he thought, with little of the kind of psychological drama that engaged him. Instead, he had joined the army, quickly finding his home in intelligence and translating that experience into a career that had been many things, but never dull.

It was, therefore, somewhat ironic that Klingsor now found himself essentially heading up exactly the kind of multinational law firm that he had taken such care to avoid. Gisler's practice may not have been traditional, and his client base was certainly more colorful than that of a white-shoe firm in New York or London, but there was no escape from the fundamental tedium of the profession. Contract negotiations, wills, and estate planning. Even Russian mobsters, it turned out, needed trust funds for their children's education and Caribbean tax shelters for their ill-gotten gains. One of Gisler's clients, a wealthy Arab who stood one hundred and seventy-sixth in the line of succession to the throne of Saudi Arabia, had retained Gisler to represent him in a zoning dispute with London authorities over plans to install a pool on the roof of his Kensington estate. It was hardly the kind of stuff to get one's pulse pounding.

Klingsor needed to keep all of the wheels and gears turning in the law firm while they searched for the package. It needed to look like the practice was functioning normally. If Marko Barcelona realized that Gisler was dead or even if he merely suspected that something was wrong, he would move quickly to set up another fail-safe. As long as he thought Gisler was still carrying his insurance policy, they had an open window.

Klingsor pushed aside the stack of folders on his desk that held the records for a senior Chinese general with an extraordinarily expensive Russian mistress. The general wanted Gisler to purchase an apartment for her, her third, it so happened. This one on Lake Como.

Klingsor stretched his back without bothering to stand up from the butter-soft executive-level chair. Gisler had been something of a hedonist. His office was beautiful, with a large mahogany desk and a wall of legal books with unbroken spines that Klingsor suspected had been purchased by the meter. There was a humidor stocked with Davidoffs and a decanter of Scotch that had no label but tasted like money.

The hum from the industrial-strength freezer in the far corner of the office was a little distracting. Echoes Two and Four had manhandled the heavy stainless-steel box up the stairs to Gisler's office. Gisler himself was stuffed awkwardly inside. Echo Four had had to break both his legs to get him to fit. By now, the lawyer was no doubt frozen solid into a rough cube shape.

If Klingsor had learned anything about Gisler since taking over his office, it was that he was secretive by nature. He had no permanent employees, relying on a temp service to provide clerical support and never keeping the same person in the job for more than two weeks. Klingsor had broken the encryption on Gisler's computer without too much trouble. He had sent an e-mail to the temp agency announcing a last-minute vacation. The office would not be requiring the services of an administrative assistant for at least the next two weeks. Two weeks. That was about as long as Klingsor thought he could keep the charade going.

The door was open, but Echo Three knocked to alert Klingsor to his presence. He was a polite kid, but Kundry had seen his file and knew that the Andy Griffith looks and his aw-shucks demeanor were misleading. Echo Three was a stone-cold killer.

"Any luck?" Klingsor asked without much hope.

"Not a fucking thing," Echo Three replied.

Klingsor motioned to the chair on the other side of the desk. Echo Three sat down and Klingsor poured him a fifty-euro slug of Gisler's Scotch.

"What are we looking at?"

"It's a mess. There are no real records. I think that Swiss son of a bitch kept most of it in his head. He didn't trust paper and he certainly didn't trust electrons. The computers are almost clean. Nothing but solitaire."

"What about the safe-deposit boxes?"

"There are bills from various banks. They're all over town, just like fatso said before his coronary. But we don't know what's where. There doesn't seem to be a master key of any kind."

"What about the ledger?"

The black leather book they had found in Gisler's desk was filled with coded entries, symbols of various kinds that did not mean anything to Klingsor or the Echoes. The code was too personal and idiosyncratic to give up its secrets easily.

"Can't figure it out. If it's coding for whatever insurance packages he's holding for his clients, there're no obvious indicators. Nothing that looks like a bank routing number or a safe-deposit box number. Any chance we could get the geeks to look at it?"

Klingsor hesitated. The nerd battalion with their pocket protectors and supercomputers could perhaps tease some meaning out of the ledger book, but there were complications with this operation, and they were not the kind that he wanted the Echoes to know about.

"Give me the book," he said finally. "I'll see what I can do."

Once Echo Three had left, Klingsor closed his eyes and massaged his forehead and temples with his fingertips. He could feel a tension headache coming on. This op had been a total cluster fuck from the beginning, and there was no clear path forward to success that he could see. The clock was ticking. The package was almost certainly somewhere in this city, but with Gisler dead, it might as well have been in Timbuktu.

The phone rang. Gisler's private line.

"Allo," Klingsor said in French. He could have gone with German, but he had the Swiss lawyer pegged as someone who preferred French

whenever possible. It was difficult to be elliptical and imprecise in German.

"Gisler?"

"No, this is his assistant. Monsieur Gisler is currently unavailable."

"That is not acceptable." The caller spoke German with an accent that Klingsor could not identify.

"I am sorry," Klingsor said in his best High German. "I can get a message to Herr Gisler."

"My name is Ibrahim Korkuti. Tell him that. He will wish to speak with me."

Klingsor knew that name. Korkuti was Albanian mafia, head of the most powerful clan in the country and the kingpin of a criminal enterprise that encompassed not only the usual drugs and guns and extortion but also manufacturing and even mainstream politics. Korkuti had his own political party and a dozen seats in the Albanian parliament. His organization was also violent enough to make the Colombians and the Sicilians look like grade-schoolers. He was not a man used to hearing no.

"I really can't interrupt him at this moment."

"I have something that I need to deliver to Gisler today for safekeeping. One of my associates will deliver it, but I want Gisler there personally to receive it. I won't trust anyone else. He will hold it for me as per the usual arrangement. For reasons that you do not need to know, the delivery must take place this afternoon. It is extremely important."

"I will give Herr Gisler that message."

"Tell me, assistant. Are your insurance premiums paid up?"

Klingsor hesitated. The last thing he needed was someone from the Korkuti clan paying a late-night visit to Gisler's office and either burning it down or breaking in to smash the place up . . . maybe checking the freezer for a late-night snack.

"Give me a minute to find Herr Gisler, please."

Klingsor held the phone with his hand over the receiver for almost two minutes as he thought through the problem set. He had an idea. It was not one that he was especially comfortable with, but at this point it was all improvisational. And improvisation, Klingsor knew, could be exceedingly dangerous.

"Herr Korkuti," he said into the receiver. "Herr Gisler has agreed to receive your materials this afternoon at four thirty. But there are a few conditions."

"What are they?" Korkuti did not bother to disguise the irritation in his voice.

Klingsor explained.

When he had finished, Klingsor called Echo Three into the office.

"What's going on?" Echo Three asked.

"We have a job to do," Klingsor said, before outlining his conversation with Korkuti.

"Where do we start?" Echo Three asked.

"By thawing the son of a bitch out."

The Albanian mob was nothing if not punctual. At 4:32 the bell rang. Echo One opened the door and escorted the courier to the outer office. To Klingsor's mild surprise, the courier was a woman. He would have expected the Korkuti clan to be somewhat retrograde in its attitude toward gender equality.

Klingsor tracked her arrival on the computer with a feed from a series of closed-circuit cameras that the Echoes had installed for that purpose. He looked up from the screen in feigned surprise when Echo One and the courier arrived.

The courier was young and attractive, with raven-dark hair and features that were just on the edge of severe. There was a slight bulge at the beltline of her tailored suit, likely a firearm of some kind. In her right hand, she carried an attaché case. Black sharkskin. Very stylish. And no doubt outrageously expensive. Who said crime doesn't pay?

"Herr Korkuti sent you?" he asked in German.

"I am here for Herr Gisler," she replied. Klingsor noted that she had not answered the question. It was a professional response.

"Herr Gisler is in his private study."

"I was told that I would be able to see him."

Klingsor nodded.

"But not disturb him. His time is exceedingly valuable. You may watch, however, as I deliver him the materials Herr Korkuti would like safeguarded. I assume that they are in the attaché."

"It is the attaché. It should not be opened."

"Very well."

Klingsor extended his hand and waited while the courier's instincts struggled against her instructions. She handed the case over with visible reluctance.

"My employer is displeased with these special arrangements," she said, seeking to salvage some kind of moral victory from the exchange.

"We do apologize for the inconvenience. This was very last-minute, is all."

"It is not always possible to plan ahead in my employer's line of work."

"I'm sure."

Klingsor opened the double doors to the study. Inside, Gisler was sitting at his desk studying a folder that was open in front of him with an intensity that brooked no distraction.

"Wait here," Klingsor whispered to the courier, trying to convey the importance of not disturbing the great man at work.

The blinds were not drawn, and this late in the afternoon the sun shone directly into the office. This would account for Gisler's decision to don tinted glasses at his desk. The large mirror on the far wall reflected the light back toward the outer office, leaving Gisler somewhat in silhouette. Echo Two had purchased and installed the mirror earlier in the day.

Klingsor saw the courier glance at her phone then up at Gisler. He knew what she was looking at. A photo of the lawyer. She seemed satisfied and slipped the phone back in her jacket pocket.

Klingsor walked the attaché case over to Gisler and placed it on the top of the desk where it would be clearly visible to the courier. Then he leaned over to whisper something in Gisler's ear, placing his hand on the lawyer's back as he did so.

From this close, the makeup job looked obvious and overdone, but Echo Four had assured Klingsor that from a distance it would look natural.

Gisler nodded his head, as though accepting something that Klingsor had told him. What the courier could not see was the handle of the screwdriver inserted into a small hole drilled into the back of Gisler's skull that Klingsor had used to manipulate his head. He would look stiff, Klingsor knew, but then he was a Swiss lawyer.

It would help that the courier seemed more interested in the briefcase than in Gisler. Whatever was inside it must be extremely important.

Klingsor did not linger. The longer he was in the office, the greater the chance of a screwup that would reveal to the courier that she was doing business with a week-old corpse. He exited the study and closed the doors behind him. They had been open for no more than forty-five seconds.

Echo One escorted the courier to the door.

When she was gone, Klingsor returned to the study and poured himself a stiff measure of Gisler's Scotch. In a slightly macabre gesture, he poured one for the lawyer as well, setting it on the desk in front of him.

"To your health," Klingsor offered, raising the glass to his lips.

It had been a hell of a day. He did not know how long he could keep the charade going.

Maybe the code geeks could get something out of the ledger.

If not, Kundry had better deliver results.

SARAJEVO
OCTOBER 28

12

She was waiting for him when he got home.

Eric's apartment was a comfortable two-bedroom in Logavina, a hip and up-and-coming Sarajevo district only a short walk from the embassy. As was the case with most apartment buildings in the city, the common space was dirty and grim. The glass over the front door was cracked. The paint on the walls was stained and peeling, and the row of metal mailboxes was dented and rusty. In the foyer, a faint scent of urine hung in the air.

The private apartments in the building were a stark contrast to the common spaces. They were spacious and elegant, and when Eric had visited the neighbors for coffee, he had been struck at the care the residents lavished on their own homes. This was one of the legacies of Yugo-style communism. What belonged to everyone belonged to no one. There was no condo board or tenants' association. A few months ago, the elevator had broken. One of the families on the seventh floor had taken up a collection to get it repaired. But the residents on the first floor refused to contribute. They did not need an elevator. Families on the second and third floors did not want to pay as much as the people who lived on six or seven. Tensions were running high and neighbors who had been friends for decades stopped talking to one another.

Eric's apartment was on the fourth floor. He routinely took the stairs for the exercise, but when the residents of the upper floor had collected half of the money they needed to repair the elevator, Eric had made up the difference. It was only a couple hundred dollars and it helped to keep the peace.

He had spent the day working with Annika on the plans for the conference. There was still a great deal of work to do, but the pieces were beginning to fall into place. Eric felt energized by the work they had been doing, and he bounded up the stairs to his apartment.

The door was unlocked.

He was always careful to use the dead bolt. Most Sarajevans were still struggling to get by and break-ins were common.

He opened the door with a sense of foreboding, expecting to see his possessions strewn about from a desperate search for valuables. Eric had a good laptop and an iPad and there was maybe fifty dollars in various currencies scattered throughout the apartment, but the burglars were hardly going to make a big score.

To his relief, everything was in place. Maybe he had somehow forgotten to lock the door.

Then he heard the music.

The unmistakable bluesy sound of Ray Charles singing "The Midnight Hour." It was unlikely that a Bosniak burglar would have put *Genius Sings the Blues* on the turntable while he ransacked the apartment.

Eric knew who it was.

They had listened to this album together on enough lazy Sunday mornings, trying to pretend for just a few hours that there was no war. Sarah had teased him good-naturedly about his fetish for vinyl. LPs were a technology that she had assigned to the same category as vacuum tubes and Betamax, losers in the march of progress.

Sarah was sitting on the couch in the living room with her shoes off and a glass of red wine in her hand. Her hair was loose around her shoulders. She looked relaxed, almost happy. Her eyes were closed as she listened to the music.

"Make yourself at home," Eric said.

"Thanks." She did not open her eyes.

"Enjoying a little R&B with your B&E?"

Sarah opened her eyes slowly, languidly, like a sleepy cat stirring reluctantly from its spot in a beam of sunlight.

"Don't be so dramatic. I didn't break anything. The door was hardly locked."

"It has a dead bolt."

"Like I said. You really should talk to the embassy security office about getting better locks. This isn't the safest part of town."

"You could have called."

"It's better to have this conversation in person, I think."

Eric did not need to ask what Sarah meant by this conversation.

He slipped his jacket off and undid his tie, draping both over the back of a chair.

"It's better to have this conversation over a drink."

Sarah poured a generous glass of Eric's wine and handed it to him. He saw that she had picked the most expensive bottle that he had in his modest collection. Sarah had good taste. She saw that he had noticed, and she held up the bottle with the label facing him.

"I assume you were saving this for a special occasion."

"Yup."

"Well. I'll see what I can do to make it special."

Eric's throat suddenly felt dry, and he took a large swallow of the wine to cover his confusion. Sarah had always blown hot and cold, and the signals she sent could be misleading, sometimes deliberately so.

"I'm sorry about Zvornik," she said. "That didn't work out the way I had hoped. It got a little out of hand."

"How far out of bounds are you, Sarah? How much are you risking on this play?"

"As much as I have to. Washington wants reward without risk. Well, you can't have that. The trick is to take smart risks. It's got to be worth it."

"And is it?"

"Without a doubt. I won't stand by and let this place fall back into the savagery of the nineties. Not if I can do something about it."

"And you think Mali is the key?"

"I do."

"And you're ready to do anything to bring Dimitrović back into our camp."

"I am."

"What is it that Mali has on Dimitrović? You know more than you told me. You told Viktor it was a disc or a tape of some kind. What is it? What's on it?"

Sarah seemed to hesitate. "We're not sure. But it's something pretty big."

"Something from the war?"

"Most likely."

"What if it's something criminal? Dimitrović had a dark past. I'm sure that you can find all sorts of slimy things under the rocks of his personal history if you turn enough of them over."

"I'm not interested in the past. It's the future I care about. Dimitrović may have been a wing-nut nationalist up until a few years ago, but he changed. I don't know why he did and I don't particularly care. All that matters is what he can do. What he can mean for the future."

"What about justice?" Eric pressed. "Who speaks for the dead? What do we owe them?"

"Nothing, Eric. We owe them nothing." Sarah leaned forward to emphasize her point. "The dead don't care."

"What about Meho?"

"What about him?"

"What do we owe him and his family?"

"We owe it to him to make this country the best place it can be. If that means that a few creeps manage to escape the consequences of their actions, so be it. It isn't personal."

"You do understand that if we have evidence that Dimitrović was culpable in serious human-rights violations or something from the war that would meet the bar for crimes against humanity, we have a legal obligation to turn it over to the tribunal in The Hague."

"To hell with the tribunal. It's a bunch of old men sitting in a courtroom a thousand miles from here splitting the few hairs they have left."

"That's pretty much the way the law works."

"I don't care. Morality trumps law."

"Who's the judge of what's moral?"

"I am. You are."

The final sorrowful notes of "Ray's Blues" faded to a close and the arm of the turntable swung up back into its cradle.

Eric rose from his seat and flipped the disc. It gave him something to do to cover his confusion. Was Sarah right? Was his own obsession with the past not only damaging to his psyche but morally misguided as well?

He watched as the arm settled back onto the vinyl disc and the first few brassy piano notes of "Mess Around" played over the Pro-Audio speakers.

He felt a hand on his shoulder gently pressing against the tension in his muscles.

"Eric . . ." Sarah said, and stopped.

He turned, taking her in his arms and pressing his lips against hers. Sarah kissed him back fiercely. She tasted of wine and chocolate. Sarah wrapped her arms around his waist. Eric stroked her hair then caressed the side of her face. She shivered slightly at his touch as though from cold, and a soft sound of pleasure and desire came from deep in her throat. It was just as it had been.

"Sarah, I . . ."

"Shhh." She put a finger to his lips. "Don't talk. Not now. Later."

She unbuttoned her jacket and let it fall to the floor. Her nipples were clearly visible under the sheer fabric of her blouse. Eric took her hand and led her back to the bedroom, remembering what it was like to be young and in love.

The morning was awkward.

Sarah was up and dressed before Eric was even awake. He threw on a pair of jeans and a T-shirt, and padded barefoot into the kitchen where Sarah was brewing coffee. She seemed distant and cool, turning away from Eric when he moved to embrace her.

Here we go again, he thought. *The emotional roller coaster.*

Sarah handed him a mug of coffee, black and strong.

"Do you want to talk about it?" he asked.

"Not really."

It was hard to believe that this ice queen was the same person who had made love to him with passionate intensity only a few hours earlier. His back stung deliciously where Sarah's nails had scraped furrows in his flesh. She was a complicated woman. She always had been. Eric had to acknowledge that his feelings for her were still strong, stronger than he had realized. But that did not mean that he had any real hope of understanding her. Sarah was a paradox, a beautiful enigma.

"Are you hungry? There's a great bakery on the corner that has the best *burek* in the city. They'd be the first to tell you that."

Sarah offered him a wan smile.

"Coffee's all I need," she said.

"The breakfast of champions."

"I thought that was cornflakes and bourbon."

"Cold pizza and warm beer, actually."

"Eric, about last night . . ."

"The night you don't want to talk about?"

"Yes. That one."

"Tell me."

"I'm sorry."

"I'm not."

"I shouldn't have done that."

"I don't think it was just you. I remember being there too."

"Okay. We shouldn't have done that. I've been under a lot of stress and I'm lonely. It just happened."

"Maybe it'll just happen again."

She shook her head and sipped the coffee. "I don't think so."

"Just try to keep an open mind."

"I should go," she said.

And Eric thought that if she left his apartment then and there she was lost to him forever.

"Actually, I was planning to call you last night and invite you to take a road trip with me today."

"Because the last one was such a success?" Sarah suggested.

"Because there's someone I want you to meet."

"Who?"

"Nikola Petrović."

"Nikola Petrović of the Social Democrats?"

"The very same."

"Kind of a small fish, isn't he?"

"Not for long," Eric assured her. "Not if I have anything to say about it. No matter what happens with Mali, I think Nikola can be part of the answer to the problem."

"Where will he be today?"

"Prijedor."

"The RS again?"

"Hey, it's gotta go better than the last time around."

Sarah was quiet, thinking through the implications of accepting or rejecting Eric's invitation. She had a sharp analytical mind and a processing speed that kept her a step or two ahead of nearly all her colleagues.

"Okay," she said, after no more than ten or fifteen seconds of contemplation. She cast an appraising look down at the outfit she was wearing, the same one she had been wearing the night before. "But I need to go home to get changed first."

Eric smiled at his little victory.

"I'll drive," he said.

The drive to Prijedor took about four hours, and he kept the conversation light, steering clear of the emotional minefield of their past and future. Eric outlined for Sarah his plan for elevating Nikola to a leadership position in the RS by virtue of his unwavering support for a European Bosnia. Sarah was skeptical. She was focused on returning Dimitrović to the pro-West camp as the answer. But she recognized that it was always good to have a fallback plan.

Sarah's trick with the license plates helped them slip past the checkpoint into the RS without being stopped. Eric's car, an eight-year-old Volkswagen Golf, was one of thousands just like it on Bosnia's roads. It was cheap, reliable, and completely anonymous. The guards, who looked to be the same trio who had stopped Eric and Annika on their visit to Banja Luka, hardly glanced up at the Golf from their card game as they sped through the checkpoint.

Prijedor was an attractive riverside town that featured an interesting mix of Austrian and Ottoman architecture. The city had been cleaned up a few years earlier in a major municipal beautification campaign, but it was harder to scrub out the bloody spots of its recent history. Prijedor had lent its name to one of the worst massacres in the Bosnian War, second only to Srebrenica. After the Serbian takeover of the city, thousands of civilians had been executed, raped, or detained without trial. A series of concentration camps in the hills around Prijedor, including the notorious Omarska camp, had been virtual abattoirs. To the survivors, as well as to the prosecutors in The Hague, what had happened in this sleepy little city was known as the Prijedor Massacre.

Eric parked a few blocks from the city center.

"Hope you don't mind a short walk. Political rallies here can generate counterdemonstrations. And cars that get caught between the two groups can suffer all sorts of indignities."

Sarah cast a disparaging eye over Eric's car, which had once been white but now could be only charitably described as "dusty." There was a sizeable dent in the driver's-side door and a spiderweb crack in the rear window.

"How would you tell?" she asked.

"I'm not much of a car guy."

"No," Sarah agreed. "Not really a clothes guy either."

Eric was wearing jeans and a light-blue oxford shirt with perhaps a little too much mileage on it.

"Harsh."

"Just saying that you look more like a start-up maven in San Francisco than a diplomat."

"It's because I'm Asian, isn't it?"

Sarah laughed at his mock indignation.

"You'll see," Eric said. "I'll be the best-dressed guy at the ball. Trust me, this will not be a black-tie event."

"Let's go see."

The SDP rally was at the town's central square in front of the city assembly building, a beaux arts behemoth that dated back to the days of Austro-Hungarian suzerainty. There were maybe five hundred people milling around the square waiting for the speeches. A local band was playing traditional folk music, not the ear-splitting version known colloquially as turbofolk, but the older, more melodic songs of love, loss, and suffering that were like windows to the Balkan soul.

"Take a look around," Eric said. "What do you see?"

"A political rally like a million others," Sarah replied. "Smaller than most."

"Look again," Eric insisted. "Look at the flags they're carrying. EU flags. Bosnian flags. There are even a few old Yugoslav flags with the big red star. No RS flags. No Serbian flags. It's an antinationalist crowd nostalgic for the days of brotherhood and unity. And there's a mix. Young people. Old people. There are pensioners who look like they don't have two marks to rub together and a guy right over there with Italian sunglasses that must have cost two hundred euros. It's a movement."

"That's a pretty big word for five hundred people."

"Wait. You'll see."

They joined the crowd, working their way up toward the front. After another couple of songs—which Eric delighted in pointing out were a mix of Serbian, Bosnian, and Croat standards—Nikola came onto the stage.

He was dressed in black jeans, work boots, and a white shirt with the sleeves rolled up. His hair was slicked back, and he had what looked like a three days' growth of beard. The crowd cheered loudly and stamped their feet on the cobblestones.

"Not your typical pol," Sarah observed.

"No. He is not."

"And good-looking."

Eric rolled his eyes.

"You can do better," he assured her. "Hell, you just did better."

Sarah stuck an elbow in his rib cage.

Nikola soaked up the applause, spreading his arms and tilting his head backward as though the heavens had just delivered a cooling rain to break a long drought.

"He looks like Jesus," Sarah suggested.

"What do you know about Jesus?"

"I've seen pictures."

"My fellow Bosnians," Nikola began, and the crowd roared.

"Bosnians?" Sarah asked

"Not Bosniak," Eric answered. "Bosnian. Bosniaks are members of the ethnic group who used to be called Muslims before and during the war. Changing that to Bosniak was part of the growing nationalist consciousness on the part of all three communities. Bosnian just means a citizen of Bosnia and Herzegovina irrespective of their ethnic identities."

"Seems like a minor distinction."

"Not to them. People here have killed and died for much, much less."

"We are here today," Nikola continued, "to send a message to

Banja Luka. That we didn't vote for what they've become. That we didn't choose what they represent. That we—the people of Republika Srpksa—have chosen peace and reconciliation and a European future for our children. That we do not believe them when they tell us to fear our brothers. That we will not listen when they command us to hate our neighbors. That if they cannot deliver on the promises they made and the future we have chosen then we will goddamn deliver it for ourselves."

The crowd roared its approval. Eric cheered along with them, abandoning any pretense of diplomatic impartiality. Dimitrović and Petrović were not equal. What they represented was not worthy of the kind of false equivalence that too often paralyzed diplomacy, making it impossible to distinguish between right and wrong, between good and evil.

"Good-looking and talented," Sarah said. Her Serbo-Croatian was rusty, but she could follow along easily enough even after twenty years. "You know, I think my organization might have some people who could help him. He'll need access to capital, expertise, pollsters. I could deliver that."

"It'd ruin him if he was ever linked to the Agency," Eric protested.

"We know that. We're patriots, not idiots. We could keep it quiet. Petrović would get money and expert help, and no one would ever need to know."

"If his circumstances changed like that, everyone would assume it was you, in the same way that they assumed it was you behind the suspiciously well-heeled group of students who brought down Milošević in Belgrade."

"I wish we had the stones and the skills to do half the stuff we get the credit or the blame for."

"Still and all, what Nikola's doing has to be natural. It has to be organic and Bosnian. If it's seen as something alien or foreign, it'll trigger the political equivalent of an immune system response."

"Well, what can you do, then, to help the good guys?"

"There are things," Eric said cryptically. "I'm doing some of them."

Nikola was just getting warmed up. He attacked Dimitrović, lambasting him as a cheat who had promised the voters a European future and delivered instead a Byzantine past.

"And Dimitrovic is not alone in this," Nikola insisted. "He has allied himself to the mysterious Marko 'Mali' Barcelona, a man no one seems to have met but who has made himself into perhaps the most powerful man in Republika Srpska. I heard that Mali went fishing the other day and caught the magic goldfish. Being a kind-hearted fellow, he unhooked the fish and tossed it back into the lake. The fish turned to him, and said, 'But wait. You forgot about the wish.' 'Okay, fish,' Mali answered. 'What do you want?'"

The crowd laughed, but the laughter was tinged with anger.

"There is a way forward," Nikola said, as though sensing that the crowd was on the edge of becoming a mob and setting fire to the parliament building behind him. "Annika Sondergaard, the Viking warrior, has put forward a peace plan that would finally make us whole. It is not a perfect plan; no plan is perfect. But it is a step forward, a step in the direction that we have chosen. I will walk this path with Sondergaard, and I hope that you will all walk it with me."

Eric scanned the crowd, hoping to gauge their reaction. This was exactly what he had had in mind when he had pitched the idea to Nikola in Mostar. Now was the chance to see whether it would play in Peoria—or Prijedor.

Twenty feet to his left and closer to the stage he saw a large man in a long coat that seemed unnecessary on such a warm afternoon. Although Eric had proudly highlighted the crowd's diversity for Sarah, this man seemed out place. He did not belong here. Eric could see a dark tattoo creeping up the side of the man's neck, but he was too far away to see if it was one of the paramilitary symbols.

In what seemed to Eric like slow motion, the man swung his coat open and pulled a wicked-looking gun from a concealed holster. An Israeli Uzi, Eric realized, and a part of his brain was unreasonably proud that he had identified the weapon.

He pushed his way toward the assassin shouting "Gun!" at the top of his voice. It was too far. There was not enough time.

Even worse, Eric saw, the gunman was not alone. There was a second man about fifteen feet farther to his left. He had drawn a handgun and was leveling it at the stage.

"Nikola! Get down!" Eric doubted that he could be heard over the crowd.

Those standing closest to the gunmen were fleeing in every direction, all except four. Eric saw two men tackle the first shooter. They did not look like amateurs. One man went for the gun, grabbing both the weapon and the shooter's forearm, and forcing it down toward the ground. The second man had a pistol in his hand that he jammed into the base of the would-be assassin's skull. Even over the crowd noise, Eric could hear the instruction.

"Drop the gun, you piece of shit."

Something similar was happening to the second gunman. He was already on his knees. A woman Eric would have taken for a middle-aged housewife was standing behind him strapping his wrists together with yellow flex cuffs. Her partner, a younger man dressed like a student, covered the second shooter with a snub-nosed pistol. It had all taken only seconds.

Nikola had not moved. He was standing on the stage straight and tall. Eric jumped up beside him. Nikola embraced him and kissed him roughly on the cheeks three times in the Serbian fashion.

"Oh, to be shot at and missed," he said.

"They didn't get a chance to shoot," Eric replied.

"That's not what the papers will say. There'll be a hail of bullets in the stories tomorrow. Those two just did me a huge favor."

Eric looked out over the crowd. Only a few of Nikola's supporters seemed to have fled the shooting. Hundreds were still milling around the square. They were keeping a respectable distance from the subdued shooters, but the atmosphere was still more that of a rock concert than a crime scene.

"My friends," Nikola said into the microphone. "We have clearly scared the powers that be. They know what we stand for and what we fight against. And we live to fight another day. Now, let us leave the authorities to do their work. We will meet again soon. Bring your friends, and your cousins and your lovers. And thank you for sharing this adventure with me today."

The crowd cheered its enthusiasm. Few seemed inclined to go home.

The uniformed police had arrived and were arguing with Nikola's rescuers about custody of the shooters.

"Are those Dragan's people?" Eric asked.

"They are." The answer came from behind Eric, and he turned to see a short man in aviator sunglasses and a brown leather jacket who looked more than a little like Telly Savalas. He was completely hairless, without eyebrows or even eyelashes, the consequence, Eric knew, of an autoimmune disease.

"Good to see you, Dragan," Eric said. "I don't suppose it was luck that had your people within arm's reach of the shooters."

"I don't believe in luck. We know those two. They're heavies for the Zemun clan who have moved over to the White Hand. We marked them the moment they stepped into the square."

The police had evidently won the argument, because they bundled the shooters into their cars, ridiculously small Czech Škodas done up in the standard blue-and-white livery of the RS police.

Sarah joined the group, and Eric made the introductions.

"Gentlemen, this is my colleague, Sarah Gold, on temporary assignment to the embassy's economic department. Sarah, this is Nikola Petrović of the SDP and Dragan Klicković of the BIA."

"State security?" Sarah asked with a raised eyebrow. BIA was the acronym for Bezbednosno-informativna agencija, or Security Information Agency, an organization that was supposed to spy on Serbia's enemies but spent much of its time and energy spying on the political opponents of whoever happened to be in power.

"Formerly," Dragan explained. "Now I'm a . . . what's the word . . . privateer?"

Eric swallowed a laugh. "That's the right word for sure," he offered.

"I run a private security firm," Dragan said to Sarah, ignoring Eric's jibe. "I have been contracted to provide security to Mr. Petrović here, and my employees, if I may say, have again demonstrated that this is a quality firm. Well worth the price."

"Who hired you?" Sarah asked.

"Your friend Eric, of course," Dragan answered.

Eric shrugged.

"It's not my money. It's Annika's. But it was well spent."

Nikola clapped him on the shoulder. "Indeed. Thank you, my friend. You kept your word."

Dragan pulled a silver flask from his hip pocket and unscrewed the cap. He passed it to Nikola, who took a deep swallow and then handed it to Eric. It was homemade plum brandy, the kind that should not be set next to an open flame. Sarah took a slug as well. Dragan raised the flask and offered a toast.

"To near things," he suggested, before downing the rest of the flask.

"Do you know the story of Mujo catching the magic goldfish?" Nikola asked.

"How many of those jokes do you know?" Eric interjected.

"More than most. Now hush."

Eric held up his hands in mock surrender.

"So Mujo catches the goldfish. The big one. The one that grants three wishes. And Mujo's first wish is that bread grows from the trees. Sure enough, the branches are soon heavy with beautiful golden-brown loaves of fresh bread. His second wish is for the river to run with brandy instead of water. The fish shakes its head and the river begins to flow with amber *rakija*. Now Mujo is stumped. 'You have a third wish,' the fish says, 'but you have to use it now. No saving it for later.' 'Okay,' Mujo answers, 'I guess I'll have just one more liter of *rakija*.'"

Sarah laughed harder than the joke merited and touched Nikola's arm. Eric felt a brief and irrational stab of jealousy. Was she flirting with Nikola or manipulating him? With Sarah, it could sometimes be difficult to tell.

Dragan looked at her appraisingly.

"So I have heard from some friends of mine . . . mutual acquaintances, I believe . . . that you are interested in the activities of a certain faux Spaniard."

"I may be," Sarah acknowledged.

"One of these acquaintances is currently eating his meals through a straw."

"Really? That must be just awful for him."

"I hear that you may have had something to do with that. It's an unusual skill for an economic officer, no?"

"Oh, I don't know. Numbers can be pesky things. A girl likes to have options."

"Indeed." Dragan's smile was as enigmatic as anything that the Mona Lisa had ever managed.

"I may be able to assist you in this," Dragan continued.

"You know something about Mali? Something useful?"

"Perhaps."

"Do you know who he is?" Sarah asked. "What he wants?"

"No, but I know where to begin."

"What do you know?"

"I know where the son of a bitch lives."

KRIVA RIJEKA
OCTOBER 28

13

Marko Barcelona examined the empire he had built with the obsessive attention to detail of the clinically paranoid. He was not satisfied. All had gone well so far, remarkably well. But there was a weak point. A vulnerability. Mali worked it over in his mind as he might probe a loose tooth with his tongue. He could not afford any mistakes. Not now. Not when he was so close.

His name was neither Marko nor Mali, and although his Spanish was nearly as good as his Serbo-Croatian, he was neither a Spaniard nor a Serb. Marko "Mali" Barcelona was a legend, a man with no past and no home and no history. He was an invention, a reinvention, really, of what he had been. His contempt for his former identity was so complete that he had all but banished it from his thoughts. It was painful to contemplate, and he had so thoroughly embraced his new identity that he thought of himself only as Mali.

Before he was Mali, he had been a worm feeding on the decayed leaf matter on the forest floor, the droppings of his betters, his self-styled "superiors." But he had spun a chrysalis around himself of power and money and knowledge, and he had burst forth a wolf. Transformed. Metamorphosed. He preferred being a wolf to being a worm by a wide margin, and he intended to keep it that way no matter what, or who, stood in his way.

Mali's office was deep inside the villa he had built for himself with the resources that flowed effortlessly from influence. He had always understood at a gut level that money was power, but it was only after his metamorphosis that he had come to appreciate the obverse. Power was money, or near enough to a one-to-one exchange rate so as to make no difference.

Dimitrović had political power and Mali had Dimitrović. That translated into a significant share of nearly every business deal done in Republika Srpska, a kind of tax on the weak paid by the sheep to the wolves. This office was Mali's wolf's lair, his retreat. It was paneled in oak and lined with shelves of books in half a dozen languages. A few paintings hung on the wall, the muted palette of Serbian masters and the bolder colors of Russian artists from the avant-garde school.

The desk was massive. It had been moved in during construction because it would not have fit through the door. A side table held a decanter of Scotch and a humidor of cigars. Crown Royal and Cohibas. Tito's favorites. It was an homage of sorts to the master manipulator, the little peasant boy from a Croatian village who had risen to a position of absolute power from which he could thumb his nose at both East and West.

Mali slapped the top of the desk, feeling the sting in his palm. It was made of solid oak. But the solidity, he knew, was an illusion. His empire was built on a foundation of lies and deception and the control he could exert over one man. As long as Mali had the tape, Dimitrović was his to control, and the dead man's switch, Emile Gisler, kept him untouchable. But if Dimitrović disappeared. If he was hit by a truck, or knocked off by a rival, or even simply lost out in a power struggle, Mali's empire would melt away like a morning frost.

He would need to build on his position, use this window to make himself independent of Dimitrović. Then, when the RS had formally separated from the horrifying accident of history that was Bosnia and Herzegovina, Mali's position would be secure. He would no longer be merely a wolf among lesser wolves. He would be a king.

It was ten o'clock in the morning, but he poured himself a drink. Crown Royal over ice from a silver bucket engraved with the Serbian seal. The seal was a cross with four C's that were really Cyrillic S's. They stood for the phrase *Samo sloga Srbina spašava*: *Only unity can save the Serbs.*

Mali did not give a shit about that. He had no interest in Greater Serbia, the pathos of a battle lost some five hundred years ago on Kosovo's field of blackbirds, or any other project of ethnic aggrandizement. Mali was interested in wealth and power. The only kind of power that mattered. Dominion over other men.

There was a knock on the door.

"Come in," Mali shouted. The door was steel with a ceramic core. It was bombproof, bulletproof, and nearly soundproof. But he could not be bothered to use the intercom system. Mali set his drink down on a coaster. It was, he understood, a bit fastidious, but that did not bother him. He considered it, together with his well-developed sense of paranoia, a source of success.

His personal secretary opened the door. Marija was a statuesque blonde with dark roots and expensive tastes. She managed his calendar and fucked him with the same cool efficiency. She was a professional.

Mali had no illusions about the nature of their relationship. He was not a handsome man. He was overweight with sallow skin and a nose that could charitably be described as prominent. In a country where a hundred and ninety centimeters was considered average height, Mali barely cracked a hundred and sixty. But he was not ashamed of his nickname. Mali might not be physically imposing, but he was the real power in Republika Srpska. That gave him stature well beyond his mere physical size. Money more than compensated for his appearance, and power, as Kissinger had famously observed, was the ultimate aphrodisiac. If that troll Henry could get laid, then it must be true.

"Darko Lukić is here," Marija said. "He's waiting upstairs."

"Is he sober?"

"Mostly."

"Try to keep him that way. Give me ten minutes and then bring him down."

"Of course."

Marija turned to open the door, and Mali had a good look at the way her perfectly shaped ass filled out her Prada skirt. He felt a brief flash of desire and thought for a moment about calling her back and delaying his meeting with Lukić another ten minutes. He had had her more than once on the leather couch in the corner.

The moment passed. There would be time for that later. He had work to do.

There was a buff-colored folder on the desk next to his drink. An Avery label stuck to the tab read DARKO LUKIĆ—SERBIA/BOSNIA. Mali sat in the leather desk chair and opened it. The first page was a biography of Lukić stamped TOP SECRET/EMERALD WAVE. The file had been stolen from the archives of the American CIA, which was not an easy thing to do.

Emerald Wave was an older project code name, a compendium of biographic material from the Balkan wars on players both major and minor who were considered candidates for PIFWC status. That was the awkward acronym, pronounced *piffwick* in international circles, for persons indicted for war crimes. Most of those included in the Emerald Wave program were either dead or serving long prison sentences. A few had escaped the long arm of international law, most for lack of evidence rather than lack of culpability. Darko Lukić was one. If there was a hell, Lukić's reprieve from the consequences of his "work" in the 1990s would be only temporary.

The Emerald Wave files were more than dry recitations of birthdays, work history, and schooling, which in the case of Lukić were February 13, 1970; spotty; and none. The prosecutors were open to offering deals to the little fish if they would turn on the big fish. The Emerald Wave files were intended to be of use to case officers in recruitment and were geared toward identifying weaknesses that could be exploited.

Darko Lukić seemed to have many of these.

Lukić was a drunk. He was a religious fanatic with an image of Saint George tattooed on his chest. His commander in the war had suspected him of being mentally unbalanced, even delusional.

But he was also a gifted shooter, an absolute ace with the Zastava M76 that was the standard-issue sniper rifle in the Bosnian Serb army. From strongpoints overlooking Sniper Alley, Lukić had routinely made shots from more than a thousand meters in the rain, wind, and fog.

Lukić seemed to have something of a sadistic streak as well. There were reports in the file from his commander that praised his skill while noting with a certain squeamishness his demonstrated preference for shooting children and pregnant women.

This was just the kind of conscienceless killer Mali needed.

Exactly ten minutes after Mali had sat down at the desk, the beautiful Marija returned with Lukić in tow.

Lukić looked at least two decades older than the age given in his file. He had the hollow-eyed look of a serious drinker. Mali hoped that alcohol had not sapped either his skills or his will. He only needed Lukić to make one shot. But he would get only one chance.

"Sit," Mali said, pointing to one of the small armchairs on the far side of the desk.

Lukić sat. He seemed tractable enough, someone used to taking orders.

"Drink?" Mali asked.

"Please." The note of eagerness in his reply was a definite warning flag, but Mali poured him two fingers of Crown Royal over ice. He wanted Lukić relaxed and pliable.

Lukić was dressed in all black, a black wool sweater, black canvas pants, and a black watch cap. The shock of hair that stuck out from under the cap was black. So were his eyes and, Mali both hoped and expected, his soul.

"Darko, do you know who I am?"

Lukić nodded. "Mali Barcelona," he said.

"Good. I asked you to come here today because I was worried about you."

Lukić looked confused, which was a perfectly reasonable response to Mali's out-of-the-blue expression of concern. It was likely that even his own mother had given up worrying over her son some years earlier.

"Worried about me?" Lukić asked.

"Yes. The last years have not been easy for you, have they?"

Lukić shook his head.

"Since the war ended, things have been hard." It was a statement, not a question.

Lukić just looked at him.

"Have you had steady work since the war?"

"Steady? No."

"There's not much work for a man of your particular skills on the outside, is there? Oh, they like you well enough when you're doing their dirty work, killing their enemies. But when the fighting's done, they act as if they've been secretly ashamed of you all along, don't they?"

Lukić nodded. His face softened, and Mali thought that he might be on the edge of tears. But the old soldier quickly swallowed whatever emotions Mali's line of questioning had uncovered, and his expression returned to its impassive norm.

"You are a son of war, Darko. You should be honored for your service."

"Yes," Lukić agreed.

"Do you still have it? Are your skills still sharp?"

The vague, glassy look in his eyes faded, and they snapped into focus. They were the eyes of a predator. A hawk or even, like Mali, a wolf. Lukić looked at Mali with the intensity he had once directed through the scope of his rifle. It was almost like a physical force, like he was seeking to impose his will on Mali's. It was its own answer to the question.

"Yes, they are," Mali said appreciatively. "Darko, I need you to kill someone for me. From a distance. A considerable distance. You would be doing a great service to your country and your people."

"Who do you want me to kill?" Lukić asked.

"A woman. That won't be a problem, will it?"

Lukić should his head slowly.

"I thought not."

SARAJEVO
MAY 12, 1993

14

He loved the world he saw through his sights. With one eye pressed firmly against the rubber seal of the German rifle scope and the other closed gently, not squeezed tightly, the world was narrow, constrained, and predictable. And Darko Lukić was its master. In this narrow world, he was a god. The god of death. He would reach out silently and unseen from his perch on Mount Olympus and deliver death unto whomever he had chosen.

The rush of power that came with each individual act of killing had no equal. No drug could match it. Even sex was but a pale shadow of killing.

The world outside his scope was a consistent disappointment. Without the German optics that brought focus and clarity, Lukić's world was a disorganized clash of stimuli. It all moved too fast, with no order or direction. He preferred the deliberate and methodical to the spontaneous and chaotic. The rifle and its scope were the single meaningful organizing principles in his life. Without them, he was nothing, an insignificant speck of protoplasm washed back and forth by tidal forces beyond his control or comprehension.

He hoped the war would never end.

But how could it? At least not until one people stood at last alone and victorious atop the piled bodies of the others. This was a conflict with no end and no beginning. It had gone too far. It had settled into the bones of all three sides. It simply was.

This conflict was timeless. It was . . . beautiful.

Lukić pulled his eye away from the pleasingly simple lines of the reticle and took a quick look around. He worked alone without a spotter, and it was important that he not get so lost in the world through his scope that he left himself vulnerable. The foreign special forces—the British SAS and the American SEALs—had taken to hunting the snipers. If they could find your nest, they would kill you. Lukić had already lost three friends to the hunter-killer teams.

They would not find him. Lukić had built his nest well. He was in an abandoned apartment block up in the hills that encircled the city. But he was not simply shooting out the window. That was the easiest way for the inexperienced to make the transition to the newly dead. Lukić would not let himself be silhouetted against the glass. There would be no muzzle flash from his rifle. Nothing to use to guide mortar teams or a countersniper. Lukić wasn't even in one of the rooms along the outside wall. Earlier, he had used a sledgehammer to knock a small hole in that wall. A second hole in a wall between the living room and an interior bedroom was located about half a meter higher up. From inside that bedroom, perched on an old mattress resting on top of a pile of shipping crates, Lukić could sight through both holes with a clean angle on the street that had come to be known as Sniper Alley. His alley. The name itself was a form of tribute being paid to the god of death.

Lukić used his pocketknife to carve thick slices off a slab of dried smoked pork. To go with it, he had a small loaf of bread and a hunk of yellow monastery cheese that was starting to dry out. He washed it down with a swallow of *rakija* from a plastic Coca-Cola bottle.

Okay, he thought, *time to get to work.*

Lukić lay back down on top of the mattress in the prone position with his legs spread for balance and the butt of the rifle pressed tightly against his cheek and shoulder. The walnut stock was smooth and cool against his skin, like the touch of a woman.

He would want a woman later. Killing always made him thirsty and horny. Fortunately, there was a camp near his base where the army kept some of the prettier Muslim girls who were made available to men who had done well. Lukić had had a few. Unlike some of the other men in the unit, he did not especially like forcing himself on them. It distracted from rather than added to his pleasure. But military life was full of compromise.

The streets were nearly empty. It was late afternoon, and the good people of Sarajevo preferred to stay home if at all possible rather than roll the dice and take their chances with the snipers and the artillery. Lukić waited patiently. He was an ambush predator.

The snipers played a game for points. Pensioners were worth half a point. They were slow. Military-age civilian men were worth one point. Children were worth a point and a half. They were smaller targets. Soldiers and women scored two points. Pregnant women three. Wounding a target and then killing one or more of the first responders trying to save the victim was worth a total of four.

Lukić was so far out in front that his fellow snipers had conceded that they were all playing for second.

A few civilians passed through his field of view, but none were at the right angle for a clean shot. Finally, his patience was rewarded. Two men appeared at the corner of Ulica Zmaja od Bosne and an alleyway too small to have its own name, the area he had identified as his primary target zone. They did not look like they were together.

Lukić zeroed in first on the man on the right, sighting in on his chest. Ordinarily, he prided himself on taking the more difficult head shot, even at distances of more than a thousand meters. But the winds were shifting, and center mass was the high-percentage shot.

His finger squeezed the trigger slowly. The discharge, when it came, would be almost a surprise, an afterthought. That was how it was supposed to be, an act free of thought, devoid of consciousness. It was a kind of communion with God.

The trigger on the Zastava was set as light as the manufacturer's specs allowed. Lukić could sense that pressure in the same way that a violinist could identify the individual notes of a chord or a painter could differentiate between subtle shades of red. With only two or three pounds of pressure standing between stasis and the release of the shot, Lukić's finger froze on the trigger. Slowly, he released the pressure.

There was something off about the target. He had dark skin like a Gypsy and a hairstyle that said "foreigner." Maybe he was a UN official or an aid worker. Maybe a diplomat or a journalist. He could be European or American. Foreigners in Sarajevo came in a limited range of flavors. None, however, were especially appetizing.

Killing a foreigner had consequences. It could trigger air strikes, manhunts, indictments, and tribunals. It was not a decision to be made impulsively.

Not when there was a second target.

Lukić slid the sight to the left, just half a degree. The second target came into focus. This one was clearly a local, a perfectly ordinary-looking Sarajevan. Just another nameless, faceless victim of the siege.

There was nothing especially difficult about this shot. He had made similar shots dozens of times before. His breathing was controlled and even. His heartbeat was slow and regular. His trigger finger was tied to his pulse to avoid even the slightest tremor that would spoil in his aim.

The crack of the shot when it came was startlingly loud in the confined space of the apartment. He saw his target stiffen as the 57mm Mauser bullet passed through his lung or his heart. The target was dead before he hit the ground. Lukić saw the foreigner jump to his target's aid rather than doing the sensible thing and seeking cover. Had he been inclined to, Lukić could have shot him too. He would have argued for the extra three points back in the barracks. But he had already decided that the risk and cost of retribution outweighed whatever gains the target offered.

He was satisfied with his day's work. It was a shot that few men in the Bosnian Serb army could have made.

Lukić was the god of death.

And he never missed.

LANGLEY, VIRGINIA
OCTOBER 31

15

VW had always been good at puzzles. Her favorites were acrostics, which required stringing together disparate data points to find the hidden pattern. It was not all that different from analytical work. She did the acrostics in pen—pencils were for intellectual cowards looking to hedge their bets—and filled in the boxes with handwriting that was so neat it looked almost machined. There were few things that got under her skin like failing to finish a puzzle did. It was almost a moral shortcoming. And it had been quite a number of years since VW had left a blank space in one of her acrostics.

Now, whether she meant to or not, VW had started a new puzzle. Parsifal. And she would be damned if she left it unfinished. Her search had so far turned up nothing useful. There was nothing in the files about Parsifal. The database was empty. The few inquiries she had dared to make had been met with blank looks. But VW had an idea. Money was every operation's Achilles' heel. The black budget was really more a dark gray. Every purchase still needed to be expensed against an authorized fund site and accounted for to the budget analysts. The beans they were counting may have been dyed black, but they were still beans.

In the old days, dissecting Parsifal would have required digging through box after box of paper records in the Agency's subbasement storage rooms. Now VW could do nearly everything without having to stand up from her desk. Or at least David Rennsler could. VW was a manager, after all.

"You wanted to see me?" Rennsler asked diffidently from right outside the door. It was typical of David that he would not come into her office without an engraved invitation.

"Yes, David. Come in, please. Sit down."

Rennsler complied reluctantly. He was a huge bear of a man with a beard that would not have been out of place on a Canadian lumberjack. He topped the scales somewhere north of three hundred pounds, and the stains on his suit testified to dining habits constructed around vending machines and the office microwave. His social skills were underdeveloped, even on the sliding scale used for grading econ analysts.

Rennsler had been sentenced to the Island largely because nobody wanted to work with him. He smelled like he had not showered in days, often because he had not. He talked to himself as he wrote or read, not muttered asides but a genuine monologue conducted at normal conversation levels. His cubicle smelled vaguely of cheese, maybe because Rennsler wore sandals with black socks rather than shoes. He was almost certainly somewhere on the high-functioning end of the autism spectrum.

But he was also a genius. And there was little enough of that to go around. VW was willing to tolerate and accommodate his eccentricities, including his almost pathological shyness. Before wearing out his welcome and being sentenced to the Island, Rennsler had been Counterterrorism's top analyst on the financing of global extremist groups. He could track a dime as it traveled from the pocket of a believer in a village near Jeddah to the tribal belt in Northwest Pakistan to a Swiss bank.

"David, I need your help."

Rennsler nodded. He spoke to himself freely and easily, but he had a marked tendency to clam up around others, especially women.

"There's a program with a director-level code called Parsifal. I'd like to know more about it. I'd like to know everything about it. Can you help me?"

Rennsler gulped for air, and he reminded VW of a fish flapping helplessly on the floor of a boat.

"With the money?" he asked finally. His voice was surprisingly thin and reedy for such a large man.

"Yes. If we know where the money's been going that should give us a pretty good idea of what the program managers have been up to."

Rennsler shifted his considerable bulk in the seat.

"Do you have the financial identifiers?"

"I do."

"Then it shouldn't be hard."

It wasn't.

The next morning when VW arrived at work, Rennsler was there, wearing the same tired suit he had been wearing the day before. A pile of empty wrappers from a variety of Hostess products offered evidence of an all-night effort.

"Looks like a late night," VW said.

"I had nowhere else I needed to be."

"Let's talk in my office."

VW had an oversize desk. But even so, Rennsler's printouts covered it several layers deep. VW scanned the data quickly. Parsifal was laid out before her like the patient in the "Love Song of J. Alfred Prufrock"—etherized upon a table. Every expenditure was exposed and frozen in place. It was always good to have hard copies. For someone who knew what he was doing, digital fingerprints were too easy to alter or erase.

Assembling the data was only the beginning, however. Now came the struggle to understand it. The puzzle.

"Let's start at the beginning," VW suggested.

Rennsler nodded vigorously.

"How far back does the spending trail run?"

Rennsler pointed to a column of numbers and letters on a legal-size printout on the far left side of the desk.

"This is the first recorded instance of expenditures linked to Parisfal," he said. "A little more than two years ago."

"July 17," VW said, looking at the entry Rennsler had indicated.

"Yes."

The rest of the entry was gibberish to VW. The spreadsheets for the black budget were written in a shorthand code that would have taken VW hours to interpret even with access to the master key. Rennsler could read them with the same ease with which a regular person could read a newspaper. He knew all the fiscal codes without having to look them up. It was a little bit like one those Asperger's kids who could reel off train schedules in Scotland or the names of thousands of Japanese anime characters. It was esoteric knowledge, but at least in this one case it was also invaluable. It would have been almost impossible for VW to sort through the mountain of data without Rennsler's help.

"What can you tell me about it?" she asked.

"It's a travel voucher. Three people to London and Athens. Those numbers"—Rennsler stabbed the printout with a thick stubby finger to indicate which column he meant—"are linked to Parsifal's fiscal data. It's an open-ended account. There's no spending limit."

VW raised an eyebrow at that. Even on the black budget, open-ended accounts were about as common as unicorns.

"Can you tell who the travelers are?"

"Not from this. The identifiers here are linked to names in a different database that requires special-access permissions. Trying to get into that would trigger all sorts of alarms. And, in any event, the names are more likely to be cover identities than actual given names."

"Why is it that the only secrets we seem really good at keeping are the ones we keep from ourselves?"

Rennsler blinked rapidly, clearly confused. His thinking was rapid, razor sharp, and almost entirely literal.

"Sorry, David. Don't worry about it. What else can you tell me from the data?"

"Most of the early expenses are for travel, but there's an uptick at about the three-month mark in cash payments that could be going to sources. Some of the payments seem pretty big, tens of thousands of dollars big, which is unusual."

"I'll say." The CIA could waste millions of dollars in operation excesses, but it was notoriously stingy with payouts to human sources who took the biggest risks on the Agency's behalf.

"The bulk of the early money seems to have been expensed in Bosnia and Serbia," Rennsler continued. "The costs are uneven. They spike and then go flat for long periods."

"Can you graph the expenses so that they're visual? Give me a sense of where and when the spikes are?"

"No problem."

Two hours later, VW had a new chart laid across her desk that looked something like an EKG from a patient suffering severe cardiac distress. VW did not need Rennsler's help to translate the data in this form. It was pretty clear and—for VW—it raised at least as many questions as it answered.

"Thank you, David," she said. "Let me sit here with this for a while. I'll call you if I need help."

Rennsler shuffled out of the room, his Birkenstocks flopping softly on the carpet.

VW looked at the chart on the top of the pile. It was a simple graph with time on the X axis and money on the Y axis. There was the initial spike Rennsler had identified. Whatever Parsifal was, it had involved substantial up-front costs. There was another significant spike about eight months ago and a third that started only about four weeks earlier and seemed to be ongoing.

VW decided to take as her working hypothesis that Parsifal was connected to the Balkans, probably Bosnia. The link to UAV time out of the eastern Slavonia airfield was the original tie to Parsifal, and until something in the data set contradicted that theory, she would work under that assumption.

Through that lens, the spikes in Parsifal spending seemed to track pretty closely to the key developments in RS politics. First, the sudden and dramatic rise to power of Zoran Dimitrović and then his retrograde slide into the swamp of ethnic nationalism and the return of the paramilitaries. The timing seemed too close to be coincidental.

The third spike was something of an anomaly. A second chart, this one set up as a bar graph, broke the spending down by geography as well as time. Parsifal expenses for the first two spikes were heavily weighted toward the Balkans, but the lion's share of expenses making up the third spike seemed to have been spent on an unrelated operation in Geneva.

VW called Rennsler back to her office.

"David, can you break this down for me? What's this bump in Geneva spending? Doesn't seem like the right environment for UAV operations."

Rennsler looked over the columns of numbers and letters, running a finger over them as though he were reading braille.

"These are payments to contractors," he answered, after a few minutes deciphering the information. "Sizeable payments."

"Can you tell which ones?"

"Yes. This group here." He pointed to a line of accounting code in the middle of a dense block of text that was meaningless to VW. "This is keyed to one of the specialty firms. True North."

"True North? I thought they were frozen out of Agency contracts after that problem in Afghanistan."

"Officially. But when I was still in Counterterrorism, the word was that True North had a certain skill set that the agency needed and didn't want to give up."

"Which is?"

"Renditions."

"So who were they going after in Geneva? George Clooney?"

Rennsler shrugged. "That's not the kind of thing you'll find in the fiscal data."

He took another look at the numbers, humming softly to himself as though to block out distractions.

"The really odd thing about this is that most of the expenses aren't tied to the original fiscal codes. They're linked to subordinate codes. It makes it hard to get a clear picture of the totality of the operation. You wouldn't stumble across this by accident. You'd have to know to go looking for it."

"Who does that sort of thing?"

"In my experience, narco-traffickers and terrorists."

"David, honey. Those two groups represent the sum total of your experience."

Rennsler blushed and looked at his feet.

"So, what does this tell us?" VW asked, trying to get Rennsler back on task.

"They're hiding something."

"Who?"

"Whoever is behind Parsifal."

"Is there any other way to look at the data?"

Rennsler shook his head vigorously in the way a terrier might do to snap the neck of a rat. "No."

"Okay. What about this last entry? What's the very latest that we have?"

Rennsler scanned it quickly.

"It's drawing from Parsifal's open-ended fund site for operations in the Balkans."

"What kind of operations?"

"UAV flights."

"And those are the most recent Parsifal expenditures?"

"Yes."

"When were the UAVs flying?"

Rennsler stabbed at one of the columns with his index finger. These numbers even VW could understand.

"Yesterday," she said.

Rennsler nodded.

VW sat at her desk sipping a cup of room-temperature coffee. Rennsler was back in his cubicle scouring the various databases for anything else he could find on Parsifal.

There was something about Parsifal that bothered VW. It stank of excess and overreach and the kind of scandal that could damage the work of the Agency for decades. She did not have the evidence to support this view yet, just a feeling. And if she was going to be brutally honest with herself, at least some of that might be attributable to her desire for revenge against the Balkan team. Even if her motivation was not entirely pure, Parsifal—she was increasingly convinced—was a cancer. She would be damned if she was going to just let it lie.

She sighed.

She knew what she had to do.

It took no more than a couple of minutes to find the telephone number she needed. VW took one final swallow of the bitter dregs of her coffee and dialed the eleven-digit number on the secure Sectéra vIPer phone on her desk. The number she dialed was an internal Agency extension, but the phone on the other end was located in eastern Slavonia.

It rang twice before someone picked up.

"Hello." Somehow these two short syllables managed to convey both boredom and impatience.

"I'd like to speak to the duty officer, please."

"That's me."

It was almost ten p.m. in Croatia. It would make sense that the duty officer would be the only one available to answer the phone.

"Excellent. I'm calling from the payroll office in Front Royal. There's a problem on this end that I'm hoping you can help straighten out so that we can pay you and the other members of your team."

Now, VW knew, she had his complete attention. The contractor force performed a wide range of functions on behalf of the Agency, but their motives were almost entirely mercenary. These were not patriots. They were—quite literally in some cases—hired guns.

"What's the holdup?"

"Well, a number of overtime charges have been submitted that the auditors want to deny. There's no justification for the claims, and they need more detail before they'd be willing to sign off on them."

"What a goddamn waste of time." VW could hear the edge of irritation in his voice.

"I agree with you . . . did you tell me your name?"

"Allen."

"I agree with you, Allen, and I'm certain we can clear this up quickly. I just need something to take back to the accountants. There's a significant overtime charge for UAV operations over the last forty-eight hours. If you can give me more detail, I may be able to shoehorn all of the outstanding overtime under the single claim."

"What do you need?"

"Justification. Was the flying time over Bosnia?"

"Allen" in eastern Slavonia hesitated. He was not supposed to discuss the details of operations with people outside his immediate chain of command, but the call was coming in on a CIA vIPer phone and VW knew that he would want to put any administrative hassles behind him as quickly as possible.

"Yes," he finally admitted.

The ice had been broken. They were talking about the operation. Now, as Churchill had put it, they were simply dickering about the price.

"Is there a flight plan?"

"Nothing written down."

"What kind of flights are we talking about? The overtime codes are different. Was it surveillance? Signals gathering?"

"Surveillance."

"Routine patrol or a specific target? It'll be harder to justify overtime for routine operations."

"It was a specific target. We had orders."

"What was the target? I need to input something into the field on the new system. Without it, I can't get the approvals I need to process the paperwork."

"A house," the man said, after another moment's consideration.

Interesting.

"Do you know whose?"

"No."

"Well, do you at least have grid coordinates?'

"Of course."

"That should be all I need."

Allen gave her the coordinates.

VW assured him that she would do everything she could to expedite the outstanding overtime claims.

"You boys are at the pointy end of the spear," she assured him. "It's my job to make sure we keep you oiled and sharp."

"Thanks," Allen had said appreciatively.

Asshole, VW thought, after she hung up the phone. Allen was cutting corners on OPSEC to make sure he got paid. And although he had done it at VW's urging, it was still infuriating. She abhorred unprofessional behavior in all its forms, even when she was the direct beneficiary.

"So what have you been looking at, Parsifal?" she asked out loud.

There was a paper map of Bosnia in the filing cabinet with air force grid markings. The coordinates Allen had so helpfully provided had the UAV loitering over a valley called Kriva Rijeka. The Crooked River.

There was only one way to find out what was there.

VW picked up the vIPer phone again and dialed another number, this one from memory.

"Bob, it's Victoria."

"How's tricks?"

"Still living the dream. Listen. I need UAV time in Bosnia. But not out of eastern Slavonia. I want a Global Hawk out of Ramstein."

"And I want to sleep with Scarlett Johansson. My chances are actually somewhat better than yours."

"Bob, get me my Global Hawk or I'll be forced to remember that time you took your girlfriend on a joyride to West Virginia on a CIA helicopter. I don't think the inspectors would take kindly to that."

"You really want to play that card, VW?"

"Not unless I have to."

"Well, I hope it's for something pretty fucking important."

"Me too."

Bob Landis sighed. "Give me two or three days."

TRNOVA, BOSNIA
OCTOBER 31

16

The bees were living up to their reputation. The pear trees were heavy with the last fruit of the season, and standing on the edge of the small orchard, Father Stefan could hear the low hum of the honeybees from the monastery's apiaries as they gathered the pollen from the purple flowers of the aster that grew in the shadows of the trees.

Stefan loved the bees. They had something of an understanding. He did not take more of their honey than he needed, and they did not sting him more than they had to. *People could do worse than to model themselves after honeybees,* Stefan thought. Hard workers. Productive. Ready to sacrifice themselves for the good of the hive. Gentle unless provoked.

Wasps were something else altogether. Nasty. Aggressive. They would sting for pleasure, and they offered nothing of value. It was no coincidence that they had lent their name to one of the more vicious of the paramilitaries. Father Stefan was a man of peace. At least now he was.

It had been a good year for honey, Stefan thought. The spring had been wet and cool, and the summer warm and dry. God was good.

There were almost a hundred glass jars of sweet-clover honey in the cellar, some with a generous piece of the waxy comb that the village children chewed like gum. There were also five big oak casks holding the pear brandy that the novices had distilled under Stefan's direction. The brandy would need at least a year to mellow, but there were four barrels from last year's harvest that were ready to be bottled and fifty glass bottles with beeswax seals from the year before that. The cellars also held wheels of monastery cheese and boxes of onions, carrots, and potatoes from the garden that would keep through the winter months. The monastery was not rich, but it had been self-sufficient even when the godless communists had been in power.

Now the monastery was more than self-sufficient. It was well-off. All thanks to the patronage of the mysterious newcomer to Bosnia, Marko Barcelona. Mali gave generously to the church, and all he had asked in return was the smallest of personal favors. Stefan tried not to think about it too much. If he did, it raised questions that he could not answer and did not want to answer.

He knew, of course, why Mali had come to him. Reputation followed a man for years, long after he had stopped doing what he had done to earn it. He had been a young man back then, or at least younger. His beard was already salted with gray when Yugoslavia had splintered into its warring parts. But he had been full of fire and passion. Attributes he had always associated with youth.

It was impossible to separate ethnicity and religion in the Balkans. The Croats were Catholic. The Serbs were Orthodox. The Muslims were what they were. The new politically correct term "Bosniak" was the misnomer meant to lay claim to all of Bosnia by one of its constituent peoples. But even so, Bosniak meant Muslim. A Catholic Bosniak was like dry water. The church had inevitably and to its detriment been sucked into the politics of Yugoslavia's disintegration. Stefan had been swept along with all the rest on the tide of religious and nationalist fervor that had blanketed the entire region. It was a kind of insanity, less temporary than latent. That was the past. You could not escape its shadow, but you could, Stefan believed, light a candle against the darkness.

He picked a yellow-green pear off a branch and took a bite. The flesh was firm, and the fruit was sweet and juicy. It was truly God's bounty.

He walked back toward the small chapel he tended. It was still early, and the field was wet with dew. It was time to treat his boots with beeswax again. The fall rains were cold, and his feet would freeze if he allowed the water to soak through the leather.

The chapel was small, not more than a single room, but it was elegant, with an octagonal design in the classic Byzantine style and frescoes of the saints and martyrs of Christendom that dated to the fourteenth century. The door to the chapel was at least two hundred years old, dark oak bound with iron and worn smooth by the elements. Nominally, the chapel was a part of the Monastery of St. Archangel Gabriel complex that had more than a hundred novitiates and a vast acreage, mostly forest and mountain slopes too steep to cultivate. In practice, this small chapel was Father Stefan's private world. He lived an ascetic life of prayer and labor appropriate to a hieromonk, a monk who had taken priestly vows. In another age, he might have been a hermit.

Inside the chapel, it was five degrees cooler and there was a damp that he had begun to feel in his joints. He was, Stefan thought with a sense of resignation to the inevitable, growing old. He would be seventy in the spring. God willing.

On the wall to the right of the door was a fresco of Saint Nikola holding in one hand a model of the chapel. He had no eyes. The villagers believed that eating even a small piece of the plaster from the eyes of a saint in a fresco could cure cataracts. It was superstition. Sympathetic magic. The disfigurement of Saint Nikola, a masterpiece of Byzantine art, depressed him. But eyeless saints were more the rule than the exception in the churches and monasteries out here in the wilds of the Bosnian mountains. He hoped someday to repair the once-elegant frescoes. The money from Mali would make that possible.

It was time for the morning liturgy. As on most mornings, there were no parishioners in this small mountain chapel. But Stefan put on the vestments and read the liturgy out loud in a clear voice as an act of devotion to God. Much of the service was conducted with his back to the door, facing the altar with its seventeenth-century icon of the Madonna and child. He was somewhat surprised when he turned at the end of the service to find someone standing at the back of the chapel, waiting patiently.

It was a woman. She was elderly, although village life in the mountains had a way of aging people prematurely. It was possible that she was as much as a decade younger than Stefan. She was wearing a head scarf, the kind that covered the chest as well. Observant Orthodox women covered their heads in the church, but this was an Islamic-style *hijab*. A Muslim woman then. *What was she doing here?* he wondered.

"Good morning," he said, after removing his vestments and hanging them back up on the altar. "It is always nice to have visitors for the service even if they are not of my flock."

The woman looked nervous, and she backed away as Stefan approached her until she was pressed up against the wall.

Reputation.

Stefan stopped. If he moved too quickly or stepped too close, he thought the woman might bolt for the door.

"You have nothing to fear here. You are in a house of God."

The woman smiled tentatively. The few teeth she had left were yellow-brown.

"Thank you, Father. I have not been here since I was a girl and Andreas looked after the church."

Father Andreas was a Greek priest the communists had just barely tolerated. He had been a senior figure at the monastery when Stefan had first arrived some forty years ago.

"It is good to meet a friend of Father Andreas's," the priest offered. "I was just about to make myself a cup of coffee. Would you care to join me?"

"With pleasure."

Stefan slept in a small room with its own entrance at the back of the church that had once been used for storage. There was also a kitchen with a wood-fired stove. Stefan packed it with dry kindling and lit it with a match. The stove heated up quickly and he set a *džezva* of water to boil for coffee.

The village woman waited outside, sitting on a bench at a wooden table at the base of an apple tree that was too old to produce fruit but that could still make shade. When the coffee was ready, Stefan carried a tray out to the table loaded with two demitasses of coffee, a bottle of pear brandy, cheese, bread, a shallow bowl of honey, and a dish of dried apricots. Hospitality was an ironclad rule that bound both Orthodox Christianity and Islam.

"My name, by the way, is Stefan," he said, pouring his guest a shot of brandy to go with the coffee.

"I know," the woman answered. "I came here to see you. My name is Orahovac. I am Ibrahim's widow."

Stefan remembered Ibrahim Orahovac as a friendly and mostly capable mechanic who helped keep the monastery's two small trucks in a semblance of working order, patching the old bald tires until they were more epoxy than rubber. He had died suddenly some four years ago, heart failure or a stroke. Stefan could not remember which. Ibrahim had two children, both girls. A terrible tragedy in a Muslim family.

Ibrahim had been drafted into the Bosnian army during the war, and he had fought at Žepa and Goražde, where he had been badly wounded by shrapnel. He had walked with a limp.

"I remember your husband," Stefan said. "He was a good man."

"Yes," his widow agreed. "He was a good provider."

"It must have been hard for you and the children after his loss."

The widow Orahovac nodded, and Stefan could see just how hard it had been from the lines etched into her face by hard work, deprivation, and fear.

"How can I help you, Mrs. Orahovac?" She was not his parishioner. She was not even a Christian. But she was clearly a soul in need, and Stefan would do what he could to help her. That was the proper role for a priest, not mucking around in ethnic politics like so many of his younger colleagues—or his younger self.

"Ibrahim always said that you were a good man, an honest man, that he trusted you to do what was right. That you didn't deserve your . . ."

"Reputation."

She nodded but said nothing in response, stopping suddenly as though at a loss for what came next. Stefan just sipped his coffee and let Ibrahim's widow organize her thoughts.

"I have tried to keep the farm and work it with the girls. But it has been hard. There are not enough men since the war. Too many dead. Others who have left for Germany or even America. One girl, my oldest, found a match and moved to Sarajevo. Her sister is still with me. We keep chickens and sell the eggs in town. We grow vegetables, and we have two cows that give good milk. We have enough to eat. But when the tractor broke, I had no money to fix it. So I borrowed three hundred euros from Zarko Golubović. But I wasn't able to pay him back, and now Golubović is going to take our house and our land. My older daughter lives in a small apartment in the city, and her husband is unemployed. They can't take us in. And we have nowhere else to go."

The widow Orahovac began to cry, and Stefan handed her one the cloth napkins from the tray so that she could dry her eyes.

"Golubović is a religious man," the widow continued. "His office has a big picture of one of your saints, and he wears a big gold cross around his neck. Would you speak to him, please? Ask him to take pity on an old woman. If you ask, I am certain he would give us more time to find the money."

Stefan was much less confident. He knew Golubović, a greedy, grasping man who would charge his mother a usurious rate of interest if he had reason to believe she was good for it or if he could get one of his siblings to cosign the note. Golubović's superficial religiosity was more a matter of fashion than faith. He would no sooner sacrifice a fat profit for Stefan and the church than he would donate to the Bosnian chapter of the Red Crescent Society.

"I would be happy to speak to Golubović, but I am afraid that it would do little good."

The widow Orahovac nodded her understanding, her eyes bright with the tears she could barely hold back. Coming to see him, Stefan knew, was grasping at straws. She must have exhausted every possible alternative before deciding on this minipilgrimage to his little mountain chapel.

Stefan was moved to pity.

The meek may inherit the earth, but not until they had paid decades of rent to the strong. It was an affront, and Stefan knew that he could not simply slough it off and tell Ibrahim's widow that there was nothing he could do to help her. He could help her. Thanks to Mali.

"Golubović will not listen to the church," Stefan said gently, and he reached across the table to cover one of her calloused, sunbaked hands with his. "But there is a way I can help you."

"Yes, Father?" she said, trying and failing to keep a note of hope out of her voice.

"Wait here a moment, Mrs. Orahovac."

Stefan got up from the table and walked around the chapel to the front door. Inside, at the altar, behind the icon of the Virgin Mary and her miraculous child, there was a loose stone. Stefan carefully lifted it out and reached into the hollow. His fingers closed around a metal box. He pulled it out and opened the lid. There was more than two thousand euros piled neatly inside the box, all in crisp new bills and all from Mali in payment for that smallest of favors Stefan did for the head of the White Hand.

Stefan removed five hundred euros and slipped the bills into an envelope. Then he replaced the box, the stone, and icon.

When he gave the envelope to Mrs. Orahovac, she again broke into tears.

"I cannot pay you back," she said.

"You don't have to. Go with God."

"God bless you," the elderly Muslim woman replied, and her invocation was wide enough to transcend the barriers between their faiths.

When she was gone, Stefan sat at the table under the apple tree eating a breakfast of bread and honey and sipping at his coffee. He was not a political man. Not anymore. He was not, however, entirely ignorant of his benefactor. The White Hand was quite possibly the driving force behind the resurgent paramilitaries and the growing threat of a new Bosnian war. He had not known this when he had first agreed to be the keeper of Mali's secrets as well as the monastery's bees, but it had become clear to him over time.

The money Mali gave him could be used for good. It could do the Lord's work, and it could provide comfort to those in need, people like the widow Orahovac. Surely, noble purpose could cleanse the money even if it had been stained with blood. Couldn't it?

Stefan poured himself a glass of brandy, uncertain about the answer to that question.

SARAJEVO

NOVEMBER 4

17

"Are you sure this is a good idea?" Sarah asked.

"Absolutely," Eric answered with more assuredness than he felt. "And besides, it's too late. We're here."

"I'm not sure she ever really liked me."

"What is this, junior high school? Grow a pair."

"You first."

"Touché."

They were standing in front of an older building. The architectural details marked it as prewar. Pre–World War II. The Balkans had seen so many wars it was often necessary to be specific. The façade was brick rather than concrete, and at least a few apartments had balconies with Ottoman-style carved wooden balustrades. To the right of the gated front door was a list of apartments and an intercom system. Eric did not need to search for the number. Muscle memory guided his finger to the button labeled ALIMEROVIĆ. This had been Meho's apartment. His mother and sister still lived here.

"Halo," said a scratchy voice over the intercom. Eric was not sure if it was Meho's sister, Amra, or their mother.

"It's us."

"Come on up."

Amra, then. Meho's mother would have greeted them with an effusive warmth. Amra had always had sharper edges.

The apartment was on the third floor. The stairwell was dark and unwelcoming. Most of the lights had burned out, and there was no condo board to take responsibility for upkeep. Neighbors competed to see who could put up with an inconvenience the longest. The loser would be the family that replaced the bulbs at their own expense or repaired the cracked tiles on the stairs. Both of those contests seemed to be ongoing.

The door to 313 was solid wood with a chunky brass lock. Eric caught Sarah looking at it with professional interest.

"How long?" he asked.

"Twenty-five seconds on a bad day."

"Sometimes it's easier just to knock."

He did.

Meho's mother, Elvira, opened the door. She was a small woman, no more than five foot four and shaped more like a barrel than a pear. Her knee-length dress was maroon and black and would have been at the cutting edge of fashion in the Yugoslavia of the nineteen seventies.

Elvira grabbed Eric's face with both hands and squeezed. Her palms were rough and calloused from a life of hard work, and her face was lined by years of still harder loss and grief.

"Zlato moje," she called him, which meant literally *my little golden one* but was closer in spirit to *darling.*

"Hello, Elvira," Eric said in Serbo-Croatian, when she had ceded control of his face. He kissed her on both cheeks. "You look fabulous."

He presented Elvira with a box of Swiss chocolates and a bouquet of lilies.

Elvira greeted Sarah next, politely but not nearly as warmly as she had welcomed Eric. They removed their shoes while Elvira took the flowers to the kitchen to find a vase. The Alimerović family was not especially religious, but removing shoes at the door was a deep-seated cultural norm among Balkan Muslims.

A striking woman in dark-blue slacks and a white blouse tailored and open at the throat stepped out of the kitchen, drying her hands on a dishtowel. Her hair was the color of sand dunes.

Amra Alimerović was almost Eric's age, but she looked considerably younger. Her skin was smooth and only a shade or two lighter than Eric's. Meho joked that his sister offered proof of the Alimerović family's Gypsy roots.

She gave Eric a kiss on the cheek, and he caught a hint of the perfume she was using, musky and unfamiliar.

Amra was much cooler with Sarah, shaking her hand and welcoming her to the family's apartment in a way that might have encouraged an independent observer to doubt her sincerity.

Eric looked around.

"The place hasn't changed," he said.

"Not really," Amra replied.

They spoke English together. Amra was fluent with just the trace of an accent.

The apartment was built around a central foyer. There were three bedrooms, a living room, a dining room just barely big enough for a table and eight chairs, and a simple galley kitchen where Elvira worked her artery-clogging culinary miracles.

There was more than enough space for the two of them. Multi-generational living arrangements were the norm in the Balkans. Amra had been married for a few years and her husband had moved in with them, but the marriage had not lasted and Amra's ex had moved to Switzerland to find work. There were no children.

Amra had once confessed to Eric that she could not see bringing up a child in a city that seemed to have no future. In this, she was hardly alone. Bosnia's demographics were both dismal and disheartening.

Elvira stuck her head out of the kitchen to announce that she needed a few more minutes, and Amra led Eric and Sarah into the living room. There were several paintings hanging on the walls, mostly landscapes but also a few abstract pieces and one portrait. Eric stopped in front of that one. It was a picture of Elvira, Amra, and Meho painted by one of the faculty members at the University of Sarajevo's Academy of Fine Arts. Eric had commissioned the painting during the siege and had provided the artist with paint and canvas as well as food and a nominal sum of money.

It was a good painting, a somewhat stylized representation of the family rather than photorealistic, but it was emotionally true. It captured something of each of them that was essential. Elvira was painted in somber dark tones. She was already a widow, and the dark colors seemed somehow to foretell the family tragedies to come. Amra's portrait was sharper and more angular than she was in real life. The artist had used that to express the intensity of her personality, and she seemed almost ready to step off the canvas. Meho was painted in lighter tones, standing between his mother and sister, and connecting them like a bridge. One arm was draped over his mother's shoulder, and the other hand firmly clasped Amra's. That was Meho, ever the conciliator. Gregarious and easygoing. A friend. Eric felt a tightness in his chest.

"I'm glad to see that this is still up on the wall," he croaked.

"It's Elvira's favorite," Amra said. Since she was a child, she had called her mother by her first name. "Mine too."

Amra poured three glasses of wine, a good-quality red from Croatia. Both Serbia and Croatia were producing excellent wine, but Bosnia's vineyards had a long way to go before they could be considered even middling.

"So how's work been treating you, Amra?" Sarah asked.

"Busy. You know how it is with us journalists. The worse things get, the better it is for business."

There was little warmth in her response. *Maybe Sarah had been right,* Eric mused, *to question whether she should have come.*

"Same in our line of work," Sarah replied gamely.

"That's right. Economic affairs, is it?" Eric could tell that Amra did not for a moment buy Sarah's cover story.

"Still stuck on the econ track. I've been doing some Balkans, but also Central Asia. I've been in D.C. for a while, but my last overseas tour was two years in Pakistan."

"Just goes to show," Amra offered. "You can take the girl out of Lahore . . ."

Amra did not finish the sentence. She took a sip of her wine, giving Eric and Sarah a moment to process the jibe that was remarkable for both its cleverness and cruelty.

Sarah arched an eyebrow. "Is that the best you got?"

"We'll see. I have a lot of material to work with."

The frost had settled over the conversation so quickly that Eric was left confused. There seemed to be a backstory here that eluded him. He was grateful when Elvira appeared in the doorway to announce that dinner was ready.

Even by Elvira's lofty standards, the dinner was a feast. The appetizers included *kajmak* and *ajvar*, pickled vegetables, potato salad in the Balkan style made with vinegar and onions, and long hot peppers grilled and marinated in oil and garlic.

Every square inch of the table was covered in platters and serving dishes, and it was all delicious. But Eric had learned from hard experience the importance of pacing at a Bosnian dinner. These were just the starters.

The next course was trout with almonds, the skin crisp and the flesh sweet and juicy. This was followed by roast lamb and new potatoes baked with rosemary.

Conversation was light and in Serbo-Croatian so that Elvira could join in. This put Sarah at something of a disadvantage. Her language was good, but it was not at Eric's level and she had to work hard to keep up. Eric had the impression that Amra made things harder for Sarah than she had to, picking obscure or difficult words when a commonplace word would have worked just as well. They had all been friends back in the war. Amra and Meho and Sarah and Eric. But there was clearly something between the two women, something that was a source of considerable friction. But Eric would be damned if he could figure out what it was or whether it was fixable.

Eric watched helplessly as Elvira spooned an enormous serving of

Turkish-style moussaka onto his plate. It was a complex dish, layers of ground beef alternating with grilled eggplants, peppers, tomatoes, and onions. Chilies gave it just a hint of heat. Its only flaw—common to most dishes in Bosnia—was the daunting size of the portion.

A sip of Sarajevsko Tamno, a dark lager with a malty sweetness and a thick white head, cut the heat of the chilies.

Amra looked at him appraisingly.

"There's something you want to tell me, isn't there?"

She was right.

"Is it that obvious?"

"Let's just say that I'm looking forward to our next poker game. Bring your checkbook."

"I went to Srebrenica," Eric said. "Sarah and I did. I went to Meho's stone." He couldn't quite bring himself to use the word "grave," not in front of Elvira.

"I'm glad you did," Amra answered. "It's hard for me to go now that the checkpoints are back. The wasps or the ants or whatever little creepy-crawlies are camped out at the border like to hassle little Muslim girls."

"There's more," Eric said. "I met a man there who was with Meho at the tractor factory."

"I know him. He found me after the war. Meho asked him to."

"Why didn't you tell me?"

"You were gone, Eric. Off to your next assignment. You'd left Bosnia behind you, left us to clean up from the war."

"I had no choice," Eric said defensively.

"I know." Amra reached across the table and squeezed his hand. "In truth, there was no great revelation. Meho just wanted me to know that he loved me."

"He had a message for me as well."

"What was it?"

Eric swallowed the lump in his throat. "He asked the old man to tell me that it wasn't my fault."

"It wasn't," Amra agreed. "There are others with more to answer for."

At first, Eric thought Amra was talking about herself and he wanted to say something reassuring, but then he saw that she was looking at Sarah, who was staring intently at the food on her plate, pointedly not meeting Amra's gaze.

There was something between these two women that Eric did not understand. They were both beautiful and intense, but so different in character. Amra was fire to Sarah's ice. Passion and heat contrasted with cool logic and self-control. Eric only now appreciated the thickness and solidity of the wall that separated the two women who had once been friends.

Now was not the time, he knew, to try to untangle the knot of this relationship. But neither would he let it rest. There would be time enough to learn what had come between them.

Over coffee and baklava, the conversation turned to politics, with Elvira excusing herself to the kitchen. Eric switched back to English, hoping that this would help put Sarah back on a more even footing with Amra.

"What are you hearing about the peace conference and Sondergaard's plan?" Eric asked Amra. "You've always had good sources. What are they saying?"

Amra seemed to weigh her response carefully, taking a bite of baklava and washing it down with a sip of coffee before replying.

"There's some hope that this time is different," she said finally.

"That Sondergaard has buy-in from the right people in the Federation and a viable partner in your friend Nikola Petrović. But there was hope the last time there was a big peace conference, and the time before that. So I expect the optimists to be disappointed."

"What do you think is going to happen?" Eric asked.

Amra looked down at the tablecloth and angrily brushed some crumbs onto the floor. When she looked up, her eyes were bright with tears.

"War," she said. "Again and forever with no victors and no end."

"Hell on earth," Sarah said.

"Yes."

"Why?" Eric asked. "Why do you see failure as a foregone conclusion."

"Dimitrović and the White Hand. They've gone too far. They have too much power, and they are prepared to drag the whole region down with them if that's what it takes to satisfy their ambitions. I don't think there's anything they wouldn't do."

"What do you know, Amra?" Sarah asked. "There's something else that you're not telling us."

"It's just rumor at this point, speculation."

"What is it?" Sarah asked insistently.

"One of my sources in Srpska, a politician with the Green Party, has a friend whose sister works for Mali. Under Mali, really, both literally and figuratively from what I understand. In any event, the word from her is that Mali has engaged the services of one or more snipers with wartime experience. The last time we heard anything like that, it ended with the Serbian Prime Minister Zoran Đinđić being assassinated with a .50 caliber sniper bullet. I can't see any use for a sniper in this political climate other than one. Murder."

"Who's the target?" Eric asked.

"My source didn't know. It could be someone high up in the Federation government. It could be Petrović. It's almost certainly political. Going after a business rival doesn't usually require more than a street punk and a cheap pistol."

"Is there anyone you know in the RS who might have a line on who the target is? Or even the identity of the sniper Mali has put on the payroll? That might at least give us an idea of what Mali has in mind."

"I don't have any way of finding out. All I know is that Mali is planning to murder someone. We've seen where that can lead."

Amra looked out the window. The view was one of the best things about the apartment. Even sitting at the table, they could see the pagoda-like music pavilion at At Mejdan Park and the red brick buildings of the Sarajevo brewery. But Eric knew what Amra was looking at.

"What is it?" Sarah asked.

"Do you see that bridge over the Miljacka?" Eric replied. "The second one."

"Sure."

"It's called the Latin Bridge now, and that was the original name, but in the Yugoslav era it was called the Princip Bridge. It's where Gavrilo Princip assassinated Archduke Franz Ferdinand and triggered World War I. One street punk with a cheap pistol. More than sixteen million dead."

"That may have been the casus belli for the Austrians, but that war was all but inevitable. The political conditions made it so. If it hadn't been Franz Ferdinand's murder, it would have been something else," said Sarah.

"Maybe so," Amra said. "But it wasn't something else. It was that. Princip and his little toy pistol laid waste to a continent."

"And there's one more thing," Eric added.

"Yes."

"Do you know the name of the organization that backed Princip, that gave him money and weapons and a cause to kill for?"

"The Black Hand," Sarah said.

"Indeed."

"I don't suppose that's a coincidence."

"Not in this part of the world."

The walk back to Sarah's apartment led them over the Latin Bridge. It was a warm night, and they stopped at the midpoint to look at the black water rushing underneath the stone span.

"What's the deal with you and Amra?" Eric asked. "What happened between you two? What was that little exchange over Meho?"

"Isn't it obvious?" Sarah replied. There was a pebble on the stone railing that ran the length of the bridge, and she picked it up and tossed it absentmindedly into the river. "Amra blames me for Meho's death."

"Why would she do that?"

"A few days before Srebrenica, we had coffee together. The three of us. You were busy with something. I forget what. Tracking down some lead for a story. In any event, Meho said he had a bad feeling about the trip and that he was going to tell you that you two shouldn't go to Srebrenica. That it was too dangerous."

"And what did you say?"

Sarah turned away from Eric. She was silent.

"Sarah," he said gently. "Talk to me." He put a hand on her arm. She turned back and looked at him hard in the eyes.

"I told him that there was nothing special about Srebrenica, that every place in Bosnia was dangerous and that there was no more reason to be afraid of Srebrenica than the coffee shop we were sitting in, which was in range of Serbian artillery. I thought I was telling the truth. There was nothing in the intel that gave any sense of the scale of what was about to happen there. I didn't know. But they knew or at least suspected who I really worked for, and I as good as told Meho that it would all be fine. Amra thinks I killed him."

"You didn't. No more than I did. We both have to live with what happened. At least now I know what's come between you two."

"Well, that's part of it," Sarah said.

"You mean there's more?"

"Of course."

"What?"

Sarah looked at him with a slightly bemused expression.

"Really? You really don't know?"

"Uh . . . no."

"God, men can be so obtuse."

"So enlighten me."

"It's you, Eric. Amra has feelings for you. She had them twenty years ago as well, and she sees me as competition."

"That can't be true."

"No?"

"She never said anything."

"That's not how this game works, Eric. If you haven't figured that out by now, it may be too late for you."

"Does she have reason to be jealous?"

"Meaning?"

"Are we together? What are we, actually?" Eric and Sarah had not slept together again since that one night. And the signals Eric had been getting from his former lover had been mixed and ambiguous.

"What do you want?" Case officers, like psychiatrists, were fond of answering a question with a question.

"I want you to come home with me and make love like a pair of wild weasels."

Sarah laughed, and there was a tightness in Eric's throat as that sound pulled him back twenty years into the past.

Sarah leaned forward and kissed him softly on the cheek. It was tender, loving even, but not sexual.

"Not now. There's too much to do. Let's get through this thing, and we can talk about it. Right now I can't afford the distraction."

Eric reached for her, and she let him embrace her—briefly. God, this woman had a grip on his psyche that was deeply troubling.

"Come on," she said, stepping back to put some distance between them. "I've got some calls to make. Walk a girl home?"

Eric offered his arm and Sarah took it. They walked into the heart of old Sarajevo, down the cobblestone streets through neighborhoods redolent of a thousand years of history. But they did not talk about the past. Eric could only hope they had a future.

SARAJEVO
JUNE 28, 1914

18

Who would have thought that it would be that hard to kill one man? Even a royal. Gavrilo Princip tried to push aside the feelings of failure and disappointment. There was still a chance, he hoped, that he could make everything right.

God was with them. Their cause was just. The South Slavs, the Yugoslavs, were a people denied their right to self-determination by their Austrian overlords. Only Serbia was truly free. The Slavs of Bosnia were little more than serfs, and the arrogant Austrians missed no opportunity to drive that point home. Today was one of these opportunities. Archduke Franz Ferdinand had come to Sarajevo in his gaudy military regalia on this of all days. Vidovdan. St. Vitus's Day. The anniversary of the Battle of Kosovo—a noble defeat that had marked the beginning for Serbia of five hundred years of Ottoman rule.

The Slavs were a proud people, and they chafed under the yoke of foreign control. It had taken five centuries for the Serbs to rid themselves of the Ottomans. Princip was determined that the period of Austrian domination would not be nearly so long.

Belgrade had already taken the first steps. The tired Obrenović dynasty had been overthrown, with the weak King Alexander I and his wife, Queen Draga, shot, stabbed, and defenestrated. Peter I of the house of Karađorđević was king now, and Serbia had won glorious victories in the wars against first the Turks and then the Bulgarians. Serbia now controlled both Macedonia and its historic heartland, Kosovo.

Princip was not yet satisfied and he was far from alone in this. He was a member of a revolutionary movement, Young Bosnia. They were students, most of them Serbs but also Muslims and Croats, and they were committed to direct action against the Austro-Hungarian Empire. Tyrannicide.

There had been seven of them spaced along the route that the archduke's motorcade would follow, all of them armed and all carrying cyanide pills to ensure that they could not betray their comrades under the pressure of torture. But somehow they had failed. The Bosnian Muslim, Mehmedbašić, had waited in front of a bank with a bomb that he did not throw. Vaso Čubrilović, a fellow Serb, had stood nearby with a pistol and a second bomb, but he too had lost his nerve and failed to act.

Nedeljko Čabrinović at least had tried. Standing on the opposite side of the street farther down the route near the Miljacka River, Čabrinović had thrown his bomb at the archduke's open-top double phaeton. The bomb had bounced off the folded roof of the vehicle and exploded under another car in the motorcade. A dozen or more people had been injured, none of them people of consequence.

Čabrinović bravely swallowed his cyanide capsule and threw himself into the Miljacka River to drown. But the pill had only made him sick and the river was only a few centimeters deep in the middle of a dry, hot summer. Čabrinović had been dragged from the nearly dry river and beaten by the crowd. They came close to finishing the job that the poison and the Miljacka had begun. Close, but not quite. Čabrinović was somewhere in police custody.

Princip and the other would-be assassins had watched helplessly as the archduke's motorcade had sped past them on their way to the town hall, now moving too fast for either bullet or bomb.

But Princip had not lost faith. There was still a chance. Now he waited for the archduke to make his return. The next stop on the itinerary was supposed to be the National Museum, but Princip suspected that Franz Ferdinand would want to visit those who had been injured in the bombing once they'd been taken to the hospital. The archduke was a royal, but he was also a politician. If he did visit the hospital, the motorcade would have to pass this spot. Princip stood in front of a small grocery near the Latin Bridge and waited.

His faith was rewarded. The motorcade was moving at speed, but the lead car made what must have been a wrong turn. Princip heard a voice he recognized as belonging to Oskar Potiorek, the governor of Bosnia, call out to the driver to back up and follow Appel Quay to the hospital. The five-car motorcade stopped almost directly in front of where Princip was standing. The young revolutionary felt a hot flush of fear, joy, and anticipation as he stepped forward, drawing the Belgian Fabrique Nationale semiautomatic pistol from his pocket.

The distance was no more than a meter and a half. He could not miss. The archduke was sitting in the backseat of the phaeton in full military peacock finery, his ridiculous handlebar mustache waxed and sharp.

Princip's first bullet hit the archduke in the throat, and a spray of blood covered the white dress of the duchess who was sitting so prettily next to him. The blood may have distracted Princip because his second bullet struck the duchess in the abdomen. He had meant to shoot Governor Potiorek sitting in the front seat.

I am sorry about that, Princip thought. It was bad luck to shoot a woman, even if she was married to an Austrian royal. He turned the pistol toward the governor, but before he could squeeze the trigger, a burly Sarajevo policeman tackled him and pinned him to the cobblestone street.

"You murdering son of a bitch," the policeman said in his ear, as he twisted Princip's arm hard behind his back and forced the pistol from his fingers. "You'll hang for this." His breath smelled of onions, and drops of spittle hit the back of Princip's neck.

Murder. Princip was satisfied. The archduke's wound, he was confident, was mortal. He could hear the death rattle.

He had succeeded. He had struck a blow for freedom.

All would be right in the end.

LANGLEY, VIRGINIA
NOVEMBER 7

19

Something was rotten in the Western Balkans Division. VW could feel it. And she was determined to do more than pace the battlements of the Island of Misfit Toys and suffer the slings and arrows, assuming that they were still outrageous fortune's weapons of choice.

Rennsler was still combing through the financial trail that Parsifal had left behind. He would do a more than thorough job. In parallel, VW was wading through the intel, looking for patterns, for a thread that would help guide her through the labyrinth of data.

The reporting from the Defense Intelligence Agency and the attachés in Sarajevo, Belgrade, and Zagreb was dull, technical, and unilluminating. This was pretty much par for the course with DIA. It seemed to VW that most of the defense attachés' reporting from the field consisted of articles from military magazines translated into English with a comment paragraph tacked onto the end that was something along the lines of "I totally agree." That was enough to justify slapping a Secret label on the product and—VW suspected—counting it against some kind of informal quota that would be used to assess the attaché's suitability for promotion and a cushy assignment in Rome.

The State Department reporting was more useful. The political counselor in Sarajevo, Eric Petrosian—VW had looked him up—had interesting contacts, and his cables were both well written and relevant. His reporting was crisp and readable, and offered a sharp contrast to DIA's cables, which were as dense and dry as a Christmas fruitcake and just about as appetizing. VW was impressed by the political reporting from Sarajevo, and she was not easily impressed. Petrosian, she remembered reading somewhere, had been working closely with High Rep Sondergaard in laying the groundwork for the upcoming peace conference.

In his reporting, Petrosian acknowledged that the obstacles to success were significant, but he nonetheless argued that there was a real and growing chance for an agreement and that the U.S. government should do everything it could to back the Sondergaard Plan. The alternative, he suggested, was another Balkan war that would likely leave Bosnia fractured beyond repair. That VW shared this view may have contributed to her respect for the quality of his work.

State Department cables were an interesting mix of intelligence collection, analysis, and policy advocacy. There was no other government agency that produced anything like it. The CIA, for one, was enjoined by its charter from advocating particular policy choices. The National Clandestine Service did collection and the

Directorate of Intelligence did analysis. They were not policy makers. But there were ways that the intel community had to influence policy, and spooks were not always shy about using them. If the president was considering three options and the CIA told him that options one and three were likely to trigger nuclear war or a global financial meltdown, the Agency did not really need to specify its preference for option two. It was implied.

It was the analysis carried out by the CIA's Balkan Action Team, however, that was the most interesting, at least for VW's purposes. The BAT was an unusual mix of operations officers from the Clandestine Service and DI analysts that was meant to ensure that the collection and analysis were synched up especially closely, but the opposite seemed to be true. The raw human intelligence, or HUMINT, was consistent with what VW was seeing in other reporting channels, but the finished intelligence that went to senior decision makers in the policy process was little short of an apologia for the Dimitrović regime in Banja Luka. Reading the finished intel, you would believe that Dimitrović's sharp turn to the right was a temporary aberration and that the risk of renewed conflict in Bosnia was low. VW did not believe either of these was true. The aberrant period was Dimitrović's short-lived embrace of Western priorities and a true partnership with Sarajevo. That period she was at a loss to explain. The thug he was now was the real Dimitrović, not the gauzy cotton-candy version that had for a short while embraced the West's vision and agenda.

VW looked up from her stacks of reports and pressed the tips of her fingers against her temples. She felt a migraine coming on.

"Why Parsifal?" she wondered aloud. Was that code name

chosen at random by a computer program? It did not sound like that. It felt deliberate, intentional.

Parsifal's quest for the Holy Grail had been the subject of both a tedious thirteenth-century poem and an opera by Richard Wagner whose music was not, as one wag had observed, as bad as it sounds.

The phone rang. Deep in the fugue state of puzzle solving, VW nearly jumped out of her skin.

"Hello," she said into the receiver.

"VW, it's me. It's time."

The voice belonged to Bob Landis.

"Already?"

"Yes."

"Shit. Give me ten minutes."

She swallowed two ibuprofen and splashed some water on her face in the ladies' room. The damn automatic faucets only offered one temperature, lukewarm. VW wanted ice-cold and there was nothing the CIA could or would do to meet that need. Typical.

Her eyes were dry and felt like they had been scrubbed with sandpaper. She took a look at herself in the mirror and immediately wished that she had not. God, she looked like hell. The bags under her eyes were dark enough that they could have been mistaken for bruises, and her skin looked waxy, with the translucent sheen of supermarket apples. She was working too hard, and some part of her understood that she was dancing on the fine line between dedication and obsession. If the UAV did not turn up any kind of solid lead, VW promised herself, she would ratchet back a bit, try to restore some semblance of normalcy to her life.

Bob Landis's domain was deep in the bowels of the CIA's old

wing, a subterranean vantage point for gimlet eyes on the far side of the world.

The elevator opened up right into the flight-control center. Banks of monitors bathed the room in a dim blue glow as operators controlled UAVs with macho names like Reaper, Global Hawk, or Predator as they tracked the movements of America's enemies. The flight center felt tacky, cut-rate, and temporary, as though the CIA did not want to overcommit to a tool—drones—and a strategy—targeted killing—it had never quite made peace with.

"'Bout time, VW. You almost missed the show."

Landis was standing at one of the workstations looking over the shoulder of an impossibly young pilot with a regulation haircut who gripped the joystick casually with three fingers.

"Not a big deal, Bob, the Preds have plenty of loiter time."

"Yeah? Well, this isn't a Predator."

"What the hell is it?"

"A Wyvern."

"Jesus, that's a toy. I need loiter time over the target."

"I'm sorry, VW. This was the best I could do, particularly because you wanted to avoid using the base in eastern Slavonia. There's a small test base for the Wyverns in Montenegro, and someone there owed me a favor. Now I owe him. The boys bolted an external fuel tank onto the fuselage for this mission. It'll make it. But we aren't getting very much time on target. Ten or fifteen minutes tops. Depends on fuel consumption. The extra tank adds weight and screws with the aerodynamics so we're not really confident in the numbers."

"Where's my goddamn Predator, Bob?"

"Predator time out of Ramstein is all blocked off with a director-level code I've never seen before."

"Parsifal."

"That's the one. If you can submit your request through that channel, I can blanket that place with twenty-four-hour coverage from every possible angle. But without that, this is what I've got. If it makes a difference, this isn't a regular Wyvern. The test birds have some cutting-edge mods. This makes us square, VW."

"Understood. Thanks, Bob. I know you did the best you could."

VW sighed. Parsifal again. It seemed to lurk under almost every rock she turned over.

"Okay. Let's see what we can see."

Landis stepped aside to give VW a look at the monitors. The unmistakable rocky landscape of western Bosnia drifted slowly across the screens. The Wyvern's current coordinates were displayed in the upper-right corner of the center screen.

"How far out are we?" Landis asked the pilot, a word that VW had always found somewhat incongruous when applied to the twenty-something operators who looked and acted more like they were playing *Call of Duty* in their parents' basement on a Saturday morning rather than flying multimillion-dollar aircraft on the other side of the world.

"About ten klicks, sir."

Definitely former military, VW decided, maybe not even former. The lines had gotten blurry since the start of the war on terror.

The Wyvern, a CIA variant of the army's Shadow drone, needed only three minutes of flight time to cover the distance. The UAV crested a final hill. The onboard cameras captured a valley with steep sides and a river running along the floor. About halfway up the sides of the valley was a house—a villa, really—with extensive interior gardens surrounded by walls. A single-lane road connected the valley with the nearest town, a small village that the tactical overlay on one of the monitors identified as Štrigova.

Half a dozen vehicles were parked in front of the villa. From this angle, VW could not identify the makes and models, but they were big, almost certainly SUVs.

It was a nice house, an expensive house. *Whose was it?* VW wondered.

"Won't they see the drone?" she asked.

"UAV," the pilot said automatically, just barely beating Landis to the same riposte.

"Of course. Won't they see it?"

The pilot smiled as he made a series of small adjustments with the joystick and keyboard that set the Wyvern onto a slow, looping course over the villa.

"Not likely," he said, glancing up briefly from his monitors. "The bird is up higher than it looks. It just looks like we're flying at fifty feet because of the magnification from the Basilisk's Eye optical system, which is totally kick-ass. What's more, the Wyvern has active camouflage. The bottom is an LED screen that projects an image of what's overhead fed to it by a camera mounted on the top. And it's whisper quiet, so they shouldn't hear us coming either."

"Those are the modifications?"

"Yep. The boys in S&T went all out on this one."

"What else can it do?"

"We can listen in."

The young pilot's fingers danced over the keyboard, and one of the screens switched from a view of the valley floor to something that looked to VW like a hospital monitor displaying a series of sine waves.

"These are the frequencies we can tap into. The one at the top looks like a satellite TV signal, not terribly interesting unless you're trying to track your target's taste in situation comedies. The one at the bottom is probably from the home-security system. High-end stuff. The middle one is more interesting. It's a radio signal. Short range. Like a walkie-talkie. Want to hear what they're saying?"

"Damn straight I do."

The pilot again tapped the keys furiously. The voice that came over the speakers was coarse and guttural.

VW could read Serbo-Croatian better than she could speak it, but she was able to follow the rapid-fire exchange, which leaned heavily on variations of the verb *to fuck*.

"Did you see the way that fucking son of a bitch Lazarević lay down last night against Red Star? That fuck cost me a hundred euros."

"Fuck you, Deki. I don't give a fuck. How about a little radio discipline for a change?"

"Fuck it."

A quick burst of static was followed by silence. VW had little doubt who those two were. Security. Muscle. But security for whom?

The Wyvern continued its looping patrol over the villa. The quality of the image on the monitor was superb. But there was little to see. There was no movement of people or vehicles, nothing that might give any kind of clue as to what the villa was used for and who—if anyone—lived there.

"Five minutes to bingo fuel," the pilot announced, referring to the point at which the Wyvern would have the bare minimum of gas necessary to get back to base.

VW prepared herself for disappointment, and she began mentally to review the other assets she might be able to beg, borrow, or steal that could help her learn more about this building that had become so interesting to Parsifal.

"Bingo plus four minutes."

A short burst of static over the speakers was startlingly loud.

"Mali is on the move." This was thug number one, the one who had lost money betting against Red Star.

VW's heart rate kicked up. There was only one Mali. The villa belonged to Marko Barcelona, the outsider who seemed to be one of the leading drivers behind Bosnia's threatened descent into madness. The Agency did not have any pictures of Mali. He was a complete cipher. America's multibillion-dollar spy apparatus had no idea where he had come from or what his intentions were. This was a coup.

"Bingo plus three minutes."

"Don't you dare move," VW said intently. "Bob, we gotta get a picture of this guy."

"What guy? I don't see anyone."

VW was so focused on the task at hand that she had forgotten Landis spoke no Serbo-Croatian.

"Marko Barcelona, one of our top intelligence targets and someone we know almost nothing about. He's in that house and he's coming outside."

"Well, he'd better do it in the next three minutes. I'm not flying a ten-million-dollar aircraft into the ground for a Kodak moment with Barcelona, Grenada, or Toledo. Bingo fuel and it's back to base."

"I know there's a safety margin built in," VW pleaded.

"Two minutes twenty seconds," the pilot said, pointing at the countdown clock on the screen.

The seconds ticked off all too quickly.

"Bingo plus two minutes."

Someone walked out into the garden. He was wearing a hat.

"Can you get in closer?"

"With the camera? Sure."

The operator zoomed in on the man in the hat. His face was not visible.

"Can you try a different angle?"

"Not enough fuel for maneuvers, sorry. We are bingo plus one minute."

VW studied the image.

"That's a baseball cap," she said, thinking out loud. *What kind of mafia boss wears a baseball cap? Look up, you bastard. Let me see your face.*

"Bingo," the operator said, reaching for the joystick.

VW grabbed his wrist.

"Wait," she said, before adding as an afterthought, "Please. We may not get another chance like this."

The pilot looked at Landis, who nodded.

"Ninety seconds, VW. If he doesn't look at the birdie in ninety seconds, we're flying home."

"Keep the camera pointed at his head," VW instructed the pilot.

She stared at the screen intently, as though she could will the image to do what she wanted. With thirty seconds left on the clock, the man VW believed to be Marko "Mali" Barcelona doffed his hat and turned his face to the sun. VW had as clear a view as she could have asked for.

It took almost ten seconds for VW to process what she was seeing.

"It can't be," she said.

"What?" Landis asked.

"Mali," she said.

"Yes?"

"I know him."

SARAJEVO
NOVEMBER 8

20

"I have someone who wants to meet with you." Nikola sounded eager, even anxious, but the cell reception was spotty, and it was difficult for Eric to judge the subtleties.

"Do I want to meet him?"

"You do."

"Who is it?"

"A colleague of mine . . . but no names over the phone."

"What's it about?"

"Our mutual Spanish friend."

"Then I am interested. When and where?"

"Tonight. Do you remember that place where you and I had too much to drink that one time?"

"Oh, god. My head still hurts."

"Do you think you can find the place?"

"I'll just follow the trail of empty tequila bottles."

"See you tonight."

Eric was now as close as you could come in the Foreign Service to being a free agent. Ambassador Wylie had essentially cut him loose to support the High Rep's peace process and Sondergaard only needed Eric's help episodically. He had found himself devoting an increasingly significant share of his time to the Mali-Dimitrović connection. And to Sarah.

For the first time in his diplomatic career he did not have to account for his whereabouts. There was no requirement to get approval for a midnight meeting with an unknown Bosnian Serb politician at an isolated farmhouse ten miles from the nearest cell reception. He had not told either the ambassador or the embassy's regional security officer where he was going and why. There was too great a risk that one of them might say no and reimpose the kind of restrictions on travel and contacts that could make a political officer's job almost impossible to do well.

Sarah was off again. Eric did not know where. He had made the decision to meet with Nikola's nameless contact on his own.

When Eric pulled his Golf up in front of the ramshackle wooden structure, he had a moment of doubt as to the wisdom of that choice. He was miles from the nearest paved road and considerably farther from the nearest town. Even with a sky full of stars, the night up here in the foothills of the Dinaric Alps was dark. There was a chill in the air, and Eric pulled the zipper of his North Face jacket closed against the cold. He turned his face up toward the night sky. The Milky Way was easily visible against the black of a moonless night. With Eric's every breath, a cloud of vapor blurred the stars for just a brief moment.

The farmhouse belonged to Nikola's cousin, who lived in Vienna and rarely visited. Nikola looked after the place and used it as he pleased. The farm had gone fallow years ago and the livestock had been sold off or slaughtered, but the plum and cherry trees still produced fruit and the house itself was in good shape. Last spring, Nikola and Eric had spent an epic boys' weekend up here with a couple of friends that had involved fishing, grilling, and more drinking than he cared to remember.

Reluctantly, Eric turned his attention away from the grandeur of the Milky Way to the job at hand, a midnight meeting with someone he did not know to discuss the activities of a ruthless gangster. Eric had friends back in California who were convinced that all diplomats did was go to cocktail parties in top hats and tails. If only they could see him now.

He pulled a small flashlight out of his pocket. The narrow beam of the LED light revealed three other vehicles parked in front of the farmhouse. The canary yellow Yugo was Nikola's and the wonder of it was that this twelve-year-old car—more rust than metal at this point in its life cycle—had made it up the twisty mountain road. The Yugo was the most basic car imaginable with the absolute minimum number of moving parts. In a day when cars seemed built around their onboard computers, the Yugo did not have so much as a radio. Next to the Yugo was a black Mitsubishi 4×4 with oversize tires and a whip antenna. This was almost certainly Dragan's vehicle. The security services in the former Yugosphere were partial to black SUVs and had never felt any compunction about being conspicuous.

The last car was a Mercedes, silver and expensive-looking. This one must belong to the guest of honor.

Nikola answered the door wearing a black sweater and jeans. He hugged Eric and kissed him on both cheeks with Balkan exuberance.

"Glad you found the place."

"Me too. Get lost out here and they'll never find your body."

Inside, the farmhouse was warm and inviting. The main room was spacious with both a living area organized around a pair of overstuffed couches and a dining area with a farm table the size of a barn door. A wagon-wheel chandelier hung from the ceiling.

A fire was burning in the stone fireplace, casting an orange glow through the room. Two men sat near the fire holding cognac glasses. One, as Eric had suspected, was the ex-spy Dragan. His bullet-shaped bald head gleamed in the firelight. The second man was someone Eric knew by sight but had never met. His presence immediately elevated the significance of the meeting several notches.

He was middle-aged with a gray beard and a substantial paunch straining against an olive green army-surplus sweater. The cigarillo in his left hand was clutched so tightly that it looked like a sixth finger.

"Eric, this is Luka Filipović."

"I know."

Filipović's handshake was firm, but his palm was damp and his eyes darted about the room as though he were expecting something terrible to happen at any moment. Filipović was one of Dimitrović's senior lieutenants in the National Party. They had been together a long time, many said all the way back to their wartime service. Given the increasingly paranoid and conspiratorial nature of RS politics there were many people in Banja Luka with good reason to be nervous. But Filipović did not belong on that list.

The four men sat by the fire. Nikola produced another snifter of cognac for Eric.

"Nikola told me that you wanted to meet, that you had something to tell me about Marko Barcelona."

Filipović nodded and took a pull from his cigarillo. The cloud of blue smoke hovered over the table, a physical reminder that all negotiations in the Balkans were shrouded in a fog of secrecy and ambiguity. "I did and I do," Filipović said.

"Are you here representing Dimitrović? I know the two of you are close."

"We *were* close," Filipović corrected Eric. "I have come to the view that my old friend now represents an unacceptable danger to my country, my family, and . . . I suppose . . . myself."

Eric raised an eyebrow at this but said nothing.

"When Zoran and I were younger, we fought together. It's an experience that bonds men closer than brothers. And that's what I thought we were. When he went into politics, I followed him. Not just because I believed in what he believed, but because he was my brother. Do you understand?"

"Yes."

"And when Zoran changed, when he embraced a different future for Bosnia, for Srpska, for all of us, a future of tolerance and peace, I followed him. And then, that Spanish gangster, or whatever he is, appeared in Banja Luka. A man from nowhere. A man with no past. Zoran chose to follow this man back down the road of violence, back down the road to war. That I could not do. I could not take my family back to this hell."

"What can you tell me about Mali?" Eric asked. "What is his relationship with Dimitrović? What does he want?"

There was a pause in the conversation. Filipović sipped his cognac and puffed on his little cigar, but to Eric it looked like studied nonchalance, like an anxious man trying to pretend a cool equanimity he did not feel. "Now, that's the bush in which the rabbit lies," Filipović finally replied. It was a Serbian idiom, something akin to the Shakespearian "Now there's the rub." Eric recognized the opening salvo of a negotiation when he heard one.

"How can I help you?"

Filipović reached into his pocket and pulled out a photograph. He set it on the table in front of Eric. It was a family portrait, Filipović, his wife, and their two sons. His wife was short and round and far from beautiful, but Eric could tell from the way Filipović's arm was draped over her shoulder, holding her close against him, that he loved her. The boys, sadly, took after their mother. They were young, neither looked to have hit puberty yet, but they were pudgy, dull-eyed, and even in the snapshot they seemed sullen. Family was family.

"This is Mileva and my two boys. I want to get them out of Banja Luka."

"To Sarajevo?"

"Chicago."

"You want to emigrate to the United States?"

"In a manner of speaking. I want to be relocated to the Chicago area, my family and I, with new identities and enough in the way of financial resources to start over."

"Why Chicago?"

"It's a good city for Serbs. Dimitrović and Mali are too well connected in Europe. No matter where we are, they would find us. None of the Europeans do witness protection in the way you Americans do. That's one of the reasons they haven't broken the back of organized crime like your FBI has. I will help you get Mali and Dimitrović, but I need protection and immunity in return."

Eric did not have the authority to offer any of what Filipović was asking for, but he wanted to explore what Dimitrović's erstwhile ally had to offer and whether he was really ready to switch teams or whether this was an elaborate con of some sort.

"Tell me something that will get me interested," Eric said.

"Mali meets with Zoran at least once a week, often more, always alone. After each meeting, there is something. Sometimes it is something small, make a list of journalists sympathetic to Dimitrović's enemies and bug their phones and offices. Sometimes it is something big like reviving the paramilitaries. That didn't just happen on its own. We did it."

"Is Dimitrović using Mali or is it the other way around?"

"Mali's in charge. He's in control of Dimitrović."

"What does he have on Dimitrović? What's the leverage?"

Filipović ignored the question.

"Mali and Zoran have been working on something important, something big and ambitious. I don't know what it is, but they've called all of the power brokers in the RS to a meeting in Banja Luka five days from now. Whatever comes out of that is going to be dark and ugly. I think this meeting will be the key to everything they are planning."

"Have you been invited?"

"Yes. But I am hopeful that I can send my regrets from Lake Forest." Filipović had evidently been reading up on Chicago's high-end suburbs.

"If you had visibility into what they were planning, it would make you more valuable, more useful to my government. It would be easier to argue for witness protection if you were bringing something like that to the table."

"It would also be extremely dangerous. I have spoken up too many times. I have a feeling that Zoran is starting to doubt my loyalty. Mali, I am certain, has been trying to turn him against me."

"I understand that, Mr. Filipović. But there is no reward without risk."

Eric was getting pretty far outside his lane. This was not diplomatic deal making. This was much closer to a case officer running an asset or, reaching back to his own experiences, a journalist working a source. If Filipović was sincere about coming over to the Americans, then he was right about the dangers. But the information he might be able to bring with him could be invaluable. It could potentially stop a war.

Filipović hesitated.

"I do this thing for you and you get my family out of Bosnia?"

There was no way for Eric to duck the moral culpability in his response. Did it matter that his motives were pure? That he and Sarah were trying to avert a genocide that they felt was coming but that their government refused to see? Did it matter if Filipović was sacrificed in the process? His own past was hardly free of blood and terror. Did it matter?

"I can't make any promises," Eric said, both because it was true and because a part of him wanted selfishly to lessen the burden of responsibility. "But it would make a stronger case if you had something to trade."

"I do have something to trade," Filipović replied, holding his cognac up to the firelight and staring at it intently as a Gypsy fortune-teller might gaze into her crystal ball.

"I have the keys to the kingdom," he continued, having evidently found the answer he was looking for in the depths of the cognac.

"Tell me. And I'll see what I can do."

"That thing you asked about, the leverage Mali has over Dimitrović. The thing he uses to control him."

"Yes."

"I know what it is."

He raised the snifter to his lips, but before he could drink, the glass disintegrated in his hand and Filipović's head exploded in a red mist that was flecked with gray and white from brain and bone.

Milliseconds later, Eric heard the windowpane shatter and the crack of a hypersonic bullet. It all happened in reverse, an illusion generated by the chasm that separated the speeds of light and sound.

Every man in the farmhouse had been under fire before and none of them hesitated. Eric and Nikola dove to the floor and sought cover behind the heavy furniture. Dragan pulled a pistol from a concealed holster and calmly shot the fuse box over the front door. The lights in the house flared briefly then went dark. The fire still cast an orange glow, but the shadows were deep and long. It would confuse the aim of whoever was shooting at them. Nikola, Eric saw, had grabbed the poker from the fireplace.

Eric crawled toward the door on his elbows and knees. Hurling himself to the floor, he had landed in a pool of Filipović's blood and his shirtsleeve was wet and sticky. The coppery smell of blood filled his nostrils. Every sense was heightened and the rush of adrenaline seemed to slow time. It took forever to make it to the door.

He pulled himself up to stand next to Dragan, just to the left of the door frame. Nikola was on the right side of the door with the wrought-iron fireplace poker in one hand. Eric wanted a weapon of some sort as well. There would be knives in the kitchen, but there were too many windows, and they did not know how many men they were facing.

"Who do you think it is?" Eric asked Dragan.

"Dimitrović's men. Mali's maybe. It looks like Filipović waited a little too long to jump."

"Do you have another gun?"

"Are you going to shoot me with it?"

"Not on purpose."

Dragan reached down and pulled a squat pistol out of an ankle holster. He handed it to Eric. For such a small weapon, it was surprisingly heavy. It was a revolver rather than an automatic, so Eric would not have to fumble with a safety. Just squeeze the trigger.

"If you're not close enough to smell his breath, don't fire," Dragan said, as though reading Eric's thoughts. "You won't hit anything with that. At least not anything you want to."

A ghost of a shadow passed in front of the window shattered by the assassin's bullet, a darker black against the black of the cold night. A soft shuffling sound came from the other side of the door, and there was a low whispered exchange. Eric could not make out the words, but the note of urgency was clear enough.

Eric held up the pistol and gestured toward the door. Dragan shook his head. The front door was made of thick oak planks. It was almost certainly strong enough to stop a pistol bullet.

Instead of a knob, the door had a European-style handle. Eric watched as it moved slowly to point at the floor. Someone was opening the door from the outside.

Nikola raised the poker straight up with two hands as if it were a samurai sword. Dragan and Eric readied their pistols.

Two muffled gunshots from the outside were followed by two more and the sound of bodies hitting the ground.

"Boss, are you alive?" The question was matter-of-fact rather than concerned.

"I'm still here," Dragan said. "So's our principal. Don't worry. The check will clear."

The door opened.

Two men came in with the black leather dusters and shaved heads that Dragan's associates seemed to favor. They were both so large that Eric thought it must have taken the skin from an entire cow to make each of their jackets. The pistols in their hands were sized to match. They were easily three times as large as the snub-nosed popgun that Eric was holding.

"Who was it?" Dragan asked.

"Paramilitaries," one of the men answered. "Amateurs." It was clear that there was no harsher epithet in his vocabulary.

"That sniper was no amateur," Nikola said angrily.

"No," the other man conceded. He looked over at Filipović's body. There was a hole the size of a quarter in the center of his forehead. The back of the politician's head was a sodden mass of blood and tissue where the bullet had made an explosive exit from his skull. "That was a quality shot."

"Is he still out there?" Eric asked. He worked hard to keep his voice calm and neutral.

"Novak sent the dogs after him. I doubt they'll get him, but they should flush him out of his nest. These sniper guys are trained to shoot and move. I don't think he'll be hanging around."

Dragan stepped outside.

"Get me a light," he commanded.

One of the men produced a flashlight, and Dragan ran the beam quickly over the two dead men lying on the ground by the door. Eric could see that each had been shot twice in the head. The patches on their shoulders were cartoon wasps dive-bombing a city with their stingers extended.

"It's a shame that Filipović wasn't able to tell us what he knows," Nikola said resignedly.

"Maybe not everything," Dragan said, "but he told us one thing that's pretty fucking important."

"What's that?" Eric asked.

"There's going to be a meeting of all the big shots in Banja Luka in five days, including Mali."

"So?"

"So he won't be home. We know where he lives, and I'm pretty confident that I can get us inside his house."

ROSULJE, REPUBLIKA SRPSKA
NOVEMBER 10

21

Darko Lukić was disturbed. It was not the killing that bothered him. He had done a great deal of killing. But he had only taken a handful of shots since the end of the war, and each one stirred up old memories that had settled into the recesses of his brain like silt at the bottom of a pond. It took little more than a single footstep to turn the water cloudy and muddy, to make it hard to see or think clearly.

For Lukić, the past and the present had blurred. They were comingled in such a way as to be indistinguishable. This had been true for a long time. Like many of his fellow veterans, Lukić had taken to drinking. Alcohol could not help him separate the past and the present, but it did make the distinction seem less important. *Rakija* had dulled the edge of the pain and confusion. Killing, however, cut through the fog of memory like a searchlight.

Drinking also made his hands shake, so Lukić had not touched a drop since his meeting with Mali. He had had a few bad nights—very bad nights—but it had been worth it. The tremors in his hands were gone. Now he could shoot.

Lukić had enjoyed killing the fat man Mali had wanted dead. He understood, of course, that it was part of some political game. It was a game in which he was completely disinterested. The technical challenge of the shot was more engaging, but there was another level of meaning. Deeper. Primal. It was killing itself. He felt it coursing in his veins the way other men felt their devotion to God or love for their children. For Lukić, killing from a distance was an act of worship.

The shot on the target at the farmhouse had been a thing of beauty. It was like meeting up with an old friend after many years and finding that nothing had changed between you, or like sex with a long-ago lover that was as sweet in the flesh as it was in memory. There were only a handful of men who could have made that shot. At night. At almost fifteen hundred meters. Through the distortion of the glass and the flickering shadows of firelight. Dead center. It was so beautiful that it had almost reduced Lukić to tears.

Only one flaw had discomfited him, something so strange that it was hard to credit. He would have blamed drink had he not been stone-cold sober to keep the shakes out of his hand. It was a phantasm. Something that made him doubt his own grasp on reality. The past had him by the throat.

He would need to be in absolute control of both himself and his environment to succeed in his assignment. Filipović was not the primary target. He was no more than an appetizer. Lukić knew that the next shot would require different tools and an even more obsessive attention to detail.

For the shot at the farmhouse, he had used a Belgian-made bolt-action .300 Winchester Magnum. The shot on the woman would be harder. He had planned and rehearsed the shot mentally. The geometry was familiar. He had made shots down that same line many times. But the city had sprawled since the war. The empty buildings he had used as a nest had either been torn down or were no longer vacant. After considerable hard work, he had found a place that would serve his purpose, which was not only to kill but also to escape.

The real challenge was the distance. It would be a long shot, almost two kilometers. One thousand nine hundred and sixty-six meters to be exact. It would take the bullet 3.6 seconds to reach the target. In flight, the bullet would arc to a height of 17.25 meters relating to the sighting plane. Then it would begin to drop as gravity did its work, inexorable but entirely predictable. Lukić knew the drop charts by heart. The unknowns included wind speed, air temperature, visibility, even humidity. This was where shooting became less of a science and more of an art.

Even for an artist, however, inspiration needed to be bolstered by practice and preparation. Lukić had identified an isolated valley in Bosnia's wild Romanija region that allowed him to duplicate the distance and angle of the shot.

It was a cold day, but he had long ago learned to ignore mere physical discomfort. Heat. Cold. Hunger. Pain. These were all states of mind. They could be blocked out, controlled by conscious acts of will.

He removed some items from his rucksack. A Swiss range-finding binocular, a PDA encased in rubber armor, and a handheld weather meter. Back in the war, the snipers had not had access to such high-end equipment, but for a shot like this, where he would only get one pull of the trigger, they were a necessity. He checked the range to the target and, dismissing the creaking pain in his knees, moved the wooden pallet he had hauled up the mountain to the right spot.

He was getting old. War was a young man's game, but what Mali needed from him was not war. It was murder.

He did not bother with concealment. He would be shooting from inside a building, and his camouflage would be to blend in with the people of the city rather than the forest floor.

He turned on the PDA, which looked like a bulky cell phone, and connected it to the binocular with a cable. The weather meter automatically fed data to the little computer. He scrolled down the PDA's screen, making sure all the fields were correct. It took every variable into consideration: the bullet's weight, how fast it would exit the barrel, aerodynamics, and a dozen other parameters.

His ammunition came from a special department located within Zastava Arms, as did his rifle. The cartridges were as long as his hand and heavy. The bullets, which had been individually turned on specialized lathes, terminated in needle-sharp points.

He assembled the rifle, which weighed as much as a small child and came in two pieces. After joining the barrel to the receiver and lowering the legs on the bipod, he laid down on the pallet.

Lukić looked through the binocular and ranged the target. A red LED indicated a distance of 1,966 meters. Perfect. The PDA used this range and information from the weather meter to produce a firing solution. He dialed the figure into the scope, correcting for elevation. He knew that the computer's estimate was just that—an estimate—one that he would fine-tune as he shot.

He considered the wind. The meter only told him the speed it was blowing and in what direction from his spot on the hillside. That tidbit of data was better than nothing, but not by much.

He switched to the rifle scope and studied the air between him and the target. To most people, wind is invisible. To Lukić, it was alive and dynamic, and it would speak to you if you knew how to listen. He divided the distance to the target in five-hundred-meter increments and changed the focus on his scope to look at each slice of air in turn. He looked at how the grass swayed in the field before him and how the leaves on the trees shook. An observer coming on the scene might have thought Lukić had fallen asleep behind the large rifle. Eventually, he lifted his head from the scope, working the stiffness from his neck. But he knew. The wind had yielded its secrets. It was his feel for the wind that separated Lukić from all but a select few snipers.

He chambered a round, sliding the bolt forward and down. There was no time to waste. The wind told him what he needed, but at some point it would change. It always did.

Lukić looked through the scope at the target downrange, a simple metal rectangle the size of a human torso that he had painted white.

He saw the plate floating in space, hanging by chains in a metal frame. In his mind's eye, the background was not the valley floor but a Sarajevo streetscape. It was Sniper Alley circa 1993 with dark-clad Turks scurrying for safety like cockroaches across a kitchen floor. The view through his scope reached not only across the distance that separated Lukić from the target but also across the years that separated him from the man he had been. It was either the power of a god or the delusion of a madman. Maybe there was no difference between the two.

This was what had happened to him at the farmhouse. He pulled back from the scope and shook his head to clear the image. His breathing was ragged, and despite the cold, he could feel himself sweating. His heart raced. It would be hard to shoot with his pulse pounding behind his eyeballs and in his fingers.

Lukić closed his eyes and slowed his breathing. He pictured the blood flowing through his veins and arteries. He willed his heart to slow. Like an obedient dog, it obeyed its master's voice.

His heart was tractable, but his brain had a mind of its own. Lukić knew that the war would be with him forever. It had marked him deeply, marked him on his soul.

He could fight the visions, he decided, or embrace them. How many men could maintain this visceral connection to their youth, reach out and caress it from a kilometer or more away? In that moment, Lukić chose power over clarity. He would not deny these visions. He would not resist them. They were a part of him. He had been touched by the divine.

Lukić settled his finger on the trigger, and as he emptied the air from his lungs, he shot.

Despite the power of the round, the rifle barely moved. Lukić didn't blink. He kept his eyes on the target and saw his bullet's impact, which made the plate dance. His wind call was perfect. But the round hit low. He shot again, and then once more. All three rounds were within a hand's breadth of one another.

He adjusted the data in the PDA to give him the correct hold. Now he was ready.

Lying prone on the wooden pallet on the cold ground, Lukić sent more rounds downrange. Each bullet struck the plate in the center in a tight group no more than twenty centimeters in diameter. Each shot was a foreshadowing.

He was the god of death.

And he never missed.

SARAJEVO
NOVEMBER 8

22

"We have a problem."

Eric knew there was no need to beat around the bush with Annika. She was tough and practical. If there was a problem, she wanted to know about it. She did not need it sugarcoated, and Eric had yet to see the High Rep lose her cool.

"Tell me," she said, gesturing to Eric to sit. They were in Annika's office. Eric still had his office in the U.S. embassy, but Annika had also made room for him at the EU mission, and he had found himself spending more and more of his time working out of the converted town house that the EU used as its Sarajevo headquarters. Even when the High Rep was back in Brussels, Eric was in no hurry to move back to his old office with its multiple layers of security and bureaucracy. The EU mission was more human in scale than the U.S. embassy, which bore more than a passing resemblance to a high-security federal prison. Avoiding the embassy also kept him away from Ambassador Wylie, who had grown sour as he watched the Sondergaard Plan for Bosnia gather momentum, leaving him stranded on the sidelines with no role and no visibility. He seemed to hold Eric personally responsible for this.

Eric sat in one of the minimalist chairs across from Annika. The whole office was decorated in a vaguely Scandinavian style with blond wood furniture that looked like it had been ordered from the IKEA catalogue. It was all uncomfortable. The High Rep liked it that way. The Nordics, Eric suspected, viewed physical comfort as a sign of moral weakness.

"I got a call about half an hour ago from a contact in the HDF." This was the Serbo-Croatian acronym for the Croatian Democratic Front, the center-right party that dominated Bosnian Croat politics. "Ante Strelić has called a press conference for tomorrow morning, and my guy tells me that he is going to withdraw his support for your plan and pull out of the talks. I didn't want to come to you with only a single source, so I asked around. It looks like an accurate report."

"If we lose the HDF, we lose the Federation," Annika observed. "The Bosniak Unity Party won't move without cover from their Croat partners."

"That's right," Eric agreed. "The HDF is just the first domino. We'd lose all the center-right parties in the Federation. The left is too small to carry the load. The whole thing would fall apart."

Annika leaned back in her chair and closed her eyes. Eric could see lines at the corners of her eyes that had not been there when they had met six weeks ago. There were a few streaks of gray in her white-blond hair. Maybe the gray had been there before, but if so, he had not noticed it. Annika was tired. She was carrying enormous responsibilities, and it was slowly wearing her down. They were in this together. If they failed, they would both have ownership of the consequences. But Eric's failure would be private and personal. Annika's would be spectacularly public.

She would be linked forever to the war they were persuaded would follow the collapse of the talks. The first Balkan war of the twenty-first century would be associated with her in the way that Chamberlain and Munich still resonated seventy years after the British prime minister's disastrously supine performance in his negotiations with Hitler. It would be the end of her political career and the beginning of a long period of soul-searching and repentance. But Eric knew enough about her to recognize that her personal circumstances were not the source of her anxiety. It was the consequences their failure would have on the lives of millions. The loss of yet another generation of Balkan youth to the insatiable maw of war.

"Why?" she asked, after allowing herself the luxury of two minutes of silent contemplation. "What does Strelić want? Why the change of heart?"

"According to my contacts, it's not about your plan or the conference at all. Strelić's number two, a guy named Arsić, is making a play for the top job. Arsić is the one who's made an issue of Strelić's support for the peace conference. I don't think he gives a damn about it, but he's targeted the party's nationalist base and Strelić is feeling the heat. If he backs off from his support for reconciliation with Srpska, Strelić has a fighting chance to get a grip on his leadership position in the party. If he holds firm, he's likely to lose control of the HDF to Arsić."

"Who would withdraw the party's support for the peace conference within hours of taking the reins."

"That's a good bet."

Annika stood up and began to pace back and forth behind the desk. It was a habit she had that Eric had observed before. It seemed to help her think.

"What if Arsić was out of the picture altogether?" she asked.

"What do you have in mind?" Eric flashed back to Filipović's head exploding into a mass of red-gray goo. But he did not believe for a moment that this was what Annika meant by "out of the picture."

"What if Arsić was gone? Just out of the equation. Could we keep Strelić onside?"

"I think so, yes. His calculus would certainly change, and it's the challenge from Arsić that is pushing him to abandon the peace process."

"Can you get me another twenty-four hours? Get Strelić to postpone his press conference by a day?"

"Maybe. But no promises. There are a few guys firmly in Strelić's camp in the HDF who owe me a favor or two. I can try to cash those in for a delay, but it depends on the dynamics inside the party. If they've decided that Arsić is the future, they may already be looking to switch sides. And if Strelić feels the walls closing in, he won't listen to anyone who's telling him to do anything other than defend his position."

"See if you can get me the time I need."

"What are you going to do with it?"

Annika's eye's narrowed and her expression was steely.

"I'm going to play politics."

"I'll do my best," Eric promised.

"And one more thing," Annika said, as though she had not already asked for the moon. "Ask Strelić to come in and meet with me tomorrow morning."

"Now I'm not just cashing in markers, I'm writing IOUs."

"That's alright," Annika said with a mischievous smile. "You're good for it."

Ante Strelić was a former semipro basketball player in Croatia's development league. Eric had to crane his neck at an awkward angle as they shook hands. Strelić still carried himself like an elite athlete, angular and confident. His suit was Italian, charcoal gray with dark-blue pinstripes. His haircut was expensive. Strelić was not your average Bosnian politician. He had a future, and he would be the first to tell you that. His personal political fortune, Eric knew, would be the single most important factor in his decision making on the Sondergaard Plan. If his personal interests led him to choose war over peace, so be it.

In that way, at least, Strelić was all too typical of your average Bosnian politician even if his sartorial splendor was not.

Eric led the HDF leader up the stairs to Annika's second-floor office. The High Rep was easily Strelić's match in the wardrobe department. Black suit with a white open-necked shirt. Blond hair pulled back in a tight bun. Single strand of pearls. She looked ten years younger than she had just the day before.

They perched more than sat on the High Rep's vaguely uncomfortable Scandinavian furniture.

"Thank you for coming on such short notice," Annika said, once coffee had been served.

"It's my pleasure," Strelić replied. His English was smooth and cultured, the accent colored by the decade he had spent living in Germany. "Your people were both persuasive and . . . insistent."

"It's all in the service of peace," Annika offered.

"Of course," Strelić said carefully. "Madam High Representative, I am happy to meet with you and I agreed to postpone my press conference at your request, but I am afraid that this conversation is unlikely to produce the results you desire. The HDF is forced to withdraw support for your plan. It's not personal. I have enormous regard for your diligent efforts in pursuit of an agreement. The time is just not right."

"Is it the HDF pulling out of the peace conference," Annika asked, "or Ante Strelić?"

"Is there a difference?"

"That's a little Louis XIV, don't you think?"

"I am the party."

"But only so long as you can hold on to the top job."

"That's the nature of our profession, alas. All political careers end in failure."

"And you're concerned that Mr. Arsić will use your support for the peace conference to move your career forward to that unfortunate end before its time."

Eric admired the way Annika controlled the conversation. She was firm but not overbearing. The High Rep was a hell of a politician.

"I'm not concerned," Strelić said. "I'm certain. If I don't pull my party out of your conference, I'm going to lose it. And Arsić will be even more difficult for you to deal with than I am. He represents the hard-liners in our party, the unreconstructed nationalists. If you are thinking that you can back them in this fight against me and make Arsić an ally, you're sadly mistaken."

"I think no such thing," Annika assured him. "We have no illusions about Mr. Arsić, his supporters, or his views."

"So why have you asked to see me?"

"I just thought that you might like to know that three hours ago Mr. Arsić accepted a position as a senior advisor for the European Commission's Western Balkans Neighborhood Program. He starts immediately."

Strelić looked stunned.

He was no more surprised than Eric. The High Rep had made these arrangements through her own channels.

"Why would he do this?" Strelić asked.

"The position pays rather well, about fourteen thousand euros a month," Annika said with a tone that implied the answer was blindingly obvious. "The job also comes with a nice apartment in Brussels and a generous expense account."

"And that was enough?"

"So it would seem."

"You know what they say about gift horses," Eric added.

"I suppose that I do." Strelić still seemed confused by the sudden change in his political fortunes.

"This would seem to solve your little problem within the party," Annika suggested.

"So it would seem," Strelić said in conscious imitation of the High Rep's own blithe reassurances.

"What can we expect about the HDF's position with respect to the peace conference?"

Strelić did not hesitate.

"Madam High Representative, I can assure you that our press conference tomorrow will focus on the importance of all of Bosnia's political leaders putting aside their personal differences and embracing your plan as the surest path to peace and prosperity."

"I'm so pleased to hear that," Annika said with a slight smile. "And I am certain you will be quite convincing. I look forward to our continued partnership."

"Partnership. Yes. I would imagine, Madam, that it is considerably more profitable to be your partner than your enemy."

"I should hope so."

After Strelić had left, Eric and Annika poured another round of coffees and shared a moment of quiet satisfaction.

"That was a pretty impressive performance, Annika."

"Thank you. You're the regional expert, but I'm the politician. Politics is the same all over the world. It's all about who gets what."

"Too many of them seem to want it all."

Annika laughed lightly. "We politicians can be limited in our outlook, I agree."

"There was more to the Arsić deal than just the job offer, wasn't there?" Eric suggested.

"Well, there was also the matter of his trading company."

Arsić ran a successful business exporting fruits and vegetables from Bosnia to supermarket chains in Western Europe.

"A stick to go along with his carrots perhaps."

"Very good. I may have suggested to Mr. Arsić that if he did not take the position the EU's health inspectors were going to find his company in breach of so many phytosanitary regulations that not a single cucumber would make it onto the supermarket shelves of Western Europe."

"Were you ready to follow through on that? Bankrupt him if he wouldn't play along?"

"Yes. I was."

"That's what we Americans call hardball," Eric said.

"Do you think it was unethical, what I did?"

It was a serious question and Eric gave it serious consideration.

"Maybe," he offered, after a minute or two of thought. "But in the service of a good cause. I think that gives you some rope."

"Thank you, Eric. I don't love playing those kinds of games even when they're necessary."

"It's a tough town. You do what you have to."

Annika nodded in agreement.

A few hours later, Eric and Annika took the short drive to the Aleksandar Hotel. In a few short days, the Aleksandar would host the conference at which the fate of the Sondergaard Plan would be decided. Annika wanted the logistics to be smooth and predictable even as the politics promised to be anything but.

The Aleksandar was a venerable establishment and the beneficiary of a major facelift that had rejuvenated the façade and brought the once-tired interior into the twenty-first century. It was one of the best on Sarajevo's hotel scene and an obvious choice for the conference. They toured the rooms that were being readied for the delegates from the three major ethnic communities, the entities of the Federation, and the two big neighbors—Serbia and Croatia—

as well as the scores of European and American officials who were descending on the conference like locusts in the hopes of claiming a slice of the credit and a share of the glory that would come with success. These same self-promoters—so instrumental to the outcome, they would say back home—would slink out the back door into the night in the event of failure. It was always like that.

"What do you think, Eric?" Annika asked at the end of the tour. "Are we ready?"

"The hotel is in good shape. The plenary rooms are big enough. The delegation hold areas are too small to be comfortable, which is good. We could use a little more office space, another couple of computers, and a better copier than the one the hotel has offered. Wylie will give you one if you ask. If the talks get traction, we're going to need the ability to adjust the texts in something close to real time. We'll need to produce a lot of paper on a short timeline."

"Anything else I should ask of your ambassador while I'm at it?"

"Other than to stay away?"

"I doubt very much that he would give me that no matter how sweetly I asked."

"You're probably right."

At the front entrance to the hotel, they paused to consider how they would coordinate the complicated protocol dance of the arrivals and departures of the assorted muckety-mucks, all of whom would want to demonstrate their power and influence by jumping to the front of the line.

The hotel was located on Ulica Zmaja od Bosne, the street that had once been known as Sniper Alley. Eric looked down the now-crowded street toward the buildings on the hills ringing the city that had once served as the vantage points for the snipers and marksmen who had terrorized the populace of Sarajevo for the better part of three years. That was all in the past.

But Filipović's murder was still fresh in Eric's mind. There was no reason to believe that the assassination was the only one that Mali and his allies had planned.

Eric had not told anyone about that night. He had not reported it to Wylie because the ambassador was likely to respond by throwing him out of the country. He had not told Sarah only because he had no idea where she was or how to reach her. And he had not told Annika, largely, he suspected, because he did not want to give her cause to doubt his judgment. He had persuaded himself that he could operate effectively on his own in a fluid and ambiguous environment, and he had put himself in a dangerous position as a direct result. Filipović's murder had raised the stakes to a much higher level than Eric had anticipated. Mali Barcelona had acquired an efficient instrument of death, and there was now empirical evidence that he intended to use it. With Mali's opposition to the peace conference, the High Representative would have to be considered among the possible targets.

"Annika," he said impulsively. "There's something I need to tell you."

"Shoot."

It was an unfortunate choice of idiom.

"You read the stories in the papers about Filipović's murder in Srpska?"

"Of course."

"I was there when it happened."

Annika's eyes widened.

"Really?"

"I was sitting two meters from him when he was shot. I believe the shooter works for Marko Barcelona. Filipović was ready to sell Mali out to save his own skin and he told me that he knew what it was Mali had over Dimitrović. So Mali decided that he'd be better off with Filipović dead. I was negotiating the terms of Filipović's defection. But we didn't get the chance to close the deal. Whatever Filipović knew, he took to his grave."

"Any idea who the shooter is?"

"None. But he's extremely good at what he does. Annika, I'm worried about you. It's possible that if Mali decides you've become a serious threat he'll move against you personally. He's not above it. Not by a long shot." Eric winced at his own poor choice of words.

Annika was not easy to intimidate.

"Eric, through all the years of fighting in the Balkans, how many of the international negotiators were targeted for violence by the belligerents?"

"None," Eric conceded.

"The risks were too high. It just wasn't worth it. That hasn't changed. They will do absolutely brutal and unconscionable things to each other, but I doubt very much that they'll extend the same treatment to you or me. The outsiders are all replaceable parts."

"I'm replaceable, Annika. But I'm not at all convinced that you are. Will you at least get close protection? A detail."

"If Mali really wants me dead, it wouldn't matter. I'll let some Sarajevo policeman follow me around if it'll make you feel better, but I'm ready to take whatever risks I have to in getting this done. There's too much at stake."

Annika's thinking paralleled Eric's own. He had been chewing over Dragan's suggestion that they use the opportunity of Mali's meeting with the political and criminal leadership of Republika Srpska to search his house. Eric did not doubt that Dragan could get them inside. He did not know what they might find there, but he knew that at the moment they were two steps behind Mali—and that the leader of the White Hand seemed bent on ensuring that the Sondergaard Plan died in the cradle.

Sarah would not hesitate. But it was her line of work. Eric was a diplomat, not a spy. In principle, he enjoyed diplomatic immunity, so he could not be prosecuted even if they were caught breaking into Mali's home. In practice, judgment was likely to be delivered outside a courtroom and the execution of the sentence would be summary. A bullet to the back of the head did not discriminate on the basis of diplomatic niceties.

Annika stepped back and looked appraisingly at the hotel. She seemed satisfied.

"Are you ready for this?" she asked. Annika was talking about the peace conference. But Eric was thinking about Mali and Dragan and Sarah. Annika was right. There was too much at stake. This was a chance to correct the mistakes of the past. Or at least make amends.

He was ready.

"Let's do this," he said with more conviction than he felt.

There was no way that Annika could know he was answering a different question.

LANGLEY, VIRGINIA
NOVEMBER 10

23

Interrogation was a kind of seduction. Done right, it required time and patience as the questioner and the questioned did their complicated dance. The interrogator was the male figure. The pursuer. The aggressor. The conqueror. The subject was the female. The pursued. The defender. The conquest. At the end of a successful interrogation, the subject should give him or herself willingly to the interrogator as though it were the consummation of a secret desire. The subject would unburden himself of his secrets; whether he did this because of guilt or pride or weariness did not really matter. Interrogation was a delicate art form that could not be rushed.

VW did not have time for that shit.

There was another kind of interrogation: short, sharp, and brutal. This was the interrogation of the waterboard, of the electric current, of sleep deprivation, of stress positions, and of fear. It was violence first, questions later. Torquemada and his Inquisition. Interrogators of this stripe did not need to worry about establishing credibility. The bruises and burns they left behind did that quite nicely.

Not long after the beginning of the Global War on Terror, in which the United States of America formally declared hostilities against an abstract noun, VW had done a short stint at the prison in Guantánamo, Cuba, where the military was holding a group of what it called "high-value detainees." Most were anything but, just angry and confused kids with delusions of jihadist grandeur. A few, however, were the real deal, men like Khalid Sheikh Mohammed. The al-Qaeda propaganda chief had been waterboarded almost two hundred times, ultimately confessing to masterminding the 9/11 attacks, the Bali bombing in Indonesia, and the attempted shoe-bombing of an American Airlines flight. If they hadn't stopped, Mohammed would have accepted responsibility for the Gulf oil spill, global warming, and Jar Jar Binks. That was the shortcoming of this approach. Push hard enough and you would always find what you were looking for. Torquemada and his team had an extraordinary batting average. In the end, everyone confessed. They would say anything to make the pain stop.

Most of the class-A interrogators at Gitmo had been patient seducers. There had been a few good ones, however, who preferred shock and awe. Done right, it could be extremely effective. It could also be efficient.

VW needed to move fast. She did not really have much in the way of hard data: a code name, some dodgy accounting practices, and a single grainy photograph. She had her suspicions, even a few theories, but the evidence was so tenuous and uncertain that she was reluctant to push it forward too soon. If VW was right about a cancer in the Western Balkans Division, it would have to be cut out ruthlessly without compunction. But the standards in place for that kind of radical surgery were high.

She needed to find someone on the inside and break him quickly before the principals could activate the force field of the Old Boys' network and destroy whatever actual evidence might be out there. VW had no charter or authority for what she was doing. She was far outside her lane and, therefore, vulnerable. If she went after the Old Boys without solid proof, they would countercharge, and VW had no illusions about which party would come out the worse in that exchange. The operations side of the Agency was tight and clannish, dominated by a group of ex–Special Operations types who drank Scotch and smoked smuggled Cuban cigars while they watched the Redskins lose to whomever they were playing that week. No more proof of VW's outsider status was necessary than her residence on the Island of Misfit Toys. The Old Boys never so much as visited the Island.

Her target was Roger Penforth. She had chosen him carefully. Penforth was a relatively junior analyst assigned to the operations team and the antithesis of an Old Boy. He had no rabbi looking after his career and no field experience working undercover in a hostile environment. He had been through the short course on the Farm, but he had had few opportunities to put his theoretical training into practice. His shell would be thin and brittle. VW thought she would crack it and feed on the information that lay within, soft and gooey and rich with data. Penforth was responsible for operations support. He would have the answers that VW was after.

She would get one shot at this. If she pushed Penforth and he didn't break, he would run back to the Balkan Action Team. The Old Boys would circle the wagons. And her investigation would be closed.

Penforth was nothing if not punctual. He knocked on her door at exactly ten fifteen, the time VW had specified. She may have been exiled to the Island, but VW still had rank and Penforth could not easily have refused her summons.

"You asked to see me?"

Penforth was young and looked even younger. VW suspected that he only needed to shave once a week. He was handsome in the kind of wholesome and nonthreatening way that no doubt had appealed to the sorority girls at the University of Virginia where Penforth had majored in political science and minored in binge drinking. Or maybe it was the other way around. The transcript of his last lifestyle polygraph exam had left this ambiguous.

There was still something of Peter Pan about Roger Penforth, the boy who had never grown up. His life had been charmed and easy, and as near as VW could tell, almost entirely devoid of the kinds of setbacks and failures that built resilience. For all of his obvious confidence, Penforth was, she hoped and expected, fragile.

Penforth was nattily dressed in a blue pin-striped suit and pink shirt. His club tie was done up in a neat half Windsor. His hair, just a little too long for the Clandestine Service's quasimilitary culture, was gelled firmly into obedience.

VW was wearing an ill-fitting pantsuit she had bought off the rack at JCPenny. There was a stubborn stain on the collar that her dry cleaner could not quite seem to remove. VW felt a sudden stab of desire to take the untroubled boy standing in front of her down a peg or two just on principle. She suppressed the thought as both unworthy and self-defeating. She would need a clear head for what she was about to do.

"I did, Roger. Thank you for making the time on such short notice. But I'd rather discuss the matter at hand in a clean room if you don't mind. Can we go downstairs?"

"Sure."

Typical Roger, VW thought, *self-assured and incurious.* She led her charge to the bank of elevators down the hall. She needed to scan her badge before hitting the button for the second basement level. It was restricted access.

VW had to scan her badge again to open the door to room B2-412. She ushered Penforth inside and closed the steel door behind them. The pneumatic seals set around the frame hissed. The room inside was featureless and gray, with metal walls and a mirror that did not even try to disguise its nature as one-way glass. The air felt heavy and oppressive. The clean rooms were pressurized. A low hum from the sound maskers made it seem as if an enormous colony of bees were crawling in the space behind the walls.

A Formica table was set at the far end of the rectangular room with a single hard-backed chair oriented to face the door.

"Sit down, Roger," VW commanded.

Penforth sat in the chair, still seemingly oblivious to the hostile nature of the upcoming conversation.

"Are you going to just stand there, VW?" he asked.

"No. I'm going to ask you some hard questions and you're going to give me straight answers."

"Questions about what?"

"Parsifal."

For the first time, Penforth looked uncertain, almost nervous. He glanced at the mirror, imagining, VW hoped, the large team of investigators gathered behind it. In reality, the only one on the other side of the glass was David Rennsler.

"The opera?" Penforth suggested. VW could see he was stalling.

This was no time for subtlety. She had no authority to hold Penforth in this room. He could get up and walk out at any moment and either report the conversation to his bosses in the Western Balkans Division or lawyer up. Neither outcome would help VW get to the truth. She needed to crack him open quickly before he had a chance to think, to orient himself.

She needed shock and awe.

"Roger, the director believes that there are elements within the Balkans team engaged in an unauthorized operation. He tasked me to investigate, and I believe you are involved. The operation is called Parsifal, the story of the quest for the Holy Grail, which makes it sound pretty damn important. It is as off-the-books as you can get. But in the world of twenty-first-century record keeping, that doesn't mean quite the same thing as it used to."

VW pulled a bright orange Top Secret folder from her briefcase and set it on the table. She opened it up and spread the papers out in front of Penforth. He glanced at the documents but did not take time to decipher them. He did not need to, VW realized. He knew exactly what they were.

"I have no idea what you're talking about." Penforth held up his hands, palms out, as though warding off a blow. He glanced again at the mirror, and VW had the impression that he was looking for allies on the other side of the glass.

"Listen, Roger. I don't think you are an important piece of this. But the fact is that a rogue operation is a crime. Technically, it's treason, the penalties for which are traditionally rather severe."

Penforth nodded and gulped. All of his ruling-class sangfroid had evaporated.

"The director's not interested in the little fish," VW continued. "We want the big fish, the decision makers. If you help me with this investigation, there's at least a reasonable chance that you can stay out of federal prison. That deal's only available until I walk out of this room. Tell me what I need to know, Roger. Now. After this, you're on your own."

"I don't know what you mean, VW. I've never heard of any operation called Parsifal. And I have no information about any operations being run out of channels." He looked at her with what he doubtless hoped was a look of guiltless confidence. It was not. Penforth was a terrible liar.

"That's interesting. Because I've already spoken to Simmons and Weinberg, and they both pointed the finger at you. Said it was your op." While not exactly a shot in the dark, there was some guesswork behind this charge. Simmons and Weinberg were senior managers on the Balkan Action Team, and it made sense that they would need to be part of any operation that deviated from the norm. VW wanted to give young Roger the impression that he had already been thrown to the wolves to lighten the sleigh.

"That's bullshit!" Penforth said vehemently, confirming for VW that she was on target.

"Are you saying that it wasn't your operation?"

"I was barely involved," Penforth said. The sudden flush to his face told VW that he realized too late that he had just confirmed Parsifal's existence. Good. She wanted to keep him uncertain. It was hard to keep your balance when you were backpedaling.

"What was the extent of your involvement?" VW asked. "What was your role in Parsifal?"

"Support," Penforth sputtered. "I provided intel support to the team."

"What team?"

"The team in the field."

"Where? Sarajevo?"

Penforth looked at her as if she were an idiot.

"No. Geneva."

VW pointed at the paper sitting on the table in front of Penforth.

"This spike in spending in Geneva. What is it about?"

"They're looking for something."

"What?"

"I don't know. The Holy fucking Grail, I suppose. I didn't need to know. It wasn't my job."

"Roger, if you don't help me, I can't help you."

"They called it the package. It has something to do with Marko Barcelona. That's all I know."

"Why Geneva?"

"There was a lawyer. Emile Gisler. He was supposed to be holding it for Mali. Parsifal wanted it. I don't know why."

"Why the past tense?"

"Gisler's dead." He saw the look on her face. "No, it's not what you think. He had a heart attack. At least that's what they told me."

"Who's in on Parsifal? How high up does it go?"

"I don't know."

"Who did you get your orders from?"

"Simmons."

Harry Simmons was the deputy director of the Balkan Action Team and a dyed-in-the-wool son of a bitch. VW had long suspected that he had been behind her exile. Now she was beginning to understand why.

"Who's running the operation?"

"Someone called Kundry. I think it's a code name."

"Tell me about Geneva."

Penforth was quiet.

"Tell me about Geneva," VW repeated, more insistently this time. She placed her hands on the tabletop and leaned in toward Penforth, trying her best to make her five-foot-six frame appear menacing.

"I think I need a lawyer," Penforth said.

Time to unsettle him some more. VW pulled another file out of her briefcase.

"Roger, three days ago I flew a Wyvern over Mali's house in Kriva Rijeka. I got a good picture of him when he stepped out into his garden.

She laid the photograph on the desk, an eight-by-ten black-and-white print. It was grainy from the high magnification but clear enough for her purposes.

Penforth looked at the picture.

"Holy shit! That's . . ." His voice trailed off as he tried to process the implications of the photograph. They were considerable.

"Yes," VW agreed. "Yes, it is."

Penforth cracked. He told her everything he knew. It was not a complete picture, but it was enough. Enough for her to take to the seventh floor.

TRNOVA, BOSNIA
NOVEMBER 12

24

Father Stefan had been in the business of saving souls long enough to recognize a troubled one when he saw it. The man who had come to his small mountain chapel seeking solace and forgiveness had the haunted look of someone who had seen too many terrible things, who had done too many terrible things. It was a look that Stefan remembered from the war, a war that this man—who had introduced himself only as Darko from Vukovar—had never, the priest suspected, left behind. Men like Darko carried the war with them everywhere they went, as though it were a religious talisman or family heirloom, something too precious or familiar to surrender. And like a talisman, it was worn close to the heart.

Stefan knew why Darko had chosen him. It was the magnetic pull of reputation. That Stefan was no longer the man he had been was irrelevant. Darko had come seeking only a shadow of the past.

That was alright. Stefan could offer him comfort, even absolution, without having to refight his own war.

He did not get many visitors out here. The monastery was not on any of the major pilgrimage routes, nor did his little chapel have the kind of high-quality artistic flourishes that might have drawn the more adventurous sort of tourist. It was simple and quiet up here in the mountains. That was how Stefan liked it.

People who came to the chapel did so purposefully. Darko was one such visitor.

He was short and dark with black hair cut close to the scalp. He was dressed in black, a color that enhanced his pallid complexion. The priest was reminded of one of those pale, blind cave fish. A creature of the night and the dark who looked out of place under a clear sky. His boots were black leather and laced up to the calf. They were polished to a mirror shine, just one more marker of his military history.

Even in repose, there was a tension that seemed to emanate from the visitor, a sense of energy bound tightly in his belly and just barely contained. It was less a coiled spring and more like a steam pipe, smooth and seamless on the surface but with pressure building up on the inside, probing for weak points or design flaws. There would be no outward sign of failure, but the pipe would eventually burst in an explosion of heat and steam. And heaven help anyone who was standing nearby. At least that was how it seemed to Stefan.

"Come," he said to Darko. "Eat and drink with me, and we can talk."

It was a cool day, but the sun was out and that made it just warm enough to sit outside in relative comfort. Stefan set out fresh bread and soft white cheese, a small plate of smoked meat, a bowl of honey, and a dish of walnuts. There was also a bottle of *rakija* on the tray with a beeswax stopper and a large wooden cross that one of the novices had patiently assembled inside the bottle.

"It's not often I have a guest for lunch," Stefan explained, as he set the food and drink on the table. "Company is always pleasant."

Darko said nothing, but he helped himself to the food and grunted in appreciation as he ate. He did not, somewhat to Stefan's surprise, crack the seal on the bottle of brandy.

"You've come quite a distance to this church," Stefan observed. "Is there perhaps some way I can be of service to you?"

Darko seemed to consider this as he chewed a handful of the walnuts that Stefan had picked and shelled himself.

"There are some things that I would like to discuss," Darko said carefully.

"What sort of things?"

"Terrible things. Dark things. Things that grab you by the throat and never let go."

"You speak of the war?" Stefan asked sympathetically.

"Yesterday and today it is all the same. The past is the future. It is a snake that circles the world thrice and swallows its own tail." As he said this, Darko's eyes darted back and forth as if he expected an enemy to emerge from the tree line at any moment.

"Our memories can seem real and immediate," Stefan said. "Especially when we dream."

"Then I dream all day, Father, of things I have done and things I have yet to do. I see the spirits of the dead mingled with the spirits of the not yet dead, for that is what we are. All of us. I want to deliver them to this higher state of being, for that is what I am. An emissary. An angel."

Stefan suspected that Darko might be more than spiritually troubled. There was something about the way he spoke and the intensity of his gaze that led the priest to suspect that the man sitting across from him was delusional, perhaps even dangerously so.

Stefan dipped a walnut in the honey and chewed it slowly, biding his time as he formulated a response.

"My son, your soul seems restless. The past is a heavy burden for us all, but I would help you bear the weight if you would let me. Confess your sins and I will offer absolution."

Darko's features seemed to soften at the idea, and his eyes ceased their rapid and unpredictable movements and seemed to focus on something comforting in the middle distance.

"I would like that," he said. "The dead won't stay dead, you see. Father, I see them. They follow me. They cloud my vision and muddle my thinking. I have hopes that absolution will banish the dead back to their graves."

Stefan led Darko into the church and up to the altar. The sacrament of confession in the Orthodox Church was different than in its Catholic cousin. There was no booth, no pretense of anonymity. The Orthodox Church had adopted a system of lay confessors to serve as spiritual guides to the village folk in times of crisis, although only an ordained priest could formally absolve a person of his or her sins.

On Stefan's instruction, Darko laid his left hand on the holy book and two fingers of his right hand on the foot of an image of Christ engraved on a wooden cross.

Stefan stood across from him.

"Tell me your sins, my son."

"They are many, Father."

"We are all but men."

"Some of us are more than that. I am an angel. An avenging angel. A fallen angel."

Darko's eyes were bright and unblinking with a hint of madness. Stefan was moved to pity tempered by fear. The violence had wormed its way into Darko's heart and folded in on itself until it had become a part of the fabric of his being. Stefan feared that this visitor was deranged beyond redemption. But he was a priest and he would try.

"Why have you come to me?"

"I have killed. I have killed many men."

Stefan nodded.

"I have killed women and children."

"The war brought out the worst in all of us," the priest said reassuringly.

"No, Father. It brought out my best. I was good at war. I have never been . . . will never be . . . as good at anything ever again."

"You are in conflict with yourself," Stefan said. "It eats at your soul. I understand this. But there is a part of you that rejects that identity. Rejects violence. Turns from death. Desires another way of living. That is why you have come here."

"Yes. There is a conflict. My nature is dual. Both angel and man. And the part of me that is still a man has a soul that is in mortal danger."

"Then repent and save your soul," Stefan said urgently.

Darko's list of sins was long even by the standards of a region that had seen too much of war.

Stefan listened with patience and sympathy, and offered his blessing.

"Go forth and sin no more," the priest commanded.

"I cannot promise that, Father."

"You must try."

"I am not done with killing. There is one more I must do."

"It is one thing to kill during war. It is another thing altogether to murder."

"Is it, Father? Is it really?"

"Why do you say you must do this thing?"

"Because he wants her dead and I have given my word."

"Who?"

"She is gold. A woman of gold." Darko seemed to be babbling nonsense.

"My son, I fear you are in the grip of a delusion. I can tend to your soul, but I cannot treat your mind. You have need of a priest, yes. But you also need a physician. Let me help you."

Darko only shook his head, and without another word, he turned and walked out of the church.

Stefan was left alone with his thoughts. He had been in the presence of something powerful, but whether it was evil or simple madness was impossible for him to tell. Was there even a difference? Was insanity simply a form of spiritual turmoil?

Was Darko merely delusional or would he act out the commands of the demons in his head? There was something about the woman of gold that almost seemed to make sense to Stefan. But he could not quite put the pieces together. It was almost there. Scattered fragments of understanding that he tried unsuccessfully to shape into a complete picture. He pushed it aside. Darko from Vukovar was insane. The war had broken him, and peace—such as it was—had failed to remake him. He was caught in a world of fantasy and make-believe. In this, he was hardly alone. There were too many of the walking dead from all sides in that terrible conflict.

Darko needed a psychiatrist, hospitalization, drugs, and therapy. That was a problem for the secular authorities. There was little Stefan could do from his isolated mountain chapel. He had already done everything in his power to help the former soldier save his soul. That was the job of a priest.

Stefan returned the cross and the holy book to their resting place, and closed the door of the church behind him.

The bees needed tending.

AGINO SELO
NEAR BANJA LUKA
1570

25

"I want you to cut the boy," his mother said. "Disfigure him. Nothing too extreme. Maybe one of his ears. A finger. He won't miss one."

His wife, Brana, was mad with worry, Radoslav knew. The fear that the scout would choose their son Uros had grown in her mind until it had become a certainty. This was the dangerous period for Uros. The scout came only once every four or five years. If they could make it through this "collecting," it was likely that Uros would be too old the next time. Radoslav understood his wife's fear, he even shared it, but it was his job to be strong.

"What's wrong with you, woman? Disfigure my son? Never. He will not be chosen. There are many boys in the village who are the right age. Many are bigger and stronger than Uros."

"And if he is chosen? What then?"

Radoslav drained his cup of *rakija* and poured himself another from the wooden cask on the table.

"We have more than one son."

"You are not his mother."

Radoslav smiled at his wife and reached for her hand. Life in the village could make a man grow hard, but he was not unkind. It hurt him to see his wife suffer, and if the scout chose his boy, he would no doubt weep himself. In private. Radoslav loved the boy too. But he was a man.

He twisted the end of his mustache, a habit he had when he was thinking about something especially serious.

"If he is chosen," he said carefully, "it might not be all bad. He would be educated in the sultan's court. He would learn to read and fight. He might come back to us one day as a bey, even as a pasha. Sokollu Mehmed Pasha was born a Serb in Sokolovići and now he is master of us all. Is that so bad?"

"He would be a slave and a Turk," his wife said. "They would circumcise him and make him Muslim. He would have no reason to love us, you and me, or even remember us. It is most likely that he will die in some foreign battle fighting the sultan's wars. That is not what I want for my son."

Uros was only eight. This was the age the scouts' preferred for their Janissaries, the privileged class of slaves who guarded the sultan's person and administered his sprawling empire. Most Janissaries came from the Balkans: Albanians and Serbs, Croats and Bulgarians. Muslims were exempt from the collecting, the *devşirme* system by which towns and villages were expected to tithe their children to the sultan's imperial ambitions. Whole towns had been known to convert from Christianity to Islam to avoid the *devşirme*.

Radoslav looked around him at what he had built. They had done well for themselves, he and Brana. They had seven healthy children and two more in the church graveyard. Their house was strong, made of wattle and thatch over stone and timber. Their farm was five acres of wheat and a small orchard that produced plums and cherries and succulent apricots in season. He had iron farm tools in the shed, a draft horse, and a cow that gave enough milk to meet their needs.

The last thing he wanted was trouble. Not with the village headman, not with the bey and, God alone knew, not with the pasha. Some families tried to hide their sons or pretend they had died. But the scouts knew. The Ottomans were nothing if not very careful keepers of records. Land records. Court records. Marriages, births, and deaths. Those who tried to cheat the scouts lost their homes and farms. It was better to take your chances with the numbers. There were many Christian sons, and few were chosen as Janissaries. But you could not expect a woman to understand numbers.

A bell rang, the church bell. It was time.

Brana gathered the children. The girls did not need to come, but if little Uros was chosen, it would be their last chance to see him.

Radoslav pulled his *kožuh*, a warm sheepskin vest, over his best shirt of embroidered linen. He wrapped a red wool belt around his waist. Red was for Christians. The Muslims wore green. His hat was also made of wool dyed dark red and embroidered in black thread. Finally, he stuck a long knife into his belt. A man never left the house without a weapon.

It was already November and the cold rain had turned the roads to mud. The sky was an iron gray. His *opanci,* shoes made from woven leather, kept his feet dry and his wool socks kept them warm. The scout always came in November. Radoslav did not know why. The walk to town took longer than it usually did, as they were weighed down by their heavy hearts. Within the hour, however, all of the families in the village assembled by the church for inspection. The priest was there with his own family, but his two sons were grown, almost old enough to marry and certainly too old to be of interest to the scout.

The agent of the sultan's army was the same man who had come for the last two cycles of *devşirme*. He had seen enough winters now that his mustache was beginning to gray. The scout's riding clothes were made of lamb's wool dyed a deep blue, and his boots were polished leather. It was his horse, however, that made the most powerful impression on the villagers. If Radoslav had sold his home and all his land, and indentured his sons and daughters as servants, he could not have afforded to buy such a magnificent animal. The horse was black and at least sixteen hands high with a broad chest and thick black mane. This was the scout's personal mount. But it was the other horses that his wife feared, the dull-brown drays yoked to the wagon that would take their son away to far-off Constantinople at the whim of the man before them. The Muslims, Radoslav knew, had another name for the city, but he could not recall it.

The sons lined up for inspection, all of the village boys between the ages of seven and eleven. Uros was one of the smallest of even the youngest boys, and Radoslav hoped that he would be overlooked because of it. He did not look like a soldier or even, Radoslav had to admit to himself, a farmer. But Uros was clever, and he had not yet learned to hide that, to dull his eyes and make his face a stone. The sultan was after more than big and strong, Radoslav knew. Uros was a curious boy and also a handsome boy. He took after his mother. The scouts were partial to good-looking sons.

The scout walked up and down the line of young boys, inspecting a few of the bigger ones the way he might look over a horse, checking their muscle tone and even looking at their teeth. One boy was nearly a head taller than the others. He was eleven and strong for his age. The agent took him. Radoslav heard his mother cry out in anguish and her husband hush her.

The scout stopped again in front of Uros, and Radoslav felt his wife's grip tighten on his arm.

"What is your name, boy," the scout asked.

"Uros."

"How old are you?"

"Nine," the boy lied. He was barely eight.

The scout seemed to recognize the lie. He smiled.

"Uros, you will come with me."

The boy did not cry. He did not run to his mother. He made his father proud.

The family was allowed to say good-bye. Brana shrieked and wailed and needed to be pulled apart from her son by two of the village women. Radoslav kept this face impassive. He would show nothing to the Turk. No pain. But he held his son tightly one last time and whispered fiercely in his ear.

"Remember us. I will remember you."

Remember.

KRIVA RIJEKA
NOVEMBER 13

26

As Eric had anticipated, Sarah was enthusiastic about Dragan's offer to help them get inside Mali's mountain villa. She had returned to Sarajevo the day after Eric and Annika had toured the Aleksandar Hotel, typically cagey and uninformative about where she had been.

"Business trip" was the full extent of her explanation. It was a familiar response to a question he had learned to stop asking back when they were an actual couple. He was not quite certain what they were now, but a couple was clearly not the right answer.

Sarah had listened carefully to the description of the attack at Nikola's farmhouse retreat and Filipović's assassination.

"You did everything right, Eric," she had assured him. "And props to Amra. She was right. It looks like our little friend Tiny has, in fact, contracted the services of a capable killer."

"For Filipović?" Eric had wondered out loud. "Or for someone else?"

"We'll see," Sarah had replied.

There was not much time to prepare. The window was one night. Both Eric and Sarah understood that they were alone in this decision. The Agency had grown increasingly conservative and risk averse. The release of the damning Senate report on the CIA's "enhanced interrogation" of terror suspects after 9/11 had only accelerated that trend. If the higher-ups in the intelligence bureaucracy knew what Sarah and Eric had in mind, they would have put the brakes on, demanding studies and quantitative analyses of the risk/reward balance that would have consumed weeks, even months, that they did not have.

The State Department, meanwhile, would not even have had the vocabulary to respond if Eric had told Wylie or anyone else in his reporting chain what they were planning to do. Eric was not entirely sure how he had found himself so far outside the carefully circumscribed lines of his profession. Part of it, he knew, was Sarah. But more than that, it was his sense of outrage. That anger had been building in him for a long time, going back to that one horrifying afternoon in an Orange County garage. This was his way of shouting, *No more!* No more to the Armenian genocide. No more to the killing fields of Cambodia. No more to Srebrenica. The risk of taking action belonged to him and Sarah and Dragan. The risks of inaction belonged to an entire country.

For Dragan, there was nothing especially remarkable about the night's work they had planned. It was almost routine. And he had a typically Serbian comfort level with improvisation.

Now, as they sat shivering in a Russian jeep with a broken heater high up the side of the valley where Mali had his villa, Eric was having second thoughts. Sarah, as usual, seemed to be able to read his mind.

"Too late, cowboy. We're committed."

"We *should* be committed," Eric replied. "All of us."

"It'll all be fine," Dragan said reassuringly from the driver's seat. "We'll be careful. If it looks bad, we can pull back and try something different."

Dragan had driven them up over the mountains that ringed the valley, following an old logging road that ran through the saddle between two of the rugged peaks. The Lada Niva had jounced down the rutted road on its inadequate shocks, but the little Russian jeep was the automobile equivalent of an AK-47, simple and tough. Russian engineers were consistently disinterested in the health and comfort of end users. Heat, for example, was evidently considered an option on the Niva. And the night was cold. The logging road took them to within a kilometer of the villa. Dragan had driven with no lights, using a set of military-grade night-vision goggles to stay on the road.

They parked in a clearing that offered a direct line of sight on the villa.

After more than an hour of patient surveillance, they saw what they had been waiting for. A convoy of three cars pulled away from the house and sped down the road toward Štrigova and on to Banja Luka.

"Get ready," Dragan said, with an edge of eagerness once the lights of the convoy had disappeared down the valley road. "Remember. There will be only two guards on duty instead of the usual four. One at the front gate. One on the inside."

"You're sure of the numbers, Dragan?" Sarah asked. "There's a lot riding on that."

"I'm quite sure. My source is very good. I could tell what those two boys had for breakfast this morning if that information was material to the mission."

Mali had a contract with a company in Banja Luka that provided his security. One of the owners used to work for Dragan, which in Bosnia's close-knit and incestuous security community was not terribly surprising. Dragan had helped the company get its start, and he cashed in that favor for a temporary administrator's password that gave him access to just about everything there was to know about security arrangements at the villa.

"What about dogs?" Sarah asked.

"Only outside. Not in the house. According to the file, the client is allergic."

From under his seat, Dragan pulled out a compact, ugly-looking handgun and offered it to Eric.

"No, thanks. I'd just end up shooting one of you."

"Suit yourself." The handgun disappeared under Dragan's coat. Eric was quite confident it was not the only one the former State Security operative was carrying. He did not offer a gun to Sarah. She had brought her own.

The three of them slipped on the night-vision goggles that Dragan had supplied from his company's inventory. It was high-end gear, comfortable and easy to use. They picked their way carefully down the slope toward the back of the villa. Both Sarah and Dragan were carrying black nylon backpacks. They took their time. In the green glow of the night-vision goggles, the shadows were dark and impenetrable. Eric was careful where he put his feet.

The stone wall that encircled the garden was more than two meters tall, but the top was smooth and free of barbed wire. It would not be too difficult to climb over. Dragan raised his hand, indicating that Eric and Sarah should hold. From his pack, Dragan pulled a small aerosol can and sprayed the area along the top of the wall. In his scope, Eric could see a bright green line running parallel to the wall. A laser beam.

Dragan reached into the bag a second time and removed a palm-size device that looked something like a camera on a tripod. He set it on top of the wall and tapped a quick sequence of buttons. The device shifted slightly on the tripod along all of its axes before settling into position. A single red light on the face of the device was the only visible indication that it was active. Dragan confirmed with another shot of aerosol that the light was a laser beam directed back down the line toward the receiver. This would fool the alarm into thinking that the laser had not been disturbed.

"Okay. Up and over," Dragan whispered. "Stay to the left of our laser."

For a large man, Dragan was surprisingly graceful. He vaulted the wall in a single smooth motion and landed soundlessly on the other side. Eric and Sarah were right behind him. Despite the cold, Eric's palms were sweaty. It may have been macho bullshit, but he did not want the others to see how nervous he was. He dried his palms surreptitiously on the sides of his pants.

The walled garden was dark and deserted. Dragan led the way, having committed the layout to memory as part of the "research" he had conducted on the ill-secured computers of Mali's security company. The door to the house looked like wood, but it was painted steel and cold to the touch. The lock was located in the center of the door, a European style that typically meant there was a mechanical system inside the door that would engage locking rods on all four sides.

Sarah had it open within forty-five seconds.

"It was harder to get into your apartment," she whispered.

Eric removed his night-vision goggles and hooked them onto his belt. The lights were on in parts of the house, and it was more than bright enough inside to find their way to Mali's basement study.

Earlier, Eric had asked Dragan about the guard posted inside the villa.

"Don't worry," Dragan had replied. "I ran a little background investigation of the guard who'll be on duty. He likes to gamble, and he put a not inconsiderable sum on Partizan to beat Red Star in the derby game. No way he won't be watching that. We should be okay, at least until halftime."

"He's going to lose his money," Eric had predicted. "Partizan is just terrible this year."

Consistent with Dragan's expectations, they could hear a television on upstairs broadcasting the unmistakable roar of a match between the two biggest Serbian football clubs. In Serbia, the yearly Partizan–Red Star game was almost a national holiday.

Mali's home was extravagantly furnished, with just a hint of the bad taste that spoke of new money. A narrow set of stairs in the back of the house led down to the basement. According to the notes in the files of the security company, Mali's office was below grade and windowless. It was also secured with a cipher lock and an independent alarm system, the override codes for which were helpfully kept on file by the security contractor for operational reasons.

Dragan keyed the six-digit code onto the keypad and was rewarded with the sharp click of the lock disengaging.

The room was dark, but Sarah found the light switch without much difficulty. When the door closed behind them, Dragan said, "We can speak normally. The room is soundproof."

This is something of a double-edged sword, Eric thought. The guard could not hear them, but neither would they be able to hear him if he pulled himself away from the football game to make rounds.

The room beyond the door was an outer office that, judging by the feminine desiderata on the desk, was used by a receptionist or secretary. Mali's personal office was in the back. It was spacious and opulent. The floors were hardwood with a few oriental rugs. There was a well-stocked bar along one wall. The opposite wall featured a pair of large paintings that Eric recognized. They were museum pieces. The artist, Nadežda Petrović, was Serbia's most famous impressionist. Her face was on the two-hundred-dinar note. There were other paintings almost as nice on the wall behind Mali's desk. The total value of the art in the office was well north of half a million dollars.

The desk was walnut, with an ornate relief carved on the front. It was a nature scene, birds and flowers and climbing vines. The style was typically Balkan, but Eric had never seen an example of this kind of work so fine and delicate. Wood carving like this was generally done by village artisans. The relief on Mali's desk was fine art.

They had divided the responsibilities. Sarah went to work on the computer while Eric went through the contents of the desk drawers. Dragan, meanwhile, searched the room for a safe. The computer was password protected, of course, but Sarah had brought a piece of CIA tech with them that she hoped would get around that.

There was not much in the desk itself. The middle drawer was full of standard office products, with the exception of a Waterman pen that had a two-carat canary yellow diamond embedded in the cap. Eric did not for a moment suspect that it was a fake. Whatever other problems Mali might have, money was clearly not among them.

"Look for anything electronic," Sarah said, as she plugged a small black box into the desktop with a USB connection. "Cameras. Tape recorders. Look out in particular for videotape or anything that can hold electronic records."

Eric was again reminded that Sarah was not searching randomly. She might not have known exactly what they were after, but she had a much clearer idea than either Eric or Dragan.

There was little of interest in the right-hand drawers. On the left side, however, Eric found a plain black ledger book and a manila folder labeled EMERALD WAVE—DARKO LUKIĆ. There was a CIA product inside the folder. Eric scanned it quickly. It seemed to be a bio-cum-psychological study of a Bosnian Serb army sniper, a man of considerable technical skill and equally outsize ethical shortcomings. The black-and-white picture in the upper-right corner showed an unsmiling bearded man in a military uniform with an intense penetrating gaze. This was almost certainly the man who had murdered Luka Filipović.

"Did you lose something?" Eric asked Sarah, passing her the contents of the folder. He spoke softly so that Dragan could not hear.

"Goddamn it!"

"How could Mali get ahold of something like that?"

"I told you we had a leak."

"What's Emerald Wave?"

"Psych profiles of likely targets for war crimes prosecution. The idea was to find little fish who might be ready to roll over on bigger fish in exchange for a deal."

"This is almost certainly the sniper Amra was talking about and probably the guy who killed Filipović."

"Odds are good."

"Dragan," Eric said loud enough to get the former spy's attention. "Ever hear of a sniper called Darko Lukić from the war?"

"Lukić?" Dragan considered the question without stopping his fruitless search of the office. "Name is familiar. There was a Lukić who was part of a special unit reporting directly to Ratko Mladić. After the war, he went to work for the Zemun clan in Belgrade, one of the nastier of the mafias. He was the chief suspect in three or four gangland murders. And then nothing. He just disappeared. Maybe into the bottle. He was a very, very good shot. Is he the one who killed our friend Filipović?"

"I think so."

"Then we are both lucky not to be dead."

Eric photographed the documents and put the file back in the drawer. The ledger book was equally interesting but considerably more cryptic. It was set up for bookkeeping, and a cursory look indicated that whatever he was tracking with it there was no money coming in. It was a record of expenditures, handwritten in neat block lettering. Most of the outflow was assigned to a category labeled GENEVA, but there was also a regular stream of payments to someone identified only as Father S.

"What's in Geneva?" Eric asked. "Maybe a bank?"

"A lawyer," Sarah answered. "Mali's lawyer."

"Could he be holding whatever it is we're looking for?"

"It's possible. What about Father S? Who's he? Or they? Maybe it says fathers."

Something stirred in the back of Eric's brain, a connection struggling to be made. It was like the feeling of having a name at the tip of your tongue. It was almost there, but the harder you tried to lock it in, the more elusive it seemed.

Eric used a small camera that Dragan had given him to take pictures of the book and the letters. Most of the correspondence was in French, a language Eric did not read. Sarah could look at them later. Her French was good enough that she could have passed as a Parisian.

"I can't find any sign of a safe," Dragan said from across the room with just a hint of frustration. "Nothing in the walls. Nothing on the floor. Maybe he doesn't have one."

"Seems unlikely for a paranoid son of a bitch like Mali," Sarah suggested. "Keep looking. We have to find his hiding place." Any possible hint of despondency was buried under a thick layer of indignation that the risks they were running should go unrewarded.

Eric looked at the open drawers of the desk. Something did not seem quite right, and it took a minute for him to realize what it was.

"The drawers on the left are shorter than the ones on the right by a good eight inches. Why would that be, unless . . ."

"There's a hollow space behind them," Sarah finished his thought.

Eric explored the elaborate carving on the back of the desk. He ran his fingers over the wood. One of the heads of a two-headed eagle—the symbol of the Serbian monarchy—seemed loose. He pushed it like a button and the back panel swung out, revealing a safe built into the desk.

"Can either of you get it open?" Eric asked.

"Unless there's something special about this lock, it shouldn't be hard," Sarah said confidently.

From her backpack, Sarah pulled out an odd-looking apparatus that Eric could not identify. A small video screen was connected by several thick cables to what looked like some kind of miniature plunger. Sarah set the head of the plunger over the spin dial. It clapped onto the steel with a force that suggested the rubber shell concealed a powerful magnet. Sarah attached four leads to the safe door in a diamond pattern around the lock. The plunger made an odd clicking noise that sounded almost like dolphins at an aquarium. Sarah looked over her shoulder at Eric and Dragan.

"Sonic pulses," she explained. "The vibrations let the computer read the location of the locking pins."

A slight whir indicated that underneath the rubber cup something was spinning the safe dial. Sarah watched the video screen and made a series of seemingly small adjustments to the readouts. Some sixty seconds later, she reached for the handle and pulled down. The door popped open without a sound.

"Easy as pie," Sarah announced.

Inside, they found stacks of bills bound with currency straps from several local banks. There were dollars bundled into bricks of ten thousand, euros, Swiss francs, and rubles. Sarah had no interest in the money. Nor in the 9mm pistol and spare magazines on the bottom shelf.

She scanned quickly through a short stack of papers that looked to Eric like land records.

"It's not here," she said.

"What is it, Sarah? What are we here to find?" Eric asked.

"A tape or its electronic equivalent, a disc or even a memory stick. This is just . . . money."

"Quiet," Dragan hissed.

They froze.

The keypad on the inside was synched to the cipher lock on the outside. It was beeping. Someone was keying in numbers on the far side of the door. The code.

"Move," Dragan said, and there was no mistaking his urgency.

Eric slammed the safe door closed with a disconcertingly loud crash. Sarah scooped her gear into the backpack she carried and Dragan scanned the room for a place to hide.

"This way," he insisted. The burly Serb grabbed Sarah and Eric by their upper arms and half guided, half dragged them behind the bar.

As they got their heads down, the door opened. Eric could see the guard in the reflection from the bar mirror, which meant, he realized, that the guard would be able to see them as well if he looked in their direction.

The guard was young and fit-looking, and he walked with the confident swagger of an athlete. He was well over six feet tall and at least two hundred and twenty pounds of muscle. But Eric was more concerned about the pistol strapped to his thigh and the radio hooked onto his belt.

The guard walked over to Mali's desk and inspected it as if something did not seem quite right. From under her jacket, Sarah produced a handgun. It was small and looked to be made of more plastic than metal, but it had a large silencer screwed onto the barrel. It did not look like a pistol. It looked like a murder weapon.

Dragan held up an index finger and shook his head slightly. The meaning was clear: not "no" so much as "not yet."

"Evo ga," Eric heard the guard mutter. *Here it is.*

He pulled something from the desk drawer and pointed it at the far wall. The television came on, already tuned to the channel showing the soccer game. If he decided to fix himself a drink, they were all screwed.

The radio on the guard's belt squawked.

"Ivan, are you making your fucking rounds?"

"Yeah," the guard replied, pressing the button on the unit without bothering to unhook it from his belt.

"Well, hurry the fuck up. It's time to switch. I get the second half."

"Cool your fucking jets."

"Fuck you."

Ivan switched the radio off. He took two steps toward the bar and then stopped. Eric was certain that he had seen them, but instead of drawing his gun, the guard turned to his right and headed for Mali's private toilet. They did not need to discuss their next move. The instant the guard was out of sight, the three of them were up and moving as quickly and quietly as they could to the door. Eric hoped that Ivan's mother had taught him to wash his hands. They needed the time.

Dragan turned the handle slowly and eased the door open without a sound. Eric and Sarah slipped through and the door closed silently behind them. Eric could feel his pulse jackhammering in his ears. His breath was ragged as though he had been running. He was grateful to see that Sarah also looked keyed-up and anxious. Only Dragan seemed unperturbed. It was easy to imagine that this was far from the most stressful situation that his particular line of work had put him in.

Fifteen minutes later, they were back at the jeep and driving in the dark down the overgrown logging road.

Sarah examined the device she had hooked up to Mali's computer to mirror his hard drive.

"Nothing," she said in disgust. "I didn't have enough time to crack the security. All that effort and risk for nothing."

"Not nothing," Eric assured her.

"What do you mean?"

"Whatever that thing is that Mali has over Dimitrović. The source of his leverage."

"Yes."

"I think I know where it is."

GENEVA
NOVEMBER 14
9:30 A.M.

27

The moment Klingsor saw the face on the monitor, he knew that everything had gone to hell.

There was nothing especially imposing about the man standing on the front steps of Gisler's law office looking directly into the camera with a deceptively pleasant smile. He was of average height and build with a nondescript tan trench coat that looked like it had been bought off the rack at Macy's or a similar middlebrow department store. His features were smooth and his face unlined by troubles. His short hair was steel gray, most of it hidden under a fedora the color of charcoal that matched his round wire-rimmed spectacles. Fashion points from the Agency's foundational era.

His reputation preceded him. He was a decade into the job and had demonstrated a real affinity for its somewhat arcane practices. Everyone in Klingsor's line of work knew who he was, and no one used his name. The moniker he carried came with the job. It was the same title bestowed on the one man on a football team who no one wanted to talk to. He was the Turk.

Coach wants to see you. Bring your playbook.

Those words marked the end of many athletic dreams and careers. The spy world was less forgiving: *Coach wants to see you . . . dead.*

The Turk cleaned up the CIA's internal messes, everything from hopeless drunks to hapless traitors. Deeply flawed individuals with highly classified and potentially valuable knowledge and experience could not simply be cut loose to wander the world at will, nursing grievances and old grudges. The Turk made the arrangements for the separation from the Clandestine Service of its more problematic members. Most could be monitored or otherwise controlled. Maybe they would be asked to surrender their passports or be subject to electronic surveillance for the rest of their lives. A few, the most troublesome, the riskiest, or the least redeemable, were eliminated on a more permanent basis. The pink slip was in the form of a toe tag.

Klingsor was not certain which category he belonged in. If he was being honest, and Klingsor prided himself on his brutal honesty, the Turk's unannounced appearance at the front door was not especially surprising. Their part of the operation was not supposed to have dragged on like this. It should have been in and out, over in a few hours at the most. Gisler would have sung like a tweety bird, and Klingsor and the Echoes would have been on a flight out of Geneva with the package secured the next day. It had not worked out that way, and as hours stretched into days and weeks and the mission had morphed from securing the package to persuading Marko Barcelona that there was nothing wrong with his deadman's switch in Geneva, the risk of exposure had grown beyond what Klingsor would have accepted at the outset. He and his team had fallen victim to the mental trap of the boiling frog. Drop a frog in hot water and it will hop out. But put it in a pot of cold water and heat it up slowly and the frog will sit there as it boils to death, ignoring the simple lifesaving option of one good hop to safety. The frog dies before it realizes there is any danger.

The Turk's presence in Geneva meant two things. Someone on the other end had screwed up in some way. And Klingsor and his people were royally fucked.

Echo Three was with Klingsor in Gisler's office, and he too recognized the Turk.

"Should we let him in?" Echo Three asked.

"We don't really have much of a choice."

"No. I suppose we don't."

Echo Three showed him in.

The Turk removed his hat and coat with a precision of movement that bordered on the fastidious, hanging them both neatly on the rack in Gisler's office.

"Please, don't get up," the Turk said, though Klingsor had given no sign that he was planning to rise from the chair behind Gisler's desk.

"Could you please give us a few minutes alone?" the Turk asked Echo Three.

Three looked to Klingsor, who nodded his acceptance. Without a word, Three stepped out into the hall, closing the double doors behind him.

"You've done well for yourself, Daniel," the Turk said, using Klingsor's actual given name, which was both an egregious violation of OPSEC and a clear threat. *All that you are is naked before me,* it seemed to say.

"You look well fed also, Turk." Klingsor had no idea what the Turk's real name was. Maybe he had forgotten it himself after so many years operating under different aliases.

"Yes. I suppose so. But one must still try to stay fit. A little time in the field always helps."

"Is that what this is? The field?"

"You tell me."

"It's fucking Geneva."

"So it is. A law office it would seem. Where is the good barrister? Tucked into that freezer in the corner?"

"That's where we keep the ice cream. The Echoes have a terrible sweet tooth."

The Turk actually cracked a smile.

"Corpsicles?"

Klingsor shrugged. "For what it's worth, I didn't kill him."

"I know."

"What else do you know?"

"I know a traitor when I see one."

"That's not fair, Turk. This operation is in the best interest of our country. It's . . . patriotic."

"It's not sanctioned. It's rogue."

"It'll be sanctioned after the fact if we succeed."

"But you haven't done that, have you? Succeed, I mean."

"Not yet."

"You're grasping at straws."

"Maybe."

The two men paused, eyeing each other like tired boxers in a clinch. Klingsor considered his options. None were especially appealing. Maybe he could make a run for it. They'd need another freezer for the Turk's body, but that would be easy enough to arrange. Klingsor had four different passports in four different names identifying him as the citizen of four different countries. Two of them were absolutely clean, meaning that the Agency did not know about them. There was a bank in Zurich, one of the small ones, with a numbered account and a safe-deposit box with a hundred thousand dollars in cash. He could disappear. South America, perhaps. He had friends in Uruguay.

The Turk seemed to be able to read his mind, or maybe Klingsor was just predictable, like every other asshole caught with his pants down around his ankles and his dick in his hand.

"Don't even think about it," the Turk said, as though offering friendly advice.

"What?"

"Killing me and making for the bushes like a rabbit. You're not my first job, you know. It won't work."

"You're sure about that? Seems like a viable option to me at the least."

"Oh, that's right. You can't see it. I'm sorry. I forgot."

"Can't see what?"

"Here." The Turk reached into his jacket pocket and pulled out a small mirror, like the kind a woman might keep in her purse. He gestured toward Klingsor's face. "Take a look."

Klingsor looked in the mirror. A red dot of light danced on his forehead just a little bit right of center. A laser sight. Klingsor glanced out the window but could not see where the shooter was located. One of the rooftops, perhaps, or an apartment. It was impossible to know.

Klingsor choked down an irrational impulse to brush the dot of laser light off his face.

"Your unfortunate barrister friend aside, you are not known as an especially brutal operator. You are a more subtle player. More cautious. I respect that."

"Is that why I'm not already dead?"

"Among other reasons, yes."

Klingsor felt himself relax just a little bit. This was beginning to look more like the opening gambit of a negotiation than the prelude to a premature and permanent retirement.

And he was ready to negotiate. Loyalty was important to Klingsor. He valued it highly. But life was complicated. There were many values that had to be balanced. Openness and security. Freedom and respect. Duty and desire. And at the very top of the pyramid perched self-preservation, the *primus inter pares* of values. It trumped loyalty every time.

"You know some things, but not everything," Klingsor suggested as casually as he could. "You'd like to know more."

"Ours is the information business, no? You can never be too rich or too thin or know too much."

"Two of the things on that list are untrue."

"I suppose it depends on the circumstances."

"What is it that I have that interests you?" Klingsor wondered if the red laser dot was still fixed to his skull. A part of him wanted to look in the mirror, but he did not want to give the Turk either the satisfaction or the leverage. It would weaken his bargaining position.

"We'd like to know just how deep the rot goes," the Turk answered. He removed his glasses and began polishing the lenses with the end of his tie. "We know about Parsifal, of course, but the chain of communication we have is all in code. Good security practice. Very admirable. You, I understand, are Klingsor, and we know that your control is Kundry. What we'd very much like to know is the identity of this Kundry. Who he is and whether he represents the apex of this unauthorized operation."

Klingsor smiled at this. He had something to trade. The rest was details.

"You're not much of an opera buff are you?"

"On the contrary, but I prefer the Italians. Wagner's a little too bombastic for my tastes. All those Valkyries and magic rings."

"So you've never seen Parsifal?"

"No. Why does it matter?"

"Because then you would know."

"Know what, please?"

"Kundry is a woman."

KRIVA RIJEKA
NOVEMBER 14
10:45 A.M.

28

Something had gone wrong. Mali was not certain exactly what, but Gisler had missed two reporting deadlines. The system was not especially complicated. It wasn't supposed to be. What it was supposed to be was reliable and regular as a fucking Swiss watch.

Every two weeks, Gisler would put a coded message in the classified section of a Zurich-based Internet jobs site. Every fortnight, the message was the same: All is well. Then he had missed two postings in a row. That had never happened. He had taken Mali's money for the month, but that was an automatic transfer out of a numbered account. Gisler did not need to be alive for the check to clear.

Mali had used an untraceable burner cell to call Gisler's office. The assistant who answered had been polite enough but evasive about Herr Gisler's whereabouts. He had even tried the one-time-use emergency number that he and Gisler had established for exactly that purpose. No answer.

He had to assume that Gisler was blown. Mali would need to make new arrangements for the safekeeping of the package, but that would take time. It would have to wait until the situation had stabilized. Until Lukić had done his job.

It was not like he had lost access to the package altogether. Gisler had been holding a copy. The lawyer was just a dead man's switch, an insurance policy. The original was hidden away someplace safe. You did not leave something as explosive as the package lying around.

Mali was not, by nature, an overly optimistic man. But events were moving in the direction he wished them to go with the seeming inevitability that was the hallmark of a well-conceived plan. There would be hiccups; there always were. Gisler's unexplained disappearance was one. But it was more an inconvenience than a cause for real concern.

The meeting last night with Dimitrović and his lieutenants had gone well. War was a complex business. Moving soldiers around the board was the easy part. There were political considerations, financial constraints, operational plans and backup plans, egos to massage and pockets to line. No one wanted to make a major decision without Mali's personal blessing, and it was easy—even gratifying—to understand why they were reluctant to cross him. Planning a war was a great deal of work with seemingly endless details, but it was almost done and it would be worth it.

Once it was all over, there would have to be some changes. In truth, Mali did not care much for Dimitrović. He was limited, undereducated, uninteresting. For the time being, he needed

Dimitrović. But if all went as Mali planned, the day would come when he could jettison the National Party leader. Until that day, Dimitrović would do what he was told.

As much as he might like to, it was unlikely that Mali would be able to rule directly. He had tried to shed his past the way a snake might shed his skin, but he knew that he would never be completely successful. His personal history was such that he would have to rule from the shadows. It would be better, of course, if he could do that through a vehicle that was less damaged than Dimitrović. The president of the RS carried a lot of baggage, psychological as well as reputational. He was a dark and twisted figure, easy to dislike. But for now Mali needed Dimitrović. For now.

Still, Gisler's disappearance gnawed at his confidence. Had that fat fuck looked at the tape he was holding for Mali? Had curiosity gotten the better of greed? Had he understood what he was looking at? And did he then decide that he could make better use of it? Mali could not afford another distraction. He had enough problems.

Nikola Petrović was one. His position as Sondergaard's pet Serb had given him a political profile well beyond anything Mali had imagined possible. His party was now the focal point of a growing political movement that had picked up support from the left, students, urbanites, and what was left of the intelligentsia. Dimitrović's local supporters were largely pensioners, villagers, and the working class. For now they had the whip hand, but it would be important to crush Petrović and his supporters at the early stages of the upcoming conflict. Once the fighting started, it would be easy to bring enough force to bear to overrun Petrović's surprisingly competent personal security.

Mali hoped it would all be over quickly, but there was a chance that fighting could drag on for months, maybe even years. He was prepared for that.

The bungled assassination attempt on Petrović had succeeded only in elevating his political profile and turning the Social Democrats into a legitimate rival of the National Party. Killing Petrović now would only solidify his status as a martyr and reinforce support for the blasted Sondergaard Plan. Mali needed to blow that up first. Then he could deal with Petrović and any other fifth columnists on the RS side.

From the bar, Mali poured three or four fingers of Chivas into a crystal tumbler. The humidor on the bar top was stocked with Cohibas and he took one of these as well. He needed to relax.

As near as he could tell, there were only three possible outcomes: victory, prison, and death. Victory was always good. Death was inevitable. It did not really matter when it came along. Mali did not believe in an afterlife and certainly not in hell. Human nature being what it is, the devil would long ago have run out of room.

Even prison would have its charms, he decided. The luxuries he enjoyed in his new life were pleasant enough, but what Mali aspired to, what he craved, was power. He could have that in prison if it came to it. A man of his talents could always find a way to rise. Power was relative. Even in prison, someone had to be on top. Did they still use cigarettes to keep score in prison, or was that something out of the 1950s? If so, Mali would corner the fucking market in cigarettes. He'd be a king. Always a king. Given the choice, it was better to rule in hell.

The Scotch and cigar numbed his tongue. A pleasant alcoholic fuzz grew like moss on his thoughts. He considered calling Marija into his office for a quick fuck, standing up at the bar or on the leather couch. Maybe later, he decided. There was work to do.

It would be better, on balance, to live and stay out of prison. He needed to know that things were on track.

Mali pulled his cell phone out of his jacket pocket. Just a few years ago, he would not have dared to use the phone. The NSA would have quickly picked up the conversation. Even the mighty United States had its limits, however, and the Balkans was now little more than a backwater. The NSA was so focused on the mess in the Middle East, Ukraine, Pakistan, China, and other hot spots that it had little time for eavesdropping in the Balkans. Once the fighting started, that would change, but for now his scrambled cell would provide sufficient encryption to deter the local services.

He had his in-house assassin on speed dial. Mali took a brief moment to savor that thought. He had come far. And he had farther still to go. He would be king.

It hurt that she was involved. That they were on opposite sides. He wished that it wasn't so. She could have been his queen.

The sniper answered on the second ring.

"Da."

"Is everything ready?" Mali asked.

"Da."

Whatever his other charms, Lukić was not one for small talk.

"Any complications?"

"Ne."

"Anything you need?"

"Ne."

"This is pretty fucking important. Just so we understand each other."

"I know."

"Once this is done, there will be others. I have a list."

"We'll see."

"You understand how important this shot is? How much depends on it? It's the trigger for a whole series of actions that will transform this country."

"I understand."

"And you understand that the only way to communicate with us if anything goes wrong is over the radio. Cell phones won't work. Landlines will be down. All starting about three hours before zero minute. We're going to take the whole system down. You'll be on your own."

"I always am."

"Tell me that you can do this, Darko. That you can get it done. No bullshit."

"She is already dead."

TRNOVA, BOSNIA
NOVEMBER 14
11:30 A.M.

29

It was like traveling back in time. As Eric and Sarah drove through this forgotten corner of Bosnia, the trappings of modern life began to disappear. There were no power lines running alongside the road. No streetlamps. Smoke coming from the chimneys in the villages they passed through was from fires that Eric knew were used for heat and cooking rather than romance and atmosphere. Mud and wattle had fallen off the sides of the farmhouses in patches, exposing the timber frames beneath. The tractors parked beside the barns were old enough to remember Marshal Tito and the all-powerful Communist Party.

The mountains that loomed over them on either side were steep and foreboding. The forests were dark and threatening, like something out of a fairy tale.

Most striking to Eric, however, was the lack of commerce. The constant blast of advertising, economic come-ons, and hustle were an inescapable part of urban life. Out here there were no ads for Coke, no billboards marketing second-rate politicians and second-division sports teams. There were no car dealerships or supermarkets or movie theaters. Other than the aging tractors and stubbly fields, the only markers of economic activity were the hand-carved signs advertising various personal services. A few farmers sold honey, jam, and *rakija* on the side. Many of the signs said simply VULKANIZER, indicating that the villager who lived there also repaired tires.

It was a wild part of the world. Out here, tradition was more important than law. And Eric knew that every single male villager, no matter how poor, had a gun.

"Have you seen a wolf yet?" Sarah asked from the passenger seat, evidently affected in the same way Eric was by the raw power of the landscape.

"Nah. The bears keep them in check."

"Do you feel bad about missing the opening of the peace conference?" Sarah asked.

"Not too much. Today is strictly ceremonial. It'll be a set piece. The real negotiations start tomorrow. Those I need to be there for. We'll have a week to do a deal, maybe ten days. After that, we'll have lost whatever momentum we have and the Sondergaard Plan will wind up on the ash heap of history alongside a hundred other Balkan peace proposals."

"You really think that this one's different, don't you?"

"I think that she's different. If anyone can pull this off, it's Annika. She's Dick Holbrooke in heels. I don't think anyone else could do what she's doing, match how far she's come."

"So this has a chance?"

"Hell, yes."

"And failure means another Balkan war?"

"That's what I think. The stakes are high. That's why we need to find Father Stefan now. If he really has something that can help us keep Dimitrović from playing the spoiler role, we need it now, not a week from now. I hope like hell he's home."

"You sure about what we're doing? That we're not wasting our time on a wild-wolf chase?"

"Sure? No. But it makes sense. You're the one who told me about the Geneva connection. The book we found in Mali's desk drawer listed regular payments to someone in Geneva. It's hard to believe that this isn't connected to this package you're so damn cagey about. The only other entry in the book was for someone called Father S."

"And you think it's this guy?"

"I do. It seems to fit. Father Stefan was the spiritual advisor to Radovan Karadžić, Ratko Mladić, and the old gang from the genocide. He was the most important figure in the Orthodox Church in Bosnia through most of the nineties. And then he just disappeared. Dropped off the grid. Word was that he became a hermit. Not a few people assumed he had gone crazy. Then a few years ago he resurfaced as a simple parish priest in a small chapel out here in *vukojebina*."

Sarah laughed. "That can't possibly be the name of this place." *Vukojebina* meant literally *the place where the wolves fuck.*

"Alas, no. It's just an expression like 'the sticks' or 'the middle of nowhere.' But I suspect that it might be literally true as well."

"I remember Stefan from the nineties, but I never met him. Is he still political?"

"Not so far as anyone can tell. He's been quiet as a church mouse for the last fifteen years or so."

"Then why would Mali go to him?"

"Because of ideology. It makes sense that Mali would have confidence in Father Stefan, that he would see him as a fellow traveler. Stefan's a right-wing nationalist with deep roots in the RS. It's easy to understand how Mali would feel that he could count on the priest to keep the faith."

"Maybe he's changed," Sarah suggested. "Fifteen years. Twenty years. That's a long time."

"Not for these guys. It's the blink of an eye. They think in centuries. And besides, you know what the Serbs say about wolves."

"What?"

"The wolf can change its fur, but never its character."

Sarah looked at him curiously. "You sure about that?"

It was not easy to find the chapel. Sarah observed that it was as though it did not want to be found, like a Bosnian Brigadoon. The locals they stopped to ask offered confusing and contradictory directions, much of it predicated on a detailed knowledge of landmarks that used to be there some decades in the past. "Drive straight until you see the place where the widower Tamjanović cut down the big oak," one older woman had suggested unhelpfully.

Finally, after almost two hours of driving around nameless back roads, they found the Monastery of St. Archangel Gabriel, a collection of neat whitewashed buildings surrounded by well-tended orchards. Although the monastery was six hundred years old, there was nothing touristy about it. There were no signs in fractured

English, no guides, not even a stand selling souvenirs and religious bric-a-brac. It looked like what a monastery was supposed to be, a working religious community.

They parked the car under a maple tree with flaming-red leaves that were just beginning to fall. As they walked up the path toward the rectory, Sarah took Eric's arm and leaned against him. It was an intimate gesture, the kind that new lovers might make as easily as a couple celebrating their golden anniversary. Eric did not know what to make of it. To call Sarah's signals mixed was to devalue the concept.

They stopped a young monk carrying a load of firewood on his back. In the Orthodox Church, except for hieromonks like Father Stefan, there was a sharp divide between monks and priests. Priests were allowed, even expected, to marry and have children. Only the monks were celibate. Priests were generally educated and drawn from the middle class, while the monkhood did most of its recruiting among the working poor. This young man could look forward to a life of hard work, but he could at least count on steady if parsimonious meals.

Eric asked the monk where they could find Father Stefan. The monk said nothing but pointed them toward a small chapel located on the crest of a hill.

"Hvala," Eric said. *Thank you.*

The monk simply nodded and shouldered his burden.

They walked up the hill to the chapel shoulder to shoulder rather than arm in arm. Stolid and serious. Representatives of the United States of America.

Two rows of white apiaries stood a hundred meters or so from the chapel. A man dressed in the rough clothes of a laborer but sporting a beard that was unmistakably priestly was tending to the hives. Eric saw him bend over to grab one of the hives from the bottom and lift. He had to strain to raise the bottom up even a few inches. Seemingly satisfied, the priest set the hive back into place gently.

"That looks heavy," Eric said, as they approached. "Do you need help moving it?"

"No, thank you," the priest replied. "I was just checking the weight. The hive needs somewhere between thirty and forty kilograms of honey to make it through the winter. I want to make sure that my little friends are prepared. Praise God, they seem to be ready. Which is a good thing. It looks to be a harsh winter."

"It could be a very harsh winter, Father. But with your assistance, it may yet be less brutal than the winter of 1993."

The priest looked at them sharply, seeing them for the first time. Eric with his dark complexion and exotic features and Sarah with her unmistakable Americanness. There was no mistaking Eric's reference to 1993. It could be to nothing except the siege of Sarajevo.

"Who are you?" the priest asked in excellent English. "You're not from here, although you speak our language tolerably well."

"Not as well as you speak ours," Eric replied in the same language. "My name is Eric Petrosian. This is Sarah Gold. We're from the American embassy in Sarajevo."

The priest looked at Sarah with an expression that was difficult for Eric to interpret.

"Gold?"

"That's right. Not literal, unfortunately, more an aspiration."

The priest nodded slowly.

"I am Stefan, the priest here at this chapel."

"We know. You're the man we've come to see."

"What is this about?" The priest made no effort to hid his suspicions.

"Is there someplace we could sit and talk?"

"There's a table and benches behind the church," the priest said grudgingly.

No matter his suspicions about the visitors and their motives, the rules of hospitality were permanent and inflexible. Father Stefan brought them coffee and sweet cakes made from walnuts and honey. It was a warm day under a blue sky, and it was pleasant enough to sit outside as long as they kept their jackets on.

Sarah complimented Stefan on the honey.

"Thank you," the priest replied. "If the bees are happy and content, the honey is sweet and pure. I try to keep them happy. Beyond that, I can take no credit for the product of their labors."

They talked about nothing in particular while they drank the coffee. The weather. The frescoes in the chapel. The bumper crop of pears and apricots from the monastery's orchards.

Eric studied Stefan's face while they talked, comparing it to the man he remembered from the war years. The priest had seemed younger than his forty-five years when he was thumping the pulpit in support of national unity and in defense of ethnic cleansing. His arctic-blue eyes had burned with a fervor that reminded Eric of the line from Yeats. *The best lack all conviction while the worst are full of passionate intensity.* Now he seemed older than his three score and five, bent under the weight of memory and—Eric dared to hope—regret. The blue eyes had grown milky and softer, the color of a hazy summer sky.

The face that had been as smooth and unblemished as that of a porcelain doll was now leathery and wrinkled from long hours laboring under the sun. His once-dark hair now more white than gray. His hands were rough and calloused.

But the most salient difference was not the physical change. The younger priest had been charged with pent-up energy, eager and focused like a dog straining on the leash. Two decades later, Stefan seemed at peace, reflecting on the world rather than seeking to bend it to his will.

There was a risk, Eric understood, that he was projecting, seeing in the priest what he wanted to see rather than what was there. He would find out soon enough what was real and what was not.

"Now," Stefan said, when a sufficient time had elapsed to permit business to be done. "Why don't you tell me why you are here. I don't expect the fame of my honey has reached as far as the embassy of the United States."

"No," Eric acknowledged. "The honey is a bonus. We are here to talk to you about a man we believe you are working with in some capacity. Marko Barcelona."

For a brief moment, Stefan looked startled, but he quickly buried that expression under a mask of priestly calm. It was too late. His reaction had confirmed for Eric his suspicions about the identity of the Father S in Mali's ledger. The trick now would be eliciting the information they had come for, the location of Sarah's mysterious "package."

"I have heard of this man," the priest admitted, after a long pause in which he seemed to be weighing his response. "And I can understand why you would think of me in connection with him. I have a reputation. That reputation may be unfair, but it is not unearned. As a younger man, I was fiery, impetuous, quick to anger, and even quicker to take offense. I am an older man now. Slower. Wiser, I would like to think. Wise enough to stay out of politics and stay away from politicians as much as I can. They speak as the serpent spoke to Eve. Up is down. Black is white. They would as soon argue the one as the other depending entirely on utility to determine their position."

None of this was an actual denial. It would be better, Eric decided, not to press the priest too hard, but rather to lead him gently to the answer he desired. As a reporter, he had interviewed countless reluctant sources. What he was doing with Stefan was closer to investigative journalism than diplomacy.

"If I understand you correctly," Eric said, "you are telling me that you are not the same man you were when the Bosnian War was at its height. The Palace Priest of Pale."

"That is what they called me," the priest acknowledged with a sigh. Pale was the ski resort not far from Sarajevo that had been the seat of government for the leadership of Republika Srpska during the war. Stefan had been a prominent figure there, offering blessings and convocations at official functions and celebrations. "I was blind. We all were. The other sides were no better, but that hardly matters. So much blood. So much suffering."

Eric could see that the priest was genuinely moved by the memories of the hardship of war.

"Father, what if I told you that it could happen again. That the Bosnia we have been trying to build for twenty years with room for all regardless of ethnic origin could fall apart. That the four horsemen could ride again through the Balkans."

"Pestilence, war, famine, and death." Stefan recited it like a liturgy. "Every generation forgets the teachings of their parents."

"Dimitrović and Marko Barcelona are setting the stage for

another war, hitting the same old nationalist chords to motivate their followers."

"Things are different now," the priest insisted. "Most Serbs will not follow the siren song onto the rocks. Not again."

"No," Eric agreed. "Most won't. But it doesn't take most; it only takes enough. And Mali and Dimitrović have more than enough. The paramilitaries are back. The Wasps and the Dragons and the Volunteer Guard. It will take only a single spark to light the fire."

"And we will all burn," Stefan said.

Sarah reached across the table and laid her hand on the back of the priest's.

"All of us," she agreed.

There was a faraway look on the priest's face, but Eric could not tell whether he was gazing into the past or the future.

"It doesn't need to be this way," Eric said softly. "There is another way."

"Sondergaard?" Stefan asked.

"You've been following this?"

"No. I try to stay away from politics, but it is impossible not to know the basics."

"This plan has a real chance," Eric said insistently. "We can undo the mistakes of Dayton, mark a path forward for Bosnia to Europe and the twenty-first century. But we need your help."

"My help? I am an old man with a small church on a small hill. I am nothing."

"But you have something important," Eric said carefully. "You are holding something for Mali, and in return he supports your church and your work. I can understand that. Maybe you don't even know what it is. But you know it's important to him. We believe it is information. Something about Dimitrović. Something that he is using to control Dimitrović, to push him down the path to war. Father, we need to know where to find it. We need to break the link between Dimitrović and Mali, and give Sondergaard's plan for Bosnia a fair chance to succeed."

The priest was quiet as he processed what Eric had said. He did not try to deny the threat to what had become a fragile peace, which itself was encouraging. Eric tried to read his face, but it was impassive. Seemingly unconsciously, Stefan picked up a walnut from the table and worked it around in his hand as though it were a prayer bead. There was a tension in the set of his shoulders that gave the impression of an internal struggle. Eric said nothing. He did not want to disturb the priest's thought process, to make him feel as if someone else were making his decisions. He would have to reach the right conclusion on his own.

Sarah seemed to understand this as well. Under the table, she took Eric's hand and squeezed it hard, but she did not speak.

"Let us assume for a moment that what you say is true," Stefan said, after almost five minutes of silence. "That there was such a package and I knew where to find it. What would you do with this thing if I gave it to you?"

Eric let the air out of his lungs, surprised to find that he'd been holding his breath. The journalist in him understood that Stefan had made up his mind. There was still delicate work to do. Like a fisherman reeling in his catch, Eric could not move too fast or too slow or the line would break. But the hook was set.

"It depends in part on what it is," Eric answered. "But we would use it to separate Mali from Dimitrović, then work to persuade Dimitrović to support the Sondergaard Plan, or at least not obstruct it."

"Blackmail, you mean. You would be no better than Mali."

"No," Eric hastened to explain, realizing that he had been careless in his response. "If what you have . . . what you might have," he corrected himself, "is criminal, we would expose it, we would be obligated to. Information about common criminal behavior would be turned over to the state-level prosecutor in Sarajevo. Information about war crimes is the property of the international tribunal in The Hague. We have a treaty obligation to share everything we know about war crimes in the Balkans with the tribunal. It's an obligation we take very seriously."

"And what about Barcelona?" the priest asked. "What becomes of him?"

"I don't know," Eric admitted. "It depends, I suppose, on what the information reveals. But I do know this. Mali is bad for Bosnia. He is a cancer, a parasite feeding on the state. He will suck it dry and leave the husk to blow in the wind. He cares nothing for Bosnia. He doesn't care about the RS either, or the Serbian people, or the church. He cares only for himself. You know this is true."

Stefan shook his head, not in denial but in resignation. "I do," he said sadly. "God help me, I do."

"So where do we go from here?" Sarah asked.

Stefan looked at her, studying her face as though the answer might be written there.

"Come with me," he said.

The priest led them back to the row of apiaries.

"It would be better if you wait here," Stefan said. "My friends are usually well behaved, but they don't know you."

The priest did not put on any special gear. He simply walked over to one of the hives and removed the top. Moving slowly and patiently, he removed two screens from inside the hive and set them on a frame next to the apiary box. A mass of bees crawled aimlessly across the screens. A few took flight and circled around the hive, seemingly disoriented by the sudden transition. One bee lit on Stefan's exposed neck, but if he used his stinger, the priest gave no sign of it.

Stefan reached into the hive with one arm, digging deep for something at the bottom. He pulled out what looked like a small metal box and set it on the grass before replacing the screens and the lid with the same slow, mechanical patience.

Eric felt his pulse quicken. Sarah had taken his hand and was digging her nails into his palm. She was coiled tightly and Eric could sense that it took all of her self-control not to leap forward and snatch the box from the ground.

"Patience," he whispered to her. "We're almost there."

Stefan walked over to them, the box and his hand both dripping with raw honey, cloudy and crystalline and spotted with clumps of waxy comb and dead bees.

"This is it," Stefan said unnecessarily. "My friends have guarded it patiently and without curiosity as to the contents. I have tried to match them, but I suppose we are past that point now. Would you like to see what's inside?"

"Yes," Sarah said. And the eagerness in her response was an almost physical thing.

TRNOVA, BOSNIA
NOVEMBER 14
12:50 P.M.

30

It was such a small thing. A steel box no more than six inches across, four inches deep, and three inches high. It was well made, with a rubber seal around the lid that looked airtight, and secured with a key lock rather than a combination.

"I don't suppose you have the key?" Eric asked Stefan.

The priest shook his head.

"No. It was not for me to know what was in the box. I was just to keep it safe."

"And Mali paid you for this?" Sarah said. There was a sharp edge to the question that Eric thought was unnecessarily cruel.

"Yes," Stefan replied, with no attempt at self-defense. "For the church."

Sarah studied the lock.

"This isn't a serious thing," she announced. "It's to deter the merely curious, not the professional."

From her jacket pocket, Sarah produced a small set of tools on a chain. Within a minute, she had the lock open.

"Took a little longer than I thought," she said. "I think there's some honey in the mechanism."

Stefan looked at her curiously.

"What exactly do you do for the embassy, Miss Gold?" the priest asked.

"Economic policy."

"Of course." The irony in his reply was as thick as honey.

Sarah raised the lid and removed a foam insert that had been cut to the shape of the box. Using a pocketknife, she peeled off the top of the insert, which looked like it had been secured with some kind of epoxy. Nestled inside was a small videotape, the kind that would fit an old-model handheld camera before everything went to solid state and high-density memory cards.

Sarah picked it up and examined it the way a jeweler might inspect an especially precious stone. There was a gleam in her eye that Eric interpreted as triumph.

"What is it?" Stefan asked.

"The Holy Grail," Sarah replied with deadly seriousness.

"Let's see what's on the tape," Eric said.

"That won't be so easy," the priest observed. "That tape will require a special player or the original camera. I don't have either of those."

"No," Eric agreed, before turning to look at Sarah. "But you do, Sarah, don't you?"

The expression on Sarah's face hardened, and for a moment, she looked ready to launch into a vigorous denial. Eric looked her hard in the eyes and shook his head slightly. *Don't even think about it.*

"It's in the car," she said.

Eric could feel the anger building in him. He had tried to deny the truth, but there was no escaping it. Sarah had been drip-feeding him the bare minimum of information to keep him engaged. She had used him in the same way she had used the set of lock picks in her pocket, as a tool to open doors that would otherwise have been closed. She had manipulated his emotions and his ambitions with ruthless efficiency.

In truth, he could not really blame her for that. That's what they taught you to do in the CIA. He should have expected nothing different from Sarah, no matter the past they had once shared.

Eric motioned for the tape and Sarah handed it over to him, doing her best to look hurt at this show of distrust.

"Afraid I'll make a run for the Mexican border?" she asked.

"The thought had occurred to me."

"You understand so little, Eric."

"I know."

Ten minutes later, Sarah set a black Kevlar computer bag on the table. She removed a laptop then a video camera. Clunky and oversize. A relic of twentieth-century technology. A time when it looked like the Japanese would rule the world.

"JVC," Eric said. "Where did you even find that?"

"On eBay."

Sarah hooked up the camera to the computer and popped the tape into place. She fiddled with the connections until the computer screen was displaying the picture from the camera.

Sarah put a finger on the play button.

"Do you really want to do this?" she asked, with a note of what Eric took to be compassion, either genuine or feigned with remarkable skill. It was possible that Sarah could no longer tell the difference.

"Yes."

She looked over at Stefan and then back at Eric.

"Let him stay," Eric said. "He earned it."

Sarah shrugged.

She pressed play.

The picture was dark and grainy. The resolution was poor, and the cameraman had had trouble keeping the image focused and stable.

It was a large room of some kind. There looked to be hundreds of people inside packed close together, some standing, most sitting on the floor with their heads bowed as though in prayer. Some of those standing were armed with rifles.

The camera panned across the room, settling for a moment on a sign painted on the wall. Eric recognized the logo and there was a hollow feeling in the pit of his stomach.

SREBRENICA TRACTOR COLLECTIVE.

Srebrenica.

It haunted him still. There was no escape from it.

Eric found himself unconsciously craning his neck as if that would somehow give him a better view of the men he now recognized for what they were. Prisoners. Men and boys condemned to die not for what they had done, but for who they were.

Eric was looking for one familiar face. For his friend. For Meho.

Sarah hit the pause bottom and turned to face him.

"Eric . . ."

Wordlessly, he reached across her and pushed play.

There was no narrative. It was a seemingly unconnected series of images and vignettes. This was raw footage. The cameraman could be heard laughing and joking with his unseen friends about what they were doing.

"Look at these sheep," one disembodied voice said.

"Sheep? I only see pigs."

The doors at the far end opened with a clang of metal, and a tall man, his face hidden under a green balaclava, strode onto the factory floor like a conquering caesar. The cameraman zoomed in for a close-up. Eric could see the lizard patch on the shoulder of his uniform. The Green Dragons. Eric did not need the unit insignia to identify the man. This was Captain Zero, the last indicted war criminal from the Balkan conflicts still at large. But Zero was known only by his nom de guerre, and the tribunal's prosecutors had long ago given up hope of bringing the infamous paramilitary leader to justice.

The cameraman settled on Zero's face. The eyes behind the mask were like black pits. There was something familiar about them, something that danced on the edge of Eric's recognition. Where had he seen those eyes before?

Captain Zero marched confidently to the middle of the large room. And Eric got his first glimpse of Meho, sitting cross-legged on the concrete floor not ten feet from the leader of the Green Dragons. Meho's head was bent to his chest, his shoulders slumped.

Eric's throat tightened. He reached for the screen as though he thought he could touch his friend, comfort him in his time of need. But Meho was long dead.

Sitting next to his friend was a man that Eric recognized as a younger version of the caretaker at the Srebrenica genocide memorial who had given him the message from Meho that it was not his fault. Eric had rejected that offer of forgiveness until just now. He had had no one to blame but himself. Eric was alone with his "if onlys." Now his rage and anguish had a target. The man in the green mask. Captain Zero. This was the monster who had killed his friend.

On screen, Meho raised his head and seemed to lock eyes with Captain Zero. The paramilitary had turned to face him, and his back was now toward the camera. With one hand, he grabbed the balaclava and pulled it off over his head. The picture quality was not good enough to read Meho's expression, but Eric had no doubt that his friend would have understood the meaning of this gesture. *Death to all.*

The paramilitaries kicked the prisoners to their feet and drove them outside with the liberal use of their rifle butts. The cameraman followed. The next scenes were a disjointed blur of groups of men walking through the dark. They knew as surely as Eric did with the benefit of hindsight what was going to happen. But there was nothing that they could do.

The prisoners were forced to kneel facing a ditch. The paramilitaries went down the line shooting men and boys in the back of the head.

The concentration camps of Auschwitz, Dachau, and Jasenovac. Tuol Sleng prison in Cambodia. The Nyarubuye Catholic church in Rwanda's Kibungo Province. The killing fields of Srebrenica. It all came down to the same thing.

Genocide.

Captain Zero himself was executing prisoners with an enormous pistol, killing each man with a single shot to the head then moving on to the next victim. The gunshots were loud barks, sharp and final. Zero's face was obscured by shadows and impossible to make out.

Meho was on his knees. Waiting for Captain Zero. Waiting for death.

Eric could only watch in horror as the paramilitary leader approached Meho, knowing that the murder of his friend and colleague was simultaneously seconds away and twenty years in the past.

Zero's advance was inexorable and pitiless. As he stepped behind Meho, the Green Dragon was caught in the headlights of one of the earthmoving machines that could be heard growling in the background. For a moment, his face was clearly visible. Eric hit the pause button and used the computer to zoom in on Captain Zero. At high magnification, the image was blurry, but the face was unmistakable.

He was a bit heavier now and a bit fleshier around the jowls. There was gray in his hair now. It had been twenty years, after all.

But the eyes were the same.

The blood drained from Eric's face and he felt light-headed.

It made so much sense. And the implications were so terrible.

He had seen those eyes before.

Captain Zero was Zoran Dimitrović.

Father Stefan looked to be as devastated as Eric by what he had seen. His complexion was ashen, his expression somber. He brushed something from his cheek that might have been dirt but might also have been a tear.

"I'm sorry," the priest said in Serbian to no one in particular. "I did not know."

"There was no way you could, Father," Eric said gently.

"Those were ideas that I once supported, giving them life and flesh," Stefan said. "I might as well have executed those men myself."

"Then it's a good thing you're in the redemption business." Eric paused. "You did the right thing, giving this to us."

"Others need to see this," Stefan said. "Everyone needs to see this. If only they knew. The Serbs need to go backward before they can go forward."

Eric understood. Too many on the Serbian side of the complex Balkan equation denied the reality of Srebrenica. The numbers were exaggerated, many claimed. It was hundreds, not thousands, as though that somehow justified industrial murder. Others acknowledged the crime, but insisted it was balanced by equivalent attacks against their own ethnic kin. Serbian civilians had been the target of ethnically motivated violence, even—in the case of the once-thriving Serbian community in Croatia—ethnic cleansing. But there was nothing like Srebrenica. Nothing that could balance the scales. Nothing but justice.

For the Serbian public, rejection of the crime of Srebrenica had left them bewildered by the way they had been cast as the primary architects of Yugoslavia's bloody breakup and the West's rush to side with the Kosovo Albanians when the fighting flared in what had been Serbia's southernmost province and was now Europe's newest country. Western resolve to prevent a repeat of the horrors of Bosnia had motivated NATO to attack Serbia even at the cost of siding with the thuggish Kosovo Liberation Army, a group that straddled the line between paramilitary force and organized-crime network.

"The world will know," Eric said. "This cannot be denied. The tribunal will be able to use this tape to put Dimitrović in prison for the rest of his life. The world will see this. I'll make sure of it."

Eric took the camera and hit the eject button. He removed the tape and stuck it in the inside pocket of his jacket. It was a kind of promise. Sarah looked sharply at Eric but made no effort to stop him.

"This is a dangerous thing you are carrying," the priest said.

"Yes," Eric replied. "But for whom?"

"For everyone."

Eric looked over at Sarah, who was now avoiding his gaze. They had a great deal to discuss.

"Stefan, could you give us a few minutes, please?"

"Of course. There is more work to be done on the hives."

Stefan returned to his bees.

They sat in silence for several minutes. Eric tried to order his thoughts.

"So, do you want to explain this to me?" he asked finally. "It seems pretty clear that you knew what was on that tape. No. Not just knew. You had seen it before, hadn't you?"

"Yes, I had."

"You had this. The CIA had this."

"Yes. One of the Green Dragons made the tape on that awful night and he kept it. God knows what he was thinking. It's like leaving a live bomb ticking in your living room. But when Dimitrović started his rise to prominence, the man recognized that he had something valuable to the right buyer. He reached out to us through a middleman with a proposal."

"What sort of proposal?"

"Resettlement to the United States for himself and his family, a new identify, and a small suitcase of cash in exchange for the keys to Zoran Dimitrović's soul. It seemed like a fair price."

"I'll bet."

"You have to understand, Eric. I wasn't kidding when I told Stefan that this was the Holy Grail. Bosnia was falling apart. Our analysts were predicting another major war within the next eighteen months. Tens of thousands of dead. Hundreds of thousands of refugees. With this tape, we could do something. We could change the trajectory of the entire country."

"We have a treaty-level obligation to turn anything like this, all of the evidence, over to the tribunal for prosecution."

"Oh, grow up, Eric. That's the past. There's nothing you can do for the dead. Our concern was for the living and the future. If that's not a higher calling, then I don't know what is."

Eric shook his head. Sarah did not see it. The past and future were the same here. Stefan was right. The Serbs needed to come to terms with the past, to go back before they could go forward.

"So what did you do with the tape?"

"We made contact with Dimitrović. Made it clear to him that he belonged to us now and that he would do what we told him to, starting with enthusiastic support for revising the Dayton agreement and building a new unitary Bosnian state."

"Was this after his election?"

Sarah's look was bemused and maddeningly confident.

"You still don't understand. Dimitrović was on his way up, but he hadn't made it all the way and there was no particular reason to believe that he would, at least not on his own."

Eric was stunned.

"So you got him elected president of the RS? Knowing what he was, what he had done."

"Well, we did our bit. Money. Information. Access. Positive press coverage. More money. These are the things on which political success is built. We didn't steal the election, if that's what you mean. It's been a while since we did that sort of thing. But we sure did make it easier for him. And when he won, we owned him. And we used him. And we were winning, Eric. We were so close."

There was more to the story, Eric understood.

"How did you lose control of the tape? Weren't there copies?"

"Not as many as you might think. We had to keep the operational circle on this thing small. Very small."

"Why? You guys don't do anything small."

"The operation wasn't entirely . . ." Sarah struggled visibly for the right word. "Official."

"Are you shitting me? You were running the president of the RS as an asset off-the-books without authorization?"

Sarah raised her chin in a gesture of defiance.

"Yes. We did that. I'd do it again in a heartbeat. If we went through channels, this thing would have gotten caught up in the same kind of legalisms that you were talking about. We'd never have gotten approval for what we wanted to do. What we had to do."

"Maybe there's a reason for that."

"Maybe. But the only one I can think of is the knee-jerk cowardice of bureaucracies, even . . . hell, maybe especially . . . intelligence bureaucracies. The whole torture-report fiasco has my headquarters afraid of its own shadow."

"All right. So you had your tight little team. And then somehow you lost control. What happened?" Eric could already imagine what the answer was to this question. There was no honor among thieves.

"One of our number, a talented but relatively junior analyst, saw an opportunity for self-advancement. He stole every copy of the tape and wiped the system down so cleanly that we couldn't recover so much as a byte."

"And he sold it to the Russians? Is that where Mali comes into the picture? Is he working for Moscow and the FSB?"

"No, Eric. You still don't see. The analyst who stole the tape was named Michael Kaspar. Yugoslav background. His father was Slovene. His mother was mixed Serbian and Croatian. He knows this place well and speaks the language like a native. He kept the tape for himself."

Sarah paused and looked Eric straight in the eyes before continuing.

"Marko Barcelona is Michael Kaspar. He is one of our own."

TRNOVA, BOSNIA
NOVEMBER 14
1:25 P.M.

31

Eric was numb. He was beyond feeling. The video and Sarah's revelations seemed to have overloaded both his intellectual and his emotional circuits. His thinking felt slow and clumsy, and he was moderately disoriented, something akin to the feeling of having had too much to drink.

He bit the inside of his cheek hard, hoping that simple physical pain could help him cut through the fog that clouded his brain. *What should he do with the new knowledge he had acquired? And what should he do with the videotape in his pocket? How much could he trust Sarah?*

This last question was the most difficult, the most layered, and the most painful. He loved Sarah fiercely and selflessly, but not to the point of delusion. She was unworthy of trust. It was hard to frame this thought. Unpleasant. But it was necessary for Eric to remind himself of this fundamental truth. Maybe she loved him back in some way, whatever minimal way she was capable of after allowing years of deceit to settle over the truth like a thick blanket of snow. Two decades in the world of espionage had done that to her, as it ultimately did to nearly every case officer working in the hall of mirrors.

Sarah would sacrifice him in a heartbeat in pursuit of her goals and call it duty. She would shed a tear for him, but it would be more to valorize her own heroism than to mourn Eric's loss.

They sat under Stefan's scarlet maple tree in a fragile silence, an uneasy truce. Sarah watched the priest work on his beehives. Eric studied her face. She was beautiful. But lots of women were beautiful. Sarah was more than that. She was powerful. She had a strength of will that would have driven Nietzsche to his knees in awe. It made her compelling, as addictive as the most powerful narcotic . . . and as dangerous.

Stefan finished up whatever he had been doing with his hives and rejoined Eric and Sarah at the table.

"May I sit?" he asked.

Sarah simply nodded as though she did not trust herself to speak.

"I have been thinking over what was on that tape and what it means," the priest said.

"You are not alone in that, Father," Eric replied.

"There is something else," Stefan said. "Something you should know. I am not certain if this thing is true, and it was entrusted to me under the seal of confession. If it is true, however, I cannot believe that God would will it to be kept secret. Although we who speak in his name would do well to preserve a little humility in our claims to understand what is in his heart. He is a mystery."

"Tell me, Stefan." Eric was still distracted and he was only half listening to the priest. He was finding Stefan's stereotypically Balkan thought process with its elaborate and elliptical digressions somewhat irritating.

"A man came to see me a week ago, a former soldier haunted by demons as too many former soldiers are. This man, Darko was the name he gave me, told me that he was a sniper in the war. He said that Marko Barcelona had ordered him to kill someone. A woman."

The priest looked at Sarah, his expression grave. "A woman of gold."

Sarah Gold smiled at that, a smile as enigmatic as any that the Mona Lisa had ever managed. "How flattering. A girl always likes to be the center of attention."

"So you think this could be the real thing?" Stefan asked. "I should caution you that this Darko seemed very disturbed. I was not at all convinced that his grip on what you and I would understand as reality was terribly firm."

An unsettling image of Luka Filipović's head exploding in a red-gray mist leaped unbidden to the forefront of Eric's consciousness. That incident was both more and less than real. It was surreal in a way that André Breton, Miró, or Dalí would have understood. Eric knew from the Emerald Wave file they had found in Mali's desk both that the priest was right and the threat was real.

"There's good reason to believe his story," Eric said. "I think the man who came to see you is named Darko Lukić. He was a sharpshooter in the Bosnian Serb army, one of the killers from Sniper Alley. And he may be crazy, but he's also very good at what he does."

"And I can think of reasons why Mali might want me dead," Sarah added.

If Stefan thought it odd that a Balkan mobster would want to put a hit on a woman who had introduced herself as an economic officer at the U.S. embassy, he gave no sign of it.

"Dead, yes," Eric agreed. "But there's something about this that doesn't feel right. Why a sniper? There are plenty of street toughs who would be happy to kill on Mali's say-so at close range. A sniper is an awkward weapon. The target needs to be in a known place at more or less a known time. Kennedy's motorcade in Dallas, for example, or Zoran Đinđić meeting the Swedish foreign minister at the government office in Belgrade. Even Luka Filipović at Nikola's farmhouse. Your movements are not exactly predictable, Sarah. Sending a sniper after you would seem an odd choice. Bizarre even. Outside of war, the kind of killing a sniper does is more a political statement. It's public and visceral. There are easier ways to get rid of an enemy."

"Maybe it was more important to Mali to avoid his assassin getting captured."

"Wouldn't that be even easier with a disposable piece who doesn't even know who hired him? That's been the MO for mafia hits in the Balkans for the better part of twenty years."

"What did Darko say to you exactly?" Sarah asked Stefan.

"He said he had one last job to do, to kill a woman of gold."

"Zlatna zena?" Eric asked, switching to Serbian.

"No. That's golden woman. He said *'zena od zlata.'* Literally, woman of gold."

Something urgent clawed at the back of Eric's brain, an insight that vanished into the shadows of his thoughts when he tried to seize it. He would need to coax it into the light. Let it show itself.

"*Zlatna zena* can mean a woman with a kind heart," Sarah

suggested. "If that's what he meant, he certainly wasn't talking about me."

"But *zena od zlata* is different. It's a physical thing, like a statue of a woman cast from gold," the priest replied.

"Oh, god," Eric said.

The priest's description of the difference between the two phrases was the clue he had needed. The insight that had been hiding at the dim edge of Eric's awareness stepped boldly into the light. He did not like the look of it. But it could not be easily denied. It felt true.

"We've been looking at this the wrong way. The three of us are verbal creatures. We engage with the world through language. That's why we're focused on the coincidence of Sarah's name. But Lukić is a sniper. His thinking would be more visual. Woman of gold is what he would see through the scope when he takes the shot."

"An actual woman of gold?" Sarah asked, confused.

Eric had a mental flash of long hair as pure as spun eighteen-carat gold dyed red with blood.

"No. A platinum blonde. Lukić's target is Annika Sondergaard. I'm sure of it."

"That would bring a pretty quick end to the peace conference," Sarah agreed. "But it's a huge risk on Mali's part."

"Not if what he wants is a war."

Sarah nodded, signaling agreement as much as understanding. "I can see that, yes."

"There's more," Eric said.

"Do I want to know?"

"To be effective, Lukić would need to know where Annika is going to be, a fixed time and place. There are not many of those opportunities. But one is the ceremonial opening of the peace conference at the Aleksandar Hotel in"—he looked at his watch—"a little more than two and a half hours."

Lukić shifted his position on the shooting platform slowly and patiently, as though he were moving only one muscle at a time. It was a routine he had worked out over the years. It was important to stay loose as well as focused, to find a comfortable and relaxed position that would keep his hands steady and sure. Even a small muscle cramp could throw off his aim or break his concentration. At this distance, any error would be compounded. If the shot was off by even a fraction of a degree, the bullet would miss the target by several feet. It was delicate work. Much of it was a science. Physics and chemistry. But the last little bit—the part that separated competence from brilliance—that was art.

He settled into his new position, releasing the tension that had been building in his left shoulder. His concentration never wavered. The reticle in the Zeiss optical sight remained locked in on the kill zone. The target would present herself soon enough and he would be ready.

She was beautiful, with alabaster skin and hair the color of pure gold. Lukić considered this simultaneously regrettable and exciting. He tried not to think about what he would do to her, not because he was ashamed but because it raised his pulse and made it harder to steady the rifle. The bond he would forge with the woman of gold, what they would do together, was more intimate than sex. It was forever. It was death.

His breathing quickened slightly, and he felt a rush of blood to his groin that was not unpleasant but it was distracting. He pushed thoughts of Annika Sondergaard out of his head and concentrated on the technical aspects of what would be a difficult shot.

He had built the shooting platform himself; it rose two meters off the floor in an internal room of the eighth floor of an unfinished building. The walls were raw concrete and brick, and the windows were open to the elements with no glass between Lukić and his target one thousand nine hundred and sixty-six meters away.

With a sledgehammer, he had knocked a hole in the wall approximately a meter and a half off the floor. Lying on the platform, he could sight through the hold and then through the window to the kill zone in front of the Aleksandar Hotel. There would be no muzzle flash, no noise, and no protruding rifle barrel to betray his position. He would be a silent killer, unseen and untraceable. One moment, Sondergaard would be standing there in her golden glory, and in the next, she would be his forever.

He looked away from the scope to rest his eyes, using the opportunity to check the weather on the PDA, which was receiving information from the sensors he had placed on the roof. Temperature and humidity were within the expected parameters. Wind speed was manageable. The flags of Bosnia and the EU flying in front of the hotel would be even more useful to him in gauging the speed and direction of the wind downrange. The conditions were perfect, just like those in the valley where he had practiced the shot.

Lukić pressed his eye back against the scope and did his best to ignore the ghosts. This angle, looking down into the heart of the city, was all too familiar. He had spent hundreds of hours tracking his prey on the streets of Sarajevo from sniper nests just like this. He remembered with absolute fidelity every shot he ever took. And the phantasms of victims—young and old, male and female, military and civilian—floated across both his memory and his field of vision like clouds drifting in a clear blue sky. At first, Lukić had been afraid that the ghosts were conspiring against him to ruin his shot. Hide his target. But they were too insubstantial for that. If he concentrated, he could see past them, burn holes through their torsos with an act of will as though he were Superman shooting laser beams from his eyes.

Maybe he was Superman, or a reasonable facsimile.

A small voice in his head whispered to him that he had lost his mind, that the ghosts he saw through the rifle sights were more delusion than illusion. Lukić knew that this was true and he did not care. What mattered was the shot. All that mattered was the shot.

Even from this distance, he could take her in the head. The blood would coat her chest and run like sweat in rivulets down her back.

A middle-aged woman in a black cloth coat ragged at the hem rose up from the ground in front of the Aleksandar Hotel. She stared at him, unconstrained by distance or the brick walls of the building. The sniper could see through her to the brass doors of the hotel behind her. She was a shadow. *You are dead, bitch. I killed you twenty years ago. You cannot stop me.*

His finger tightened involuntarily on the trigger, and he was a hair's breadth from sending a copper-jacketed .30 slug through a ghost into the front door of the Aleksandar. He forced his trigger finger to relax. This would ruin everything. He could no more kill this specter than he could slay his own memories. This Muslim woman in her patched coat was a part of him.

Soon, the woman of gold would be a part of him too. He would need to be patient, but not for too much longer.

After no more than thirty seconds of macho bullshit, Eric gave Sarah the keys. Twenty minutes later, he was questioning the wisdom of that decision as Sarah manhandled the Golf around a series of twisting turns on the narrow mountain road at speeds well beyond what either the car or the road were designed to handle. The State Department taught its officers defensive driving before sending them to dangerous assignments overseas. The CIA evidently trained its personnel in offensive driving as well.

"Any luck getting a signal?" Sarah asked.

Eric checked his BlackBerry, which was still reading NO SERVICE. They should have been within range of a cell tower by this point.

"Still nothing, but I'm not sure if the problem is with the phone or the cell system."

"Let me check my phone," Sarah said, taking one hand off the wheel. The speedometer read eighty-five miles an hour.

"I'll get it."

Eric fished Sarah's phone out of her jacket pocket.

"Nothing."

"Something's not right."

"Let's see if we can find a place with a landline."

Eric wanted to call ahead to warn Annika. He wanted to get through to the police, the embassy, Annika herself, Dragan, anyone who might be in a position to disrupt the assassination attempt on the EU High Representative that Eric feared was already under way. Annika had a chance to save Bosnia. Her death might destroy it.

Five miles down the road, they came to a small village with a gas station that served double duty as a convenience store. Sarah pulled up to the door.

"Wait for me here," Eric said.

There was no one minding the store. It had the unmistakable air of a business that compensated for a lack of customers with a dearth of effort. Bags of assorted snacks were lined up on a shelf by the register. A thick layer of dust had settled over the display. No one had disturbed the potato chips and peanuts in quite some time. An idea sprang almost fully formed into Eric's head, and he acted on it impulsively without taking the time to think through the risks. It took almost no time and required little more than a furtive glance over his shoulder to see if anyone was watching.

When he was done, he rang the bell on the counter, summoning a teenage attendant with stringy blond hair and bad acne from some back room.

"Just some cashews, please," Eric said, dropping the dusty bag next to the register. "And would it be possible to use your phone?" Eric asked.

"Sure. No problem." The boy pointed to a cheap Chinese handset at the far end of the counter.

Eric picked it up. There was no dial tone. He tapped the plastic switchhook repeatedly but with no result, nothing but dead air.

"It's not working," he said, trying to keep the edge of desperation out of his voice.

The boy shrugged. "Sorry."

Eric dropped two marks on the counter.

Back in the car, he told Sarah what had happened. "Both cell phones and landlines. Coincidence?" he asked.

"No way."

"Could Mali or Kaspar or whatever you want to call him do this?"

"Absolutely."

"Drive faster."

She did. There were other cars on the road, but Sarah blew by them as though they were standing still, taking chances on a few blind curves that had Eric reconsidering his committed atheism. They made it to the outskirts of Sarajevo in a little more than two hours, but there the traffic came to a complete stop. To avoid rear-ending a van, Sarah had to slam the brakes on the Golf so hard that she left skid marks. Eric could smell the burned rubber.

"What's going on?" Sarah asked.

"Police checkpoint."

The road was a tangled mess, cars and trucks had tried to drive around the line of vehicles in all directions. The gridlocked vehicles were going nowhere.

"Wait here," Eric said. "I want to see if I can get one of the cops to call in on his radio."

Eric picked his way through the traffic jam as quickly as he could. At the front of the line, the police had set up a roadblock and they were letting one car through at a time, opening both the trunk and the hood, and using mirrors and flashlights to explore the undercarriage. For good measure, a bomb-sniffing dog circled the vehicle, wagging its tail to signal its approval.

No one was in a rush. Even past the checkpoint, cars were lined up, not moving. The police must have closed off so many blocks downtown that traffic had ground to a halt across the city.

The checkpoint was manned by the Federation's Ministry of

the Interior. Like almost every other institution in the country, the police were split in two. The Federation had one structure and the RS had its own police force, with its own command and its own political overlords. There was little communication and almost no cooperation between the parallel police forces.

Eric picked out the one cop who did not seem to be doing anything. He was almost certainly the one in charge.

"Officer," he said urgently, "I have an emergency."

"Everyone here has a fucking emergency," the cop answered. He was middle-aged and thick around the middle, and wore a dark-blue uniform and an NYPD-style peaked cap. His features were all oversize. His ears and nose seemed too large for his head. There was an automatic pistol holstered to his belt and, most important for Eric, a radio.

"My name is Petrosian. I'm an American diplomat and I have reason to believe that EU High Representative Annika Sondergaard is the target of an assassination attempt. I need to get in touch with your headquarters."

To Eric's surprise, the cop laughed. It was not the reaction he had anticipated.

"Sure. Go ahead and file a report. So far we've had sixteen bomb threats, two of them nuclear; four reports of a sniper; three calls from people with information about plans to crash the High Representative's motorcade with a garbage truck or a cement mixer; and one call from a man who insisted he was Gavrilo Princip reborn and Sondergaard was his Franz Ferdinand. Which one are you?"

"There is a shooter," Eric insisted, but even to himself he sounded slightly deranged, just one in a series of fanciful reports. "I work with High Representative Annika Sondergaard and her life is in danger. I want you to use the radio to put me in touch with your headquarters."

The policeman looked at him dismissively.

"We're already doing everything we can to ensure security." He gestured at the long line of cars backed up for hundreds of meters. "Now please get back in your vehicle."

Eric fumbled in his pocket for his wallet and pulled out his diplomatic ID card.

"I'm an American official and I am asking for your assistance."

"You can submit the request in writing to the Ministry of Foreign Affairs. I'm sure they'll be interested in helping you."

Eric looked at his watch. Sondergaard would be meeting the delegations arriving at the Aleksandar Hotel in less than thirty minutes. He had no time to argue with a beat cop at a checkpoint.

From up here in the hills, Eric could almost see the hotel. He thought about running but doubted that he could make it in the time available. The Aleksandar fronted the old Sniper Alley. It was just a few blocks from the intersection where Eric's ghost made his home. His eyes tracked Sniper Alley back up to the hills on the far north of the city. A building halfway up the slope caught his attention. It was unfinished, but it had an almost perfect line of sight to the Aleksandar. It would be an ideal location for a sniper nest except that it would be a very long shot. A mile, maybe more. The shooter would have to be very, very good. Dragan had assured him that Lukić was the best. And Eric had seen his handiwork up close. He had no doubt that the veteran was capable of making the shot.

"Officer, I need you to do something for me. I need you to get a message through your channels to Dragan Klicković at the Aleksandar Hotel and tell him to meet me at that building over there right now. Do you see which one I mean?"

Almost involuntarily, the Bosnian cop looked where Eric was pointing.

"Yes."

"Will you make that call?"

"You have to understand. We're all overloaded. There's only so much we can do."

"I just need you to make this call. Can you do that?"

The cop sighed as though he were being asked to carry the weight of the world. "I'll do what I can."

It was the best Eric was going to get. He turned and ran back to Sarah.

SARAJEVO
NOVEMBER 14
3:26 P.M.

32

Sarah pushed the Golf through the backstreets as if she were on the final lap at Le Mans, downshifting into the turns and accelerating hard into the short stretches of straightaway. Her eyes were fixed on the road and her movements were sharp and economical. But she somehow managed to keep up an almost nonstop stream of chatter.

"You understand that we have almost no evidence to back up this theory you've constructed. Golden girls. Middle-aged snipers. Penitent priests. It has a lot of moving parts, none of them solid."

"I know," Eric said, hanging on to the grab handle tightly to keep himself from being bounced around the inside of the car. "But the pieces fit together in a way that makes sense. You feel it too."

"How do you know?"

"You wouldn't be driving like this if you didn't."

"You may have a point. But you haven't seen my commute to Langley."

"If I'm wrong, we've lost nothing. But if I'm right, we could lose everything. We have to assume this is real."

The side of the Golf scraped a lamppost with an ear-splitting screech as Sarah cut a turn a little too sharp. She did not even bother to slow down.

"Sorry about the paint job."

"It's okay. I never liked this color. Keep driving."

Like Bosnia itself, the building in which Eric suspected the sniper was hiding was an ambitious project that was only half finished. The contractors had completed the ten-story shell of reinforced concrete and red brick before running out of money. It was a common problem in the region. Capital was always in desperately short supply. Construction projects, even big ones, often went forward right on the bleeding edge of solvency. Undaunted by failure, bankrupt builders would often scrape together just enough money to try again on a different project with a new set of investors, abandoning their earlier effort to the weeds and rats.

Half-built apartment blocks were common on the city's fringe, leering down from the hillside like desiccated skulls. What differentiated this zombie building from all the others in Sarajevo was that this one had a perfect line of sight down Sniper Alley to the Aleksandar Hotel.

Sarah stopped the car a block from the building.

"If the shooter is really in there, we don't want him to see us coming," she explained to Eric. "Plus, he could have a spotter or a lookout of some kind."

"Okay. I'll follow your lead. I've never done anything like this before."

"Baby, no one has done anything like this."

Sarah reached into her purse and pulled out a small pistol.

"You get the girl gun," she said. "It's only a .22, so aim for the head. If the shooter is wearing body armor, those dainty little bullets will bounce off him like he was the Incredible Hulk."

"What about you?"

"I have a SIG Sauer under my jacket. I'll be fine."

"I'm still hoping that Dragan shows up with the cavalry."

"Don't count on it. We're on our own."

They worked their way to the back of the building, trying to stay out of the sight lines of a shooter or spotter in one of the apartments facing the city. The street was lined with modest older two-story homes. There were a few people on the street, most of them modest and older as well. The pavement ended abruptly, and the last fifty meters to the abandoned apartment building were across a litter-strewn field of weeds that glittered with broken glass. A few large chunks of rusted twisted metal stood in the field like a modernist sculpture.

Weeds were growing up the side of the building, the wind-blown seeds having taken root in the mortar between the bricks. A few weeds big enough to be classified as saplings poked out of some of the windows on the higher floors.

Eric looked at his watch.

"The delegates will start arriving in ten minutes. We've got to hurry."

Sarah nodded in agreement but gestured helplessly at the apartment block in front of them.

"This is a big fucking building. I'm not even sure where to start."

"Right there," Eric said, pointing to a Mitsubishi 4×4 parked near the back door to the building. There was only one reason for a jeep to be parked there. It was a getaway car.

They moved quickly to the door. Eric grabbed Sarah's arm before she could step across the threshold. He pointed at the floor, which was covered in a layer of concrete dust a quarter of an inch thick. A set of boot prints was easily visible in the dust. The sharp patterns seemed to indicate that the prints were fresh.

"That's the trail," Eric said. "We have eight minutes."

The prints led upstairs. There were multiple sets of tracks, but they all had the same tread pattern, seeming to indicate that a single person had made several trips.

Eric and Sarah took the stairs two at a time. Sarah had drawn her SIG Sauer and carried it in a two-hand grip at shoulder height pointed at the ceiling. The .22 in Eric's hand felt too light to be a real weapon. It seemed more like a toy. Eric had no illusions about his abilities. He had fired pistols at paper targets in a State Department counterterrorism training program, but that was about it. The man they were pursuing was a battle-hardened veteran with a serious rifle. Eric carried the small pistol away from his body and pointed toward the floor, trying to shake the feeling that this was all some kind of game, like an elaborate form of laser tag.

By the time they reached the third story, Eric's breathing was ragged and uneven. It was not from exertion, but from fear.

"Be careful," Sarah whispered in Eric's ear. "There could be traps or alarms of some sort on the stairwell. Look where you step."

"Will do," Eric croaked. It was the shortest reply he could think of. He could barely speak. His throat was tight. His mouth was as dry as sandpaper and tasted of bile.

Just ahead of him, Sarah climbed the stairs with the grace and surety of a big cat stalking prey. Whatever she was feeling, her surface mask was all calm confidence. Eric envied her.

Windows were cut into the walls of the stairwell at each landing, letting in enough light to navigate. They had also let in the rain, which had mixed with the concrete dust to create a viscous sludge that clung to their shoes. As they moved higher, the Aleksandar Hotel came into view rising with each successive level like the moon. They were getting close.

The boot prints led them to the eighth floor. The interior corridor had no windows, but light leaked through from the empty door frames to the apartments on both sides. Still, the corridor was dim and musty. The tracks diverged. The bulk of the prints, however, pointed to one apartment in the middle of the corridor, right next to the gaping hole where the elevators were eventually supposed to go. Sarah nudged Eric and gestured with her head toward the door frame. Eric strained to listen for any noise coming from inside. There was nothing.

Whatever gods had conspired to put a diplomat armed with a toy pistol in this position must be having a good laugh about now, Eric thought. *Maybe this would all turn out to be about nothing, just a squatter or a drug den.* But while Eric's doubts about himself were eating away at his confidence, he had no doubts about the danger Annika was in. He would rather Dragan were here instead of him, or one of Sarah's snake-eating colleagues from the CIA's Special Operations Group. But it was just he and Sarah. There was no one else.

They lined up on opposite sides of the door. Sarah held up three fingers and counted them off.

Three . . . two . . . one . . .

They stepped through the door, guns leveled, scanning for signs of the shooter. The apartment was bigger than Eric had expected. They were standing in a center hall or sitting room of some kind with doors on all three of the interior walls leading to other rooms. The boot prints were not much help. There were tracks just about everywhere. Eric saw sawdust mixed in with the reddish gray dirt on the floor and he could smell freshly cut wood.

Sarah gestured toward what Eric supposed was to have been the living room, with big picture windows looking out on the city. Eric shook his head. The snipers in the war, the professionals, at least, if not the weekend Chetniks who looked at long-distance murder in the same way they might have looked at a hunting trip with the boys, had preferred interior rooms for their nests. The sawdust, he suspected, was from the construction of a shooting platform. It was just like old times.

Darko would be in one of the interior rooms. But which one? He glanced quickly at his watch. Three minutes until three o'clock. Maybe the delegates would be late. They usually were. But he did not want to bet Annika's life on it.

The room to the left looked brighter than the one on the right. Maybe that room had a door toward the outside wall of the apartment. There were several small metallic objects on the floor of that room. They looked like shell casings. Eric touched Sarah's arm and pointed to them. She nodded.

Without the frame, the doorway was wide enough for them to walk through together. On Sarah's signal, they stepped into the room, guns leveled. Eric's foot caught the edge of the door frame and he stumbled, his finger slipping off the trigger of the small pistol. There was a platform along the back wall that smelled of green wood. A sniper's nest.

It was empty. The room was empty.

There was a hole in the wall across from the shooting platform. Someone had smashed through the bricks with a sledgehammer. Each brick was about the size of a cinder block, but they were hollow and the composition was more like ceramic tile than stone. Through the hole in the wall, Eric could see one of the apartment's gaping picture windows, and through the window, he could see the Aleksandar Hotel a mile away.

The shooting platform was here. So where the hell was Lukić?

The delegates should be arriving right about now. The sniper should have been here waiting for the shot.

Eric stepped closer to the platform. There was a thin blanket laid over the wood as a cushion. An iPad was lying flat on the blanket. The screen was dark. He touched the home button and a picture appeared on the screen upside down relative to Eric. It took a moment to process what he was seeing. It was a split-screen image of the front and back entrances to the apartment building. The sniper had seen them coming on closed-circuit TV.

"Where is he?" Sarah hissed.

From somewhere in the apartment, Eric heard the distinctive metallic click of a rifle bolt being pulled back.

Eric understood what had happened. The shell casings on the floor were bait. They were trapped.

"Where the fuck is he?" Sarah said again, more urgently this time.

Sarah was pressed up against the wall to the entryway. One of the large bricks no more than a foot from her head exploded like a bomb, sending shards of sharp ceramic shooting across the room. A piece of brick grazed Eric's forehead, opening up a long cut. Blood started to run down the side of his face.

From the other side of the wall, the rifle bolt clicked shut.

Another brick exploded, this one to Sarah's left. Eric ducked as pieces of brick shot past his head.

He looked around the room for cover of some kind. There was nothing. But his eyes lit on the hole in the wall that Lukić had made for his shot. It was just barely big enough.

Without thinking about what he was about to do, Eric ran toward the wall and leaped headfirst through the hole. He gripped the pistol tightly. If he lost it, he would have nothing.

Eric tried to roll, but his landing was more of a sprawl that knocked the wind from him. His chest tight, he scrambled to his feet and shot wildly through the door into the front hall. Sarah, he could hear, was firing through the holes that Lukić had made shooting at them through the wall.

Eric stepped through the doorway into the front room, blinded by a deep anger that had hovered over his whole life. He fired his pistol at the sniper, but he was also shooting at Pol Pot and Brother Number Two of Cambodia's Khmer Rouge, Slobodan Milošević and Radovan Karadžić, and Mehmed Talaat Pasha and the Ottoman elite who ordered two million Armenians to their death. He was shooting at the agents of genocide, the nameless soldiers and thugs who killed under orders from a corrupt and twisted leadership. He kept firing his pistol until the trigger clicked on an empty chamber.

The shooter was gone. He was hiding somewhere back in the dark rooms of the unfinished apartment. Eric had no way of knowing how far back the warren of rooms might run and had no desire to chase the armed sniper back into the dark. He felt drained, as though he had just run for miles in thin Alpine air.

Sarah appeared at his side.

"We should go after him," she said.

Eric shook his head and pointed wordlessly toward the front door. Sarah understood.

They stood on either side of the door in the hallway outside of the apartment pressed up hard against the wall. Better to make Lukić come to them, Eric reasoned.

They did not have long to wait.

The rifle barrel emerged slowly from the apartment, weighed down by the bipod at the end of the muzzle. It was a heavy weapon, not well suited to this kind of close-quarters fighting. Eric grabbed the barrel and pulled forward and down, hoping to get Lukić off balance and give Sarah a clean shot. But the old soldier was quicker than Eric had anticipated. Instead of following the weapon, he leaped at Eric, grabbing his jacket collar and his wrist, and taking him to the ground.

Eric fell backward and they rolled on the ground struggling for leverage. The heavy rifle was in between them, and Eric's right hand got wrapped up in the harness webbing. He lashed out ineffectually with his left hand. Lukić's elbow caught Eric on the jaw, and there was a sharp pain as a tooth cracked. Eric grabbed the rifle with his free hand and used it as a lever to roll Lukić hard to his right.

The sniper landed in space. They had been fighting right next to the open elevator shaft and Darko was now dangling eight stories up. The only thing that kept him from falling was the harness webbing wrapped tightly around Eric's right hand. Eric felt himself slipping toward the edge. There was nothing to grab onto, and the concrete dust everywhere made it impossible for Eric to get any kind of grip on the floor. The sniper was shouting foul Serbian curse words strung together in a nonsensical fashion. He was trying to swing to safety on the floor below but succeeded only in tangling himself further in the harness. With each failed lunge for safety, Lukić dragged Eric another quarter inch toward the edge.

Just when Eric felt that he was about to go over, Sarah grabbed one of his legs and pulled hard. She climbed onto his back, and Eric saw that her right hand was holding a six-inch knife with a black ceramic blade. Fearlessly, Sarah leaned forward into the open space of the elevator shaft and slashed at the webbing wrapped around Eric's wrist. The blade sliced through the nylon like it wasn't even there, and Darko Lukić screamed as he plunged eighty feet down the dark elevator shaft to the concrete floor.

Eric's wrist burned where the nylon webbing had rubbed it raw. He tried to sit up, but Sarah was still lying on top of him, pressed tightly against his spine. He felt the sharp tip of her knife touch lightly on his neck right along the carotid artery.

"Sorry, lover," she said, "but I need that tape."

SARAJEVO
NOVEMBER 14
4:15 P.M.

33

Eric was disappointed but not especially surprised. When Sarah wanted something, she went after it hard. And God help whatever or whoever was in her way. Eric had seen it before, but never quite so personal.

The knife was wickedly sharp. The point of the blade stretched the skin on Eric's neck taut. Sarah would need just a slight increase in pressure to slip the knife into the artery in his neck.

"Are you really going to kill me, Sarah?"

"I don't want to, but I need that tape. Hand it over."

"That's going to be something of a problem," Eric said.

"What kind of problem?"

"I don't have it."

The pressure on his neck eased and Eric rolled over onto his back. Sarah was still on top of him, straddling his thighs. It was intimate. Erotic. Her left hand pressed down on his right shoulder. The right hand held the blade against his neck. Loosely now. Blood ran down the side of Eric's face from the cut on his forehead, mixing with the concrete dust.

Sarah leaned forward until her face was no more than inches from his. Her breath was warm on his cheek. If it wasn't for the knife at his throat, he would have taken it as an invitation to kiss her.

"What do you mean, you don't have it?" she asked incredulously. "It was in your jacket pocket."

With her left hand, Sarah patted his chest and sides, feeling for the telltale boxy shape of the videocassette. She found nothing.

"Where is it? Where did you put it?"

"Someplace safe."

"Why?"

"I thought you might try to steal it. It never occurred to me that you might be willing to kill me to get it. I'm still not entirely persuaded."

"No? Care to place a little wager on it?"

"Not really, no."

Sarah stood up slowly, tossing her hair to the side of her face with a quick shake of her head. It was a thing she did that Eric had always liked. Sarah knew it and she used it. When Eric looked at her hands, the knife was gone, back in its hidden sheath. Where the knife had been, Sarah was holding her SIG Sauer. It was sleight of hand worthy of a stage magician.

"Let me reason with you, lover," she said, as Eric stumbled clumsily to his feet. His body felt stiff and sore from the fight with the sniper, and his muscles were tense and soaked with adrenaline. He felt he might vomit.

"Reason was never really your strongest suit," Eric said. He leaned on a concrete pillar for support.

"I have the facts on my side," Sarah replied. She was pointing the gun at his feet rather than at his chest, but it was menacing enough. The steel beneath the velvet glove. "We want the same thing, Eric. To stop a war. No more killing. No more genocide. We can do that, but I need that tape."

"No, you don't, Sarah. With this tape as evidence the tribunal will take all of ten minutes to issue an indictment against Dimitrović. With Dimitrović gone, Mali—Kaspar—is nothing. He loses all of his influence. That opens the political space for people like Nikola and the peace movement in the RS. The Serbs are as sick and tired of the killing as anyone. The public wants peace. They want a deal. Annika can deliver that. Putting Dimitrović in prison will guarantee it."

"Guarantee? Really, Eric? What kind of assurances can you offer? How the fuck do you know what's going to happen with the Sondergaard Plan? Maybe it'll all work out and we'll all join hands and sing 'Kumbaya' around the campfire. Or maybe it'll fall apart like every other Bosnian peace plan and they'll all go back to killing each other, only this time our leverage over the sides won't amount to diddly-squat because you'll have wasted it putting one guy in a cushy Dutch prison with cable TV and turndown service.

"We saw what we can do with that tape. With it, we can control Dimitrović and make him dance to our tune. Then we can force the sides to a permanent peace whether they want it or not. I have real empirical evidence to back up my position. Hard facts. You have hopes and a saccharine-sweet belief in human perfectability.

People aren't like that, Eric. People are rat bastards who will rob you blind if you give them a six-inch opening. It's in our nature."

"You're wrong, Sarah. About me. About Annika. About Bosnia. You don't know this place like I do. You don't know these people."

"These people have been fertilizing their fields with the blood of their neighbors for a thousand years. You can't believe that they've put that behind them. You can't trust them to know what's in their own best interest. We saw that in the nineties in spades."

Sarah's eyes were tough and flinty. Eric could hear the passion and intensity in her voice. She believed what she was saying, believed absolutely.

"I don't give a shit who did what to who in the last century or six centuries before that, and neither do the vast majority of people on any side. They just want it all to be over."

"But you do care about who killed who two decades ago, don't you?"

Eric could see the blow coming as though in slow motion, but there was nothing he could do to protect himself from it. There was no defense against the truth.

"Is this all about you, Eric?" Sarah continued. "You get on your high horse and spout righteous nonsense, but this is really about Meho. Your guilt and your need for absolution. It's selfish and narcissistic. Is it so important to you to punish your friend's killer that you'd risk the lives of thousands of others? Tens of thousands? How many is too many? How many does it take to tip the scales?"

Eric was at a loss. He did not know the answer. Sarah had put her finger right on a question that had been scratching on the edge of his conscious thinking. Sarah was both well trained and intuitive. She sensed his confusion, and as was standard practice in her profession when finding a soft spot, she drilled down until she hit bone.

"That's it, isn't it?" she said almost triumphantly. "This is all about you. You feel bad and you think exposing Dimitrović as Captain Zero will make it all square. That it will fix whatever's wrong with you. And maybe it's about your mother as well. The Khmer Rouge killed her as surely as if they had put a gun to her head. You couldn't get Brother Number One, but maybe Captain Zero will make up for that in some way. Why not? Ones and Zeros. But life isn't binary, Eric. It's all gray. And what's at stake right now in this country is a damn sight bigger than you and your burden of guilt."

"What about justice?" Eric asked, and he could hear the weakness in his response, feel himself losing the argument.

"What about it? Does it bring the dead back to life? Does it make the trauma of rape fade into the background for the thousands of victims? Justice is an abstraction. But what is going to happen here if you don't give me that tape is going to be very, very real. The past is a foreign country. The past is history. What matters is the future."

"Without the past, there is no future." It sounded lame even as he said it. Trite. Empty.

"Where's the tape, Eric?"

"You don't need it. This can work. What Annika and I are doing. With Dimitrović gone, it can work."

"You can't know that."

"I believe it."

"I can't afford to believe."

"I can't afford not to."

"I don't give a shit."

"So what happens now?"

Sarah shot him.

It was intensely painful, and the pain as much as the force of the bullet knocked him hard to the concrete floor. But he knew that Sarah had taken careful aim. She had hit him in the upper leg, missing the bone. The bullet had carved a deep gash in his thigh. Blood was running freely from the wound and pooling on the floor, but there was none of the arterial gushing that would have indicated a serious injury. Eric had no doubt that Sarah could inflict that kind of wound if she chose to. This was a warning.

He struggled to a sitting position, back pressed against the pillar and his hand pressed against the wound in his thigh.

"Was that really necessary?"

"You tell me."

"Goddamn it, Sarah, you shot me."

"Yes. And I'll shoot you again if you don't give me the tape. The next one's going to hurt."

"So that's how it is with you now? Torture's okay as long as the ends justify the means. Did you guys learn nothing from Guantánamo and Abu Ghraib?"

The flow of blood from his leg was already beginning to slacken. It hurt like hell, but it did not seem dangerous. He stretched the leg slightly to see if he might stand on it. A white-hot sheet of pain made him think better of it.

Sarah saw what he was doing.

"You'll live, Eric. But I'm not screwing around here. The next round takes a knee. That one's forever. I'm sorry about this. I really am. But there's too much at stake."

"I can't believe you would really do that."

"Try harder."

Sarah swung the SIG Sauer to point at his right kneecap.

"Please, Eric," she said, and there was a note of desperation in her voice. "I don't want to do this. Don't make me do this. Don't make me be the monster."

"Then don't be one."

"Give me the goddamn tape."

"No."

His obstinacy was surprising even to himself. But he believed every word of what he had said to Sarah even if he had not persuaded her. Maybe she was right about his guilt over Meho driving him. Maybe it was because of the ghosts that had haunted him from the day he had found his mother's body in the garage. But there was more to it than that. Without justice, without an honest accounting of the past, whatever future was built in Bosnia would be unstable. Brittle. The peace plan that Annika and he had been fighting for could work. But only if the foundation was strong. Sarah's way was an illusion. A shortcut. There were no shortcuts.

"I'm sorry, Eric," she said. "Sorry about what I've done and sorry about what comes next."

He felt it before he heard it. Vibrations in the concrete that became footsteps. Someone was coming up the stairs.

Sarah sensed it as well. She turned toward the stairwell as two black-clad policemen rushed toward them through the gloom. These were not traffic cops. Their uniforms marked them as Special Police, expensively trained by the United States as part of the Global War on Terror. They wore body armor and tactical helmets, and carried evil-looking machine pistols.

Eric realized that Dragan must have gotten his message and that he had sent in the heavies. The job of the Special Police was not to make arrests.

"Sarah, don't!" Eric shouted, as she raised her weapon unthinkingly, reflexively.

The U.S.-trained antiterror police did not hesitate. They had rehearsed this scenario or one like it a thousand times. This was combat and Sarah was a target.

"Ne pucaj!" Eric called out helplessly, as he rose to his feet ignoring the pain in his thigh. *Don't shoot!*

But they shot, first and expertly.

Eric saw three holes appear in Sarah's back where the bullets from their machine pistols had passed straight through her torso.

The SIG clattered to the floor and Sarah spun to face Eric before collapsing into his arms. Eric went to his knees, cradling her head to keep it from hitting the floor.

Dragan appeared at the top of the landing, puffing and red with the exertion of the climb. He was no longer a young man. It took the former spy no more than a few seconds to process the scene.

"Kreteni!" he bellowed at the two men who had shot Sarah. *Idiots!*

Eric held Sarah to his chest as if they were lovers again. He could feel the sticky warmth of her blood soaking his jacket and shirt.

Her eyes were vacant and lifeless.

Just like he felt.

TRNOVA, BOSNIA
NOVEMBER 16

34

The bees were settled in for the winter. Soon Stefan and the monks down the hill would be doing the same. Winter in the mountains could be long and hard. The monks had laid in their store of provisions to see them through to spring. Cheese and smoked meat. Preserved fruit and jars of honey. There were potatoes and parsnips in the root cellar and oak barrels full of brine and cabbage heads that were slowly pickling. They would bake fresh bread in the monastery's wood-fired ovens and wash it all down with the occasional glass of brandy.

The monastery had survived more than five hundred winters, and there was no reason to believe that it would not last for five hundred more.

Stefan had just finished installing the entrance cleats that would keep field mice from seeking shelter in the hives from the winter cold. He had also sealed the hives to guard against condensation. Bees were like people. They could survive the cold, but cold and wet would lead to hypothermia and that could kill the colony.

With that done, the bees would need little enough from him until spring. Winter was hard, but it was also a peaceful season. There was less labor and more time for quiet reflection. Even after twenty years, Stefan still had a great deal to reflect on. He remembered reading somewhere that the Chinese had a curse: May you live in interesting times. His time had certainly been interesting, and he understood full well what the anonymous sage from the Far East had meant. Interesting times required a man to choose. Stefan had chosen poorly. He would spend the rest of his life atoning for the choices he had made as a younger man when the times in Bosnia had been at their most interesting.

He had also made a mistake in agreeing to be the keeper of Mali's secrets. He knew that now. After he had watched the tape of the Srebrenica murders, that conclusion was unavoidable. But it had been a deal with the devil from the very beginning and he should have seen it. He should have been stronger. No matter the good he had been able to do with Mali's money, nothing pure could grow from an evil seed.

Stefan was glad that he had given the tape to the Americans. They were an odd people, Americans. They were like the Romans, vital and energetic, but limited in ways that they did not seem to understand. Their penchant for messianic thinking, for believing it their responsibility to remake the world in their own image, was especially hard to understand. You would think the Americans would learn from experience, but they seemed to repeat the same mistakes from Vietnam to Yugoslavia to Iraq to Afghanistan. The

Americans were like some medieval physician prescribing a cure that was too often worse than the disease.

Still, he had liked the two who had come to see him. They seemed different. Less arrogant. Less entitled than the politicians and "peacemakers" he remembered from the 1990s.

They had taken the time to learn the language and the culture of the society they were working in, and they did not pretend to have all the answers. There had been something between those two, a spark of attraction and conflict that was unmistakable. They made an interesting pair, the man with dark skin and the woman of gold. He hoped she lived. Stefan did not listen to the news anymore, but if Darko from Vukovar had succeeded in murdering either the EU High Representative or an American embassy official, it was likely that he would have heard about it in some fashion.

Stefan stood by the chapel looking out across the valley. The sky was iron gray and it looked like it would rain soon. It would be a cold rain, the harbinger of winter.

A black jeep, one of the big ones, crested the rise and bounced down the uneven road to the monastery trailing a brown cloud of dust. Stefan knew that it was not a local vehicle. Farmers and villagers did not drive cars like that. Neither did monks or pilgrims. The big black jeeps were for politicians and businessmen and gangsters. It could sometimes be hard to tell them apart. Those groups mixed easily, often within the same person.

The jeep parked by the monastery and two men in dark suits got out. Even from his distant vantage on the hill, Stefan could see that they were large men. Tall and broad. Muscle rather than brains.

The men stopped one of the young monks and spoke to him. The monk pointed up the hill at Stefan's chapel. At Stefan.

The two men climbed the hill through the tall grass. For such big men, their steps were oddly light and mincing as they dodged piles of sheep shit.

Stefan waited for them patiently, for the unavoidable, the inevitable.

When they reached the top, the men walked straight toward him. Their shirts and ties matched their shoes. All black. All they needed were hoods and a scythe to complete the look. For these men, the priest knew, were death itself.

"Father Stefan?" the larger of the two large men asked. His hair was cut military short and he wore dark sunglasses on an overcast day. His partner had longer hair pulled back in a ponytail and a three-day growth of beard.

"Yes," Stefan said. "That is my name and title."

"Mali sent us," the man with the ponytail said, as though that were at all necessary. Who else would have sent men like these?

Stefan nodded his acknowledgment of their bona fides.

"You have something of his that you are keeping for him." This was the larger man again. They seemed to take turns like two priests sharing a benediction.

"Marko Barcelona gave me something to look after," Stefan answered.

Ponytail's eyes narrowed some as he considered the carefully worded response. Muscle, but not stupid, the priest realized.

"Mali would like it back. He sent us to fetch it," Ponytail said.

"How interesting. You're too late, I'm afraid. The other two already came for it."

The look of alarm on their faces was understandable, and Stefan felt himself moved to sympathy. Mali was not the kind to limit the responsibility for failure. The consequences for which could be severe.

"What do you mean, priest?" It was Crew Cut's turn. "There is no one else. We are the ones Mali sent."

"The others came here two days ago. A man and a woman. They knew what I was holding for Mali and they asked for it. I gave it to them."

"How did you know that they worked for Mali?"

"Same way I know that you do. Who else would know about our arrangement? I certainly didn't tell anyone."

Stefan was careful in his responses. He did not want to meet his maker with a lie on his lips. There had been enough lies. But the truth was a malleable thing, not fixed and firm. If anyone knew this, it was priests.

Ponytail unbuttoned his suit jacket and reached inside with his right hand.

"If we can't bring Mali the package, we will have to bring him your head. Tell us everything you know about the people who came here and told you they were with Mali, and it will be quick. Otherwise this could take some time."

"You wouldn't kill a priest, surely. It's a grave sin."

"No, Father. I am a godly man. But Suleiman here is from Sandžak and he's a follower of Muhammad. I don't think your death will disturb his sleep."

"No," Stefan agreed. "I don't suppose it will matter much to anyone. Just to my bees."

KRIVA RIJEKA
NOVEMBER 18

35

It had all fallen apart so quickly. Mali still could not understand where he had gone wrong. The first sign had been Gisler's unexplained disappearance. Then, Lukić's failure to kill that Danish bitch, Sondergaard. And finally Stefan's betrayal. Sarah had beaten him. And Sarah was dead. Even in death, she was screwing up his plans. Goddamn her.

She had demeaned him and disrespected him so many times back at Langley that he had lost count. When Michael Kaspar had skipped town and become Marko "Mali" Barcelona, he had more than evened the score, ruining her clever little Parsifal ploy. Sarah had struck back, however, and now it was Mali who was undone. His paid informants had told him that the tribunal had physical evidence that it was going to use to bring genocide charges against Dimitrović. They had the tape. Sarah must have given it to her puppy from the State Department before she was shot, reportedly by a Bosnian SWAT team in a case of mistaken identity. Served the frigid bitch right.

Once the tribunal went public with the tape and the indictment, it would all be over. Mali would lose his hold on Dimitrović and then on power. Then his enemies would step out of the shadows, and he had no illusions about their number. They were numerous and influential, and they would sing glad songs as they drank a victory toast from his skull.

It was time to run.

No one would ever call the CIA nimble.

The bureaucracy could be dense and impenetrable. Getting the Agency to change direction was like turning an ocean liner. It took time and space.

Once VW had jumped through the initial hoops, however, this action had been surprisingly easy to arrange. She had filled out more forms the last time she had needed to change the toner cartridge in her printer.

It shouldn't be this easy. It shouldn't be so simple to kill a man.

What VW had found most shocking was that there was an existing protocol to manage this kind of situation. It happened often enough that it had its own rules and procedures. The first and most important rule was never to write anything down. No memos. No e-mails. Nothing discoverable by a congressional committee. No phone calls. No texts. Nothing that could be tapped by a foreign intelligence service. This was all managed in face-to-face discussions in secure rooms.

The protocol was called Red Elegy. But those read into the program had a different name with the same initials. Rogue Elephant. A bull that had broken faith with the herd. It was a problem that had only one solution.

"Okay, Victoria. This is your show. Are you ready?"

It took VW a moment to realize the man was talking to her. Not many people called her Victoria. And she was not at all certain that she wanted to think of this as her show.

"I'm ready, Walther."

Walther Menendez was a genuine big shot. He was the deputy director for operations, and he was here as the personal representative of the CIA director herself. It was Menendez's job to make sure that no one at the White House or the Office of the Director of National Intelligence ever learned about it. The Agency cleaned up its own messes. And it was Menendez who ultimately had to give the thumbs-up or thumbs-down on a Rogue Elephant operation.

After hearing what VW had to say and seeing the pictures for himself, it had not taken him more than five minutes to give the green light.

"Let's get started."

Menendez was a veteran of the Clandestine Service, but he was more like a smooth political operator than the used-car salesmen and knuckle draggers VW had come to expect as the norm on the operations side of the house. His blue suit had creases so sharp, it looked like origami. His red tie stood out in bold relief against a striped shirt with French cuffs. His thinning hair was slicked back and gelled tightly against his scalp like a monk's cap.

They were in the drone-operations room in the subbasement where VW and Landis had flown the Wyvern on its initial reconnaissance of Kaspar's mountain sanctuary. But now the room had been cleared of all but a handful of people. Those present carried secrets inside their heads that could start half a dozen wars, unsettle the global economy, and bring down governments, including, no doubt, their own. It was better not to think in those terms, or the secrets would begin to feel like a crushing weight.

"Bob, can you put it on screen, please?"

The giant LED screen that dominated the room flickered briefly and displayed a sweeping view of a rugged mountain valley. Technical data was overlaid in yellow in the upper-right corner.

"Tell me what I'm looking at, Victoria," Menendez said. He knew perfectly well what this was. VW understood that he was trying to keep her cool and focused. His faux ignorance ensured that there was nothing condescending in the gesture. VW was confident that Menendez had been a hell of a case officer in his day.

"This is the Kriva Rijeka Valley. It's where Kaspar built his little retreat, running his empire out of splendid isolation. He must have known that Sarah Gold and the Parsifal team would come after him. This was his solution. I think he wanted to be like Peachey Carnehan in that Kipling novella, *The Man Who Would Be King*."

"Interesting," Menendez said. "You remember what happened to Carnehan in that story after he set himself up as a god-king? The thing that brought him down?"

"Yes," VW replied. "His subjects saw his partner bleed. They realized that they weren't gods."

"Indeed. Can you see the villa from here?"

"Almost. Bob, how far out are we?"

"Twenty seconds."

The young pilot at the controls used a joystick and track pad to input commands, and the picture of the valley swung sharply to the left as the Wyvern-B adjusted course.

The Wyvern-B was top of the line, larger and heavier than the Wyvern-A that VW and Landis had used on their last visit to the valley. It had a greater range, better optics, and certain additional capabilities.

The high-resolution camera and the enormous curved LED screen in the drone-operations suite resulted in an image that was so real, VW felt her stomach jump as the Wyvern banked. This was a far cry from the grainy black-and-white feed from the early days of drone warfare. It was closer to a Disneyland ride than a video game.

The villa came into view and the Basilisk's Eye camera system zoomed in for a close-up. The optical quality was so good that the quick change in perspective on the giant screen made VW feel as though she were falling. She had always hated roller coasters.

"What's the tactical situation?" Menendez asked.

"We had a pair of Wyvern-Bs passing the baton all night, keeping watch over the villa. Kaspar arrived home last night at eleven twenty from Banja Luka with two men we believe are security. One guard is posted outside. The other is somewhere in the house. It's now oh six thirty in Bosnia. Kaspar is most likely in the master bedroom. We have acquired the floor plans for the building through an asset on the ground. We know which room is Kaspar's from the plans. There's a chance he's in his study. It won't matter either way. According to the plans, the study is hardened, but only against something on the order of a car bomb. Not this."

"Okay. Let's do this thing. VW, we're here because of you. You give the orders."

VW swallowed hard. She understood the nature of their business, the hard choices they had to make. But she had always found a way to duck direct responsibility for this kind of thing up until now. It wasn't that Kaspar did not deserve this. He did. But that didn't make what she had to do any easier.

"Get me a lock," VW said, and she was pleased with herself that there was no wavering in her voice.

A red targeting reticle appeared on the screen and lined up with one of the windows, fixing into place even as the UAV continued to turn in lazy circles high up and out of sight over the villa.

"Lock established," the UAV pilot said. "Clean and clear."

"Open the doors."

"Doors are open."

VW paused for an extra beat. This next step could not be undone. There was really no choice.

"Fire."

There was no sense thinking of himself as Mali anymore, he decided. Marko Barcelona was dead. Michael Kaspar was dead as well. He had been dead for more than a year. If he was being honest with himself, Kaspar had been dead for decades. He may never have truly been alive, at least not the way Mali had been alive. Energized. Powerful.

He would not give that up without a fight. But not this fight. This fight was lost. There would be battles to come. He would rebuild his kingdom. Eastern Ukraine was wide-open territory now. It would be perfect for a man of his talents. He would ally himself with the rebels in Donetsk or Mariupol and carve out a little kingdom for himself equidistant from Moscow and Kiev, East and West.

The seams and fissures of the international system presented opportunities that only men like him could capitalize on. Men who had what was necessary to take advantage of open space.

He spun the dial on the safe in his office. The sound it made as the door opened was like the popping of a champagne cork. From inside, he retrieved two thick stacks of hundred-dollar bills and five-hundred-euro notes. The eurocrats in Brussels had decided to print the large-denomination bill precisely to appeal to those who operated in a cash economy on the margins of the law: drug dealers and smugglers and tax cheats. It was their way of challenging the supremacy of the dollar as the currency of choice for international crime and in this, at least, they had been remarkably successful.

The stack of passports was shorter but no less valuable. There were a number of nationalities to choose from. He settled on Malta. It was in the EU, which would make travel easier, but the justice system was weak and corrupt, and the Maltese were infamous for selling citizenship at reasonable prices. It was a country that no one had strong feelings about, or feelings of any sort, for that matter. As identity documents went, a Maltese passport was as close as one could get to a blank piece of paper. It would do nicely.

The picture in the passport was his. The name he had given himself was Sergei Tarullo.

Sergei, for it was not too early to start thinking of himself by his new name, returned to his room to pack his bag. He opened the shutters of the big picture window to give himself a view of the mountains. He loved the Dinaric Alps. They were in his blood. He would miss them, but Sergei was confident that he would grow to love the flat plains of eastern Ukraine in time.

The sky was a blue the color of a California swimming pool. It was clear and open and full of promise.

What the fuck is that?

The black dot grew bigger. It seemed to be coming toward him, growing rapidly, moving at speed.

Michael Kaspar understood what it was. The false identities were stripped away, and for the last few seconds of his life, he stood at the window stripped bare to his core self. He did not especially like that man, and it galled him to have to die in his company.

Shit happens.

The Hellfire was moving at almost a thousand miles an hour when it shattered the glass on the bedroom window. The missile slammed into Kaspar like a giant bullet, liquefying everything above his waistline through sheer kinetic energy. His body was not solid enough to trigger the warhead, but within a millisecond, the missile impacted the back wall of the bedroom, and the fireball and overpressure vaporized what was left of the would-be king.

The Basilisk's Eye captured the destruction of the villa in glorious Technicolor. VW was not quite certain what to feel. She had just killed a man, a man she had neither liked nor respected, but a man nonetheless. Someone she had known. They had attended the same office parties and sat in on the same endless staff meetings. Now he was dead at her hand. She had likely killed one or two others as well. Kaspar's bodyguards. Men she did not know who had just been doing their jobs. Those deaths would be harder to live with, she knew. Kaspar, at least, had made a choice.

Sarah Gold had made her choices as well. It was at last clear to VW why she had been exiled to the Island of Misfit Toys, an exile that would end in two days with her appointment as director of the Balkan Action Team. Sarah had arranged to have VW wander in the bureaucratic wilderness to keep her away from Parsifal. She knew that VW would not have agreed with the logic behind it. It was truly amazing the evil that people could do when they think they are doing good.

VW had seen the tape. It was extraordinary documentary evidence of the single worst crime on the European continent since Auschwitz. Officially, the CIA was pleased that the tribunal was in a position to issue an indictment against Zoran Dimitrović, aka Captain Zero. Privately, there was some unhappiness that a striped-pants-wearing State Department cookie pusher had gotten the better of a decorated CIA case officer, even one who had wandered pretty far off the reservation.

VW had seen the reporting. Petrosian had evidently suspected that Sarah would try to take it from him, so he had hidden the tape behind a pile of potato-chip bags in a gas station in the middle of nowhere. It was a pretty ballsy move on his part, she had to admit. But then he had sent the tape on to the tribunal without any decision on the part of the government that this was what the United States would do with the evidence.

Petrosian had no more right to give that tape to the prosecutors than Sarah had to use it in her private little game of blackmail. Both were arrogant and undisciplined.

The system existed for a reason, VW believed. It was not perfect, but it at least reflected a comprehensive debate that was supposed to take into account the full range of U.S. interests. No one person, not even the president, could make those kinds of decisions alone. The issues were too complex.

No one person was above the system. Trying to do the right thing was no excuse for circumventing the checks and balances of government. Both Eric and Sarah had been convinced of the fundamental righteousness of their cause.

Who was Sarah to decide what was right?

Who was Eric?

Who was anyone?

POTOČARI
DECEMBER 22

EPILOGUE

The first snowfall of winter had blanketed the memorial, softening the sharp lines of the steles. Against the stark white snow, the marble grave markers were a dull gray. The bare trees encircling the memorial hung heavy with snow that seemed to absorb and muffle all sound. The memorial was eerily quiet. It was as if the whole world had stopped. A moment of silence in respect for the dead. It was cold enough that their breath condensed into ephemeral clouds that lasted no longer than a heartbeat. They were the only visitors. Even the caretaker had seemingly chosen to stay in bed on such a cold morning. But he was an old man, and Eric did not hold that choice against him.

He bowed his head and blinked back frozen tears. Meho would not have approved of any maudlin display of sentiment. He would have skewered it mercilessly. Meho would have preferred a joke and a laugh. Had he been there, he would have been more than happy to supply the humor. At the very least, he would have wanted those coming together in his memory to take not just comfort but pleasure from the company of friends.

And Eric was flanked by friends. Amra was on his left and Annika was standing by his right side. They helped to steady him—literally as well as emotionally. The leg that had taken the bullet was still weak. It was growing stronger through intense and painful physical therapy sessions, but it would be some time before it was really healed. And it might never be as strong as it had been.

"Maybe it's an illusion," Eric said. "Maybe Sarah had it right after all. But coming here makes me feel as though I did the right thing giving the tape to the tribunal. Meho was a part of that decision, I have to be honest. But it's bigger than that. The thousands murdered here deserve justice."

"You did the right thing, Eric," Annika said, putting a hand on his upper arm. "Left to its own devices, your government probably would have handed the tape over to the tribunal . . . eventually. But it could have taken weeks, even months, before the Washington machinery reached that conclusion. By forcing their hand, you helped secure the early indictment against Dimitrović that got him out of Banja Luka into a cozy holding cell in The Hague. With your friend Nikola running the show in the RS, at least temporarily, the New Compact for Bosnia has a fighting chance."

"You mean the Sondergaard Plan?"

"I'm Danish, Eric. Modesty prevents me from calling it that."

Things can change quickly in politics. The peace plan that had once been a long shot was now established policy, and as was so often the case, it seemed inevitable in hindsight. Eric and Annika both knew that it had been anything but. The peace conference itself had gone well, but overcoming Dimitrović's opposition in Banja Luka had always been the most uncertain part of the process. With Mali's death and Dimitrović's arrest, the RS political establishment had been turned upside down. Dimitrović's party had fragmented into a dozen squabbling factions. Snap elections had produced a stunning victory for Nikola and the Social Democrats, who were aggressively pursuing a new pro-reconciliation agenda. The checkpoints at the border of the RS had come down and the paramilitaries had slunk back into their holes. The leaders of the three major ethnic groups were building real Bosnian institutions and the economy was at long last starting to grow. The voices of the majority in all three communities, hungry for peace and opportunity and disinterested in the old fights, were being heard. There was still a great deal of work to do, but it was a start.

"It may have been the right decision," Eric said, "but Washington doesn't like to get sandbagged that way. It will probably cost me my job. Wylie has been blasting me at every opportunity. Do you know anyone who's hiring?"

"Funny you should ask. I had a nice chat with Hank the other day." Hank was Henry Pembroke, secretary of state of the United States of America. Waspy. Patrician. Aloof. Independently wealthy. His great-great-grandfather had been secretary of state to President James Buchanan. It was hard for Eric to think of him as Hank.

"He mostly wanted to talk Iran, but he knows how much I've invested in shaping a post-Dayton Bosnia, so we talked a little Balkans as well. I told him that U.S.-EU cooperation had been the key to success so far and that we should continue that. The long and short of it is that Hank agreed to second you to my staff for at least a year. Bosnia can't be my full-time job. The world's too big. But I need a strong representative on the ground here to bang heads together and make sure this thing works. I'd like that to be you, Eric. What do you think?"

"He'll do it," Amra interjected, as she squeezed his hand.

"I rather thought so," Annika said, with evident satisfaction.

"Don't I get a vote?" Eric asked.

"If you insist," the High Rep replied graciously. "Although it is only fair to point out that even if you say no the vote would still be two-to-one against you. Nothing to be done about it. That's democracy."

"Then I might as well say yes."

"Good. It's agreed. You should have pretty decent job security. After all, your boss owes you her life."

"That *will* look pretty good in my evaluation."

"Yes. Thank you, Eric. I know how much that cost you."

"She was a stone-cold bitch," Amra said angrily.

Eric said nothing. He understood Amra's anger, but he could not bring himself to see Sarah that way. She was more complicated than that. Sarah certainly did not belong in the same box as people like Kaspar and Dimitrović. They operated solely on the basis of self-interest. Sarah had a moral compass, her own understanding of right and wrong. But her magnetic north was not the same as Eric's.

"I'm glad that you're going to stay in Sarajevo," Amra said. "And I am happy about the progress you've made. But I do wonder sometimes . . ." She stopped, seemingly at a loss for words.

"About what?" Eric asked gently.

"About whether any of this will last. Srebrenica was just the latest outrage in a cycle of violence and revenge that stretches back a thousand years. Look around. Every village, every hill, every fort or monastery or mosque or bridge has a story to tell. And none of the stories are about unicorns or buttercups. The blood has soaked so deeply into the soil that I wonder whether this place can ever recover, whether we can ever really overcome our addiction to the past."

Eric and Annika were quiet as they considered what she had said.

"There's a risk," Annika conceded. "But we have to operate as though it isn't so. Eric is the one who persuaded me that history is not destiny. We have to believe that. The alternative is to build a wall around these countries and let the strongest prevail. Twenty-first-century Europe is not willing to accept that outcome. I'm not willing to accept that outcome. Neither are you. We can succeed here. The desire for peace will ultimately outweigh the desire for revenge."

"I hope you're right," Amra said. "Men like Mali and Dimitrović see only the worst in us. We can be better than that. We are better than that."

"You certainly are," Eric agreed. "Meho was. Nikola is. Even Dragan, in his own way. But there are still so many who are stuck in the past. It isn't going to be easy."

"Then it's a good thing that you've got the job," Annika said, with a finality that brooked no further argument.

"I do love a challenge."

"Well," Amra said, leaning into Eric and resting her head on his shoulder momentarily. "You've certainly come to the right place."

BOSNIA: THE REAL STORY

We saw it coming. Analysts at the CIA and elsewhere in the U.S. government predicted the breakup of Yugoslavia. Nationalist sentiment, suppressed for more than forty years by Marshal Josip Broz Tito and the communists, was once again bubbling to the surface. Nationalist politicians rose to positions of power and influence, most notably Slobodan Milošević in Serbia and Franjo Tuđman in Croatia. The pressures building within Yugoslav society were enormous, the fault lines increasingly visible.

What no one predicted, however, was just how violent the breakup would be. On June 25, 1991, Slovenia and Croatia became the first two Yugoslav republics to declare their independence. Slovenia made a clean break, winning recognition of its independence after a ten-day fight that resulted in fewer than seventy fatalities on all sides. Croatia's road to independence was considerably rockier. The sizeable

Serb minority in Croatia considered the new nationalists in power in Zagreb as a straight-line continuation of the fascist Ustaše, the Nazi puppet regime from World War II. The fighting in Croatia between Croat forces on one side and the Yugoslav National Army and Serbian paramilitaries on the other was vicious and protracted. The siege of Vukovar and the slaughter of several hundred people, mostly patients at a local hospital, presaged the horrors that were to follow in Bosnia.

Bosnia was divided among three major ethnic groups—Serbs, Croats, and Muslims, who would later come to be called Bosniaks. In Yugoslavia, Muslim was considered an ethnicity rather than a religion, and religious practice was officially discouraged by the powerful Communist Party. Bosnia was a classic Balkan powder keg just waiting for a spark. The independence referendum organized in February and March of 1992 was just that spark. The Serbs of Bosnia, who made up about a third of the population, opposed independence and boycotted the referendum. Fighting broke out within days of the declaration of Bosnia's independence, and within a month, the city of Sarajevo was under siege. The siege of Sarajevo would last 1,425 days, three times longer than the siege of Stalingrad.

The war in Bosnia dragged on for years, prolonged by Western dithering and ambivalence. All three groups fought one another until the Washington Agreement of March 1994 forged an alliance between the Bosniaks and Croats against the Serbs.

UN peacekeepers and international aid workers functioned, in effect, as de facto hostages, discouraging military action by NATO countries that might have brought an early end to the fighting. Europe and America hoped that economic sanctions alone would be enough to force Belgrade to sue for peace. They were not. It was the massacre of some eight thousand Bosniak men and boys at Srebrenica in July 1995 that finally pricked the conscience of the West and set the stage for military intervention. Srebrenica had been designated a UN safe area, although it was protected by only a handful of ill-equipped Dutch peacekeepers who could do nothing to avert the worst atrocity on European soil since the Second World War.

NATO launched Operation Deliberate Force a month later, ostensibly in response to an artillery attack on a Sarajevo market that killed some thirty-seven people, but really in response to the evil of Srebrenica. Three weeks of bombing and a series of battlefield reversals forced Milošević and the Serbs to accept an invitation to a peace conference in Dayton, Ohio. Sequestering the presidents of what was then the Federal Republic of Yugoslavia (Serbia and Montenegro), Croatia, and Bosnia at Wright-Patterson Air Force Base in dreary Dayton for three weeks proved to be a stroke of genius. The talks, led by the talented American diplomat Richard Holbrooke, produced the Dayton Peace Accords, an awkward power-sharing arrangement that preserved Republika Srpska as one of two "entities" in Bosnia and Herzegovina along with the Federation. The RS controlled 49 percent of Bosnia's territory as compared to the Federation's 51 percent. It was, by any reasonable definition, a very good deal for the Serbs.

The Dayton Peace Accords brought an end to the fighting in Bosnia. In this, they must be considered a success. The political structure it created, however, with decision making divided in the center among the three major ethnic groups and real power vested in the entities, was largely nonfunctional. Bosnia became a ward of the international community, dependent on a European High

Representative to make all of the hard choices. The economy stagnated. Those who could left the country for opportunities in the West. And Belgrade and Zagreb continued to manipulate their fellow ethnics in Bosnia in pursuit of their own ambitions.

To be fair, the negotiators recognized from the outset that Dayton was deeply flawed. The idea was that over time practical realities would force the three parties to the conflict together and that the parallel structures would gradually be integrated. The one big success was an agreement in 2005 to create a unified military. Beyond that, Bosnia remains as deeply divided as it was in 1995.

Predictably, some individuals on all sides have taken advantage of the awkward political arrangements to make themselves phenomenally wealthy, while most people—irrespective of ethnic origin—have struggled to get by. Public frustration with the situation boiled over in 2014 in violent demonstrations across the country. Demonstrators targeted government buildings, protesting unemployment, poverty, corruption, and nepotism.

Within a few weeks, however, the protests had run out of steam. The system remained unchanged. Periodically, political tensions in Bosnia threaten to reignite serious ethnic violence. So far, cooler heads have always prevailed, but the underlying dynamic of dysfunction and rampant corruption has kept Bosnia both poor and unstable.

Although the scars of conflict remain, there is no Captain Zero still at large. Those judged to have held command responsibility for crimes against humanity in Srebrenica have been brought to justice. But there are others. In March 2015, Serbian authorities arrested seven people on war crimes charges, including Nedeljko Milidragović, the commander of a special police brigade of Republika

Srpska's police force, who was known as Nedjo the Butcher. Milidragović had reinvented himself as a successful businessman in Serbia after the war. But there is no statute of limitations for genocide.

At the time of this writing, the U.S. immigration authorities are planning to deport one hundred and fifty Bosnians living in the United States who had concealed their involvement in acts of genocide. Some have been implicated in the Srebrenica massacre, including a soccer coach in Virginia and an Ohio metal worker. Authorities in Washington believe there could be hundreds more still at large.

Back in Bosnia, tens of thousands displaced in the war have been unable or reluctant to return to their homes. Mixed communities have become ethnically homogenous, and Bosnia's once-famous culture of tolerance has been deeply damaged, perhaps beyond repair. Closure remains elusive.

It is possible that Bosnia could once again slide into open conflict, but it is neither certain nor inevitable. The people of Bosnia, on all sides, deserve better. They deserve leaders who will act in the public's interest rather than in their own. They deserve a better future for themselves and their children. The wars in the former Yugoslavia once dominated the headlines as the fighting in Ukraine and Syria does today. It would be a mistake to turn away too quickly from the Balkans. The risk of conflict remains, and Bosnia will need help from the international community to escape the shadows of its recent past and chart a sustainable course forward to a European future. They can do it. But not without our help.

As always, the opinions expressed here are my own and do not necessarily reflect those of the Department of State.